SOMNA

A BEDTIME STORY

DSTLRY

DAVID STEINBERGER *Co-Founder & CEO*
CHIP MOSHER *Co-Founder & CCO*
SEAN EDGAR *Sr. Marketing Director*
SADÉ PAIGE *Social Media Lead*
MELISSA GIFFORD *Proofreader*

Standard ISBN: 978-1-962265-01-0 · Direct Market Exclusive ISBN: 978-1-962265-08-9
Sign up for the latest info at dstlry.co

SOMNA

Collected Edition

❧ BY BECKY CLOONAN AND TULA LOTAY ☙

BECKY CLOONAN AND TULA LOTAY *story & art*

LEE LOUGHRIDGE, DEE CUNNIFFE & TULA LOTAY *colors*

LUCAS GATTONI *letters*

WILL DENNIS *editor*

ERIKA SCHNATZ *design*

TINY ONION, INC *packaging*

*"When we look into the nature of demonic power,
we find it to be insatiable,
in its lust for destruction and chaos."*

—Heinrich Kramer, *Malleus Maleficarum*

CHAPTER I.
A LILY ON THY BROW

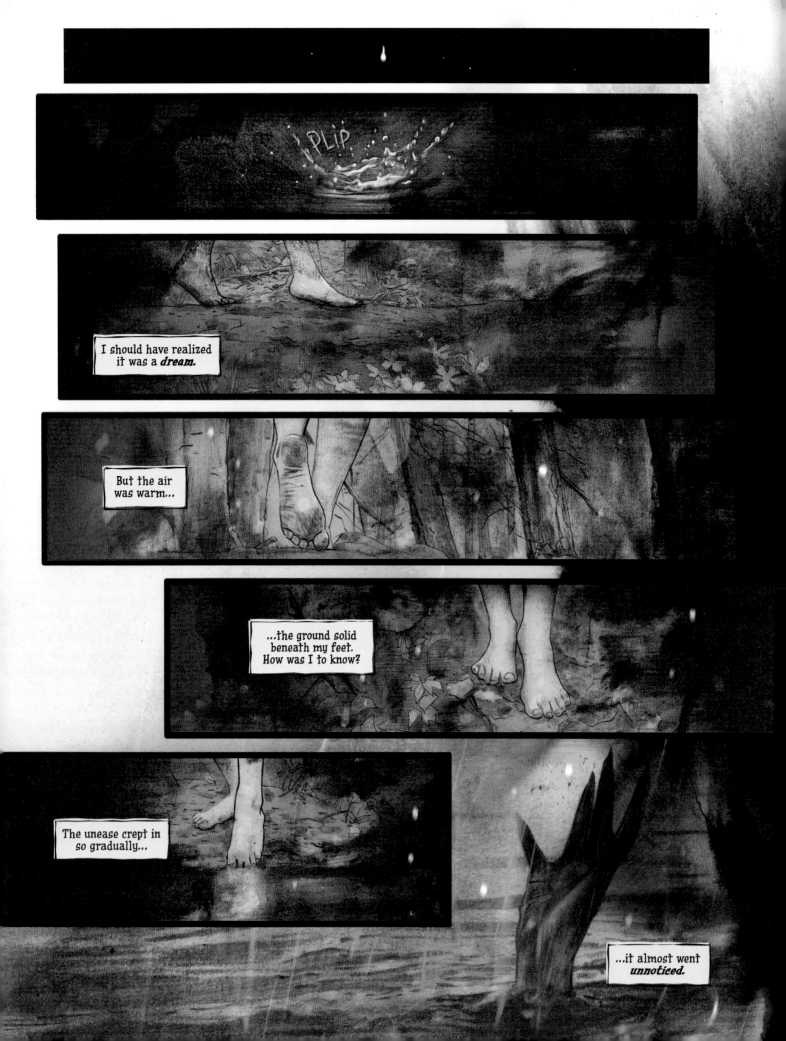

PLIP

I should have realized it was a *dream.*

But the air was warm...

...the ground solid beneath my feet. How was I to know?

The unease crept in so gradually...

...it almost went *unnoticed.*

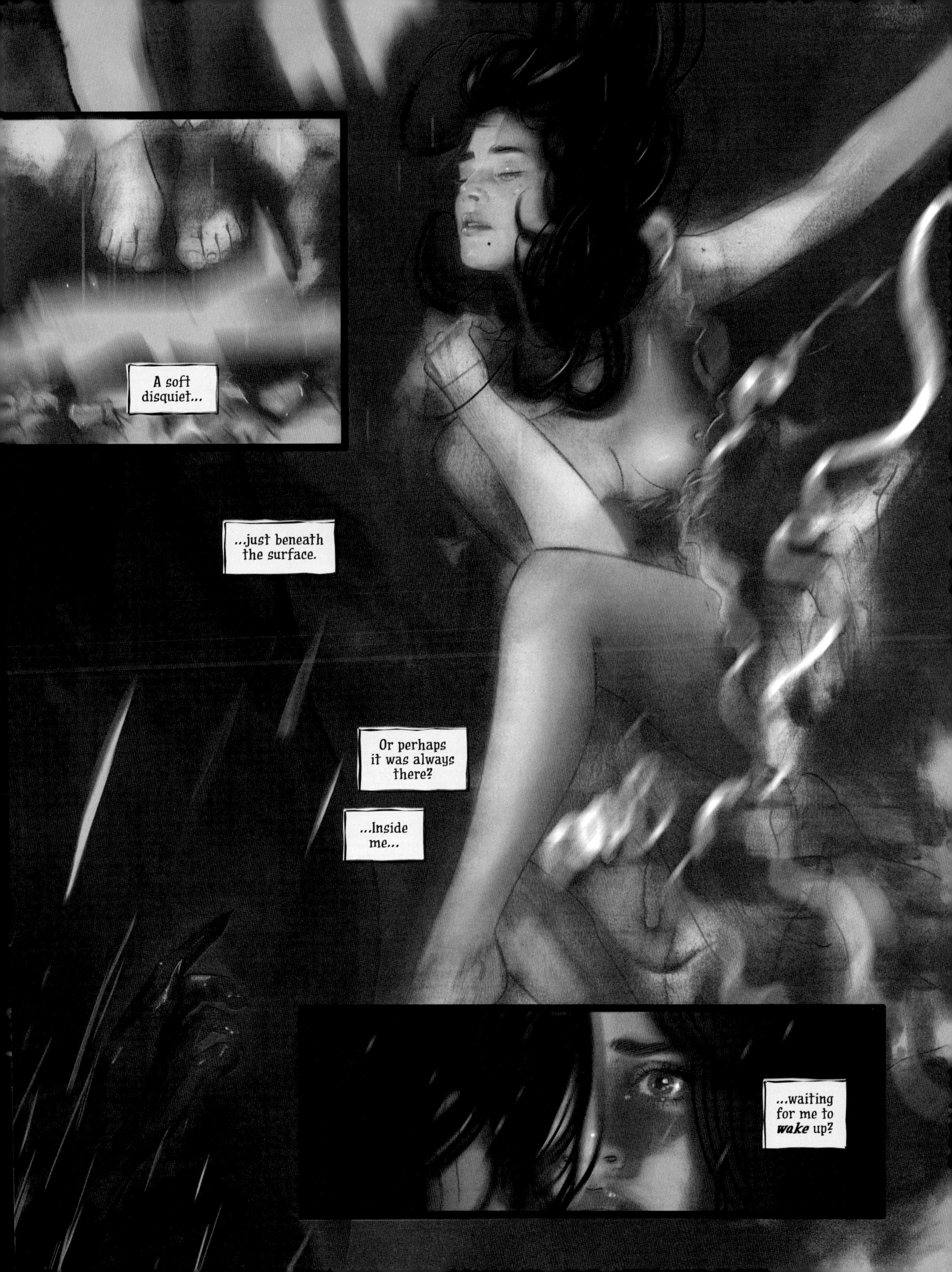
A soft disquiet...
...just beneath the surface.
Or perhaps it was always there?
...Inside me...
...waiting for me to **wake** up?

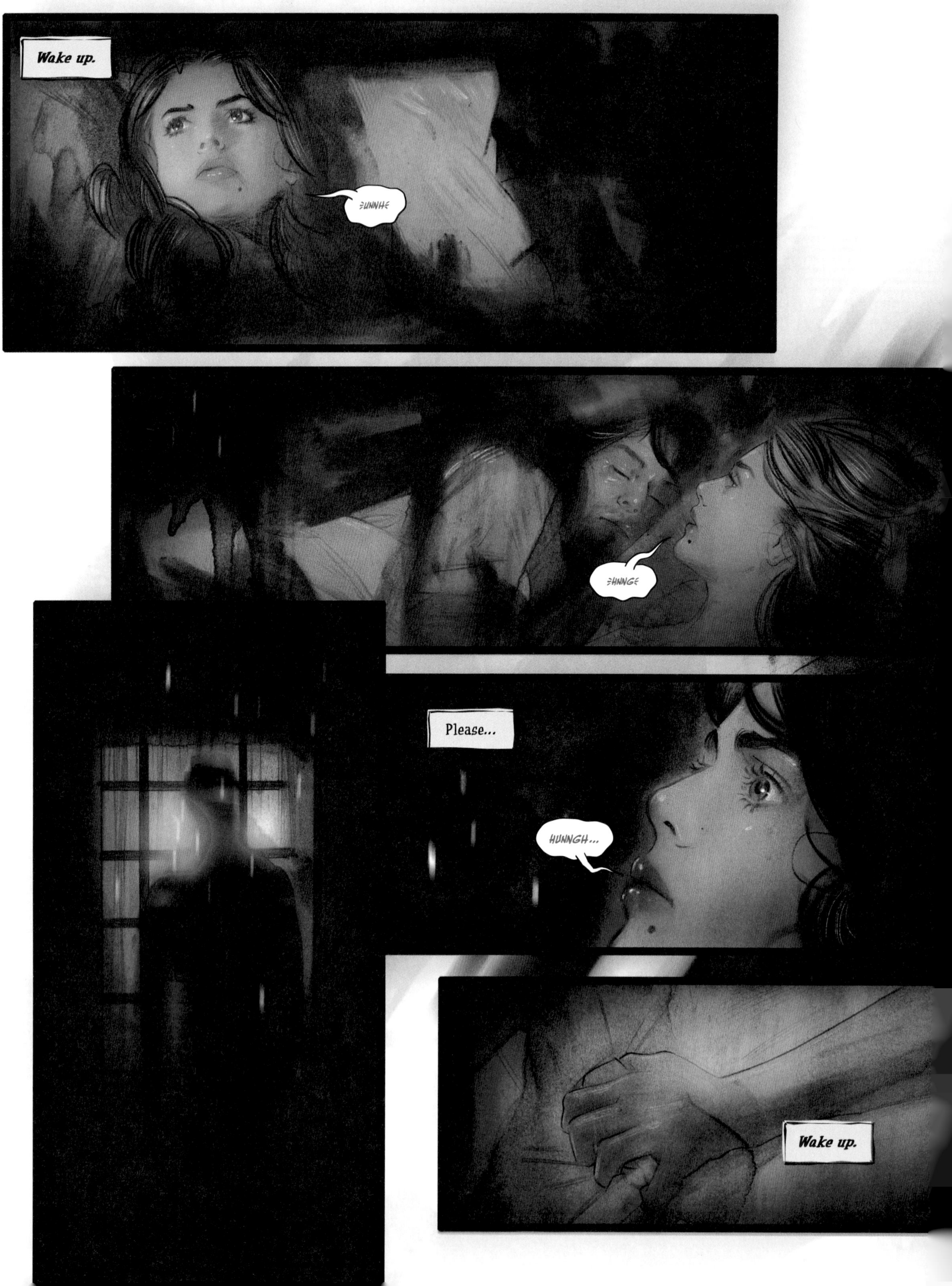
Wake up.
UNNH
HNNG
Please...
HUNNGH...
Wake up.

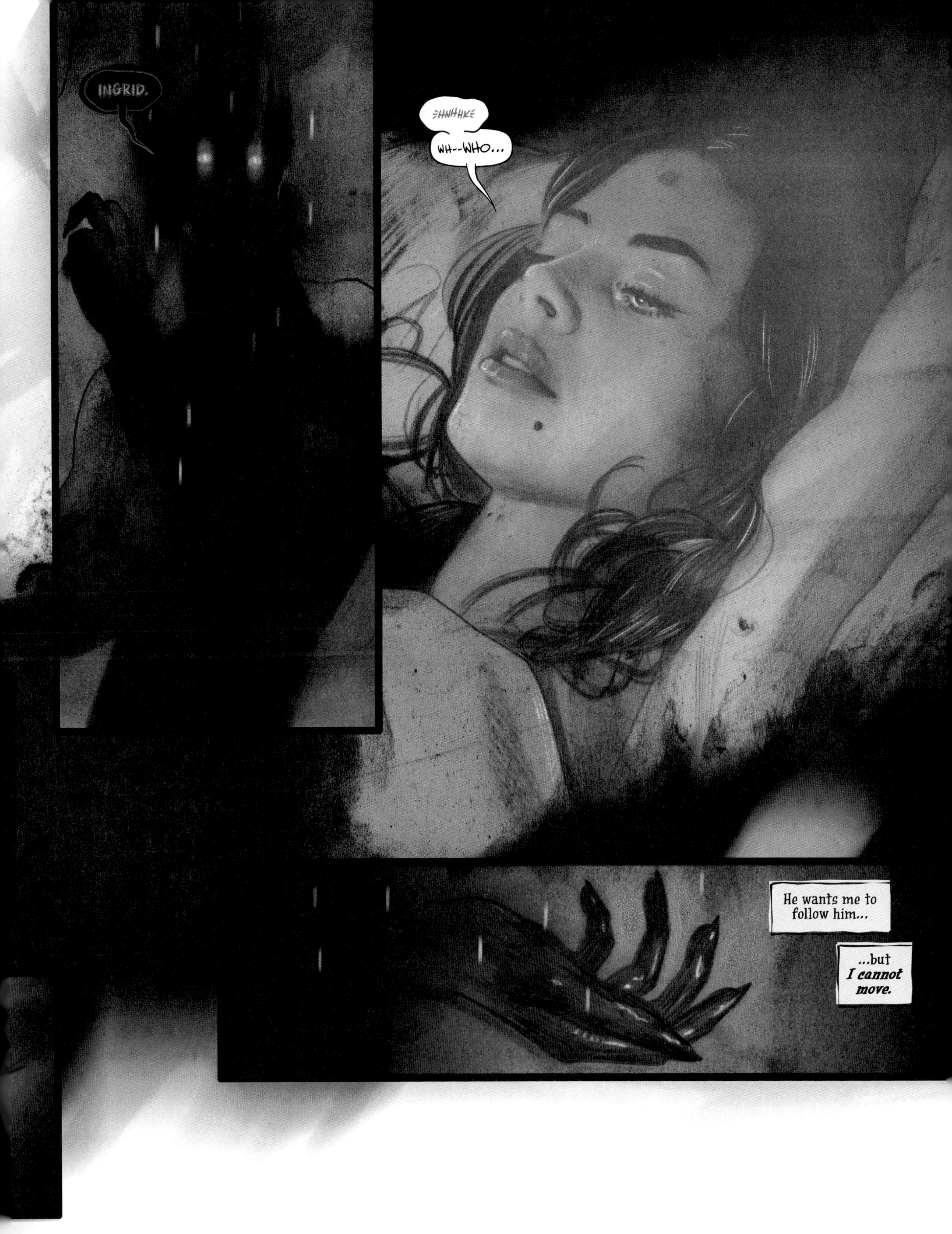
INGRID.
HNHHK
WH--WHO...
He wants me to follow him...
...but *I cannot move.*

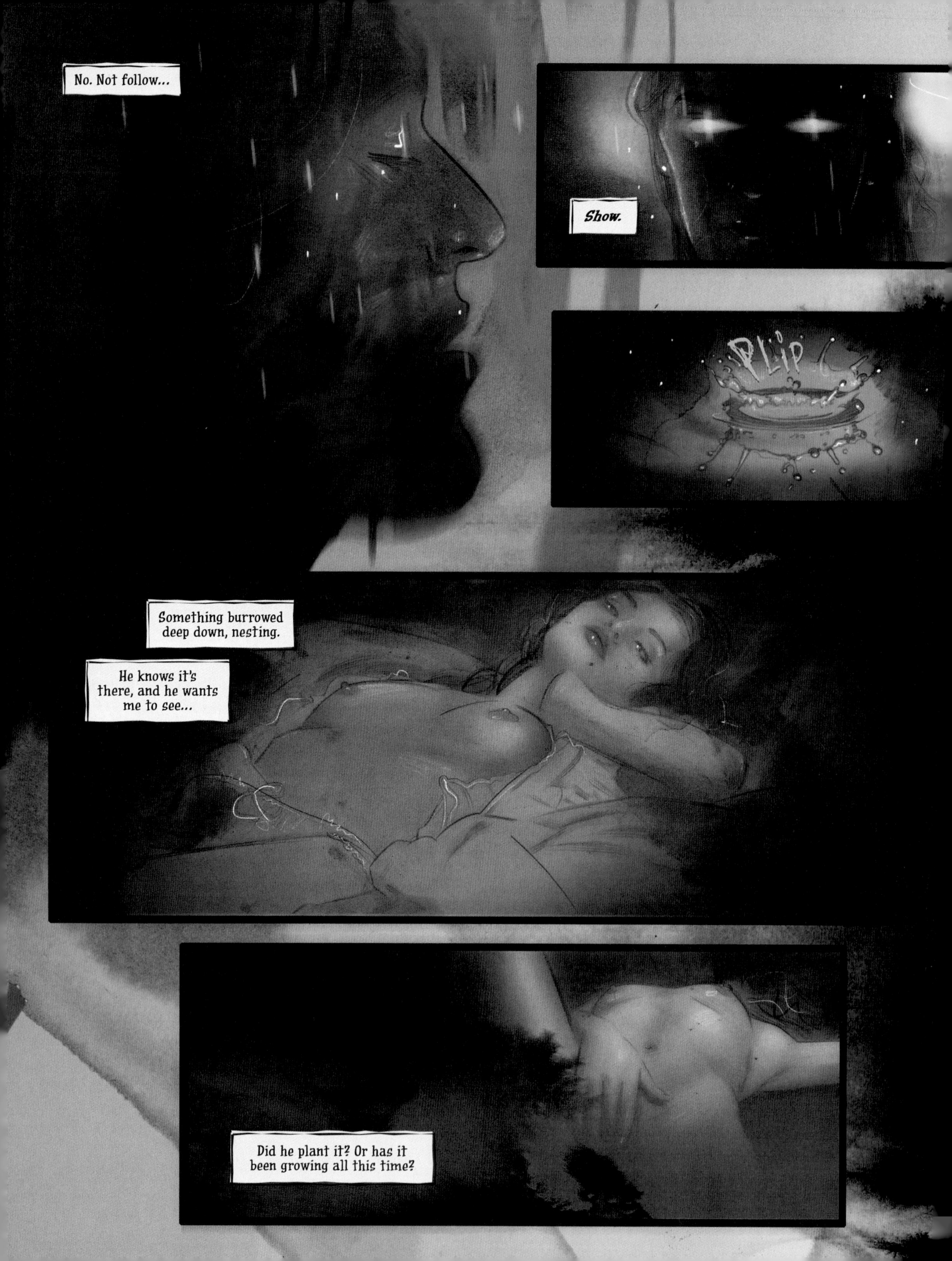
No. Not follow...
Show.
PLIP
Something burrowed deep down, nesting.
He knows it's there, and he wants me to see...
Did he plant it? Or has it been growing all this time?

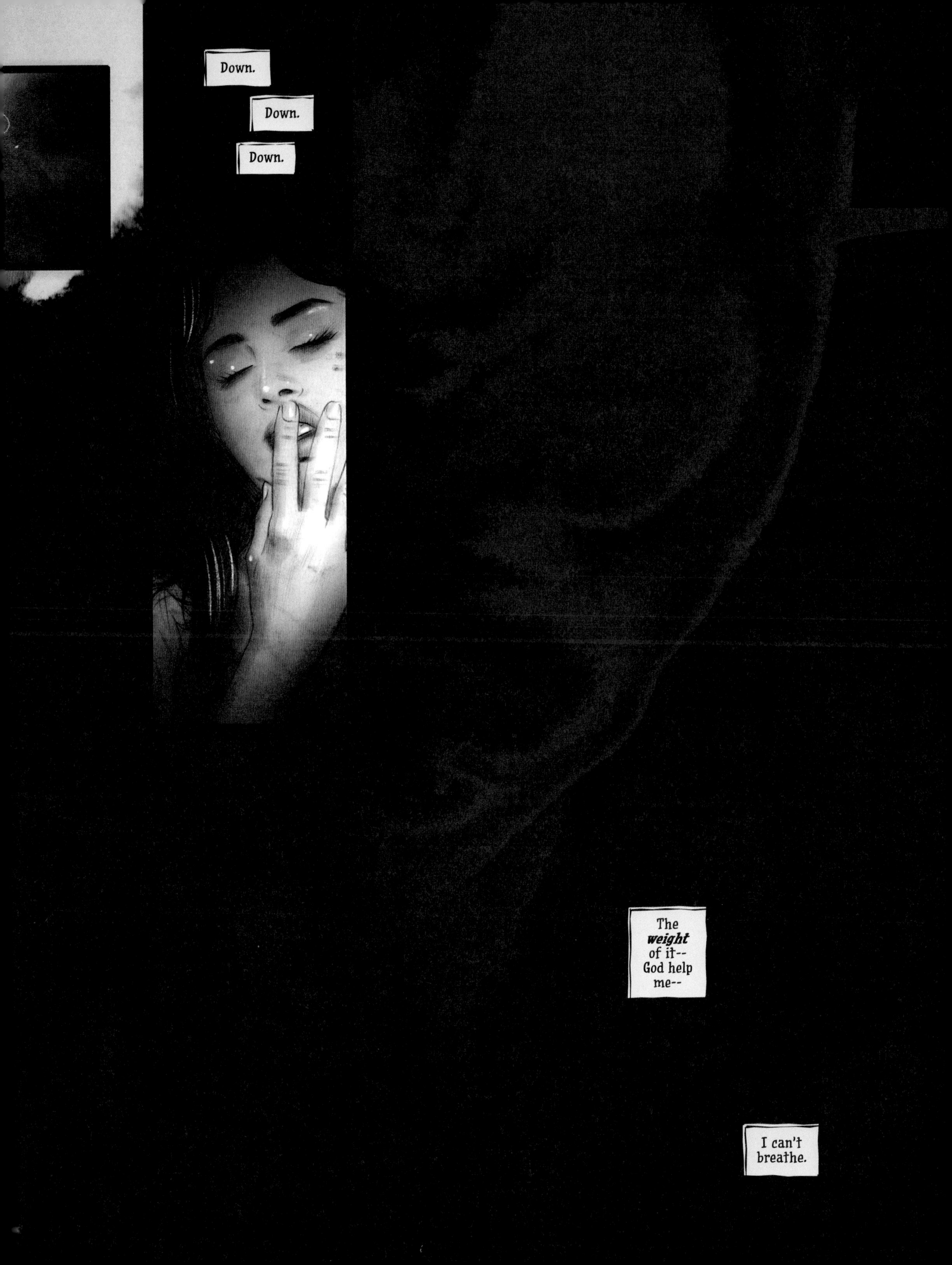
Down.
Down.
Down.
The *weight* of it-- God help me--
I can't breathe.

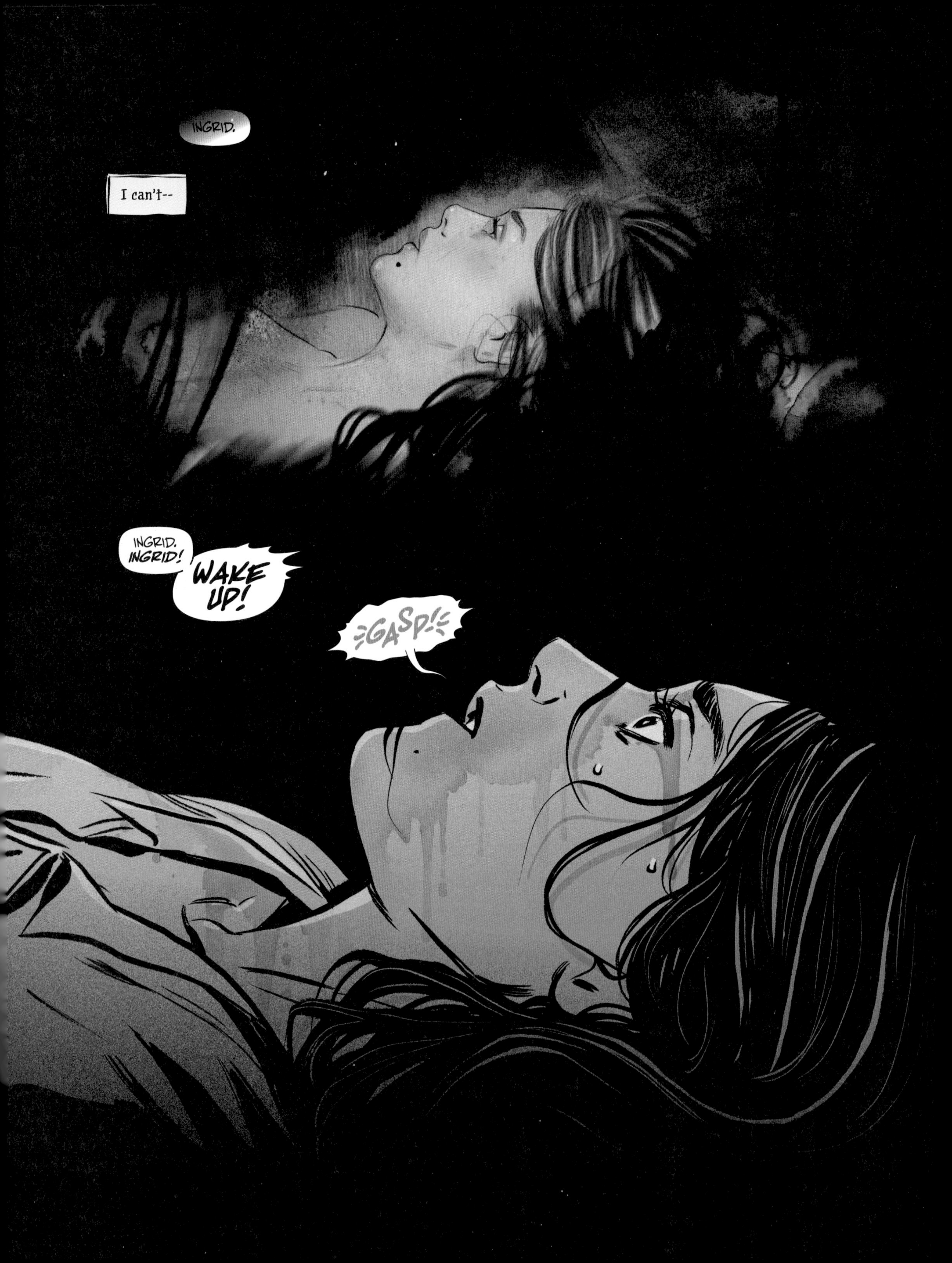
INGRID.
I can't--
INGRID. INGRID!
WAKE UP!
GASP!

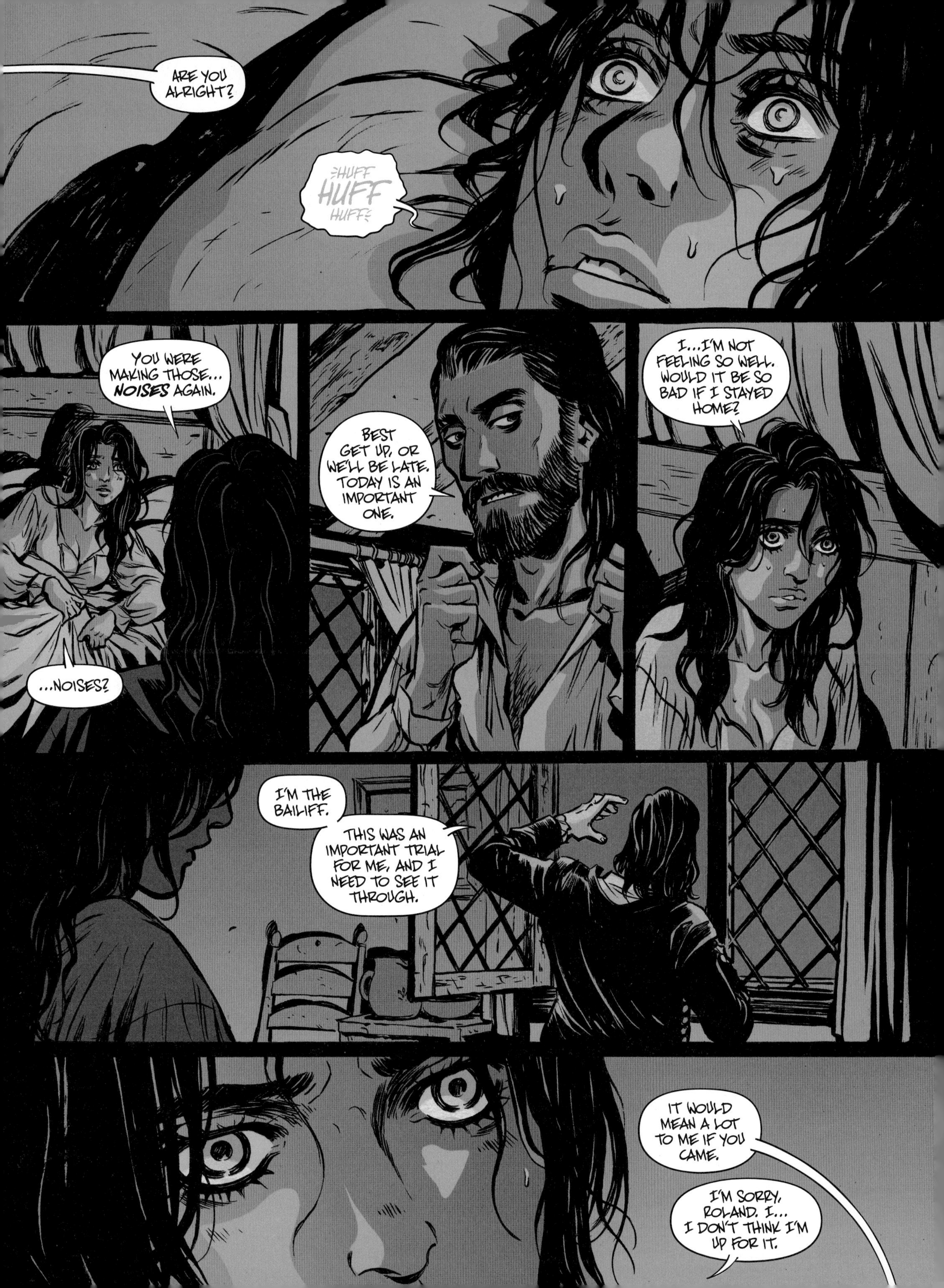
ARE YOU ALRIGHT?
HUFF HUFF HUFF
YOU WERE MAKING THOSE... NOISES AGAIN.
...NOISES?
BEST GET UP, OR WE'LL BE LATE. TODAY IS AN IMPORTANT ONE.
I...I'M NOT FEELING SO WELL. WOULD IT BE SO BAD IF I STAYED HOME?
I'M THE BAILIFF.
THIS WAS AN IMPORTANT TRIAL FOR ME, AND I NEED TO SEE IT THROUGH.
IT WOULD MEAN A LOT TO ME IF YOU CAME.
I'M SORRY, ROLAND. I... I DON'T THINK I'M UP FOR IT.

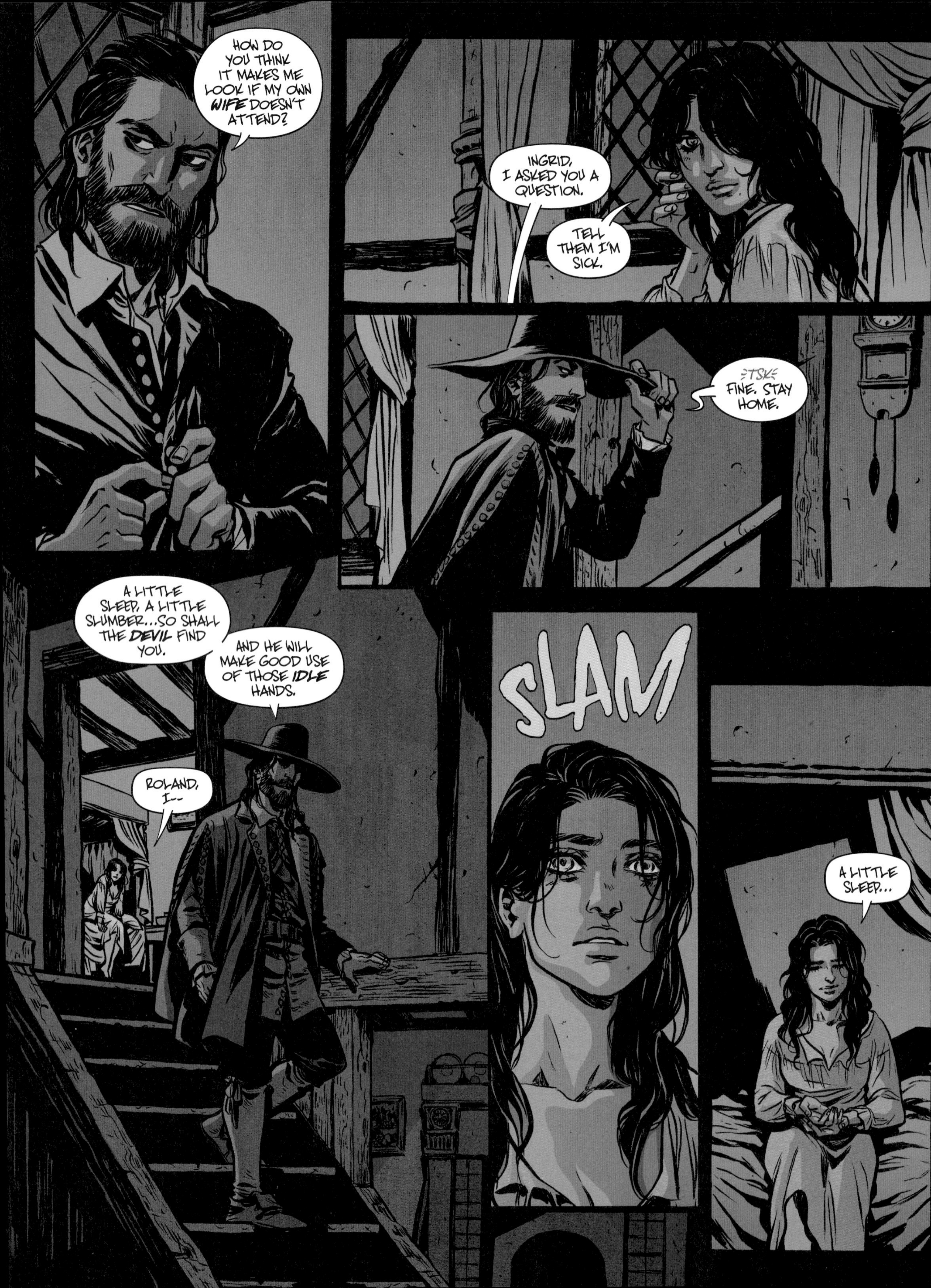
HOW DO YOU THINK IT MAKES ME LOOK IF MY OWN WIFE DOESN'T ATTEND?
INGRID, I ASKED YOU A QUESTION.
TELL THEM I'M SICK.
TSK
FINE. STAY HOME.
A LITTLE SLEEP, A LITTLE SLUMBER...SO SHALL THE DEVIL FIND YOU.
AND HE WILL MAKE GOOD USE OF THOSE IDLE HANDS.
ROLAND, I--
SLAM
A LITTLE SLEEP...

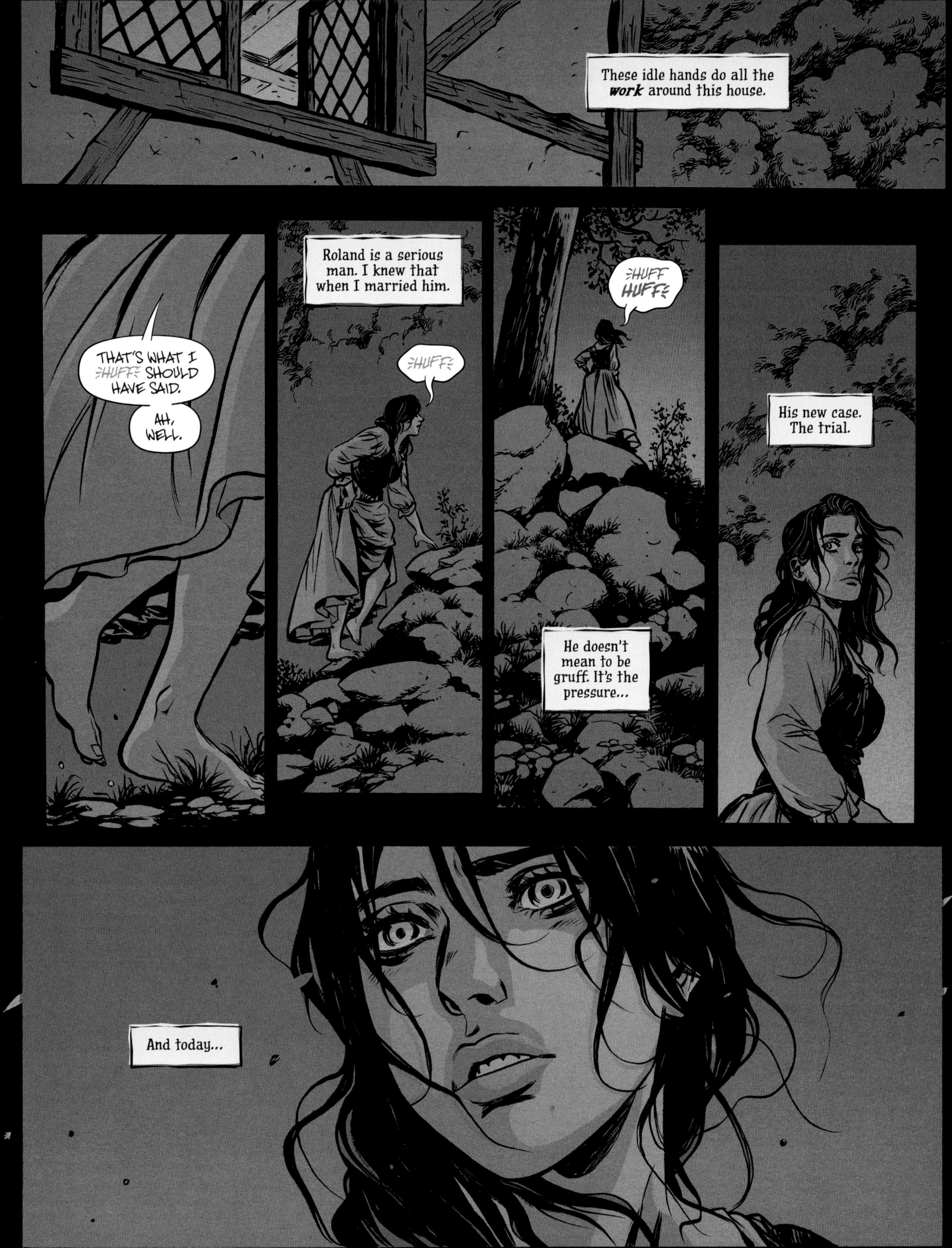

These idle hands do all the **work** around this house.
THAT'S WHAT I HUFF SHOULD HAVE SAID.
AH, WELL.
Roland is a serious man. I knew that when I married him.
HUFF
HUFF HUFF
He doesn't mean to be gruff. It's the pressure...
His new case. The trial.
And today...

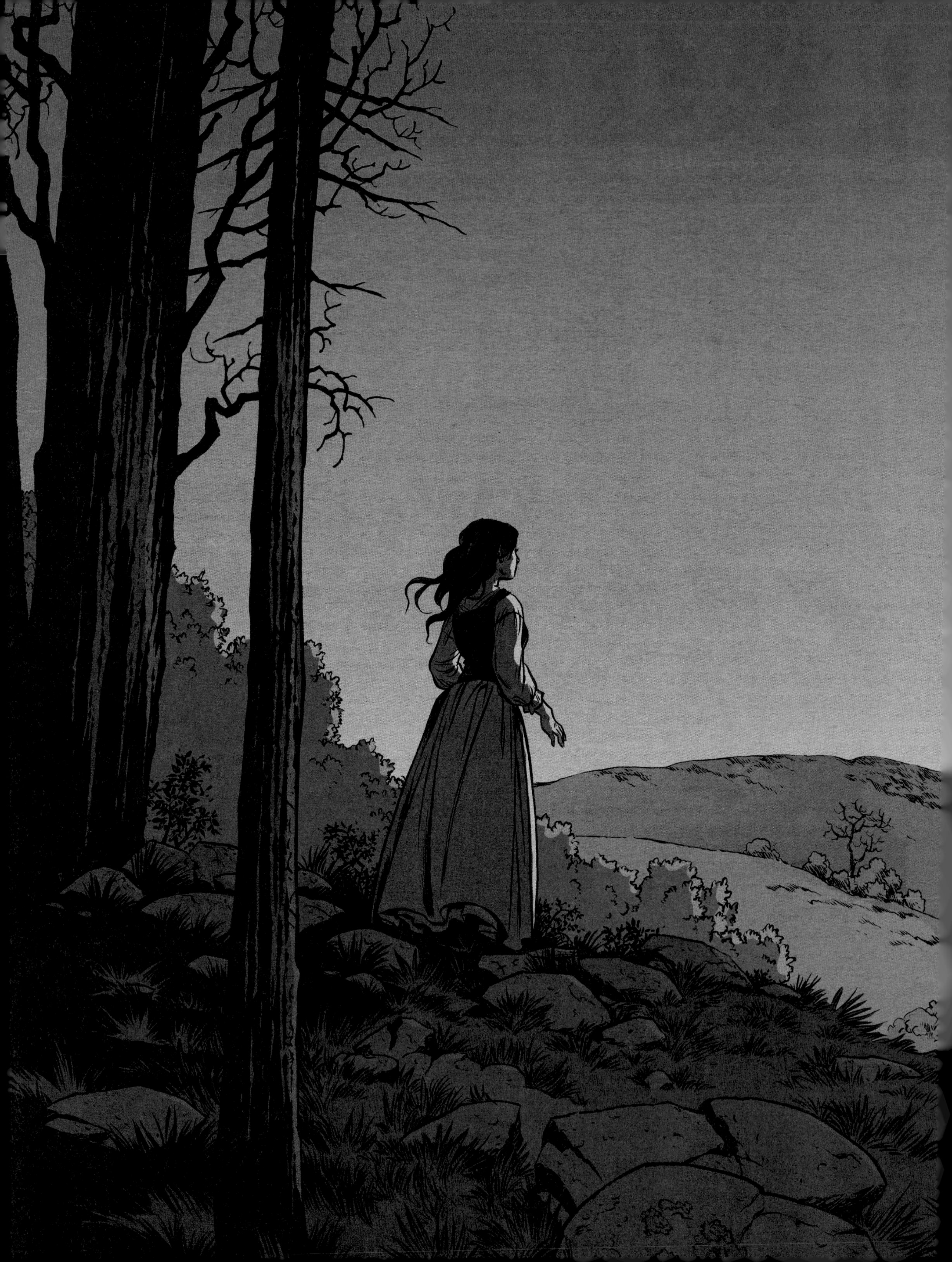

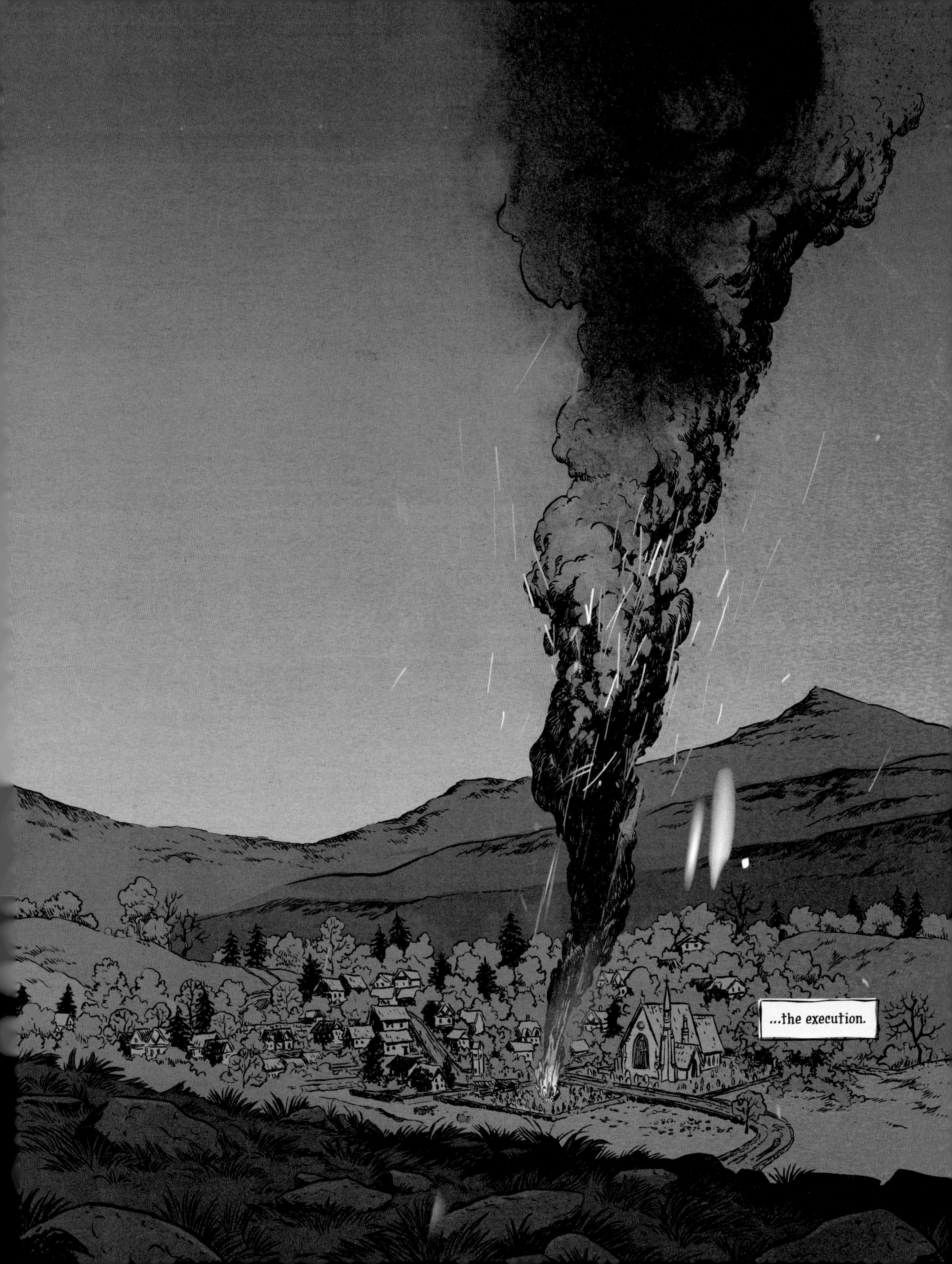
...the execution.

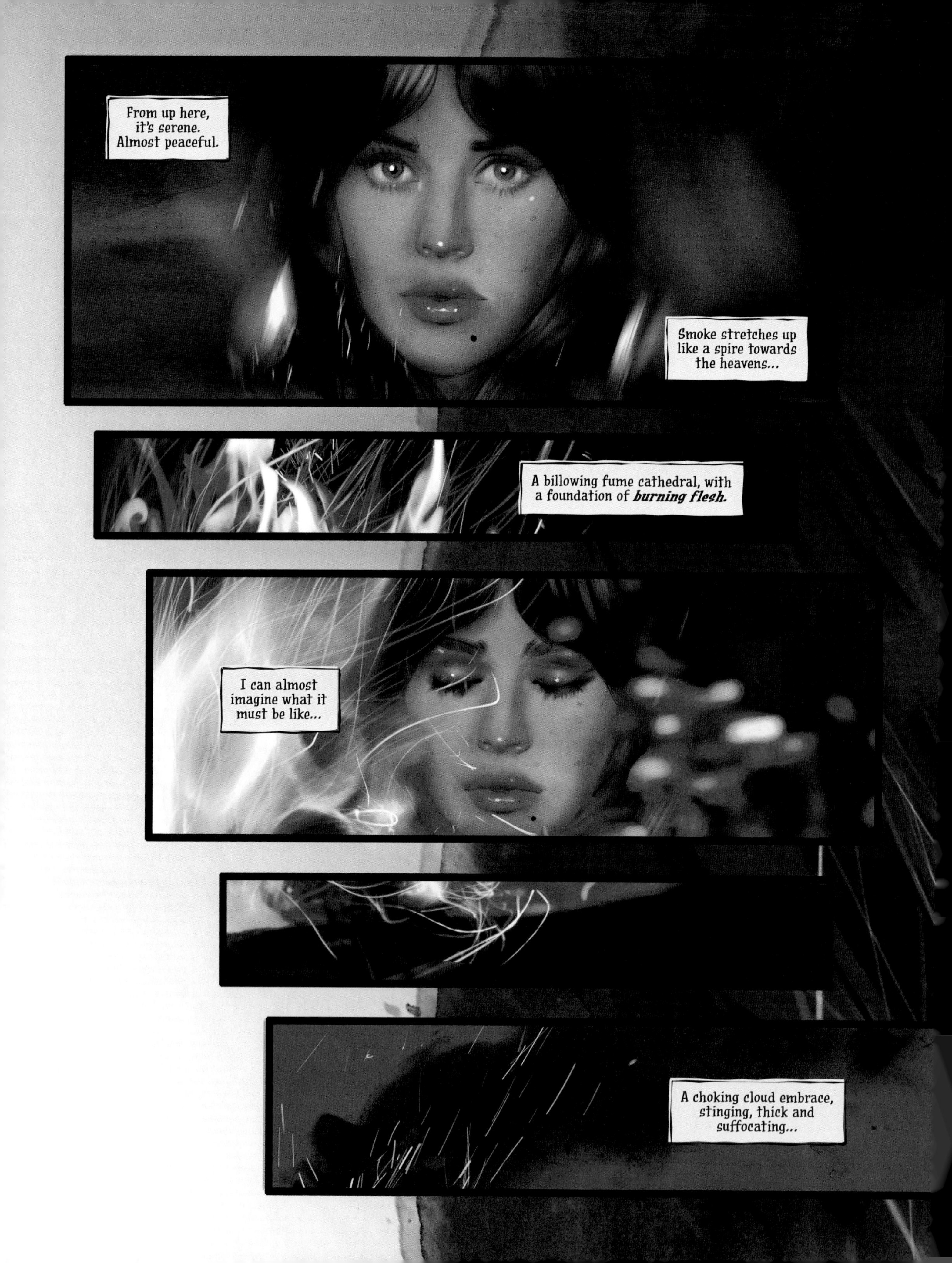
From up here, it's serene. Almost peaceful.
Smoke stretches up like a spire towards the heavens...
A billowing fume cathedral, with a foundation of ***burning flesh.***
I can almost imagine what it must be like...
A choking cloud embrace, stinging, thick and suffocating...

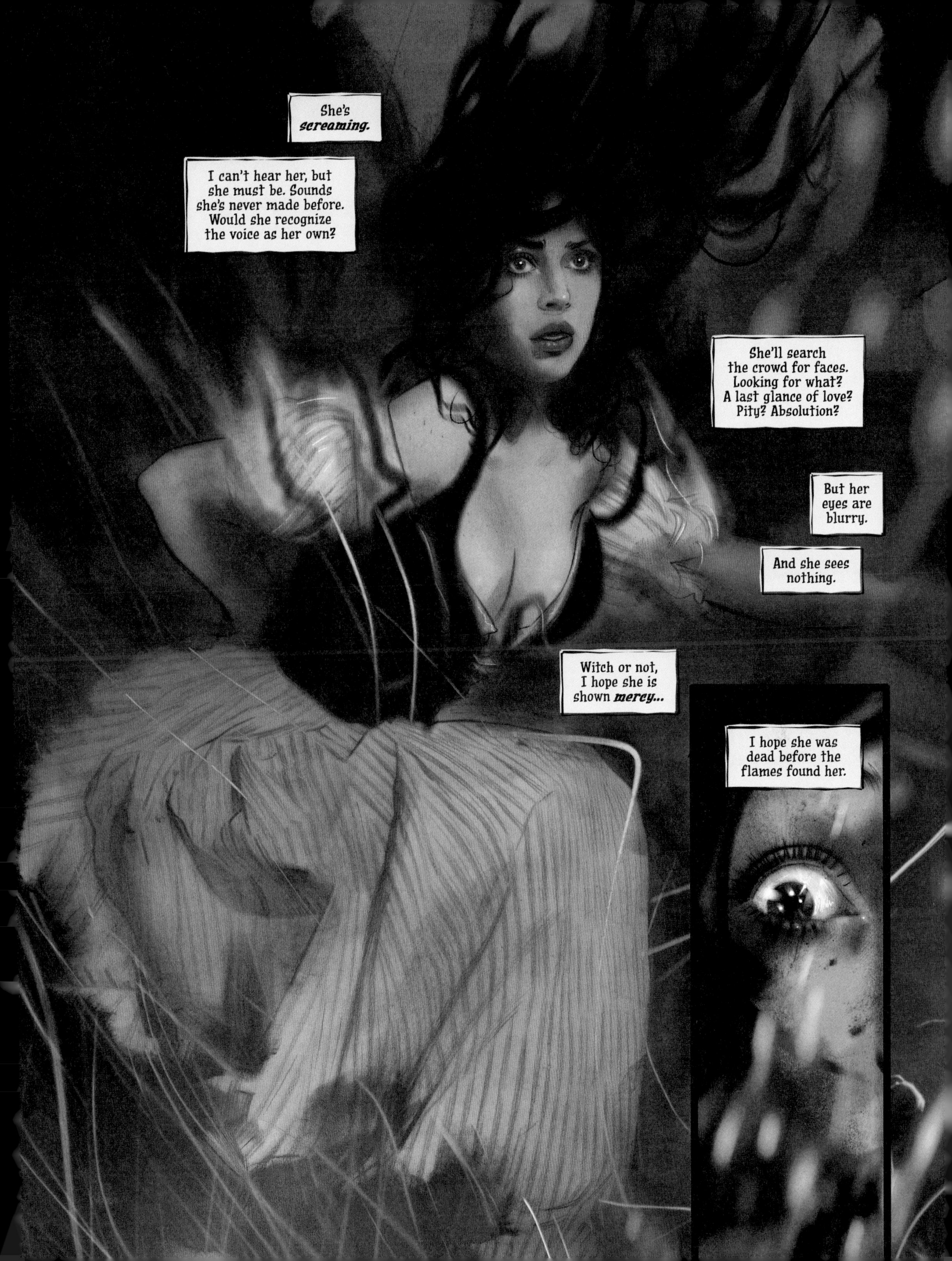
She's *screaming.*
I can't hear her, but she must be. Sounds she's never made before. Would she recognize the voice as her own?
She'll search the crowd for faces. Looking for what? A last glance of love? Pity? Absolution?
But her eyes are blurry.
And she sees nothing.
Witch or not, I hope she is shown *mercy...*
I hope she was dead before the flames found her.

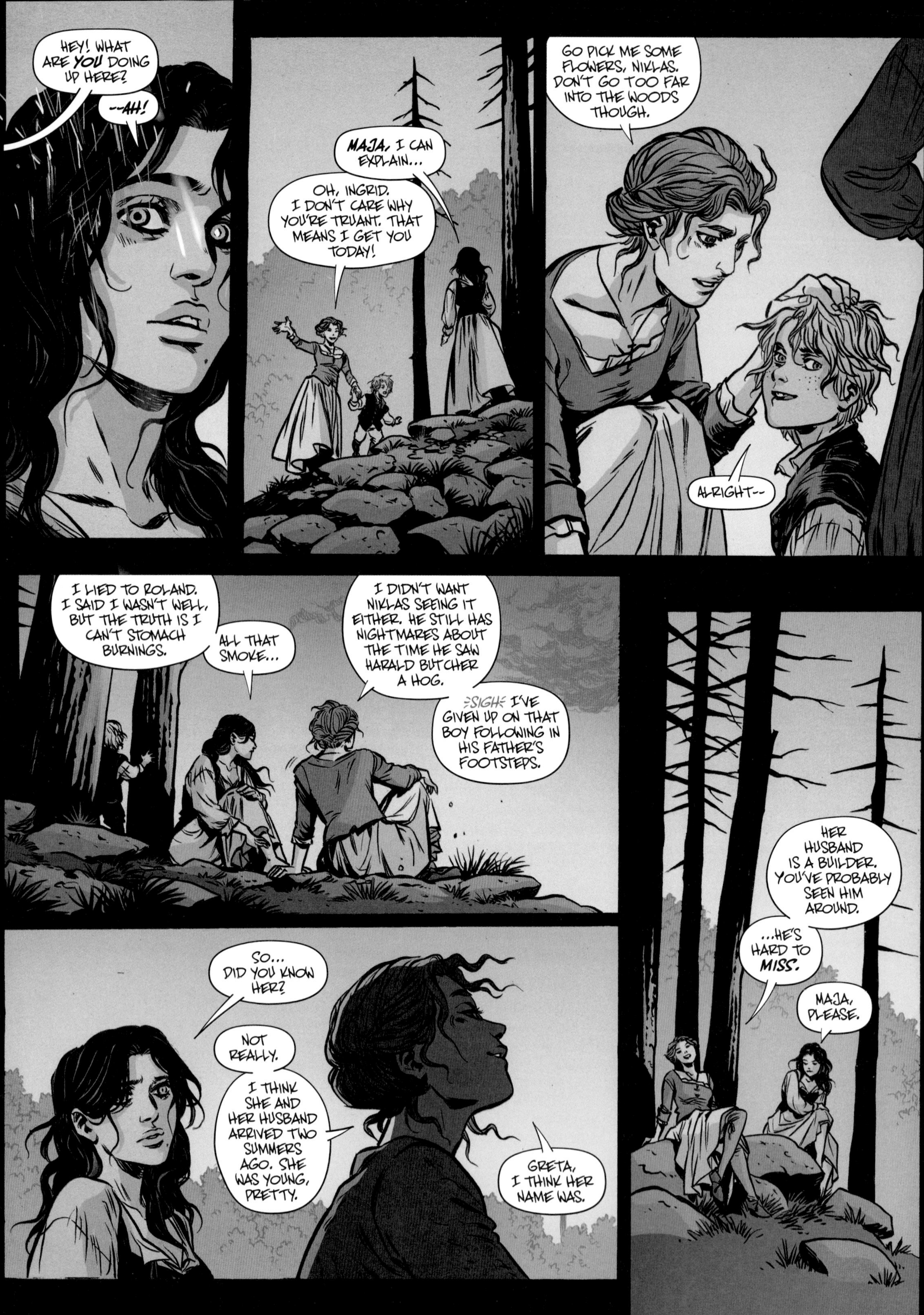
HEY! WHAT ARE YOU DOING UP HERE?
--AH!
MAJA, I CAN EXPLAIN...
OH, INGRID. I DON'T CARE WHY YOU'RE TRUANT. THAT MEANS I GET YOU TODAY!
GO PICK ME SOME FLOWERS, NIKLAS. DON'T GO TOO FAR INTO THE WOODS THOUGH.
ALRIGHT--
I LIED TO ROLAND. I SAID I WASN'T WELL, BUT THE TRUTH IS I CAN'T STOMACH BURNINGS.
ALL THAT SMOKE...
I DIDN'T WANT NIKLAS SEEING IT EITHER. HE STILL HAS NIGHTMARES ABOUT THE TIME HE SAW HARALD BUTCHER A HOG.
SIGH I'VE GIVEN UP ON THAT BOY FOLLOWING IN HIS FATHER'S FOOTSTEPS.
SO... DID YOU KNOW HER?
NOT REALLY.
I THINK SHE AND HER HUSBAND ARRIVED TWO SUMMERS AGO. SHE WAS YOUNG, PRETTY.
GRETA, I THINK HER NAME WAS.
HER HUSBAND IS A BUILDER. YOU'VE PROBABLY SEEN HIM AROUND.
...HE'S HARD TO MISS.
MAJA, PLEASE.

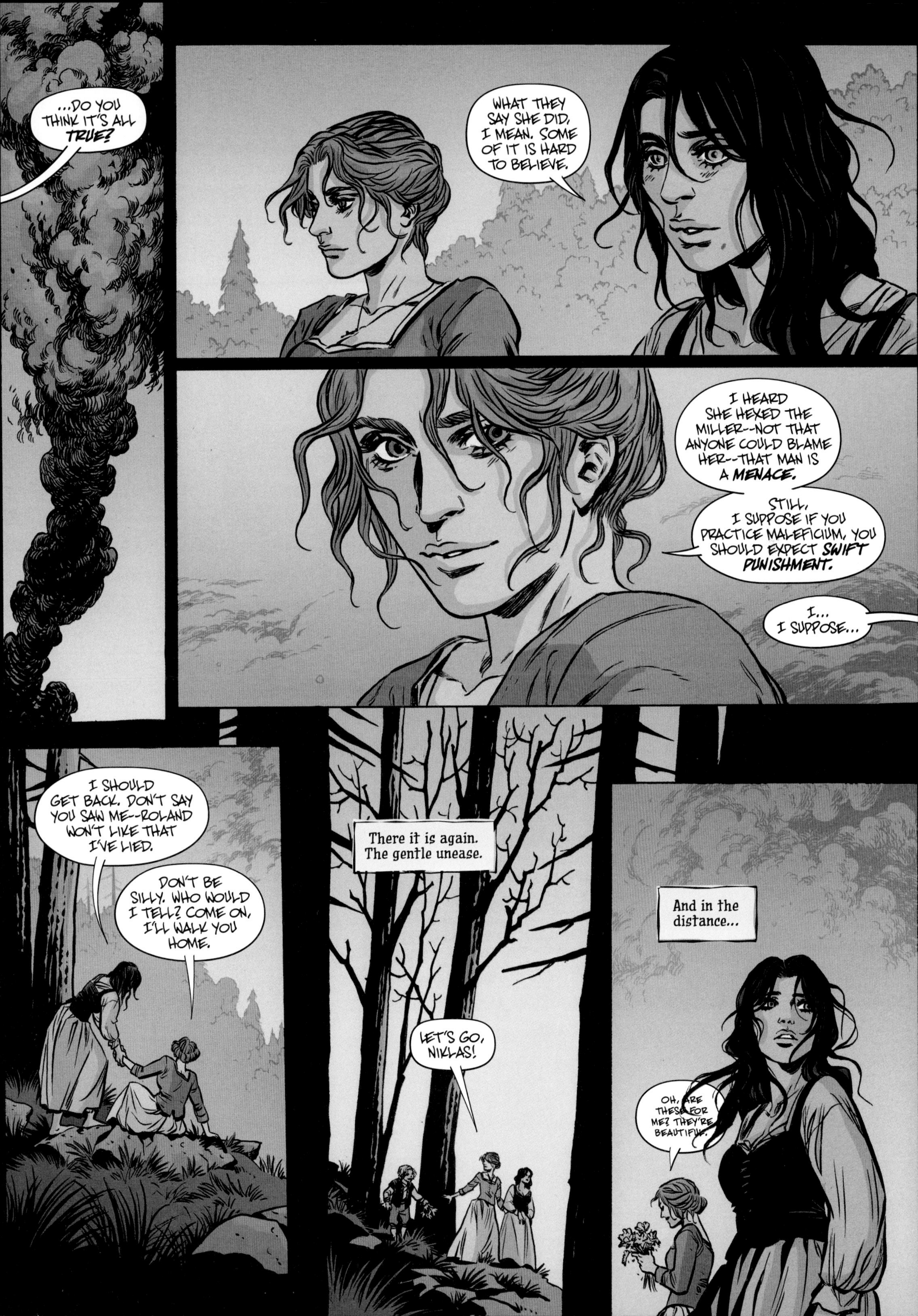

...DO YOU THINK IT'S ALL **TRUE?**
WHAT THEY SAY SHE DID, I MEAN. SOME OF IT IS HARD TO BELIEVE.
I HEARD SHE HEXED THE MILLER--NOT THAT ANYONE COULD BLAME HER--THAT MAN IS A **MENACE.**
STILL, I SUPPOSE IF YOU PRACTICE MALEFICIUM, YOU SHOULD EXPECT **SWIFT PUNISHMENT.**
I... I SUPPOSE...
I SHOULD GET BACK. DON'T SAY YOU SAW ME--ROLAND WON'T LIKE THAT I'VE LIED.
DON'T BE SILLY. WHO WOULD I TELL? COME ON, I'LL WALK YOU HOME.
There it is again. The gentle unease.
LET'S GO, NIKLAS!
And in the distance...
OH, ARE THESE FOR ME? THEY'RE BEAUTIFUL.

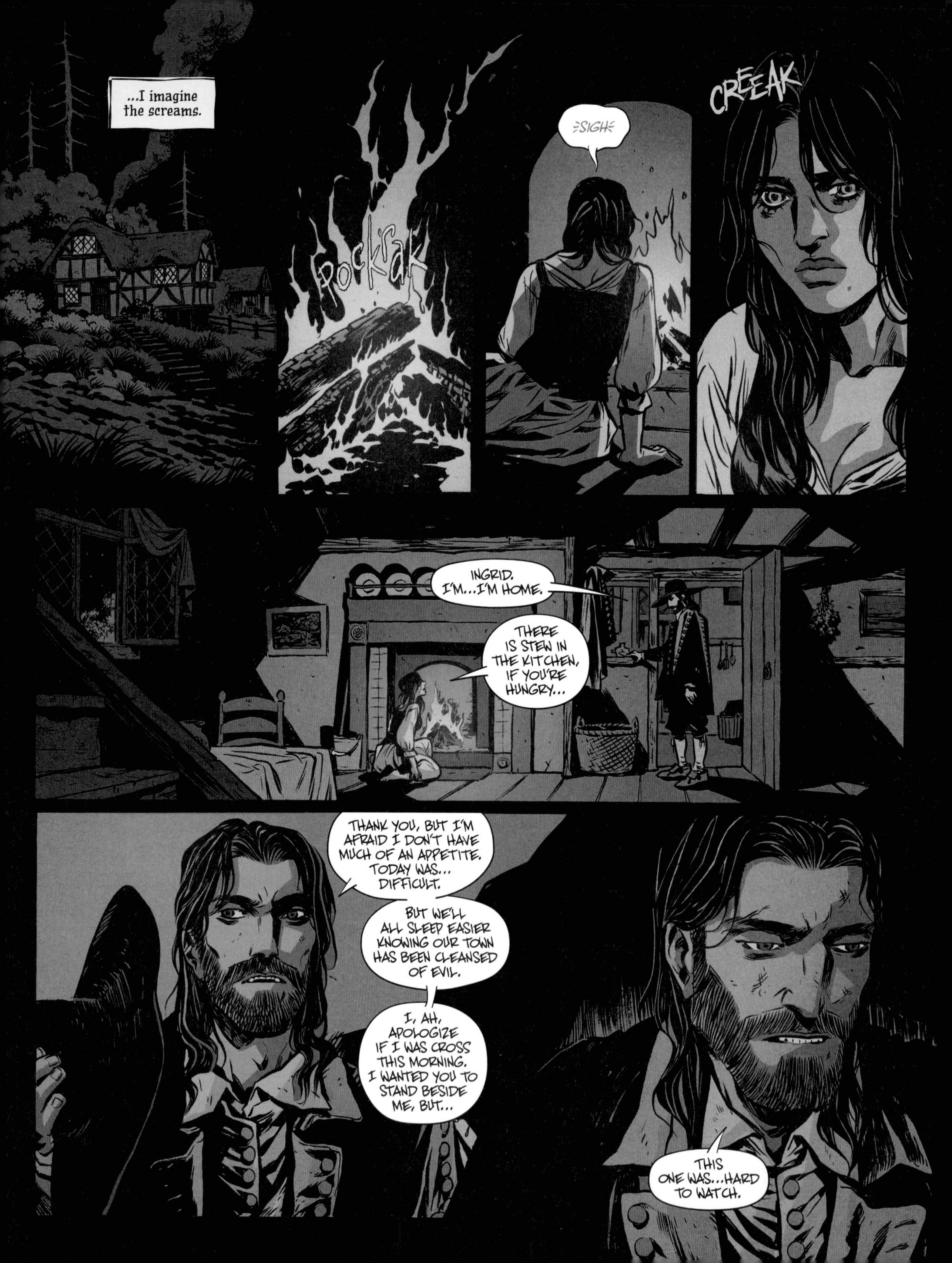
...I imagine the screams.
POCKRAK
SIGH
CREEAK
INGRID. I'M...I'M HOME.
THERE IS STEW IN THE KITCHEN, IF YOU'RE HUNGRY...
THANK YOU, BUT I'M AFRAID I DON'T HAVE MUCH OF AN APPETITE. TODAY WAS... DIFFICULT.
BUT WE'LL ALL SLEEP EASIER KNOWING OUR TOWN HAS BEEN CLEANSED OF EVIL.
I, AH, APOLOGIZE IF I WAS CROSS THIS MORNING. I WANTED YOU TO STAND BESIDE ME, BUT...
THIS ONE WAS...HARD TO WATCH.

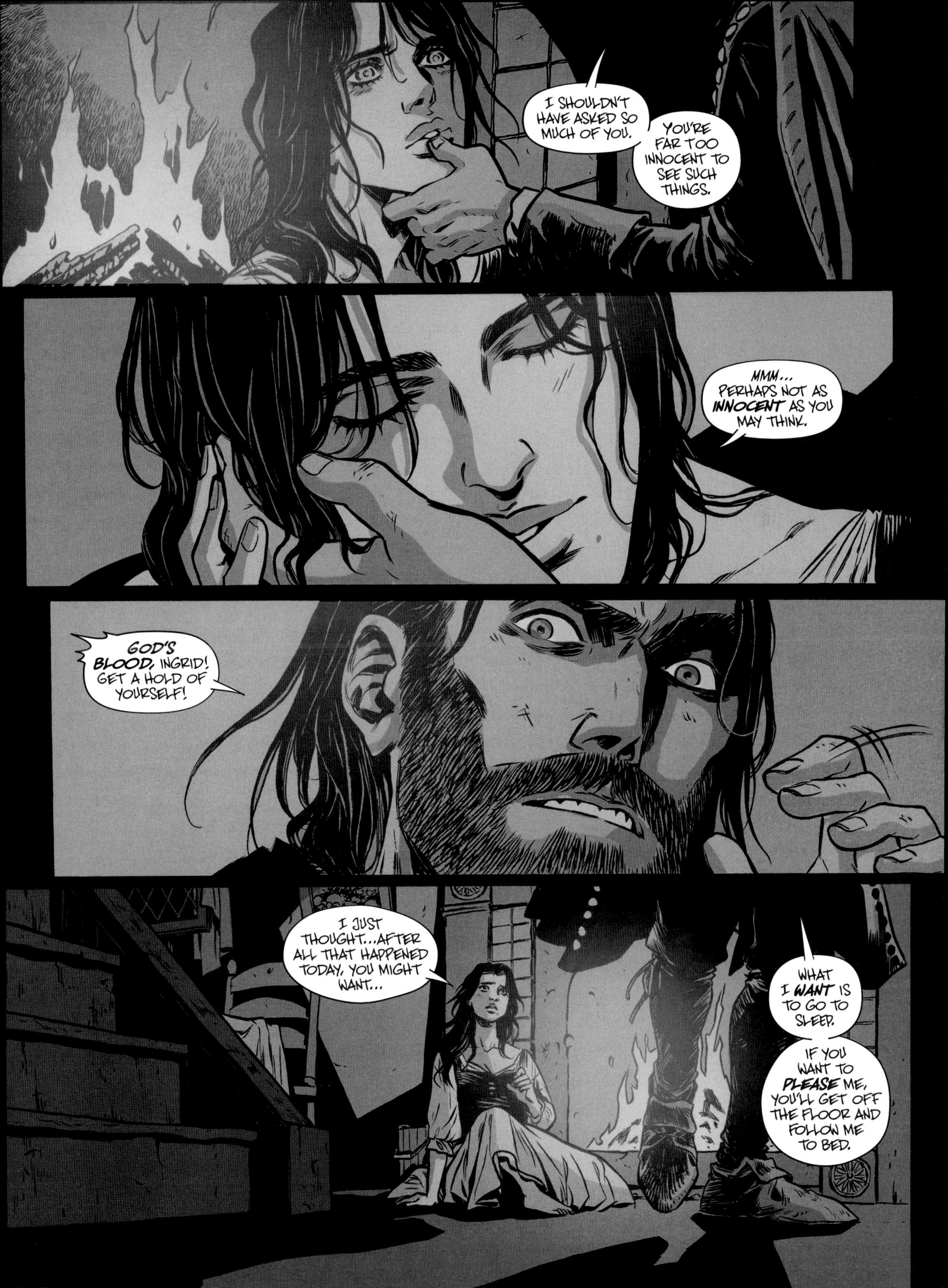
I SHOULDN'T HAVE ASKED SO MUCH OF YOU.
YOU'RE FAR TOO INNOCENT TO SEE SUCH THINGS.
MMM... PERHAPS NOT AS ***INNOCENT*** AS YOU MAY THINK.
GOD'S BLOOD, INGRID! GET A HOLD OF YOURSELF!
I JUST THOUGHT...AFTER ALL THAT HAPPENED TODAY, YOU MIGHT WANT...
WHAT I ***WANT*** IS TO GO TO SLEEP.
IF YOU WANT TO ***PLEASE*** ME, YOU'LL GET OFF THE FLOOR AND FOLLOW ME TO BED.

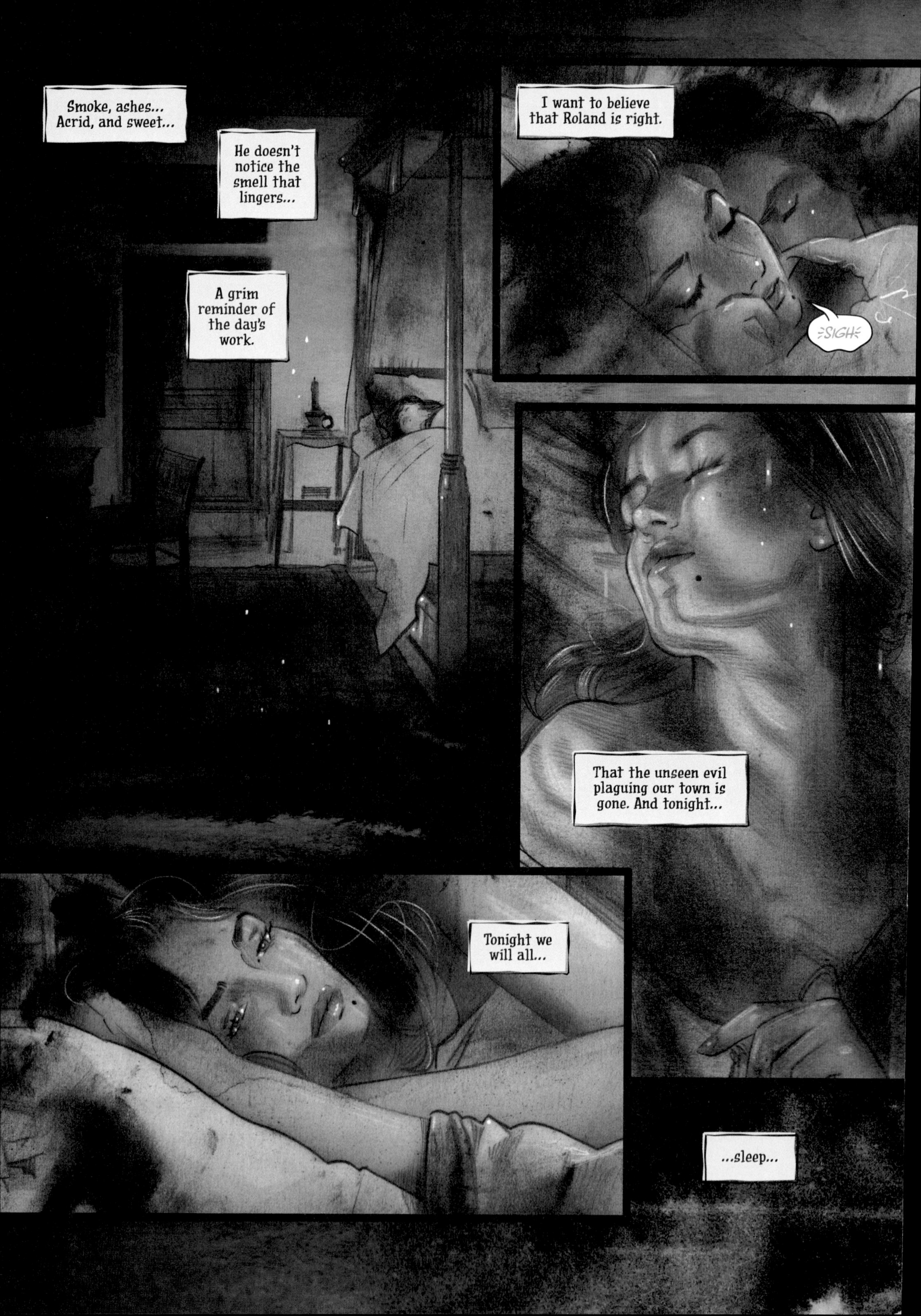
Smoke, ashes... Acrid, and sweet...
He doesn't notice the smell that lingers...
A grim reminder of the day's work.
I want to believe that Roland is right.
SIGH
That the unseen evil plaguing our town is gone. And tonight...
Tonight we will all...
...sleep...

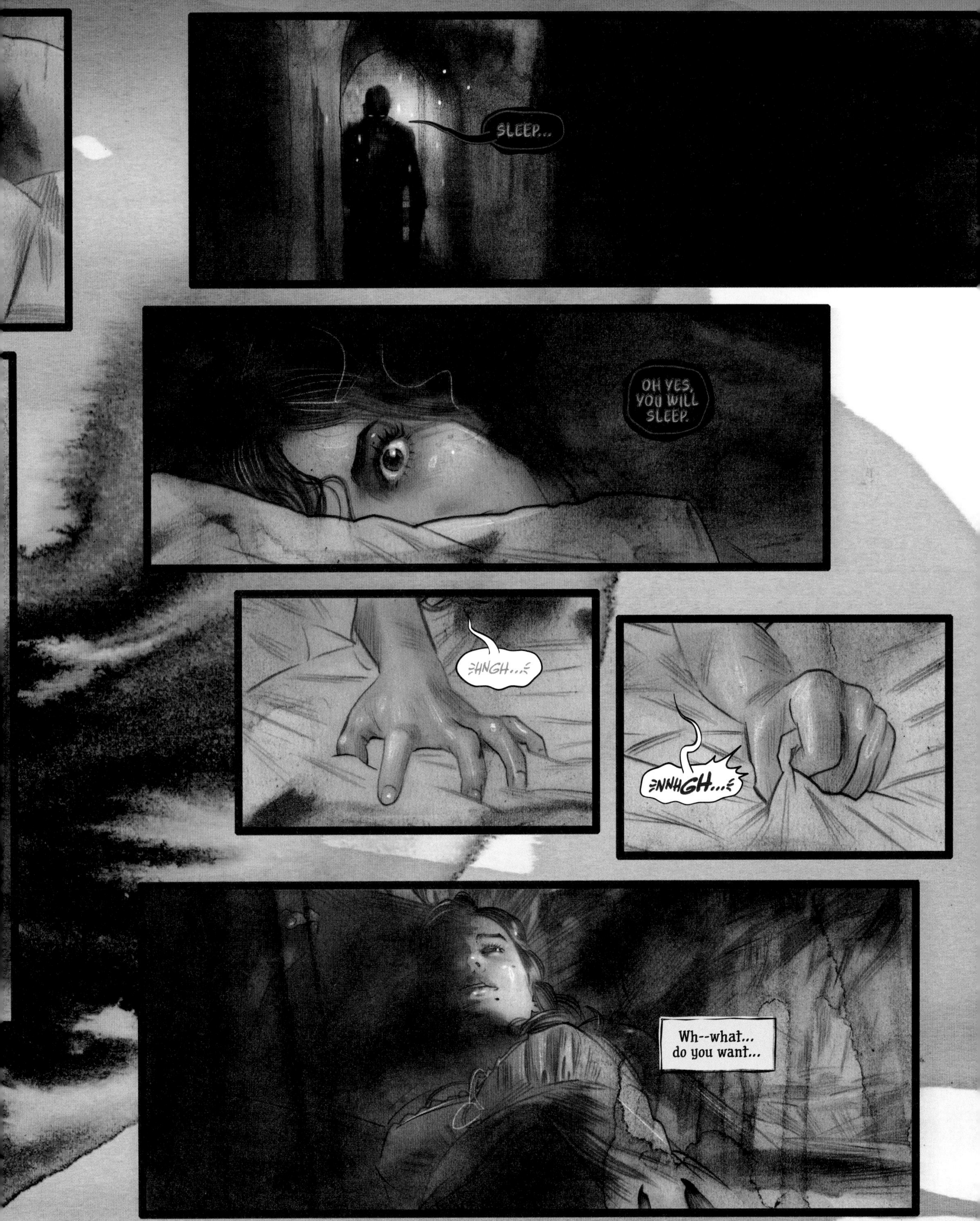
SLEEP...
OH YES, YOU WILL SLEEP.
HNGH...
NNHGH...
Wh--what... do you want...

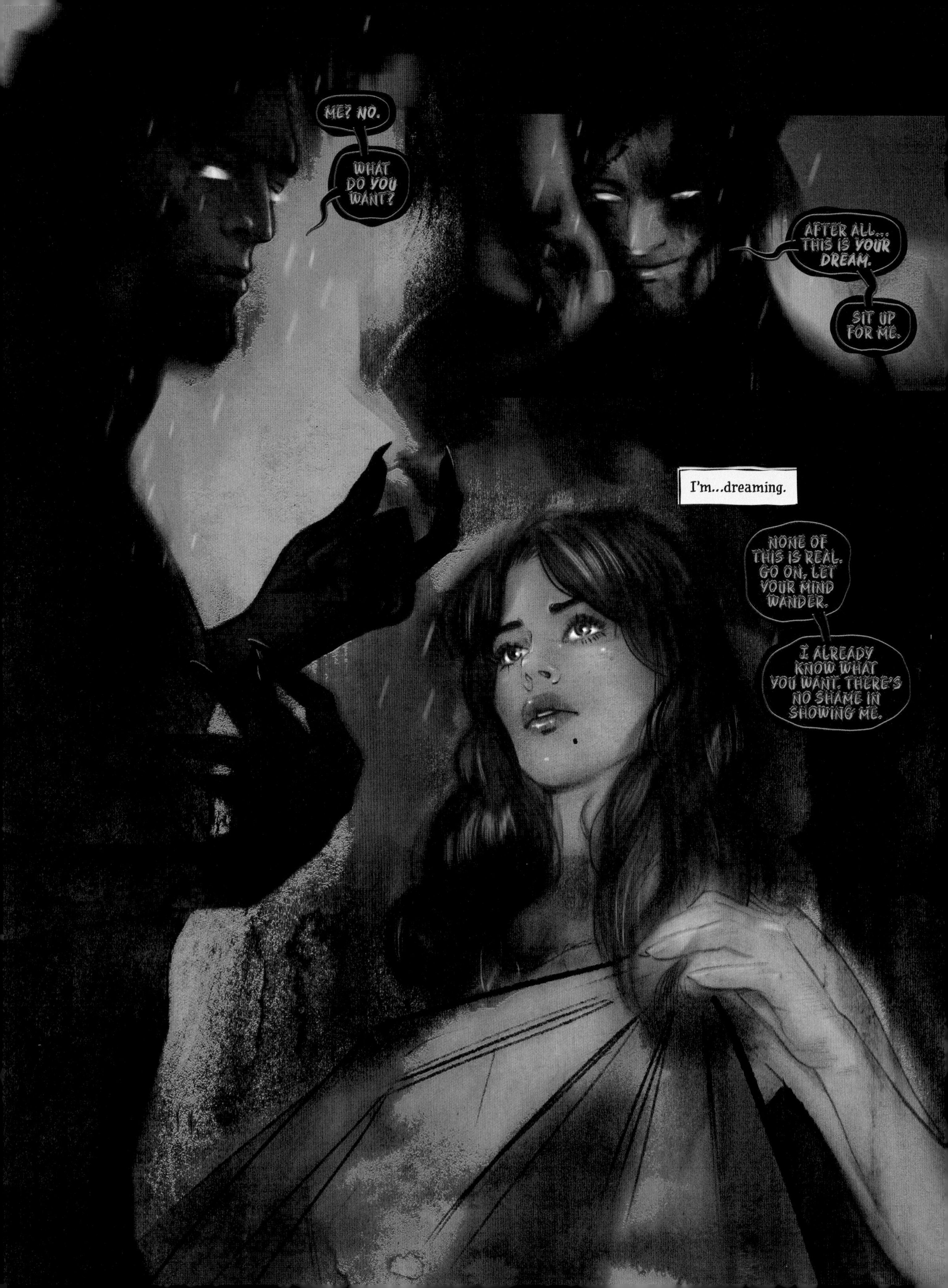

ME? NO.
WHAT DO YOU WANT?
AFTER ALL... THIS IS YOUR DREAM.
SIT UP FOR ME.
I'm...dreaming.
NONE OF THIS IS REAL. GO ON, LET YOUR MIND WANDER.
I ALREADY KNOW WHAT YOU WANT. THERE'S NO SHAME IN SHOWING ME.

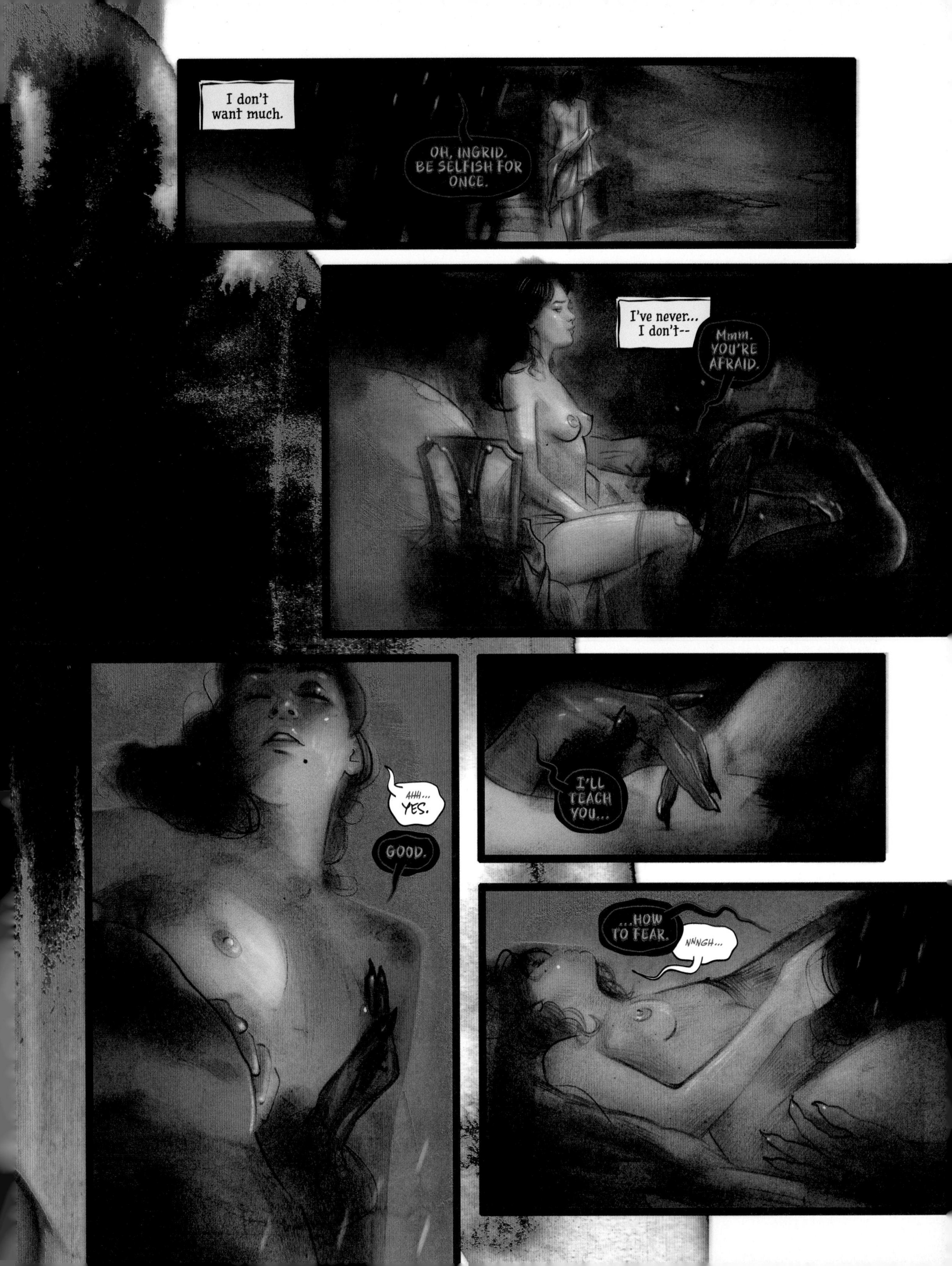

I don't want much.
OH, INGRID. BE SELFISH FOR ONCE.
I've never... I don't--
Mmm. YOU'RE AFRAID.
AHH... YES.
GOOD.
I'LL TEACH YOU...
...HOW TO FEAR.
NNNGH...

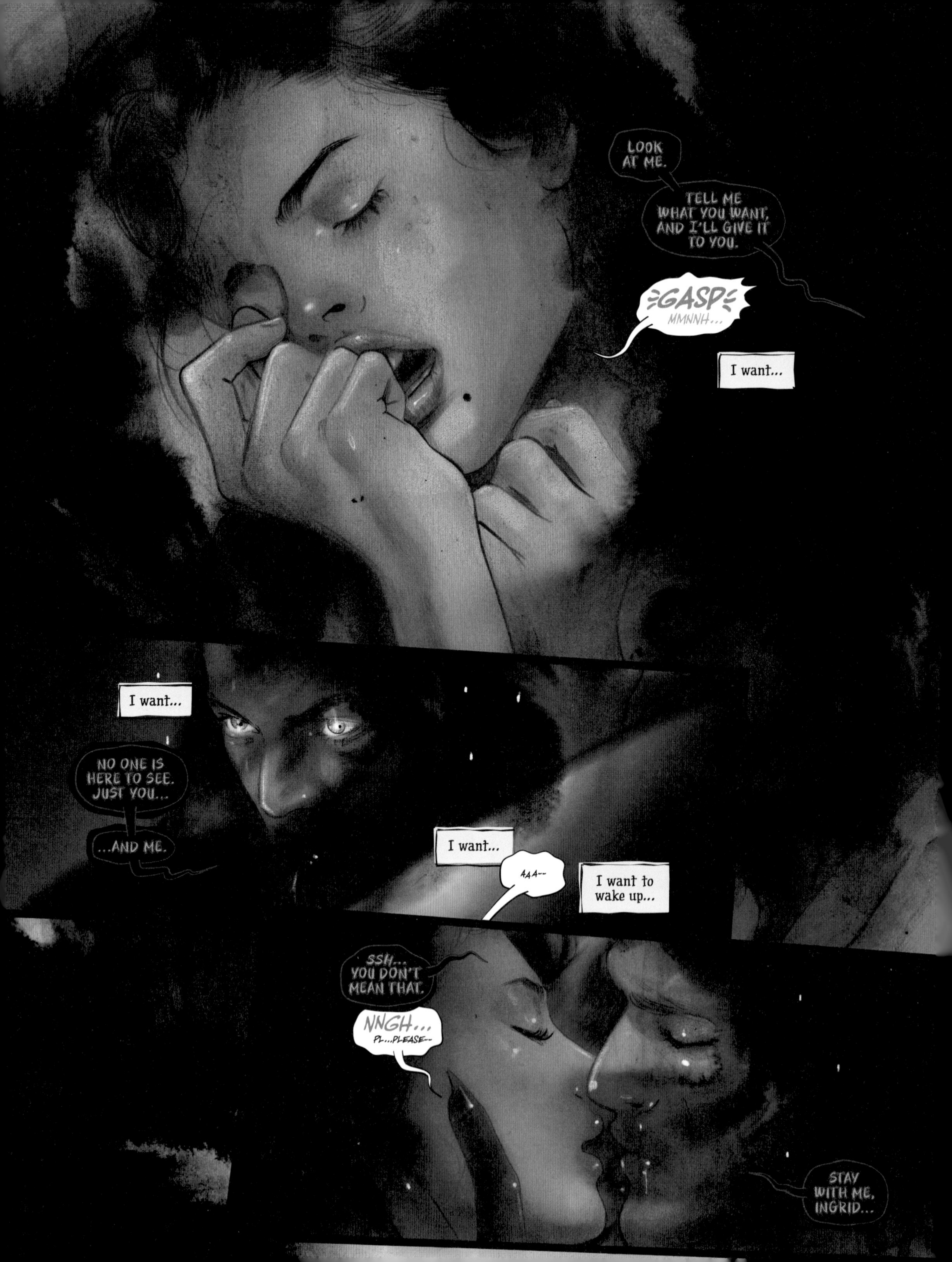
LOOK AT ME.
TELL ME WHAT YOU WANT, AND I'LL GIVE IT TO YOU.
GASP MMNNH...
I want...
I want...
NO ONE IS HERE TO SEE. JUST YOU...
...AND ME.
I want...
AAA--
I want to wake up...
SSH... YOU DON'T MEAN THAT.
NNGH... PL...PLEASE--
STAY WITH ME, INGRID...

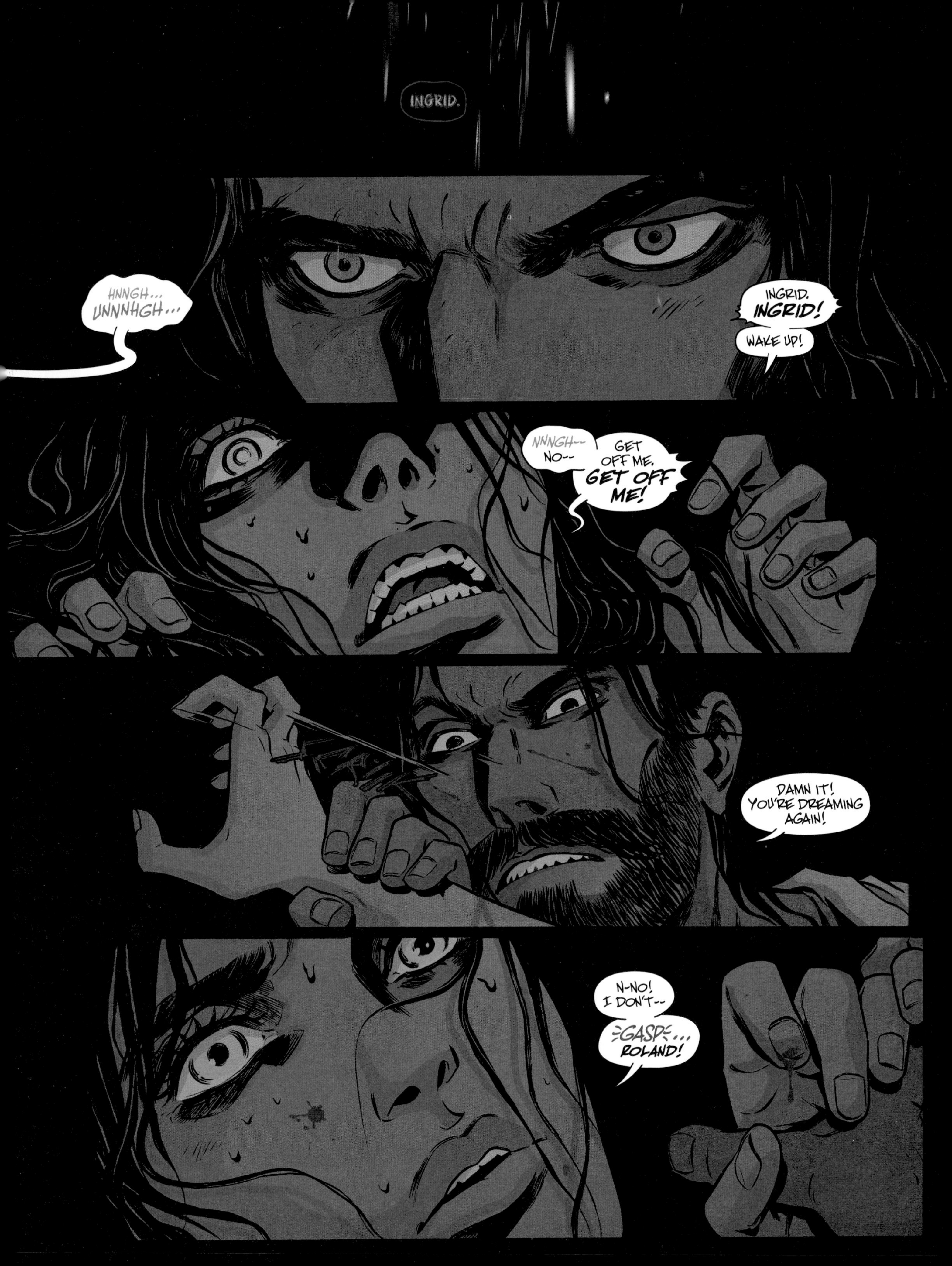

INGRID.
HNNGH... UNNNHGH...
INGRID. INGRID!
WAKE UP!
NNNGH-- NO--
GET OFF ME. GET OFF ME!
DAMN IT! YOU'RE DREAMING AGAIN!
N-NO! I DON'T--
GASP... ROLAND!

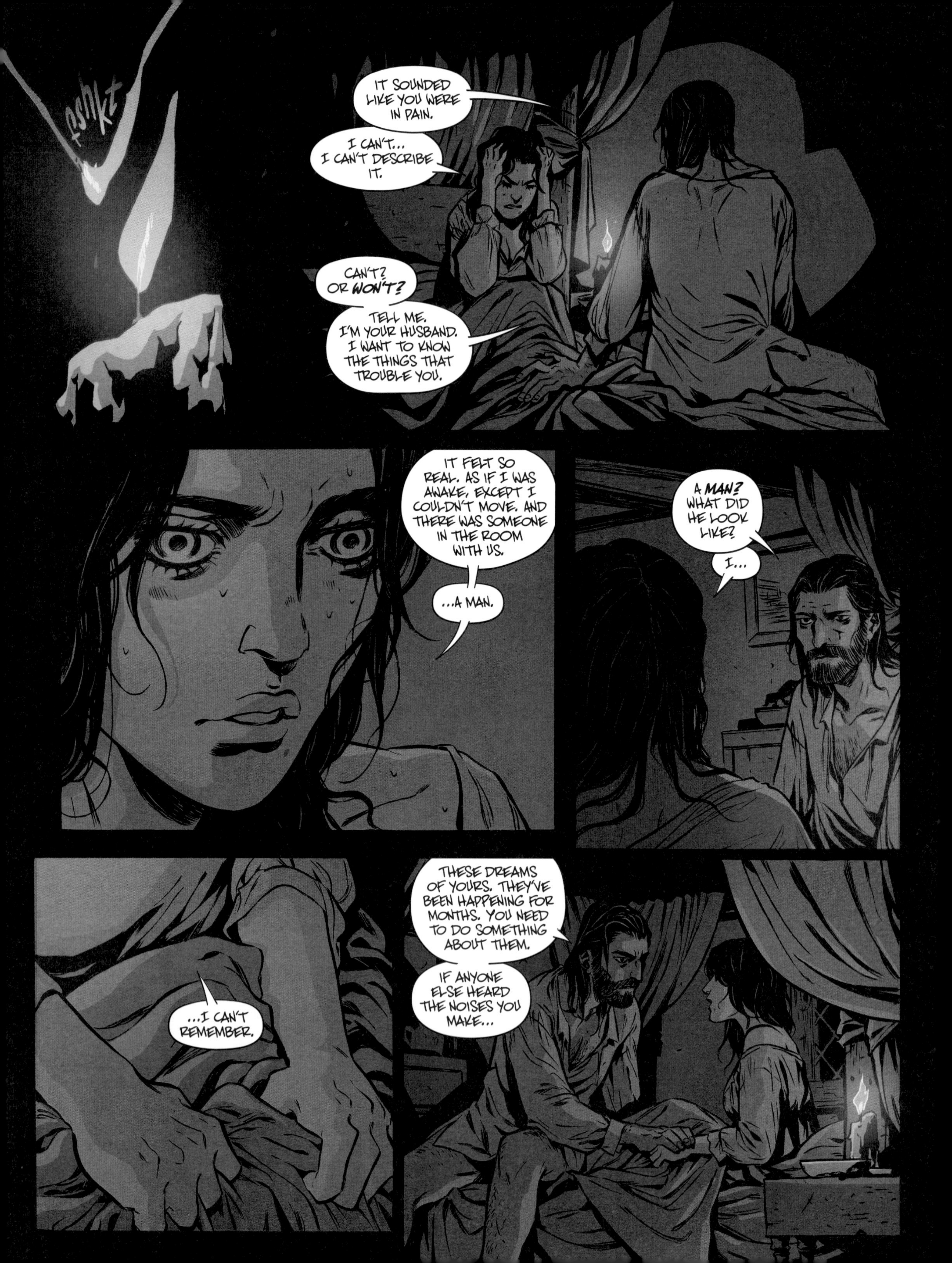
FSHKT
IT SOUNDED LIKE YOU WERE IN PAIN.
I CAN'T... I CAN'T DESCRIBE IT.
CAN'T? OR WON'T?
TELL ME. I'M YOUR HUSBAND. I WANT TO KNOW THE THINGS THAT TROUBLE YOU.
IT FELT SO REAL. AS IF I WAS AWAKE, EXCEPT I COULDN'T MOVE. AND THERE WAS SOMEONE IN THE ROOM WITH US.
...A MAN.
A MAN? WHAT DID HE LOOK LIKE?
I...
...I CAN'T REMEMBER.
THESE DREAMS OF YOURS. THEY'VE BEEN HAPPENING FOR MONTHS. YOU NEED TO DO SOMETHING ABOUT THEM.
IF ANYONE ELSE HEARD THE NOISES YOU MAKE...

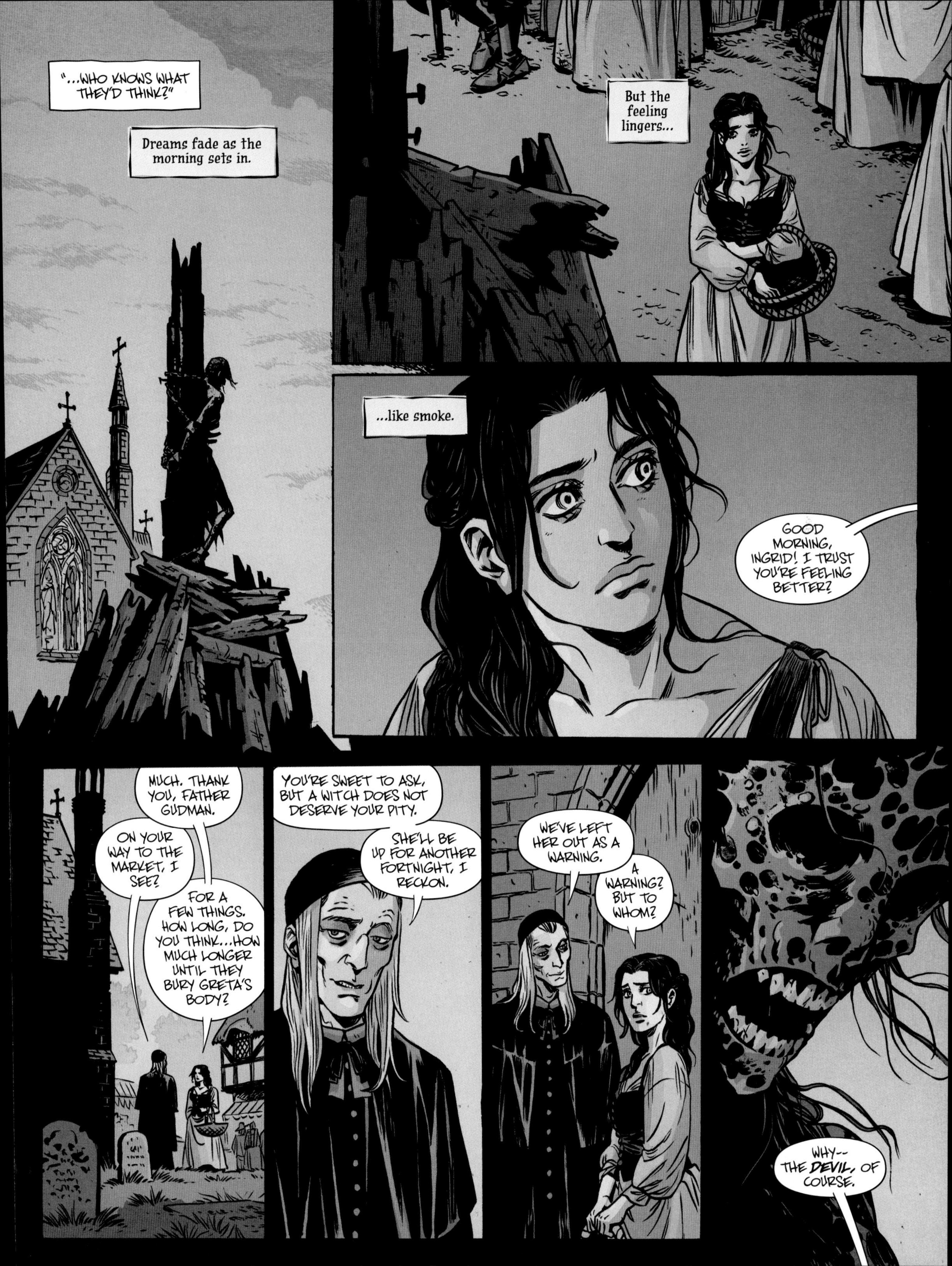
"...WHO KNOWS WHAT THEY'D THINK?"
Dreams fade as the morning sets in.
But the feeling lingers...
...like smoke.
GOOD MORNING, INGRID! I TRUST YOU'RE FEELING BETTER?
MUCH. THANK YOU, FATHER GUDMAN.
ON YOUR WAY TO THE MARKET, I SEE?
FOR A FEW THINGS. HOW LONG, DO YOU THINK...HOW MUCH LONGER UNTIL THEY BURY GRETA'S BODY?
YOU'RE SWEET TO ASK, BUT A WITCH DOES NOT DESERVE YOUR PITY.
SHE'LL BE UP FOR ANOTHER FORTNIGHT, I RECKON.
WE'VE LEFT HER OUT AS A WARNING.
A WARNING? BUT TO WHOM?
WHY-- THE DEVIL, OF COURSE.

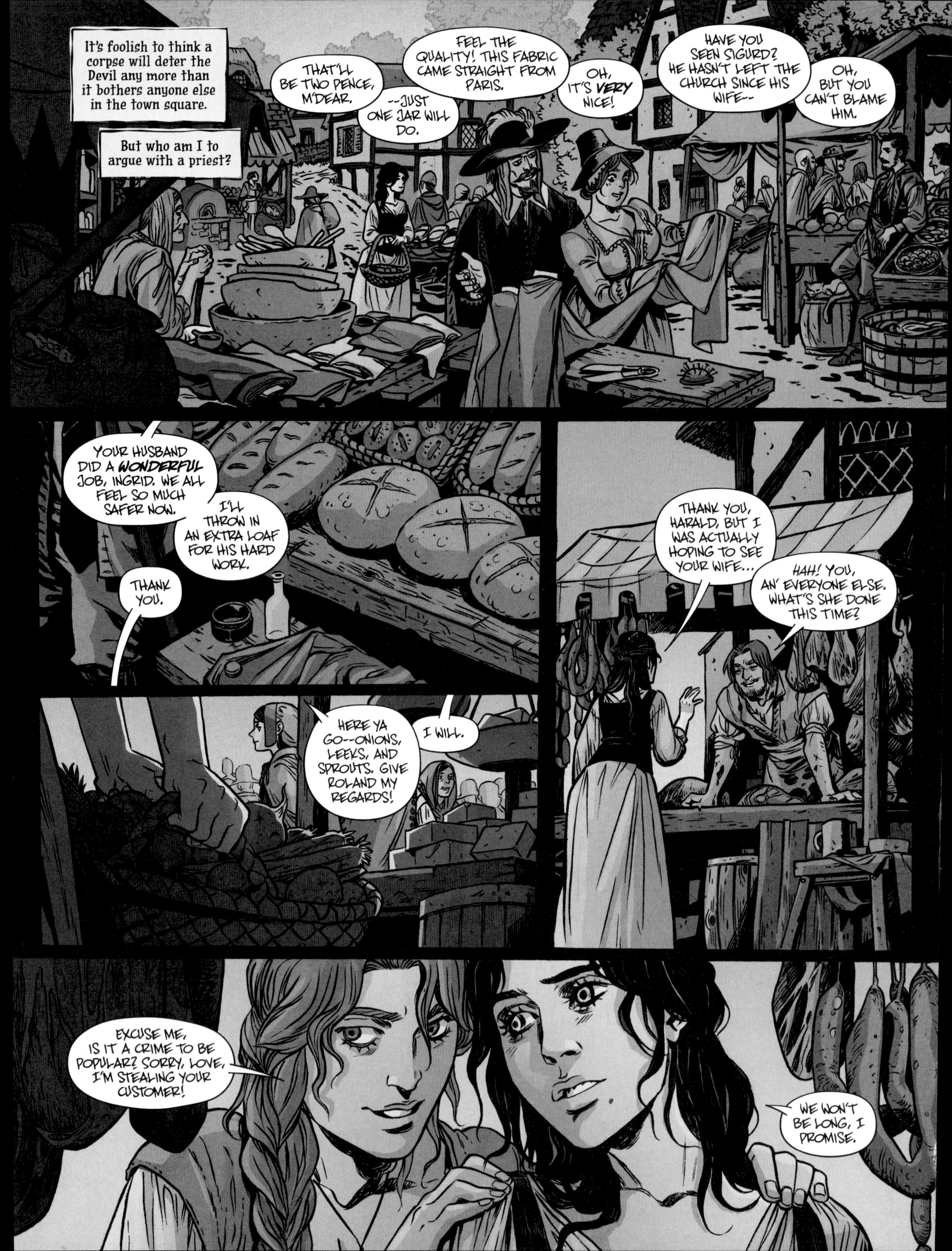
It's foolish to think a corpse will deter the Devil any more than it bothers anyone else in the town square.
But who am I to argue with a priest?
THAT'LL BE TWO PENCE, M'DEAR.
--JUST ONE JAR WILL DO.
FEEL THE QUALITY! THIS FABRIC CAME STRAIGHT FROM PARIS.
OH, IT'S VERY NICE!
HAVE YOU SEEN SIGURD? HE HASN'T LEFT THE CHURCH SINCE HIS WIFE--
OH, BUT YOU CAN'T BLAME HIM.
YOUR HUSBAND DID A WONDERFUL JOB, INGRID. WE ALL FEEL SO MUCH SAFER NOW.
I'LL THROW IN AN EXTRA LOAF FOR HIS HARD WORK.
THANK YOU.
HERE YA GO--ONIONS, LEEKS, AND SPROUTS. GIVE ROLAND MY REGARDS!
I WILL.
THANK YOU, HARALD, BUT I WAS ACTUALLY HOPING TO SEE YOUR WIFE...
HAH! YOU, AN' EVERYONE ELSE. WHAT'S SHE DONE THIS TIME?
EXCUSE ME, IS IT A CRIME TO BE POPULAR? SORRY, LOVE, I'M STEALING YOUR CUSTOMER!
WE WON'T BE LONG, I PROMISE.

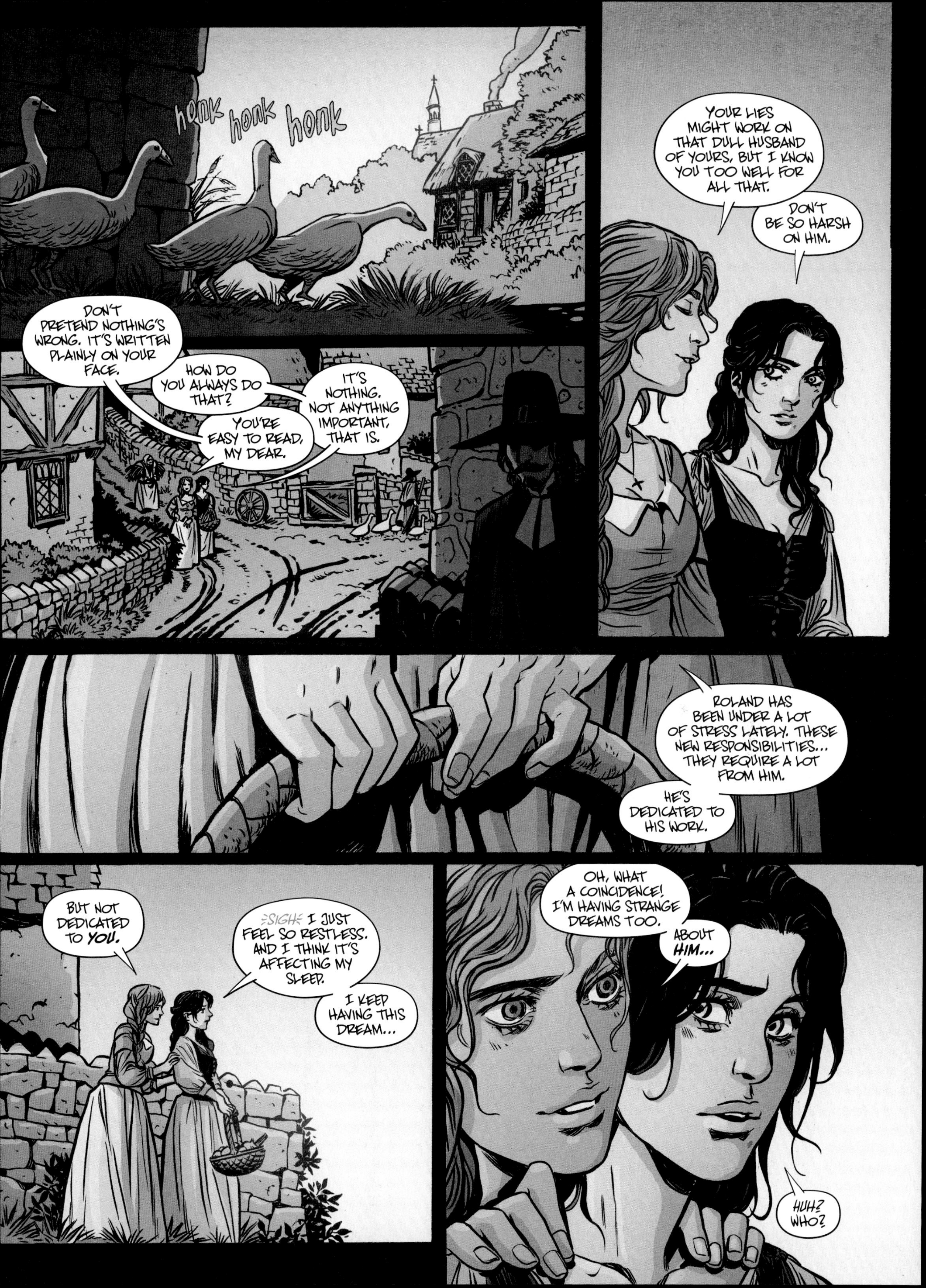
honk honk honk
YOUR LIES MIGHT WORK ON THAT DULL HUSBAND OF YOURS, BUT I KNOW YOU TOO WELL FOR ALL THAT.
DON'T BE SO HARSH ON HIM.
DON'T PRETEND NOTHING'S WRONG. IT'S WRITTEN PLAINLY ON YOUR FACE.
HOW DO YOU ALWAYS DO THAT?
YOU'RE EASY TO READ, MY DEAR.
IT'S NOTHING. NOT ANYTHING IMPORTANT, THAT IS.
ROLAND HAS BEEN UNDER A LOT OF STRESS LATELY. THESE NEW RESPONSIBILITIES... THEY REQUIRE A LOT FROM HIM.
HE'S DEDICATED TO HIS WORK.
BUT NOT DEDICATED TO **YOU.**
SIGH I JUST FEEL SO RESTLESS. AND I THINK IT'S AFFECTING MY SLEEP.
I KEEP HAVING THIS DREAM...
OH, WHAT A COINCIDENCE! I'M HAVING STRANGE DREAMS TOO.
ABOUT **HIM...**
HUH? WHO?

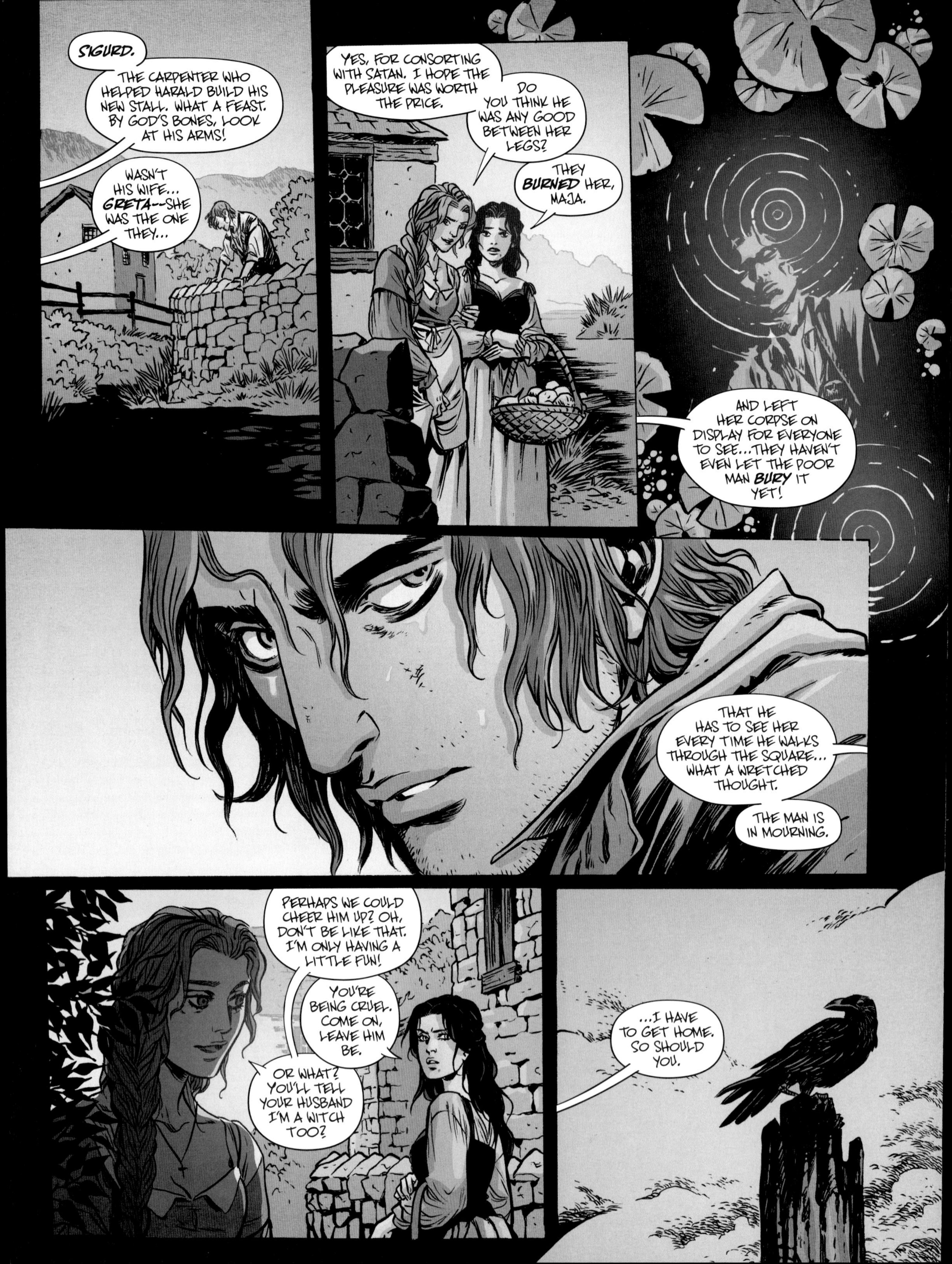
SIGURD.
THE CARPENTER WHO HELPED HARALD BUILD HIS NEW STALL. WHAT A FEAST. BY GOD'S BONES, LOOK AT HIS ARMS!
WASN'T HIS WIFE... GRETA--SHE WAS THE ONE THEY...
YES, FOR CONSORTING WITH SATAN. I HOPE THE PLEASURE WAS WORTH THE PRICE.
DO YOU THINK HE WAS ANY GOOD BETWEEN HER LEGS?
THEY BURNED HER, MAJA.
AND LEFT HER CORPSE ON DISPLAY FOR EVERYONE TO SEE...THEY HAVEN'T EVEN LET THE POOR MAN BURY IT YET!
THAT HE HAS TO SEE HER EVERY TIME HE WALKS THROUGH THE SQUARE... WHAT A WRETCHED THOUGHT.
THE MAN IS IN MOURNING.
PERHAPS WE COULD CHEER HIM UP? OH, DON'T BE LIKE THAT. I'M ONLY HAVING A LITTLE FUN!
YOU'RE BEING CRUEL. COME ON, LEAVE HIM BE.
OR WHAT? YOU'LL TELL YOUR HUSBAND I'M A WITCH TOO?
...I HAVE TO GET HOME. SO SHOULD YOU.

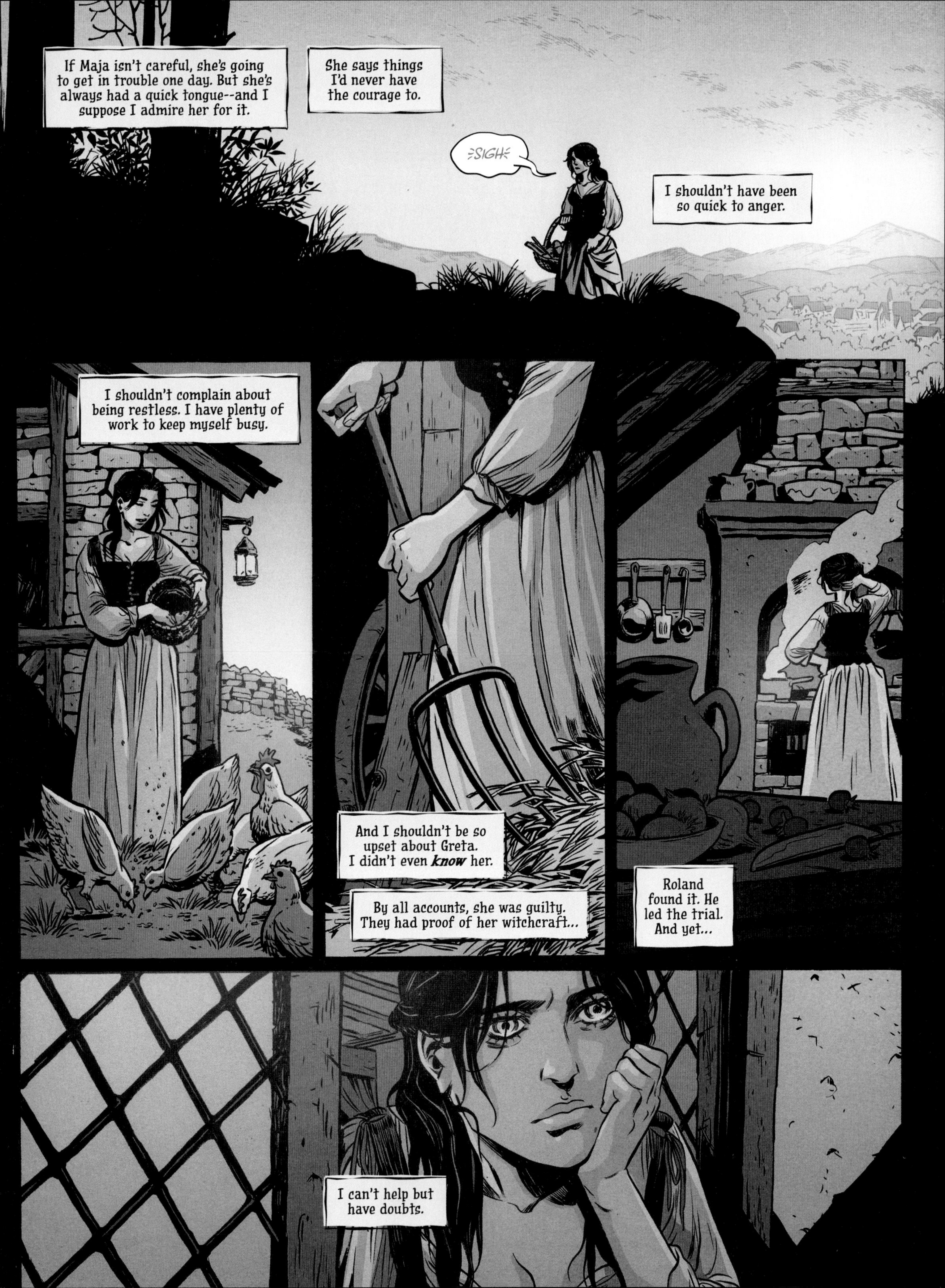
If Maja isn't careful, she's going to get in trouble one day. But she's always had a quick tongue--and I suppose I admire her for it.
She says things I'd never have the courage to.
SIGH
I shouldn't have been so quick to anger.
I shouldn't complain about being restless. I have plenty of work to keep myself busy.
And I shouldn't be so upset about Greta. I didn't even know her.
By all accounts, she was guilty. They had proof of her witchcraft...
Roland found it. He led the trial. And yet...
I can't help but have doubts.

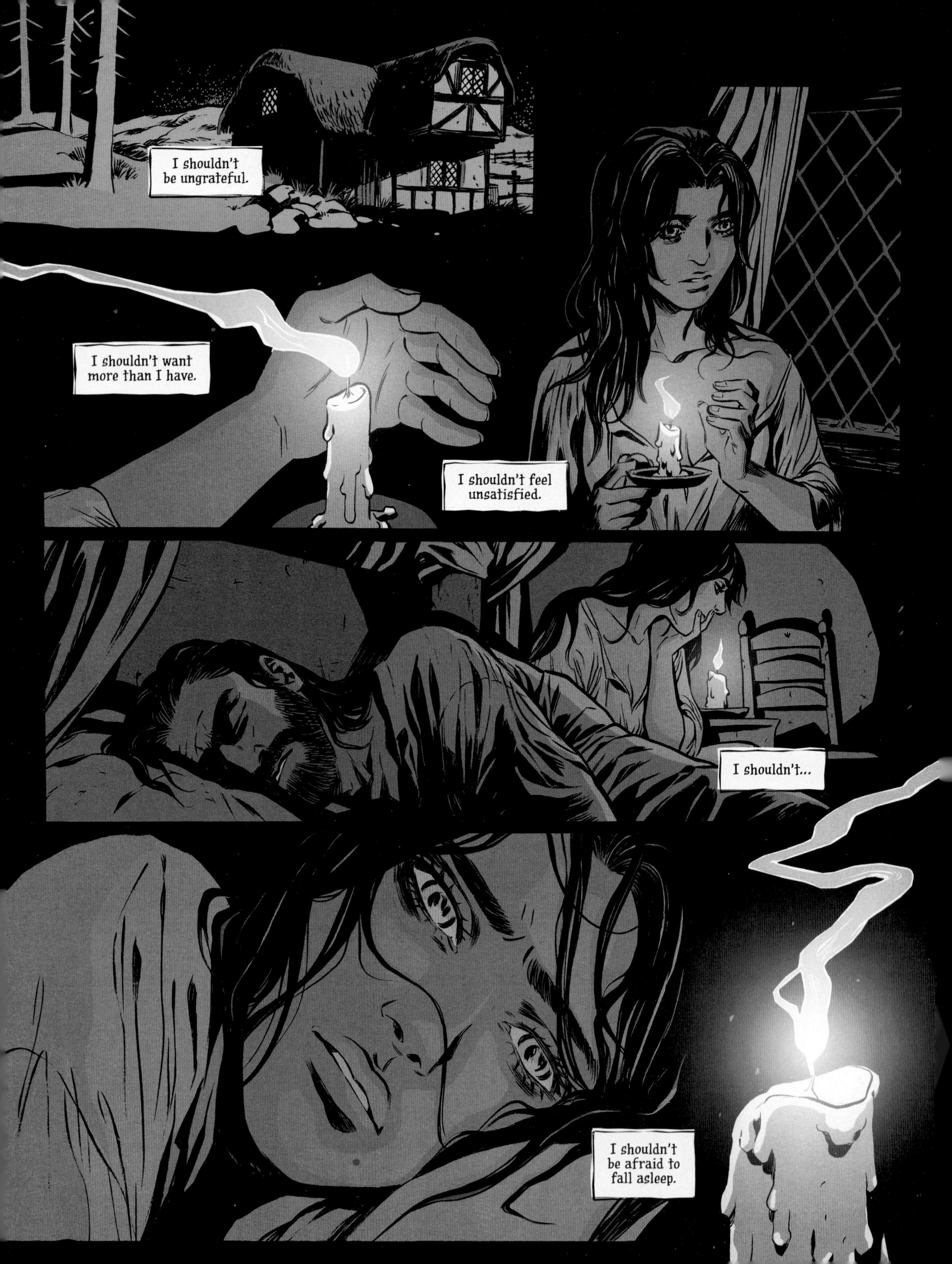
I shouldn't be ungrateful.
I shouldn't want more than I have.
I shouldn't feel unsatisfied.
I shouldn't...
I shouldn't be afraid to fall asleep.

CHAPTER II.
O FOR THIS QUIET

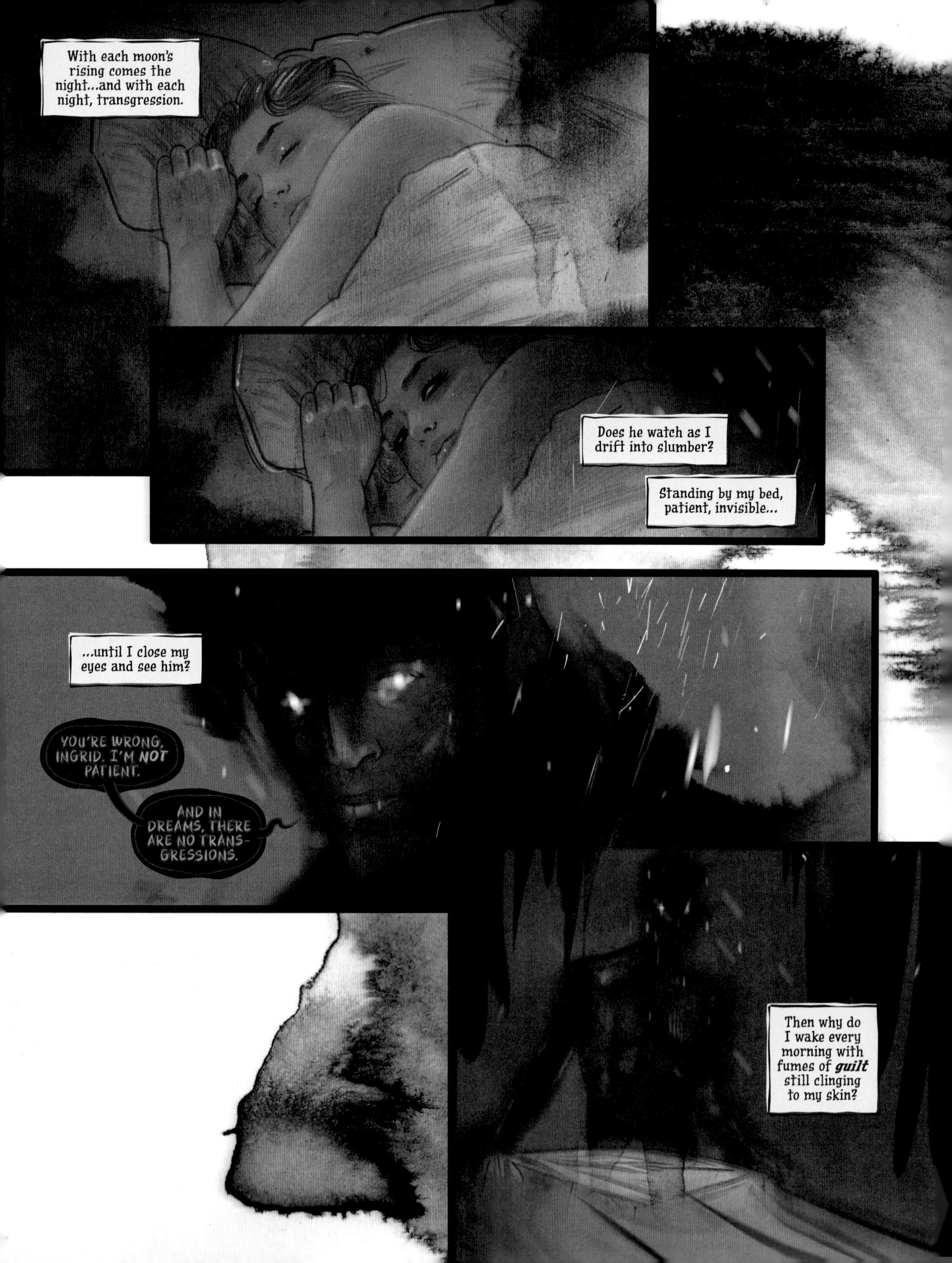

With each moon's rising comes the night...and with each night, transgression.
Does he watch as I drift into slumber?
Standing by my bed, patient, invisible...
...until I close my eyes and see him?
YOU'RE WRONG, INGRID. I'M **NOT** PATIENT.
AND IN DREAMS, THERE ARE NO TRANS-GRESSIONS.
Then why do I wake every morning with fumes of ***guilt*** still clinging to my skin?

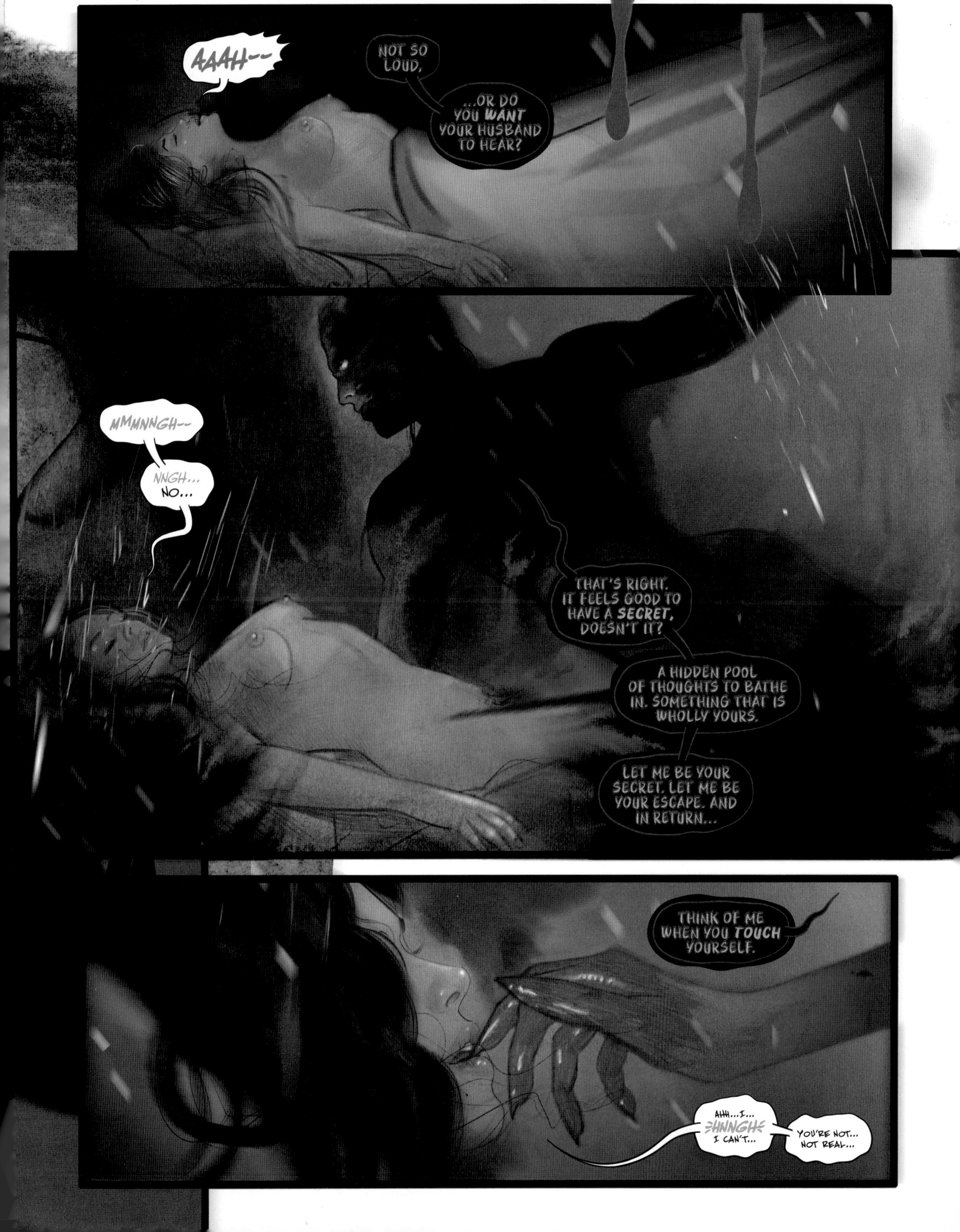

AAAH--
NOT SO LOUD,
...OR DO YOU WANT YOUR HUSBAND TO HEAR?
MMMNNGH--
NNGH... NO...
THAT'S RIGHT. IT FEELS GOOD TO HAVE A SECRET, DOESN'T IT?
A HIDDEN POOL OF THOUGHTS TO BATHE IN. SOMETHING THAT IS WHOLLY YOURS.
LET ME BE YOUR SECRET. LET ME BE YOUR ESCAPE. AND IN RETURN...
THINK OF ME WHEN YOU TOUCH YOURSELF.
AHH... I... HNNGH I CAN'T...
YOU'RE NOT... NOT REAL...

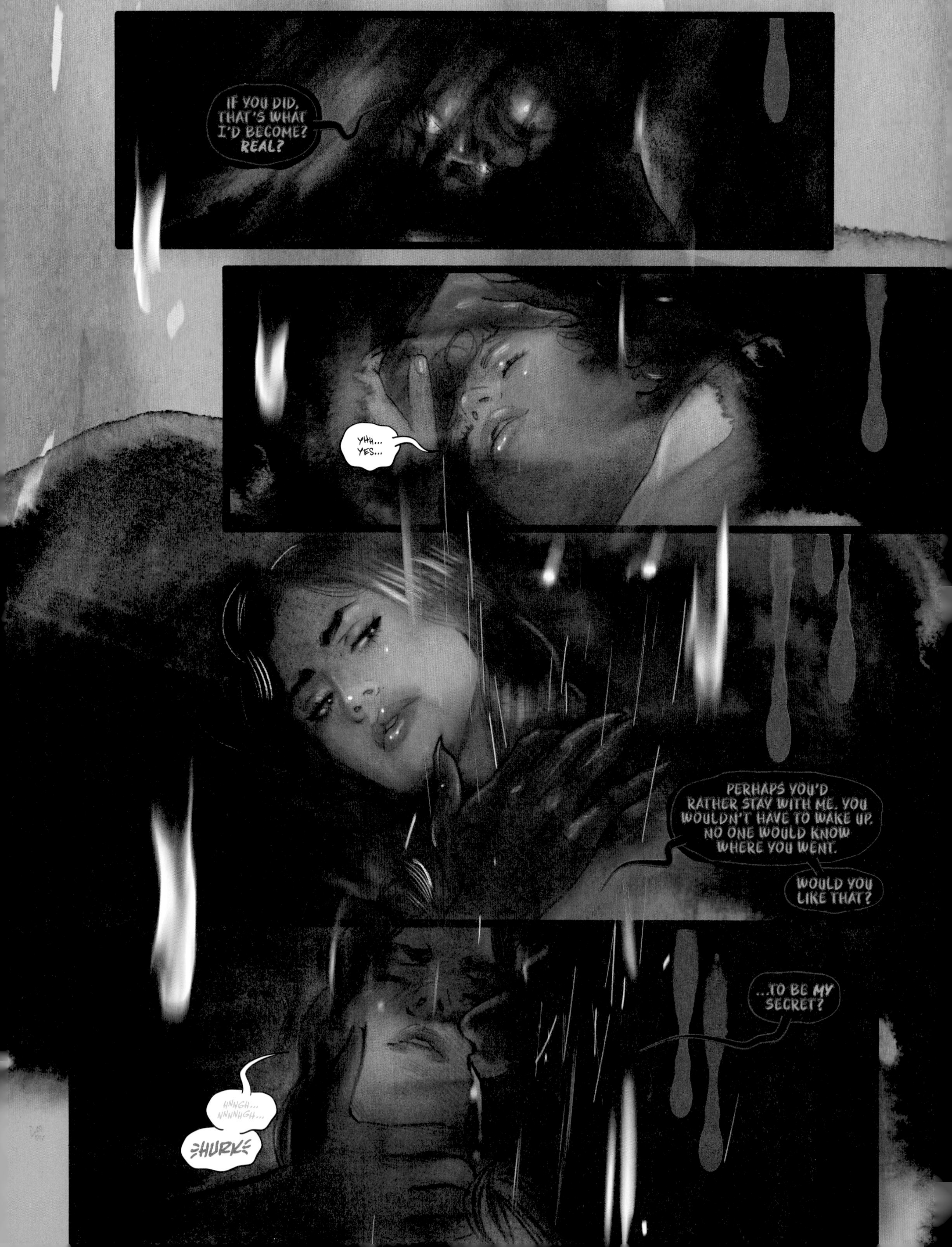
IF YOU DID, THAT'S WHAT I'D BECOME? REAL?
YHH... YES...
PERHAPS YOU'D RATHER STAY WITH ME. YOU WOULDN'T HAVE TO WAKE UP. NO ONE WOULD KNOW WHERE YOU WENT.
WOULD YOU LIKE THAT?
...TO BE MY SECRET?
HNNGH... NNNNHGH...
HURK

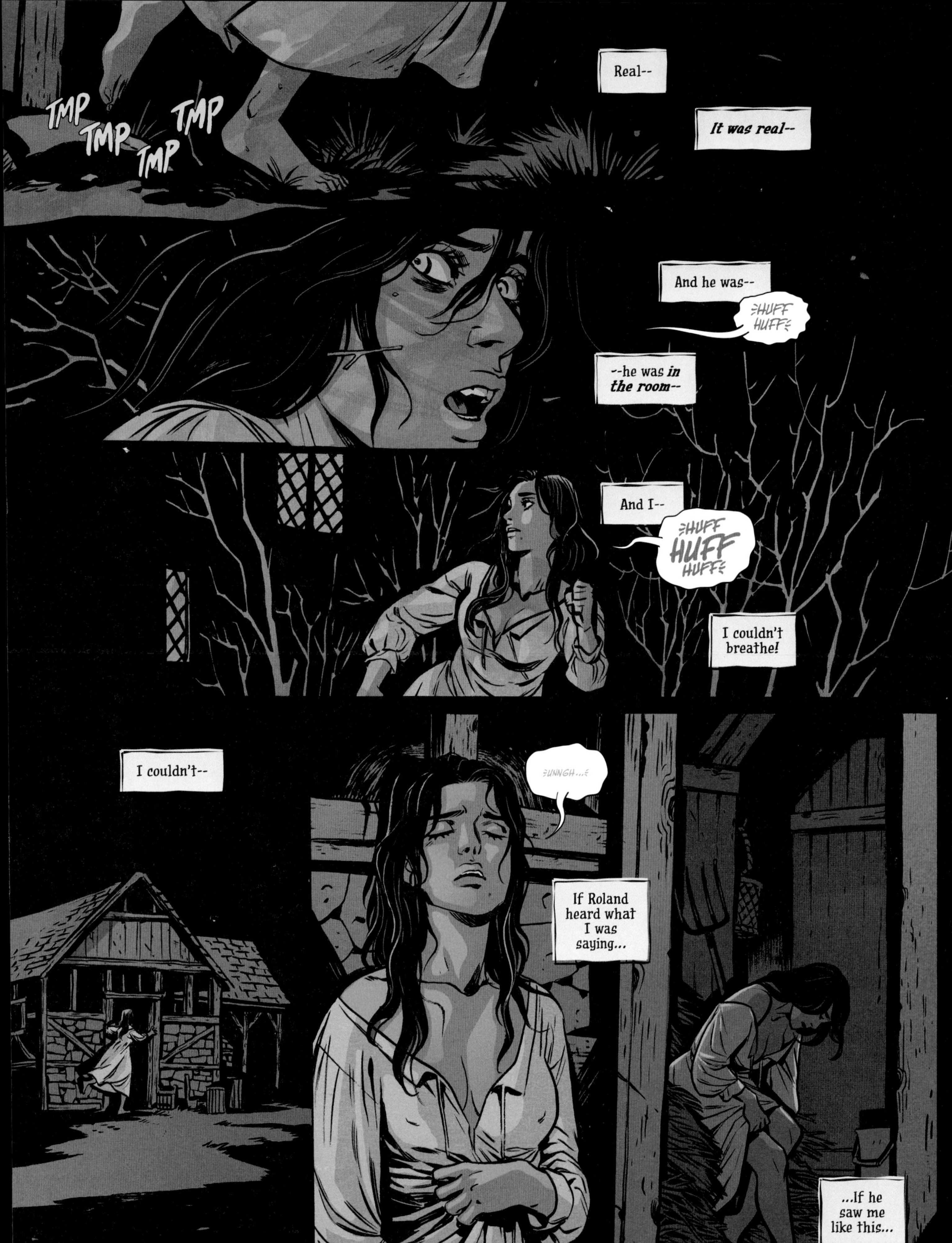

TMP TMP TMP TMP
Real--
It was real--
And he was--
HUFF HUFF
--he was in the room--
And I--
HUFF HUFF HUFF
I couldn't breathe!
I couldn't--
UNNGH...
If Roland heard what I was saying...
...If he saw me like this...

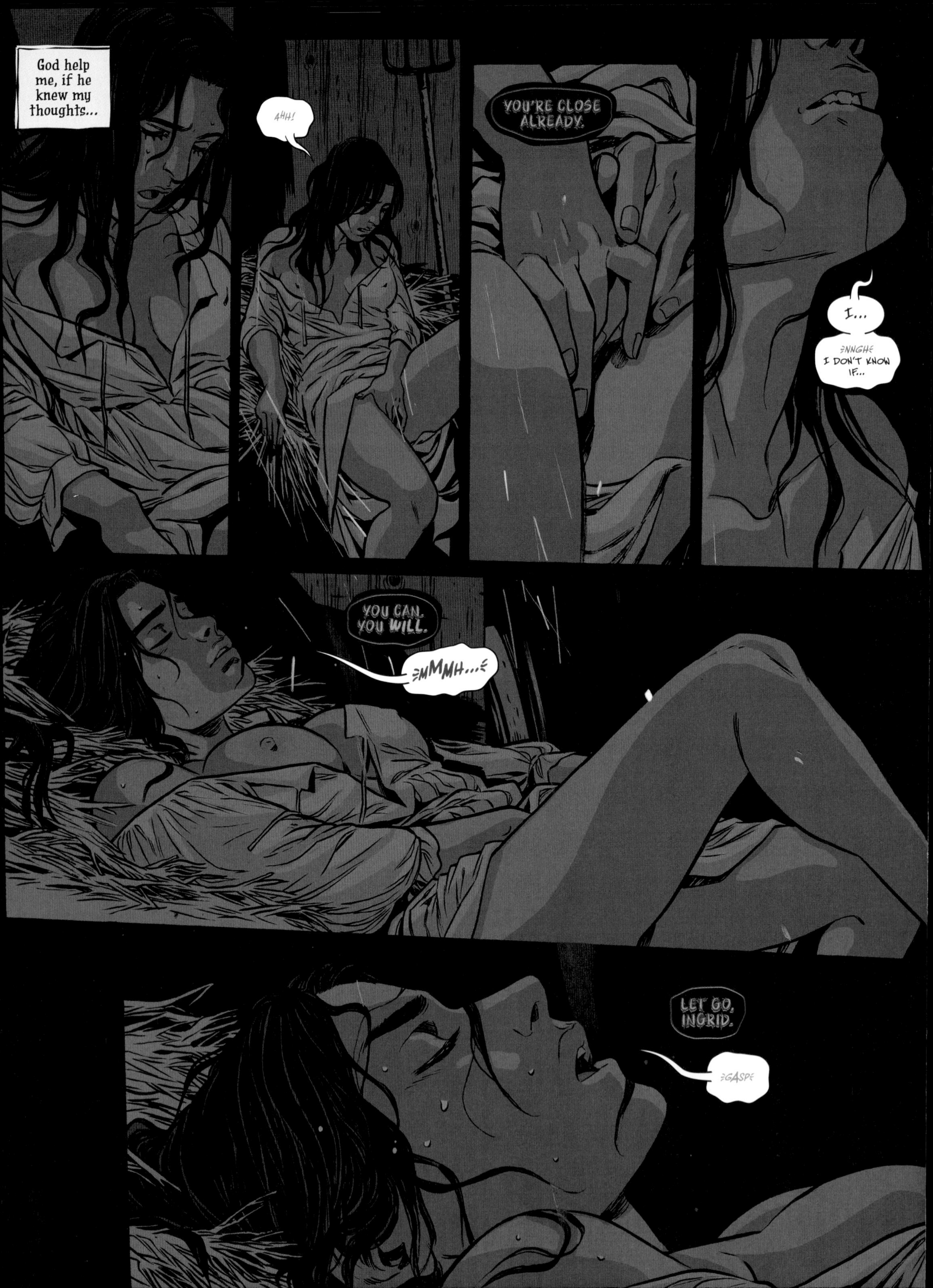
God help me, if he knew my thoughts...
AHH!
YOU'RE CLOSE ALREADY.
I...
NNGH
I DON'T KNOW IF...
YOU CAN. YOU WILL.
MMMH...
LET GO, INGRID.
GASP

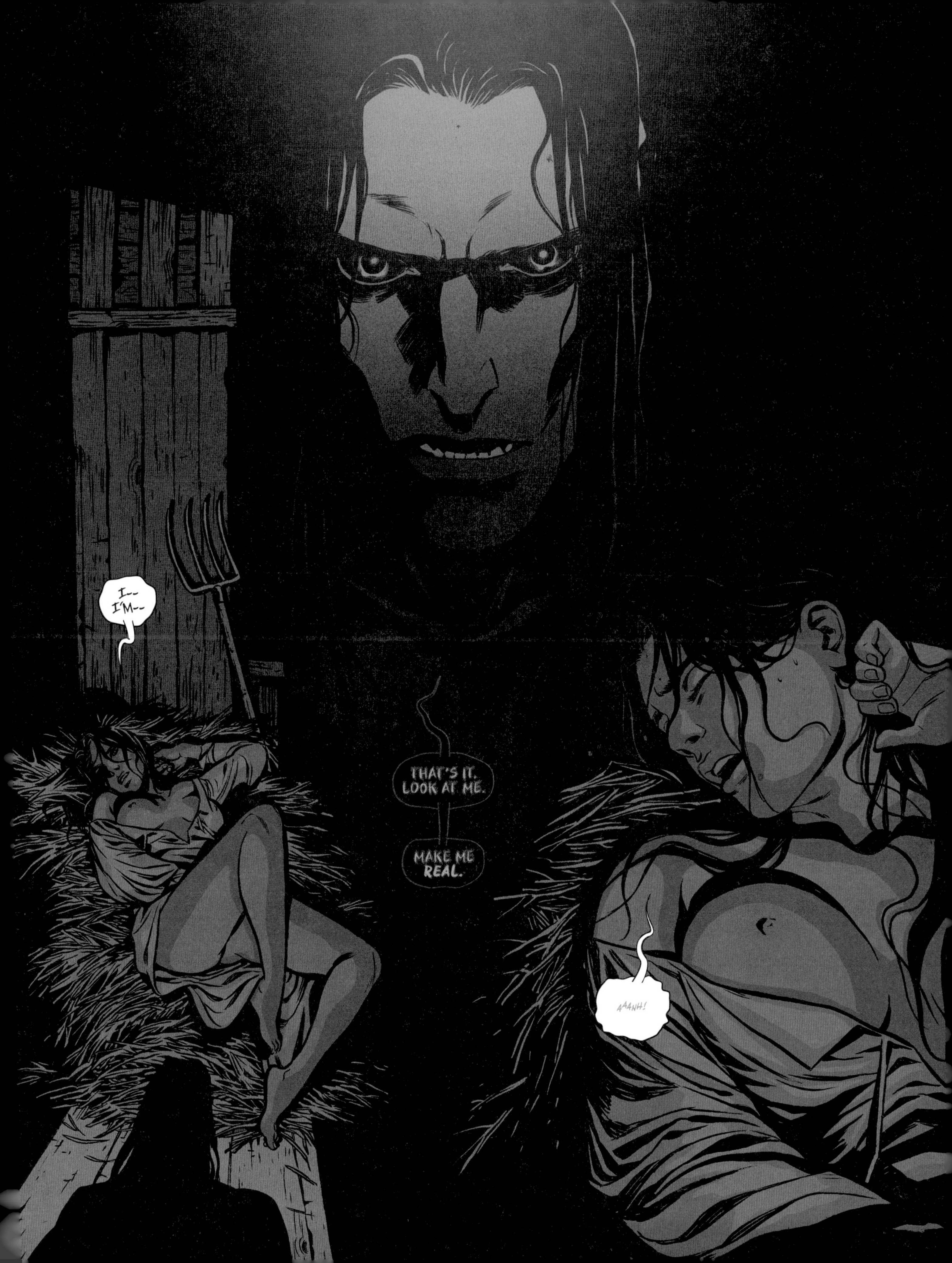
I-- I'M--
THAT'S IT. LOOK AT ME.
MAKE ME REAL.
AAANH!

YOU SLEPT WELL, I TAKE IT?

MMM... HOW DID...

I SEE YOU CLEANED THE STABLE YESTERDAY.

DIDN'T I TELL YOU? IF YOU WORK HARDER, YOU'LL BE TOO TIRED TO DREAM.

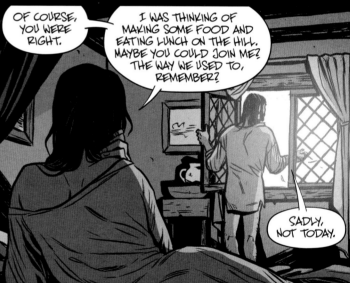

OF COURSE, YOU WERE RIGHT.

I WAS THINKING OF MAKING SOME FOOD AND EATING LUNCH ON THE HILL. MAYBE YOU COULD JOIN ME? THE WAY WE USED TO, REMEMBER?

SADLY, NOT TODAY.

I'VE BEEN CALLED TO THE CITY FOR A TRIAL. THEIR COURT NEEDS AN EXPERT, AND, WELL...

I SUPPOSE WORD HAS GOTTEN AROUND THAT I'M GOOD AT FINDING WITCHES.

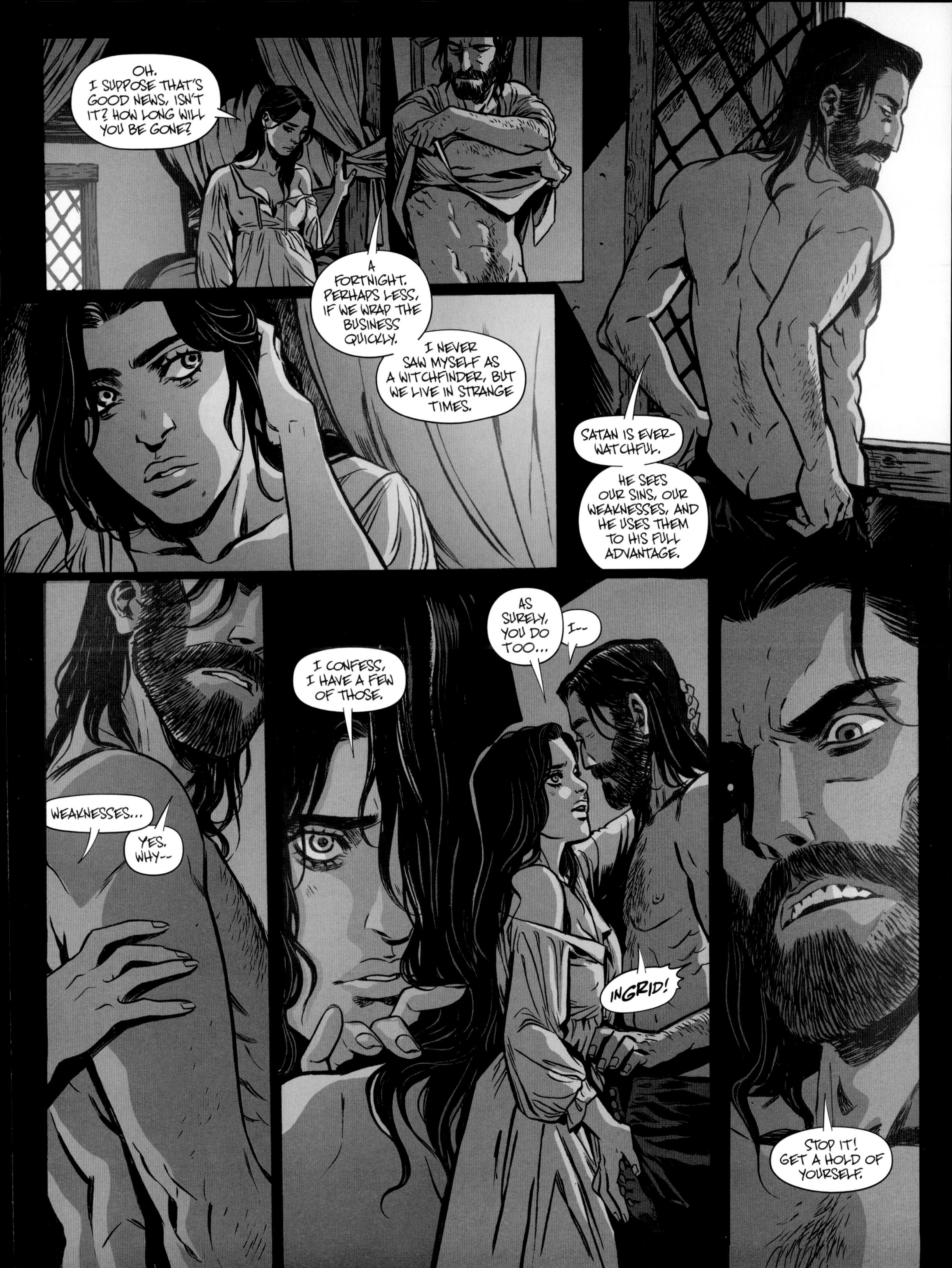
OH. I SUPPOSE THAT'S GOOD NEWS, ISN'T IT? HOW LONG WILL YOU BE GONE?
A FORTNIGHT. PERHAPS LESS, IF WE WRAP THE BUSINESS QUICKLY.
I NEVER SAW MYSELF AS A WITCHFINDER, BUT WE LIVE IN STRANGE TIMES.
SATAN IS EVER-WATCHFUL.
HE SEES OUR SINS, OUR WEAKNESSES, AND HE USES THEM TO HIS FULL ADVANTAGE.
WEAKNESSES...
YES. WHY--
I CONFESS, I HAVE A FEW OF THOSE.
AS SURELY, YOU DO TOO...
I--
INGRID!
STOP IT! GET A HOLD OF YOURSELF.

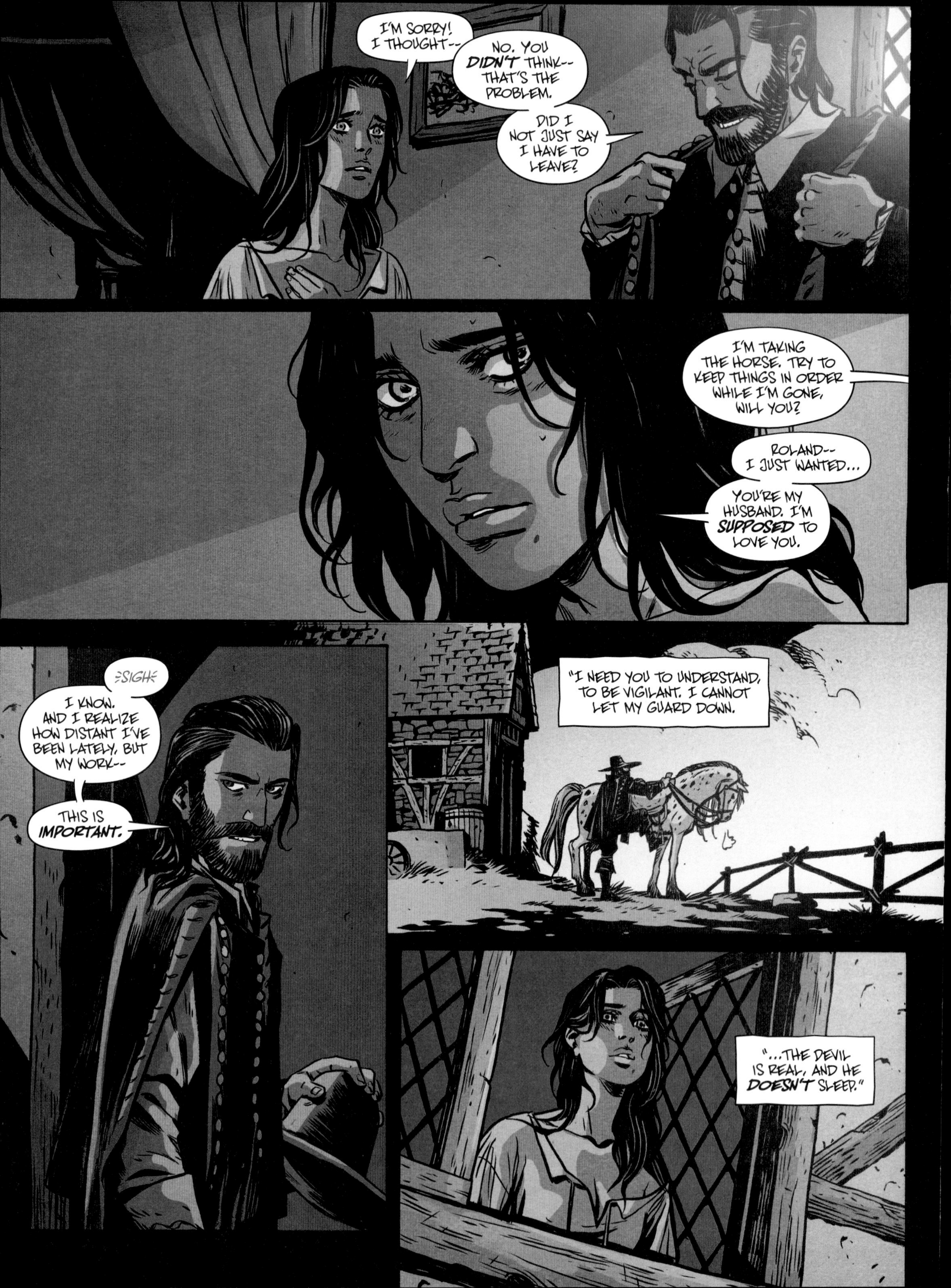
I'M SORRY! I THOUGHT--
NO. YOU **DIDN'T** THINK-- THAT'S THE PROBLEM.
DID I NOT JUST SAY I HAVE TO LEAVE?
I'M TAKING THE HORSE. TRY TO KEEP THINGS IN ORDER WHILE I'M GONE, WILL YOU?
ROLAND-- I JUST WANTED...
YOU'RE MY HUSBAND. I'M **SUPPOSED** TO LOVE YOU.
SIGH
I KNOW. AND I REALIZE HOW DISTANT I'VE BEEN LATELY, BUT MY WORK--
THIS IS **IMPORTANT.**
"I NEED YOU TO UNDERSTAND, TO BE VIGILANT. I CANNOT LET MY GUARD DOWN.
"...THE DEVIL IS REAL, AND HE **DOESN'T** SLEEP."

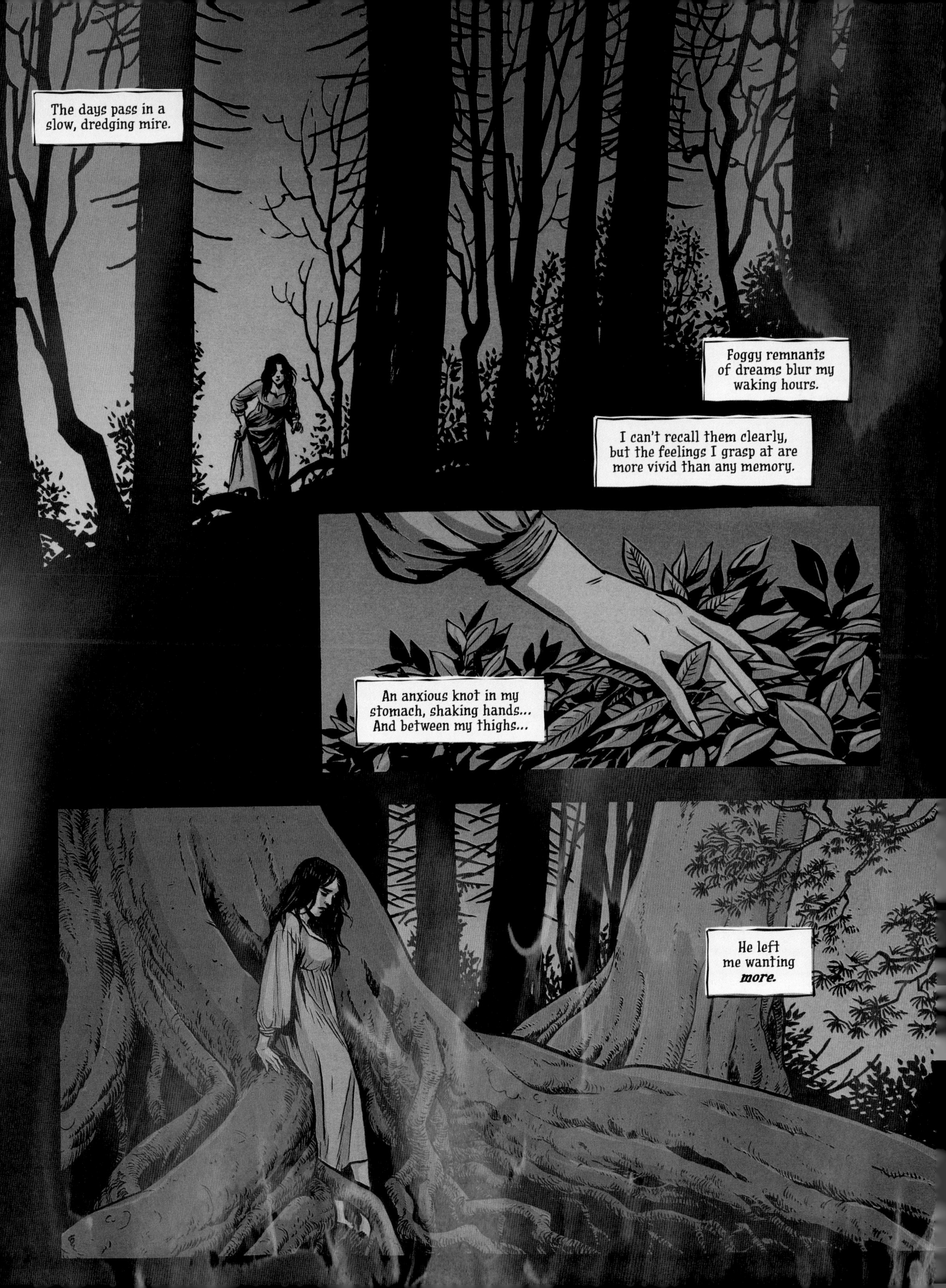
The days pass in a slow, dredging mire.
Foggy remnants of dreams blur my waking hours.
I can't recall them clearly, but the feelings I grasp at are more vivid than any memory.
An anxious knot in my stomach, shaking hands... And between my thighs...
He left me wanting *more.*

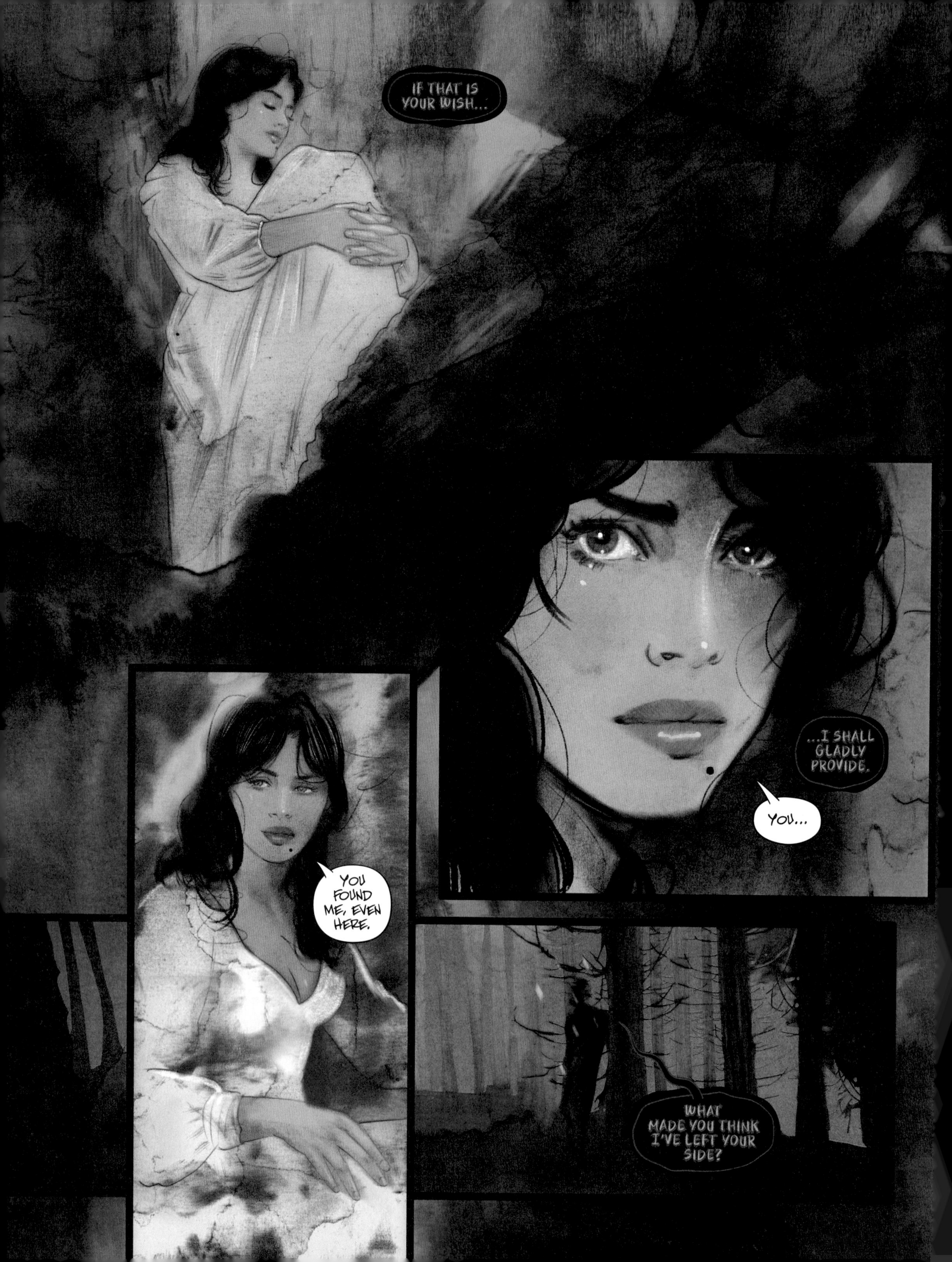
IF THAT IS YOUR WISH...
...I SHALL GLADLY PROVIDE.
YOU...
YOU FOUND ME, EVEN HERE.
WHAT MADE YOU THINK I'VE LEFT YOUR SIDE?

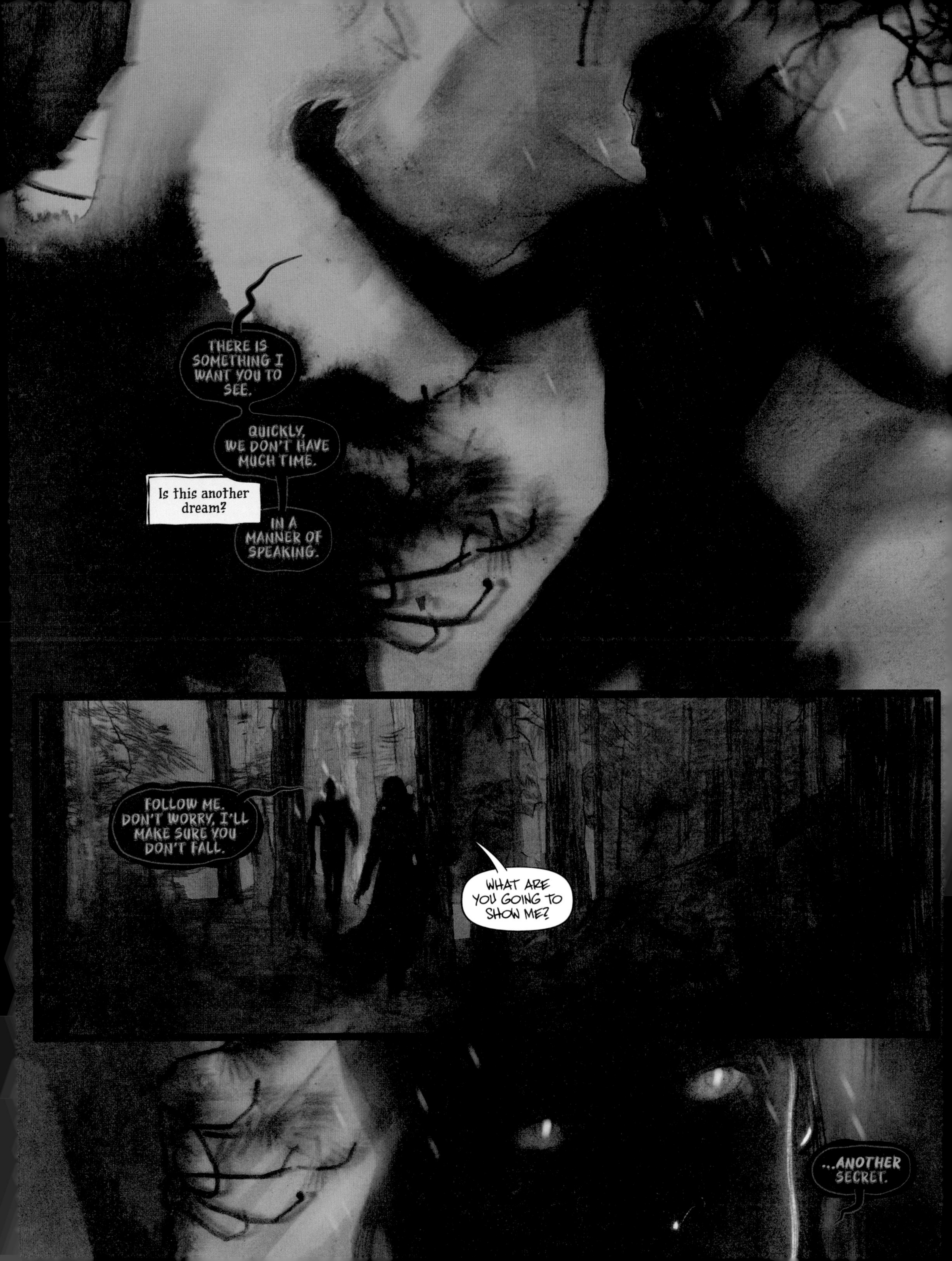

THERE IS SOMETHING I WANT YOU TO SEE.
QUICKLY, WE DON'T HAVE MUCH TIME.
Is this another dream?
IN A MANNER OF SPEAKING.
FOLLOW ME. DON'T WORRY, I'LL MAKE SURE YOU DON'T FALL.
WHAT ARE YOU GOING TO SHOW ME?
...ANOTHER SECRET.

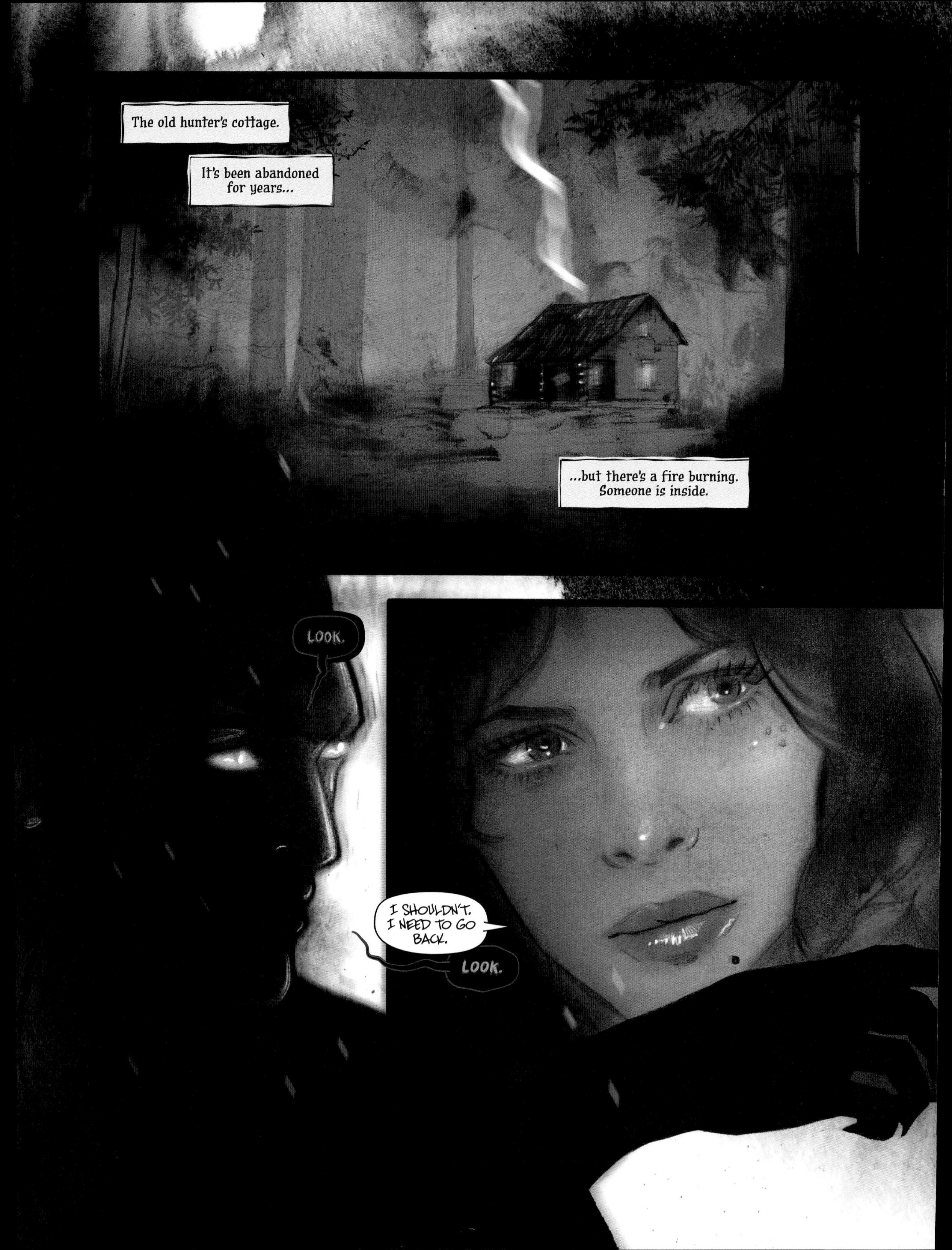
The old hunter's cottage.
It's been abandoned for years...
...but there's a fire burning. Someone is inside.
LOOK.
I SHOULDN'T. I NEED TO GO BACK.
LOOK.

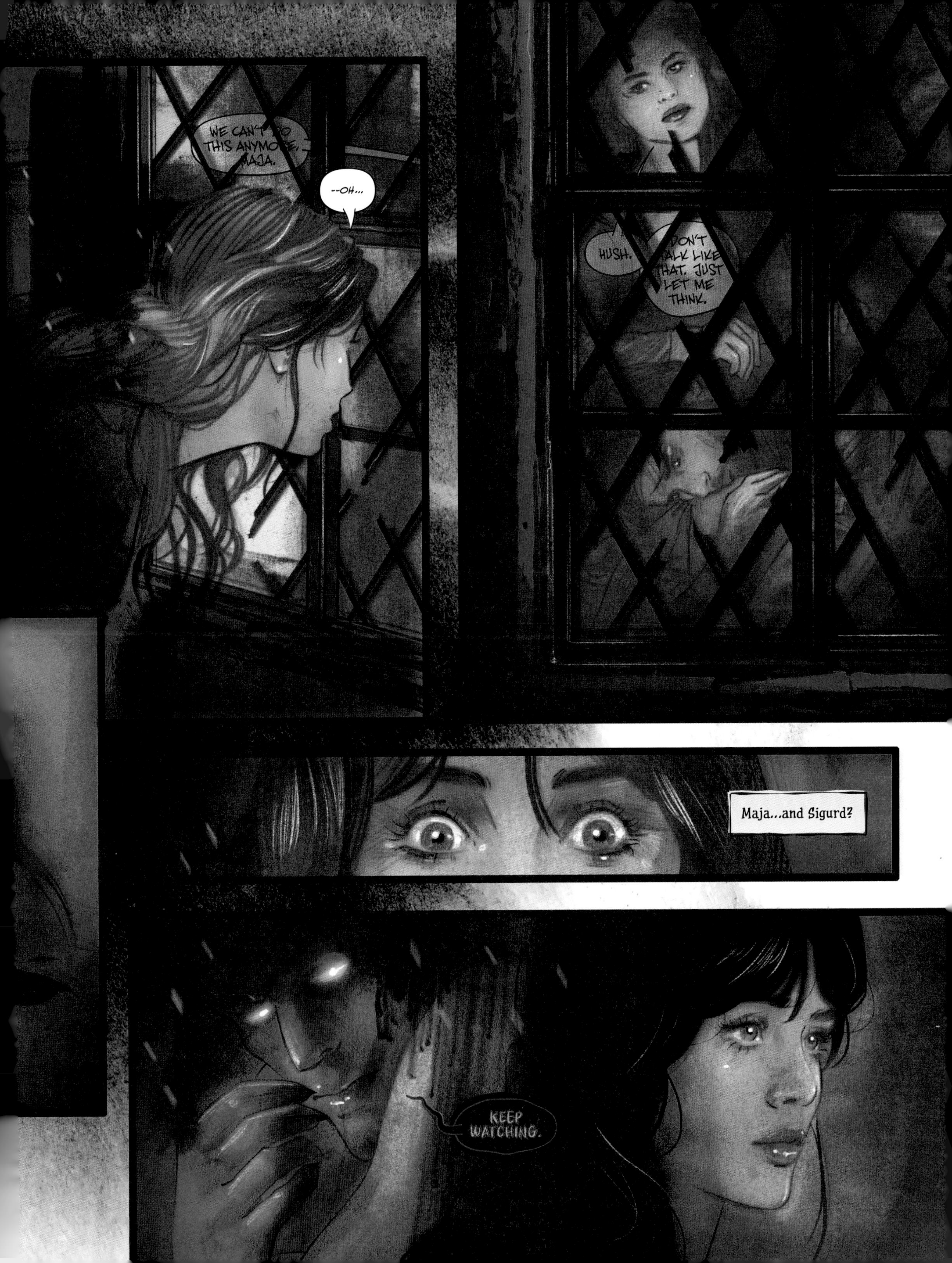
WE CAN'T DO THIS ANYMORE, MAJA.
--OH...
HUSH.
DON'T TALK LIKE THAT. JUST LET ME THINK.
Maja...and Sigurd?
KEEP WATCHING.

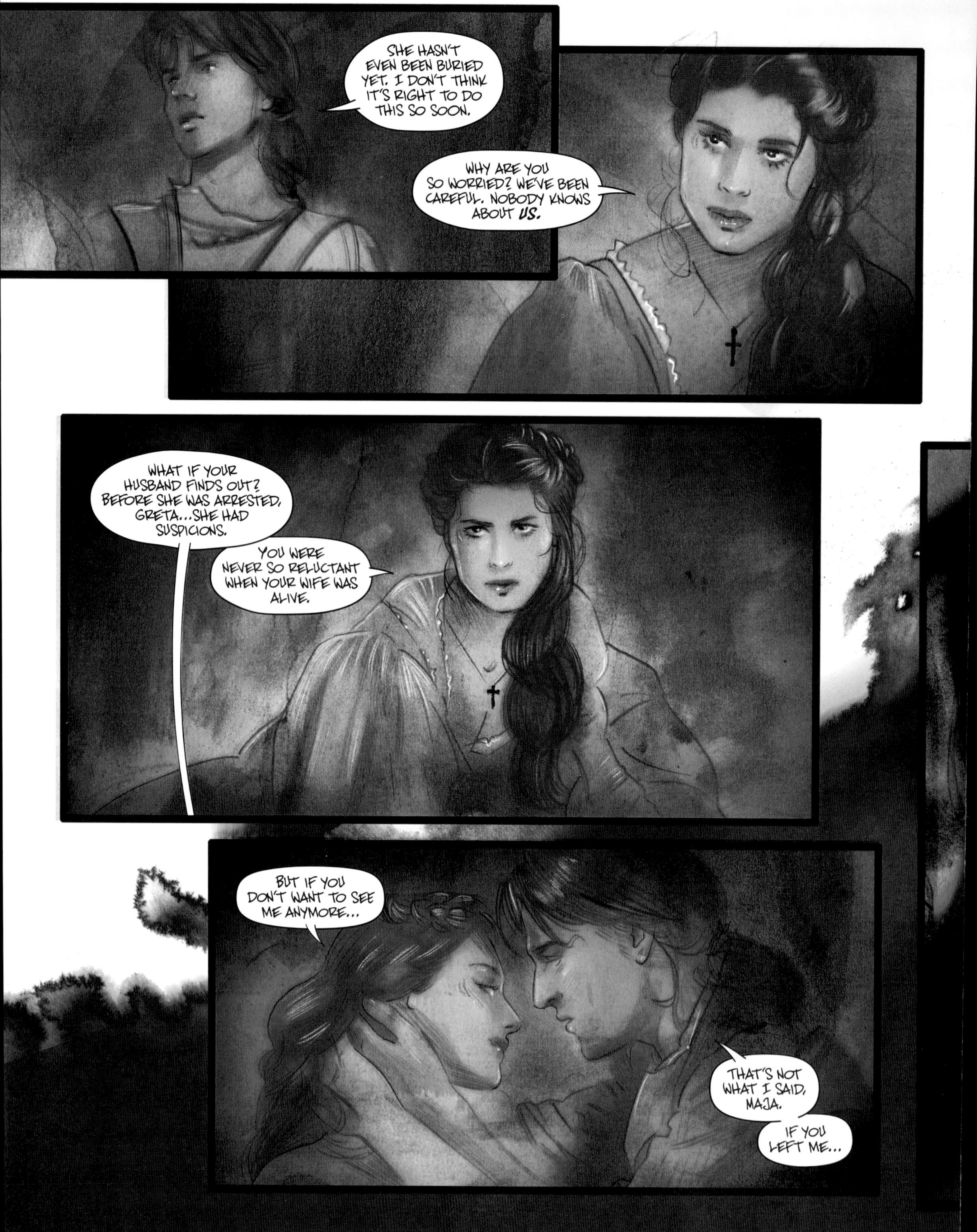
SHE HASN'T EVEN BEEN BURIED YET. I DON'T THINK IT'S RIGHT TO DO THIS SO SOON.
WHY ARE YOU SO WORRIED? WE'VE BEEN CAREFUL. NOBODY KNOWS ABOUT *US.*
WHAT IF YOUR HUSBAND FINDS OUT? BEFORE SHE WAS ARRESTED, GRETA...SHE HAD SUSPICIONS.
YOU WERE NEVER SO RELUCTANT WHEN YOUR WIFE WAS ALIVE.
BUT IF YOU DON'T WANT TO SEE ME ANYMORE...
THAT'S NOT WHAT I SAID, MAJA.
IF YOU LEFT ME...

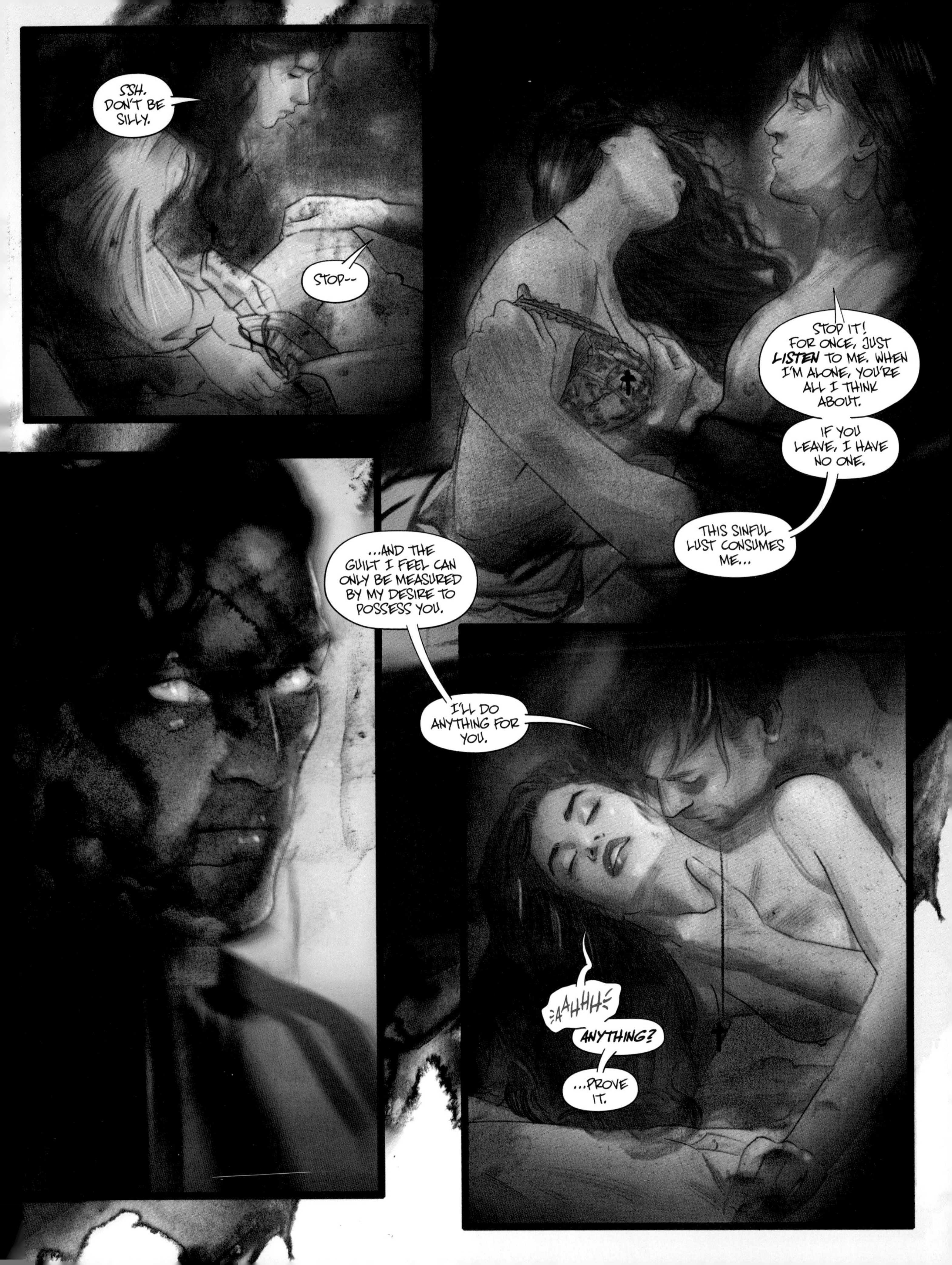
SSH. DON'T BE SILLY.
STOP--
STOP IT! FOR ONCE, JUST LISTEN TO ME. WHEN I'M ALONE, YOU'RE ALL I THINK ABOUT.
IF YOU LEAVE, I HAVE NO ONE.
THIS SINFUL LUST CONSUMES ME...
...AND THE GUILT I FEEL CAN ONLY BE MEASURED BY MY DESIRE TO POSSESS YOU.
I'LL DO ANYTHING FOR YOU.
AAHHH
ANYTHING?
...PROVE IT.

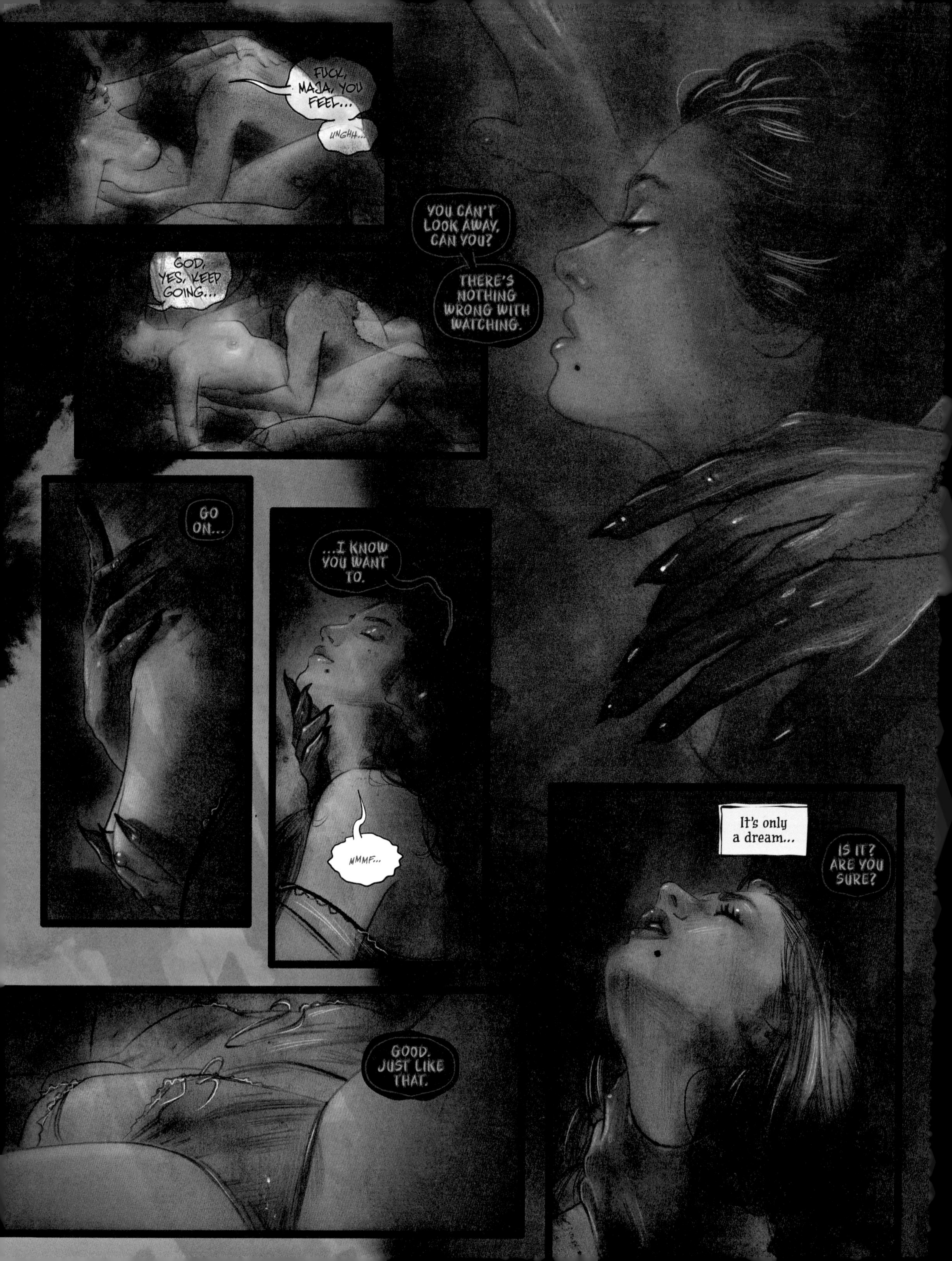
FUCK, MAJA, YOU FEEL...
UNGHH...
YOU CAN'T LOOK AWAY, CAN YOU?
THERE'S NOTHING WRONG WITH WATCHING.
GOD, YES, KEEP GOING...
GO ON...
...I KNOW YOU WANT TO.
MMMF...
It's only a dream...
IS IT? ARE YOU SURE?
GOOD. JUST LIKE THAT.

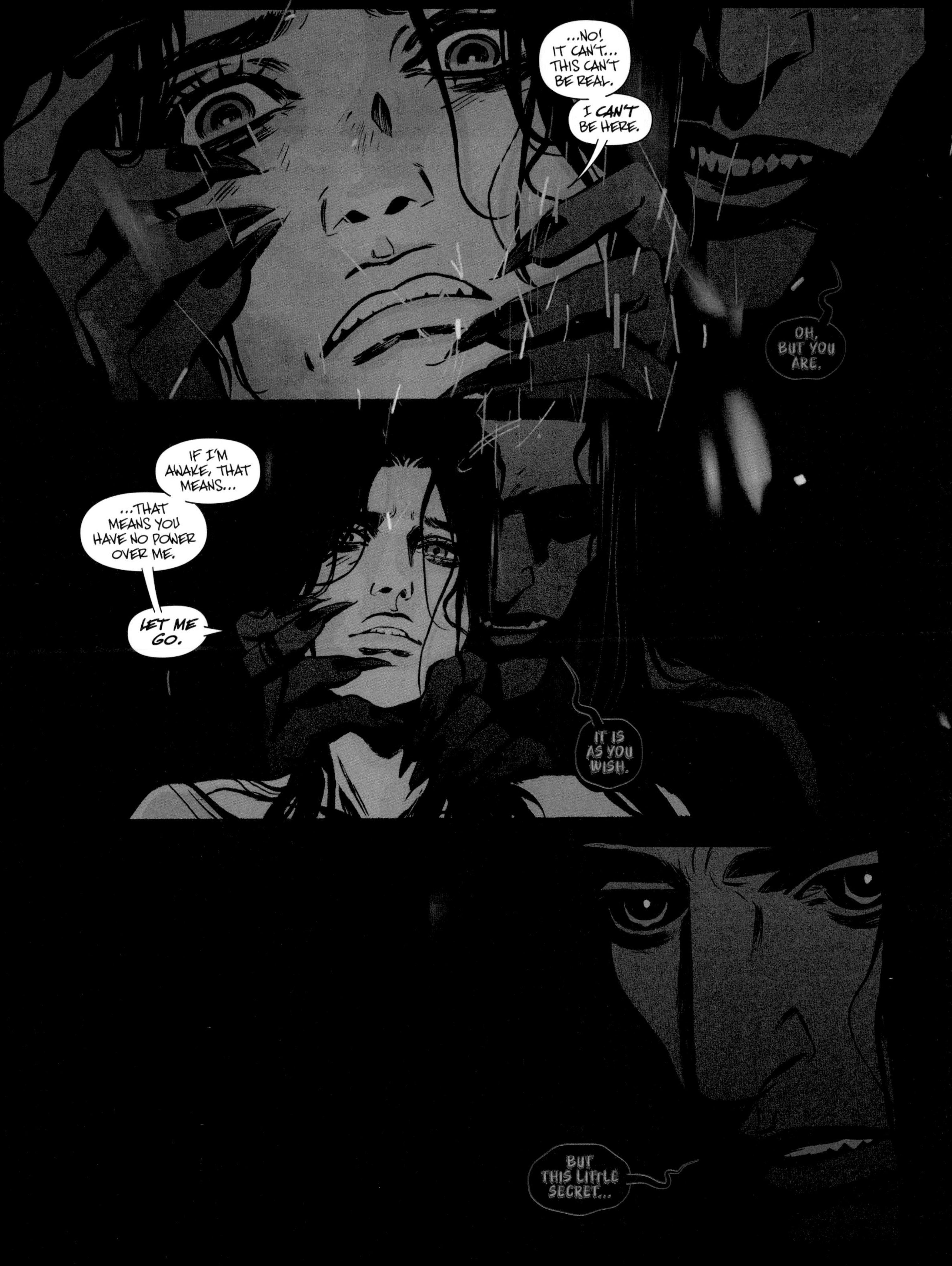
...NO! IT CAN'T... THIS CAN'T BE REAL.
I CAN'T BE HERE.
OH, BUT YOU ARE.
IF I'M AWAKE, THAT MEANS...
...THAT MEANS YOU HAVE NO POWER OVER ME.
LET ME GO.
IT IS AS YOU WISH.
BUT THIS LITTLE SECRET...

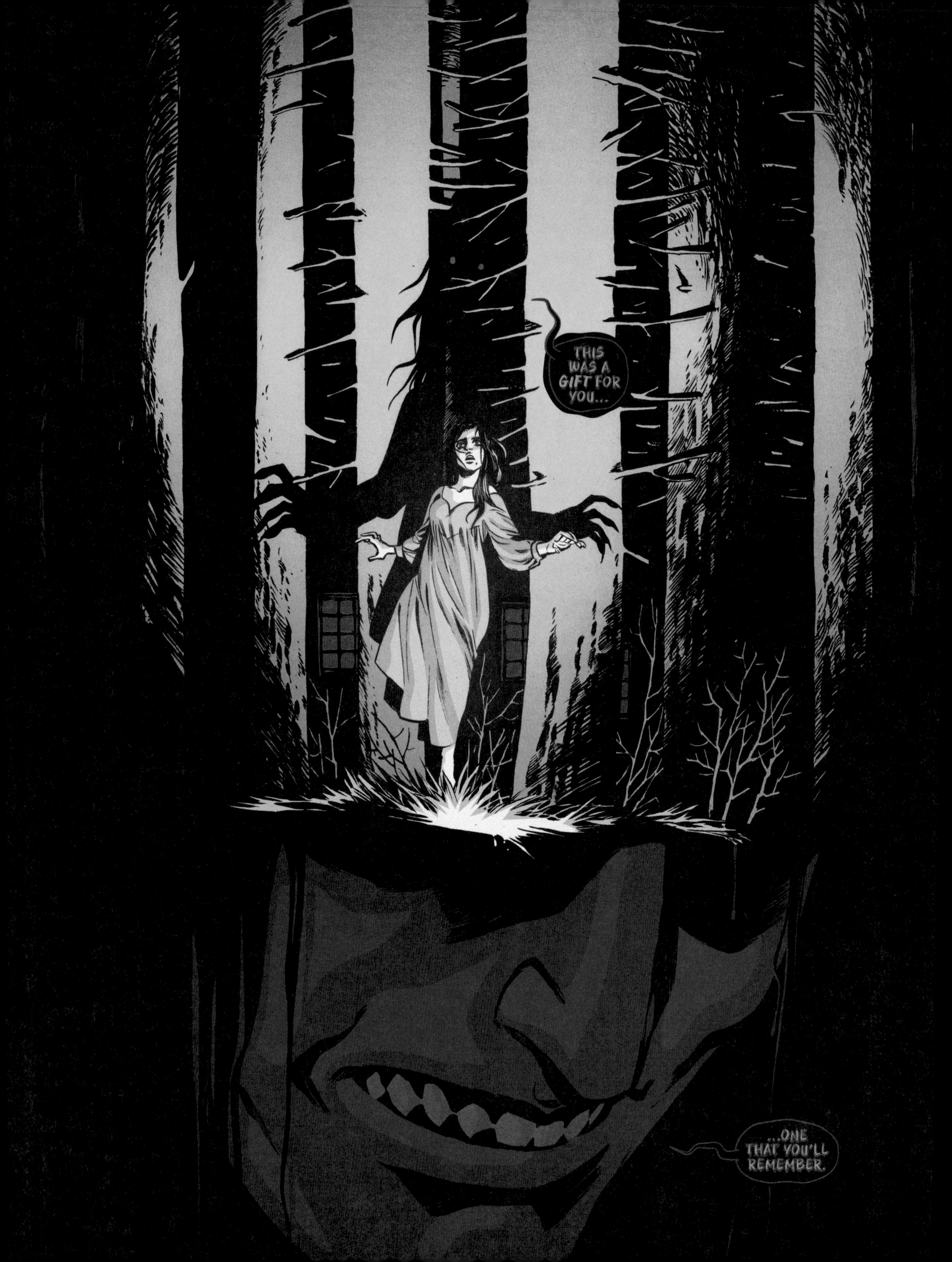
THIS WAS A GIFT FOR YOU...
...ONE THAT YOU'LL REMEMBER.

CHAPTER III.
WHISPER AND I'LL COME TO THEE

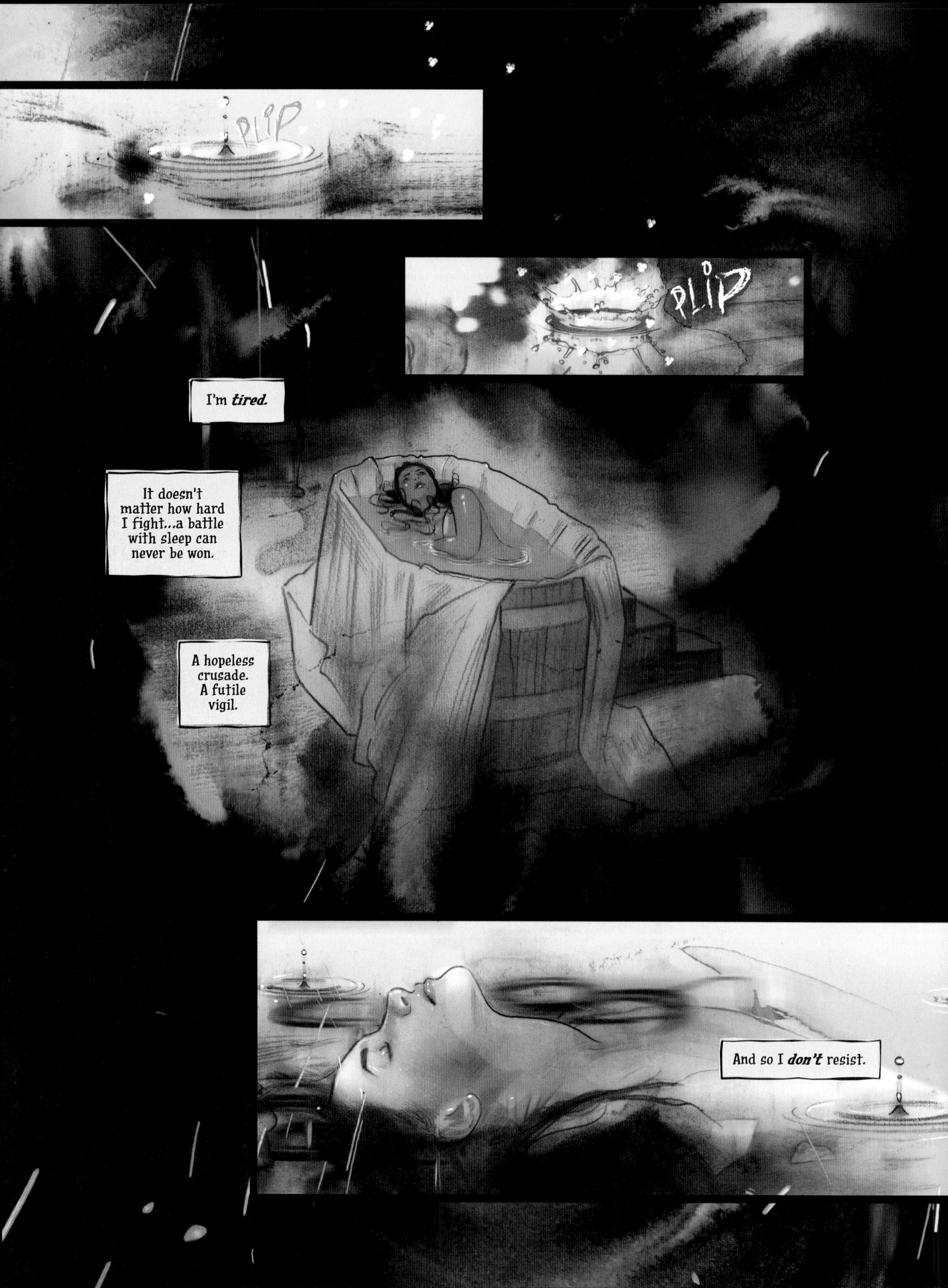
PLIP
PLIP
I'm *tired.*
It doesn't matter how hard I fight...a battle with sleep can never be won.
A hopeless crusade. A futile vigil.
And so I ***don't*** resist.

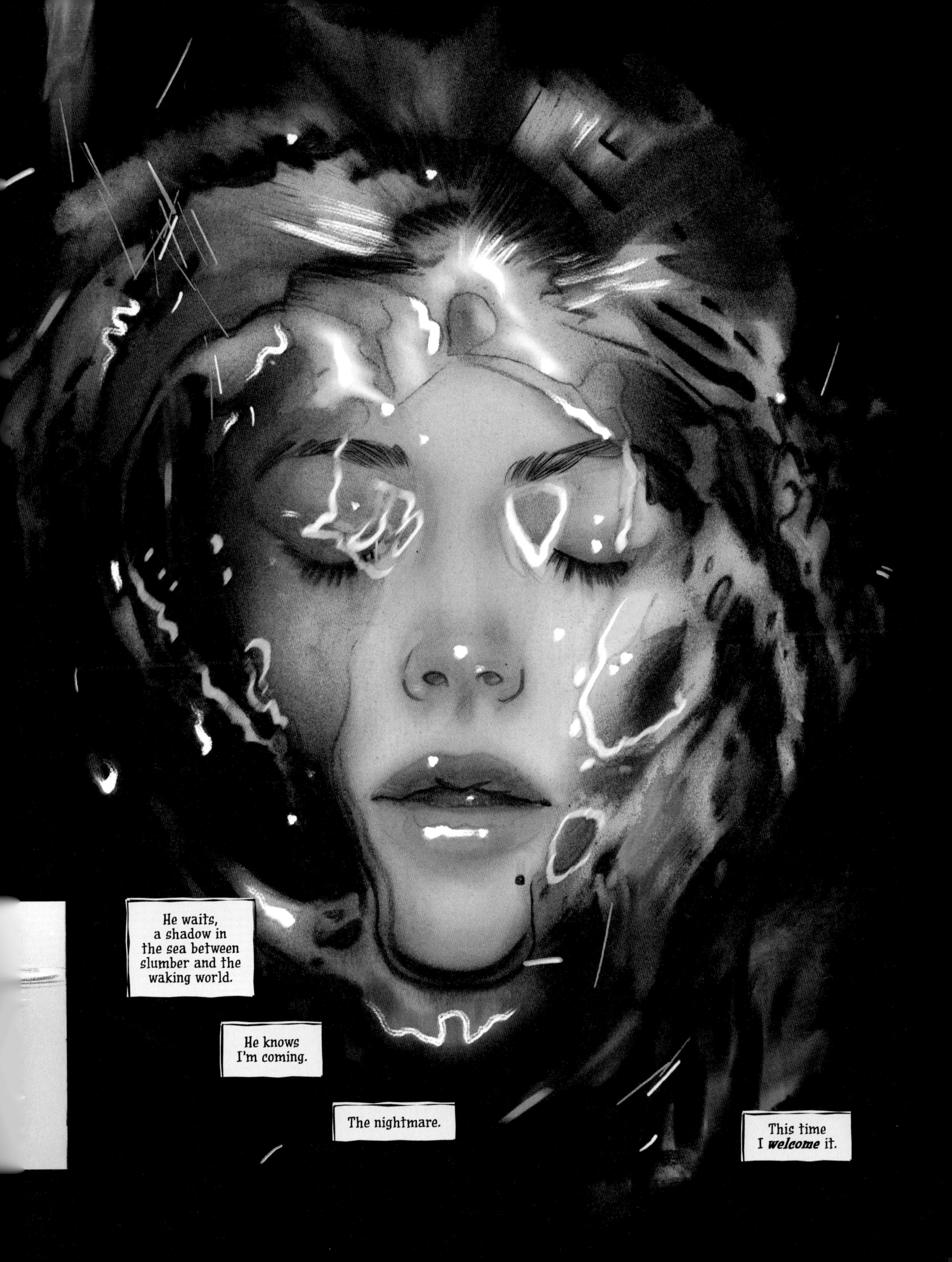
He waits, a shadow in the sea between slumber and the waking world.
He knows I'm coming.
The nightmare.
This time I ***welcome*** it.

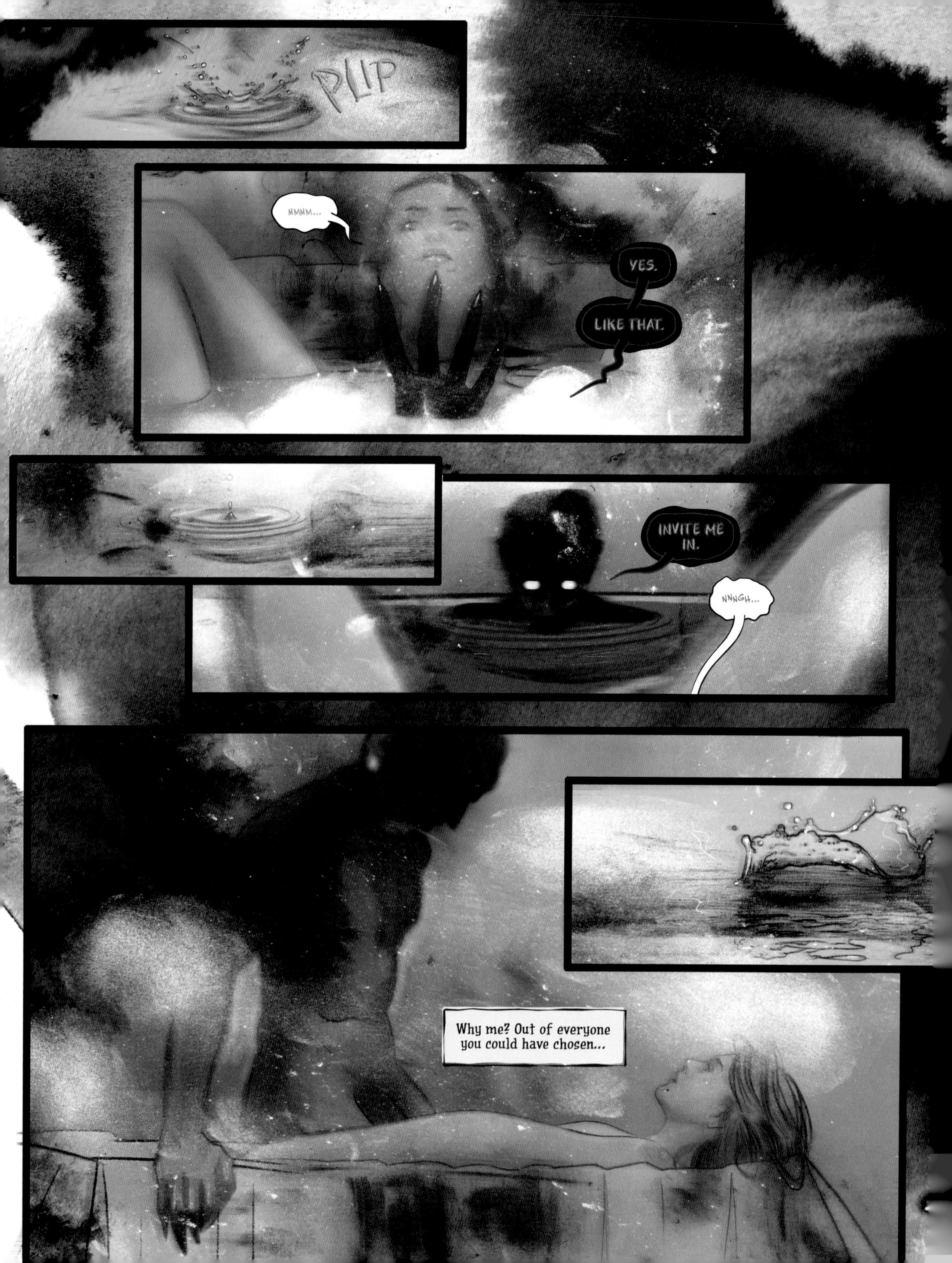
PLIP
MMMM...
YES.
LIKE THAT.
INVITE ME IN.
NNNGH...
Why me? Out of everyone you could have chosen...

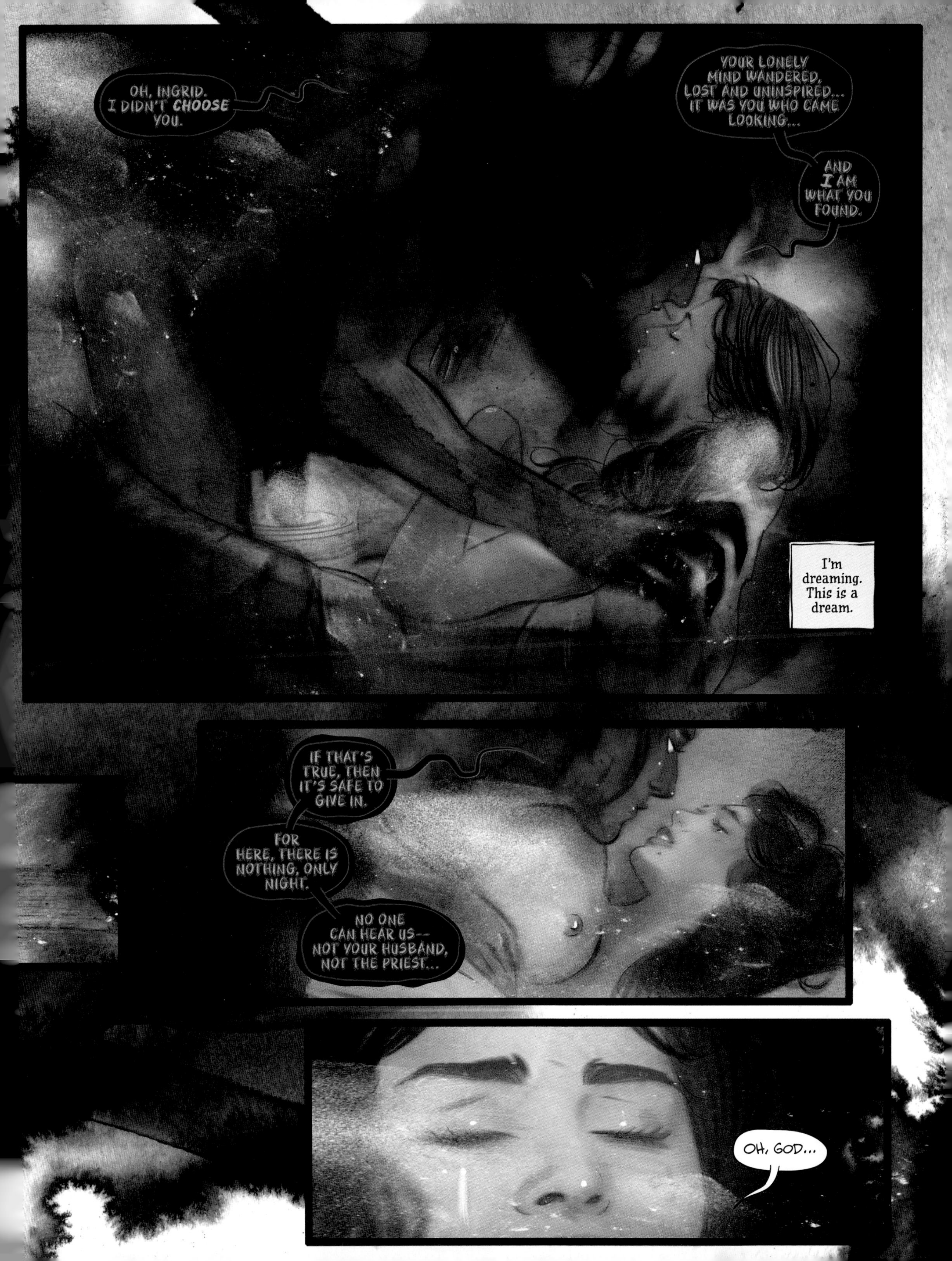
OH, INGRID. I DIDN'T CHOOSE YOU.
YOUR LONELY MIND WANDERED, LOST AND UNINSPIRED... IT WAS YOU WHO CAME LOOKING...
AND I AM WHAT YOU FOUND.
I'm dreaming. This is a dream.
IF THAT'S TRUE, THEN IT'S SAFE TO GIVE IN.
FOR HERE, THERE IS NOTHING, ONLY NIGHT.
NO ONE CAN HEAR US-- NOT YOUR HUSBAND, NOT THE PRIEST...
OH, GOD...

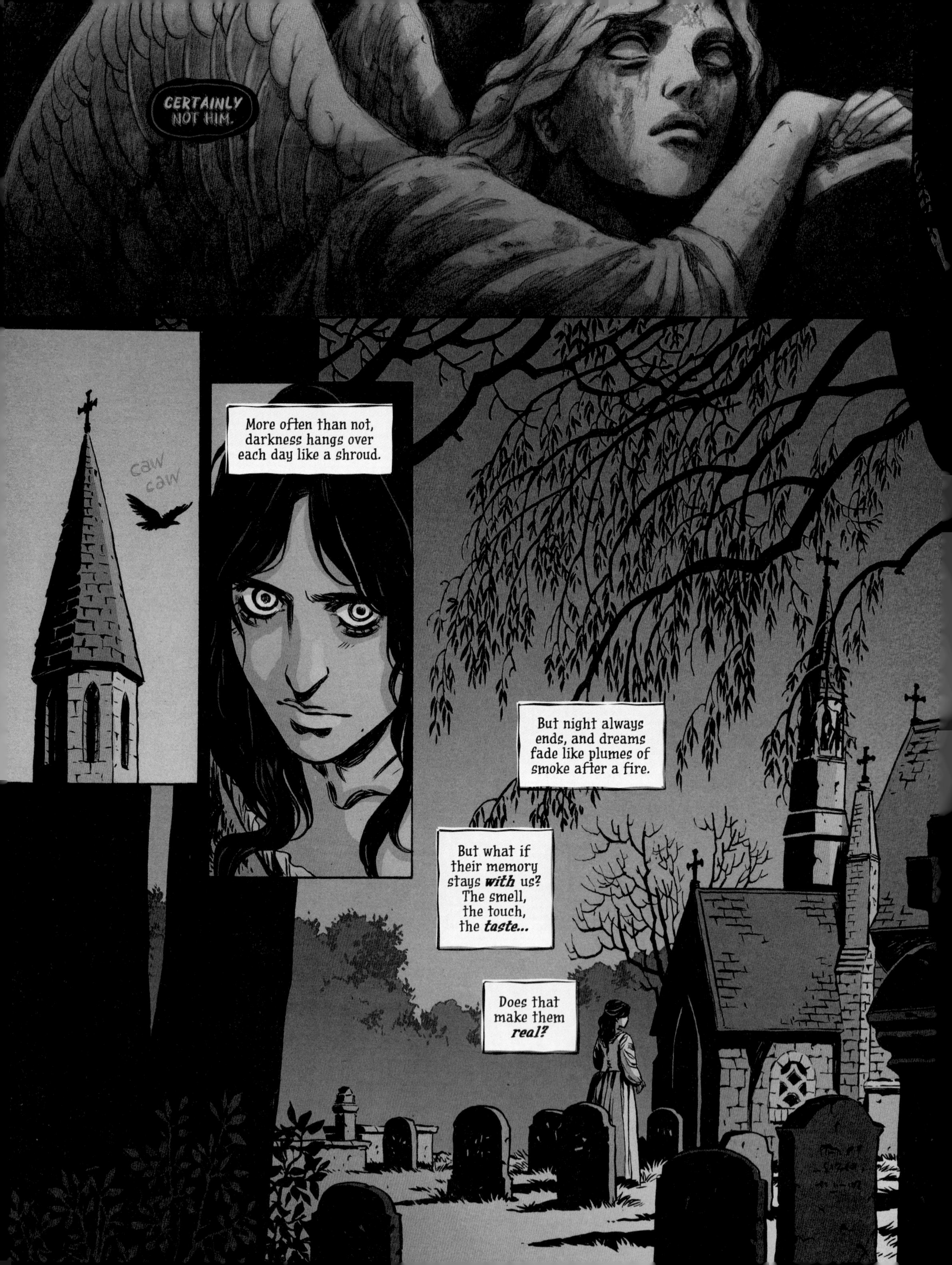
CERTAINLY NOT HIM.
More often than not, darkness hangs over each day like a shroud.
caw caw
But night always ends, and dreams fade like plumes of smoke after a fire.
But what if their memory stays *with* us? The smell, the touch, the *taste...*
Does that make them *real?*

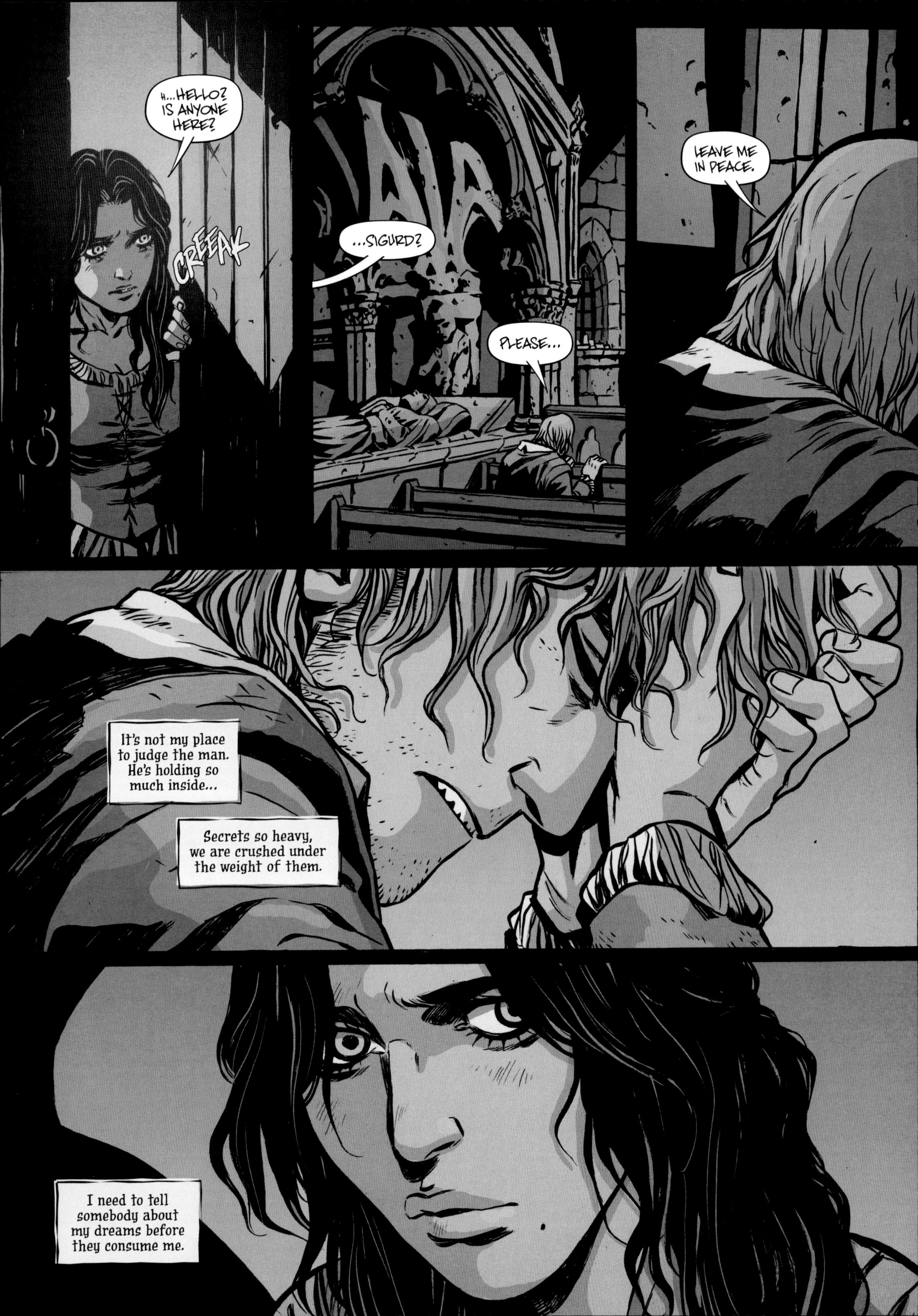
H...HELLO? IS ANYONE HERE?
CREEAK
...SIGURD?
PLEASE...
LEAVE ME IN PEACE.
It's not my place to judge the man. He's holding so much inside...
Secrets so heavy, we are crushed under the weight of them.
I need to tell somebody about my dreams before they consume me.

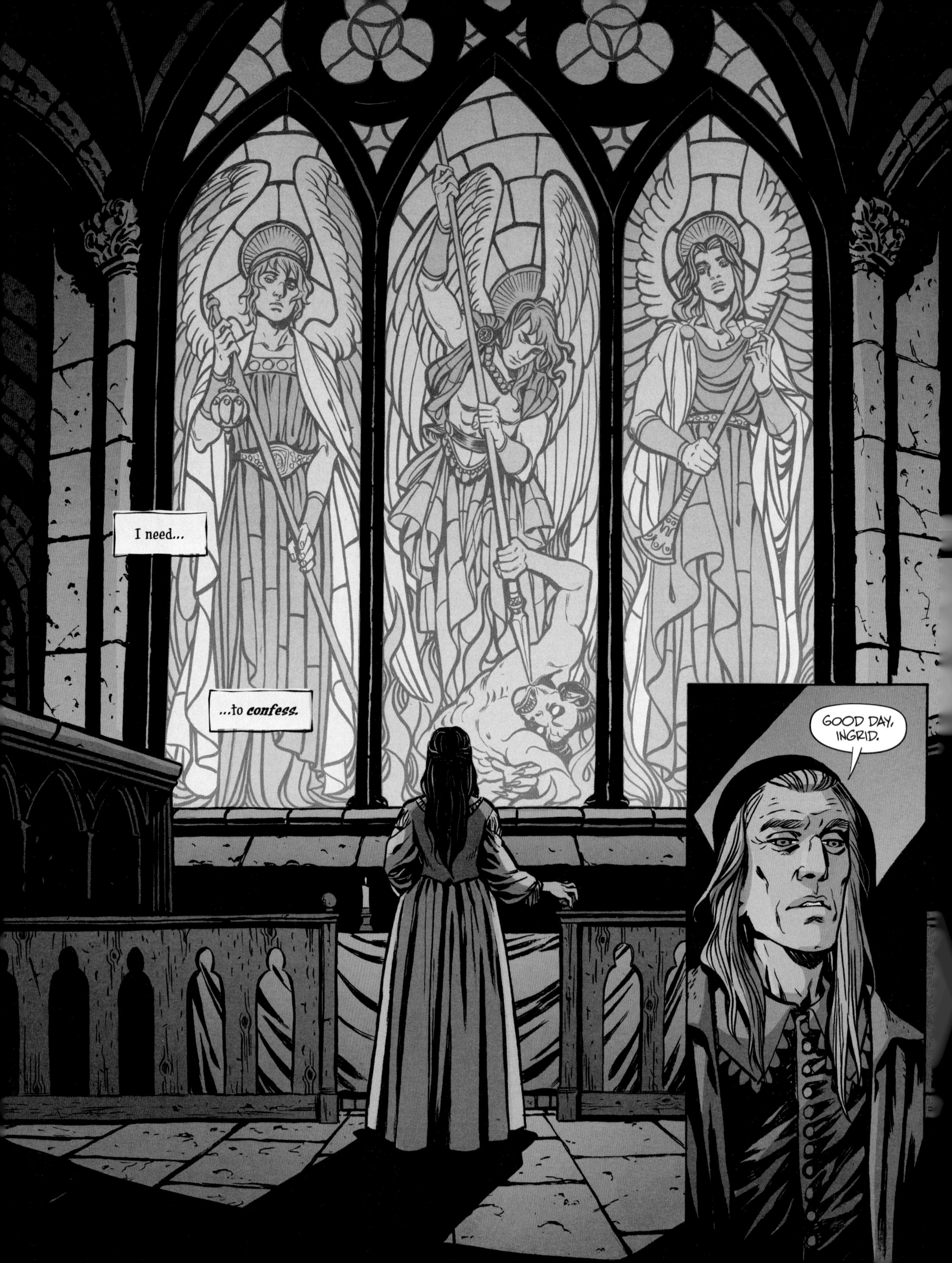
I need...
...to *confess.*
GOOD DAY, INGRID.

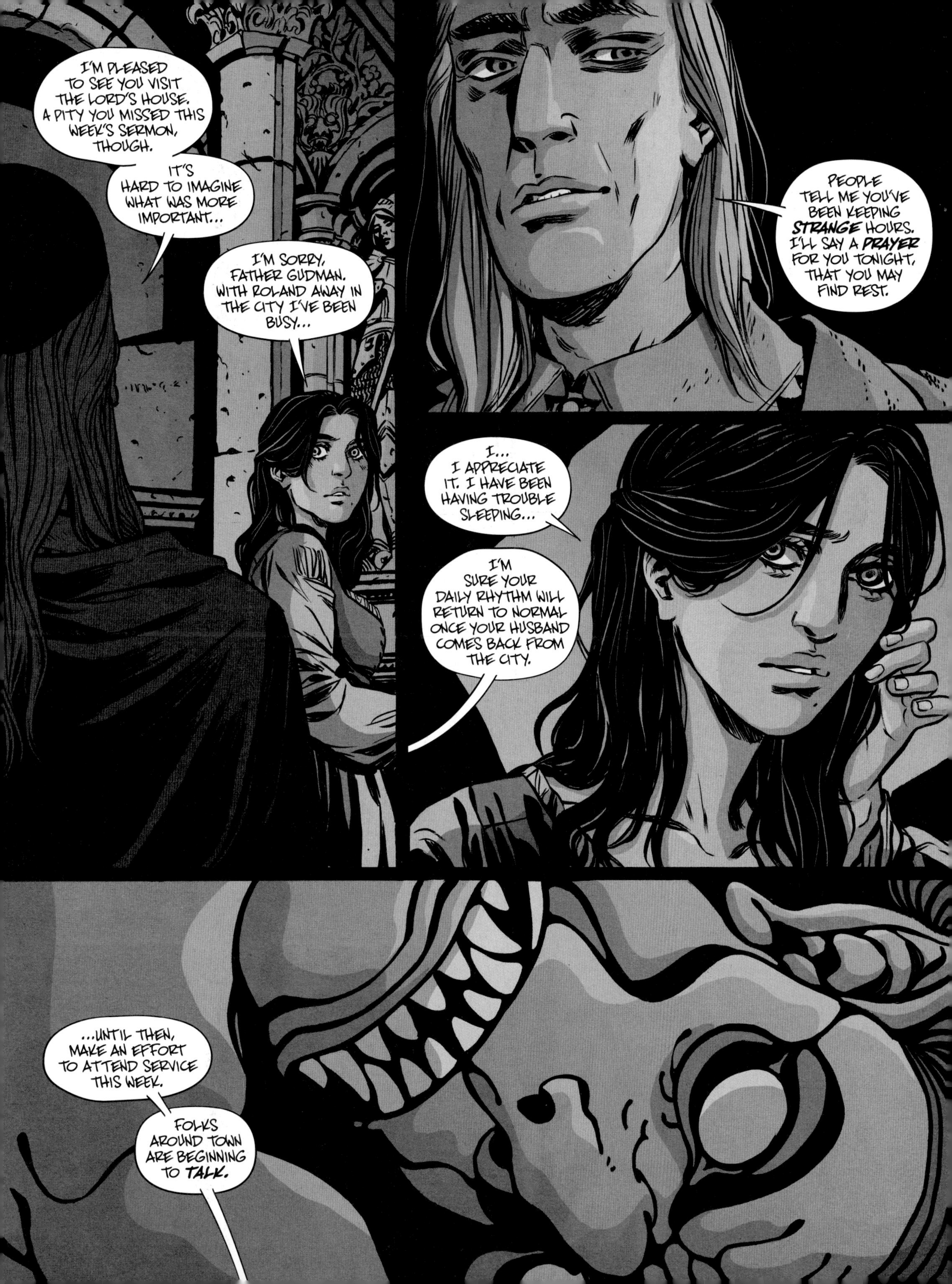
I'M PLEASED TO SEE YOU VISIT THE LORD'S HOUSE. A PITY YOU MISSED THIS WEEK'S SERMON, THOUGH.
IT'S HARD TO IMAGINE WHAT WAS MORE IMPORTANT...
I'M SORRY, FATHER GUDMAN. WITH ROLAND AWAY IN THE CITY I'VE BEEN BUSY...
PEOPLE TELL ME YOU'VE BEEN KEEPING **STRANGE** HOURS. I'LL SAY A **PRAYER** FOR YOU TONIGHT, THAT YOU MAY FIND REST.
I... I APPRECIATE IT. I HAVE BEEN HAVING TROUBLE SLEEPING...
I'M SURE YOUR DAILY RHYTHM WILL RETURN TO NORMAL ONCE YOUR HUSBAND COMES BACK FROM THE CITY.
...UNTIL THEN, MAKE AN EFFORT TO ATTEND SERVICE THIS WEEK.
FOLKS AROUND TOWN ARE BEGINNING TO **TALK.**

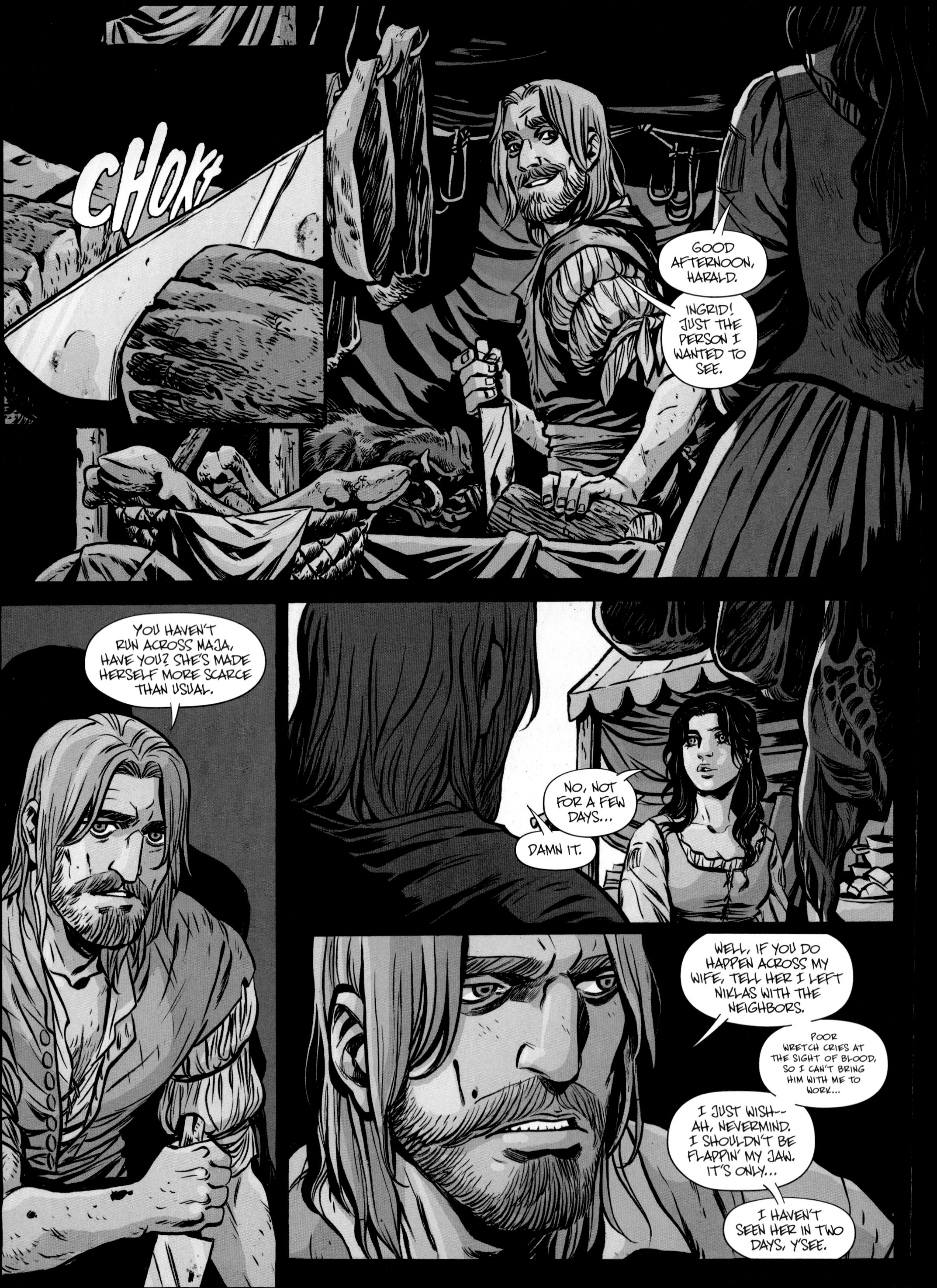
CHOK!
GOOD AFTERNOON, HARALD.
INGRID! JUST THE PERSON I WANTED TO SEE.
YOU HAVEN'T RUN ACROSS MAJA, HAVE YOU? SHE'S MADE HERSELF MORE SCARCE THAN USUAL.
NO, NOT FOR A FEW DAYS...
DAMN IT.
WELL, IF YOU DO HAPPEN ACROSS MY WIFE, TELL HER I LEFT NIKLAS WITH THE NEIGHBORS.
POOR WRETCH CRIES AT THE SIGHT OF BLOOD, SO I CAN'T BRING HIM WITH ME TO WORK...
I JUST WISH-- AH, NEVERMIND. I SHOULDN'T BE FLAPPIN' MY JAW. IT'S ONLY...
I HAVEN'T SEEN HER IN TWO DAYS, Y'SEE.

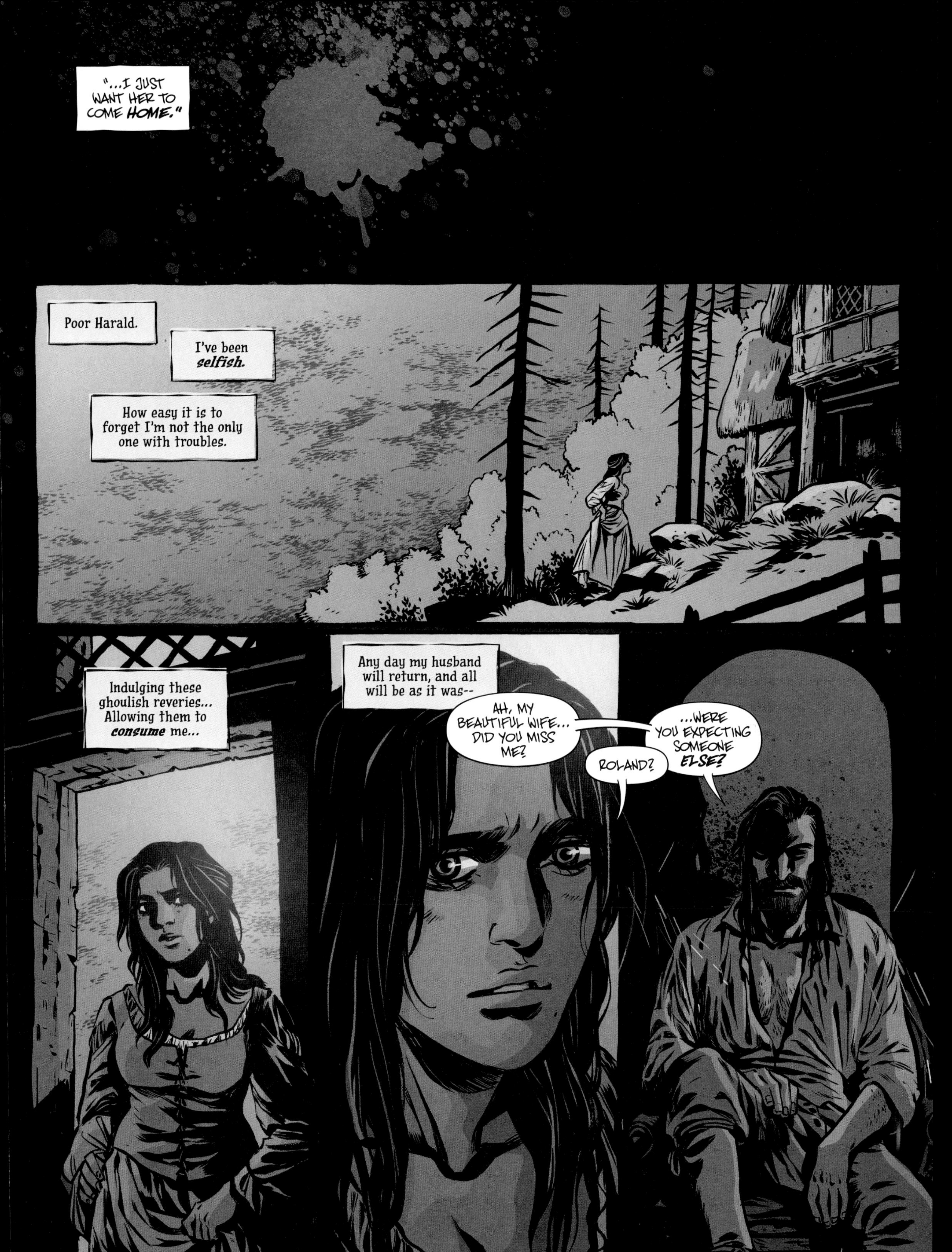
"...I JUST WANT HER TO COME HOME."
Poor Harald.
I've been selfish.
How easy it is to forget I'm not the only one with troubles.
Indulging these ghoulish reveries... Allowing them to consume me...
Any day my husband will return, and all will be as it was--
AH, MY BEAUTIFUL WIFE... DID YOU MISS ME?
...WERE YOU EXPECTING SOMEONE ELSE?
ROLAND?

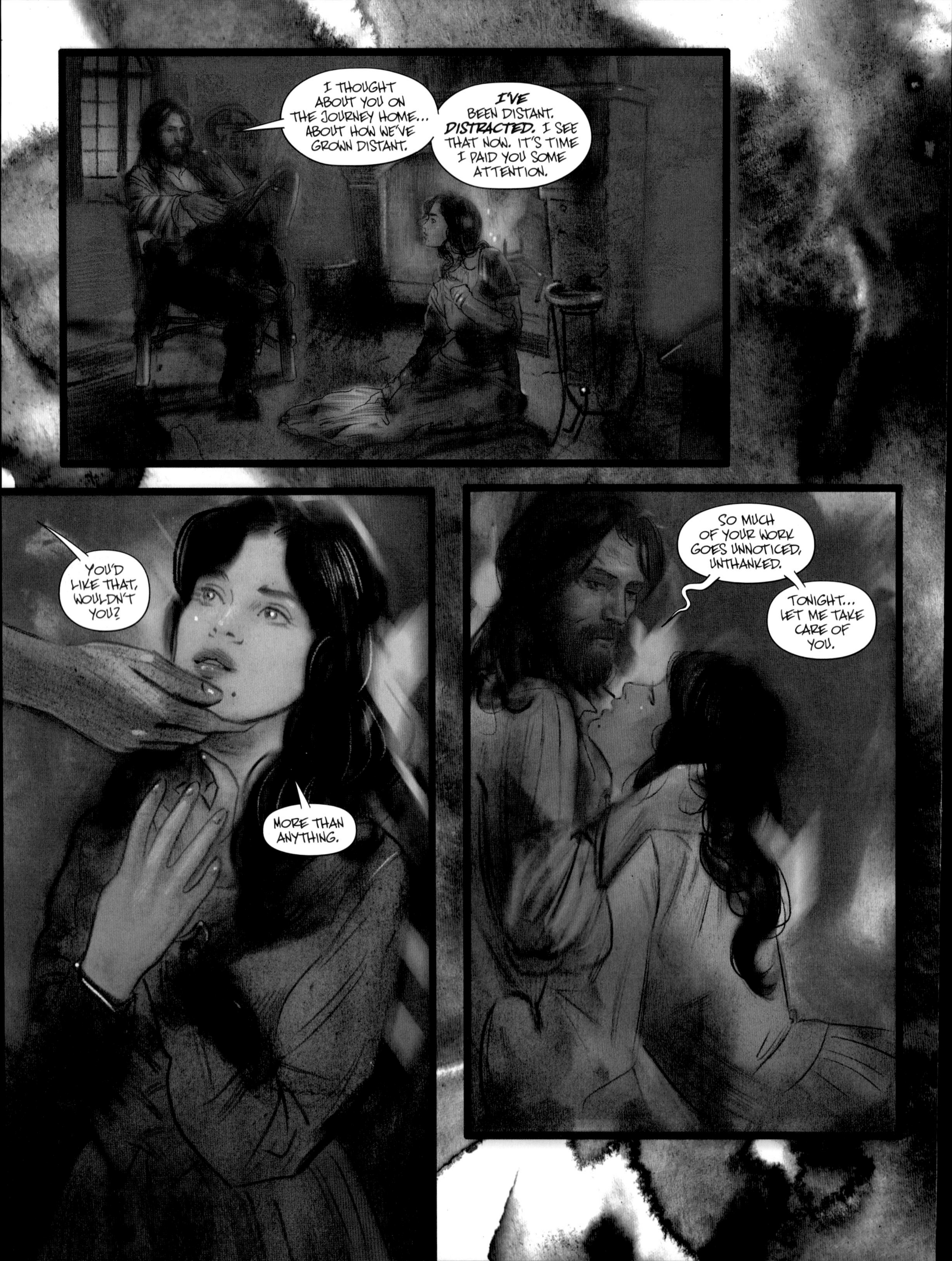
I THOUGHT ABOUT YOU ON THE JOURNEY HOME... ABOUT HOW WE'VE GROWN DISTANT.
I'VE BEEN DISTANT. ***DISTRACTED.*** I SEE THAT NOW. IT'S TIME I PAID YOU SOME ATTENTION.
YOU'D LIKE THAT, WOULDN'T YOU?
MORE THAN ANYTHING.
SO MUCH OF YOUR WORK GOES UNNOTICED, UNTHANKED.
TONIGHT... LET ME TAKE CARE OF YOU.

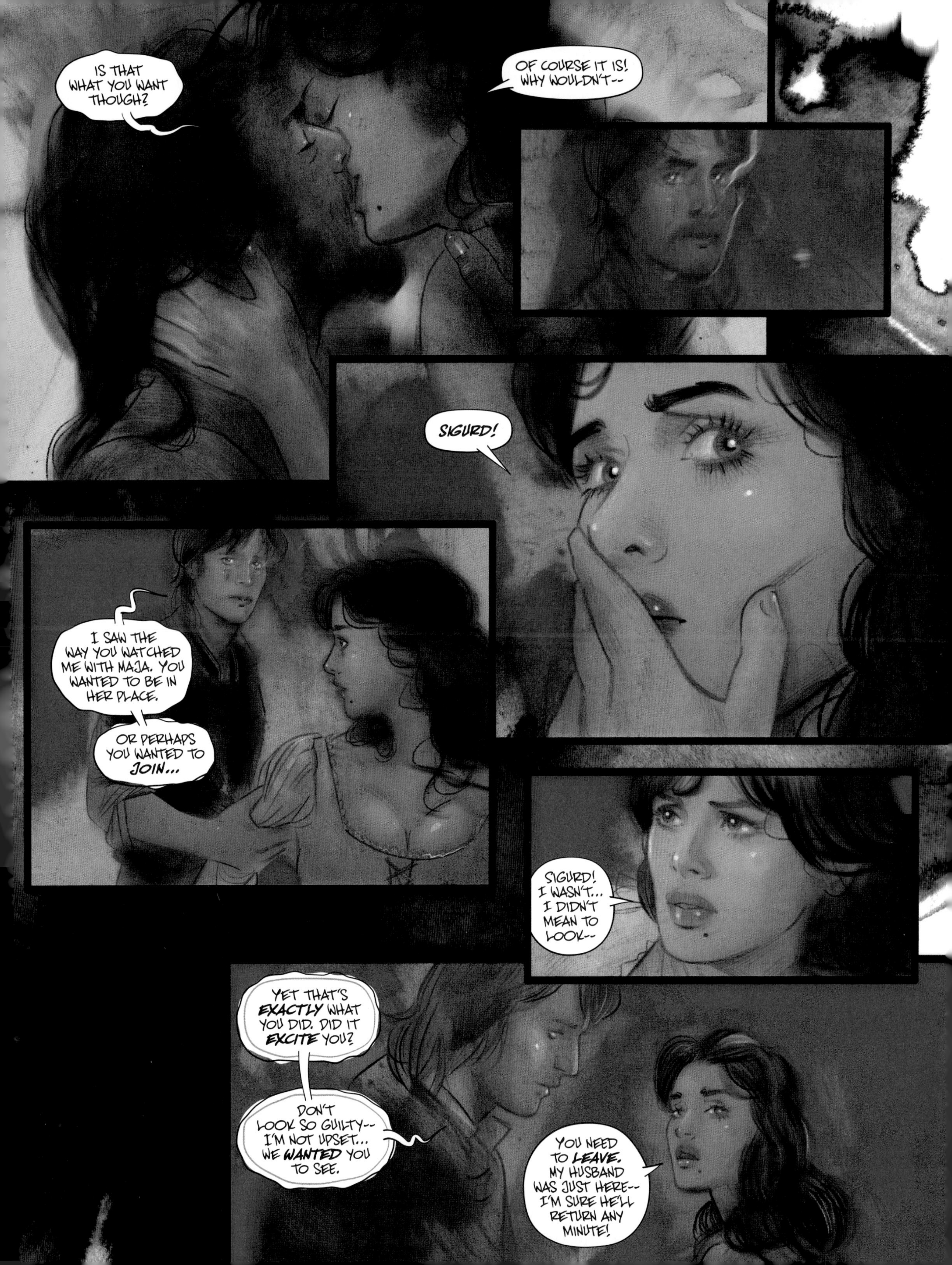
IS THAT WHAT YOU WANT THOUGH?
OF COURSE IT IS! WHY WOULDN'T--
SIGURD!
I SAW THE WAY YOU WATCHED ME WITH MAJA. YOU WANTED TO BE IN HER PLACE.
OR PERHAPS YOU WANTED TO **JOIN...**
SIGURD! I WASN'T... I DIDN'T MEAN TO LOOK--
YET THAT'S **EXACTLY** WHAT YOU DID. DID IT **EXCITE** YOU?
DON'T LOOK SO GUILTY-- I'M NOT UPSET... WE **WANTED** YOU TO SEE.
YOU NEED TO **LEAVE.** MY HUSBAND WAS JUST HERE-- I'M SURE HE'LL RETURN ANY MINUTE!

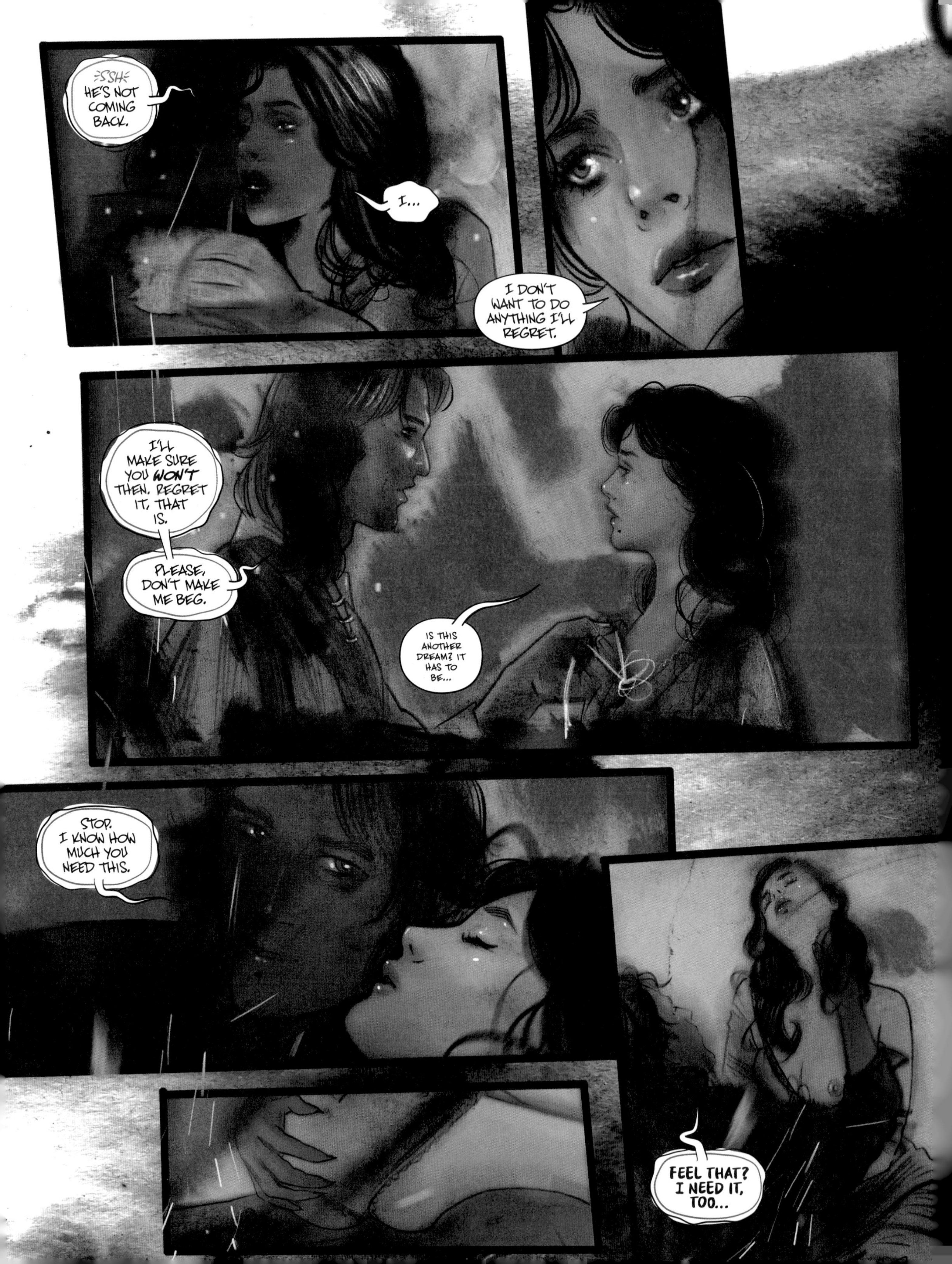
SSH
HE'S NOT COMING BACK.
I...
I DON'T WANT TO DO ANYTHING I'LL REGRET.
I'LL MAKE SURE YOU **WON'T** THEN. REGRET IT, THAT IS.
PLEASE, DON'T MAKE ME BEG.
IS THIS ANOTHER DREAM? IT HAS TO BE...
STOP. I KNOW HOW MUCH YOU NEED THIS.
FEEL THAT? I NEED IT, TOO...

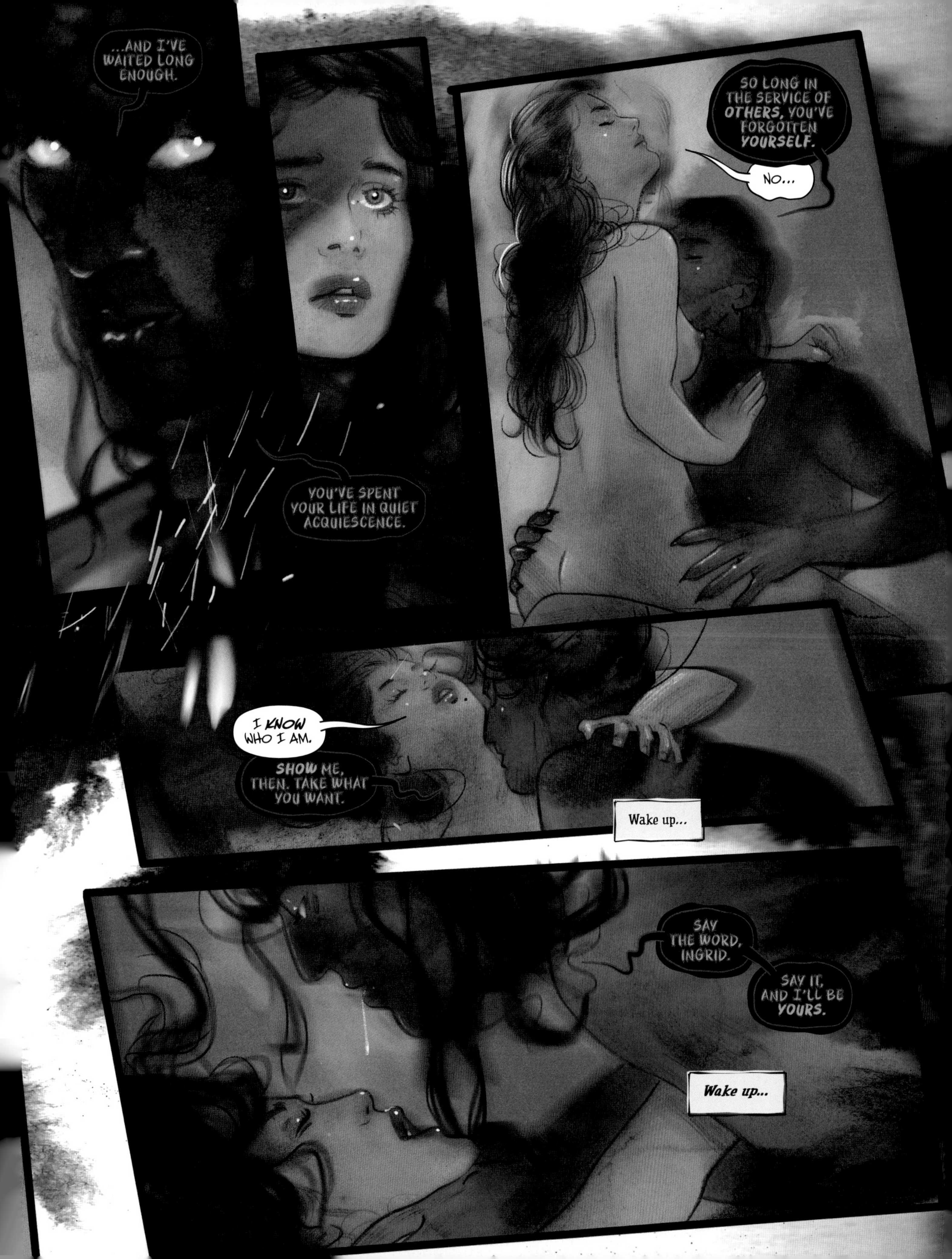
...AND I'VE WAITED LONG ENOUGH.
YOU'VE SPENT YOUR LIFE IN QUIET ACQUIESCENCE.
SO LONG IN THE SERVICE OF OTHERS, YOU'VE FORGOTTEN YOURSELF.
NO...
I KNOW WHO I AM.
SHOW ME, THEN. TAKE WHAT YOU WANT.
Wake up...
SAY THE WORD, INGRID.
SAY IT, AND I'LL BE YOURS.
Wake up...

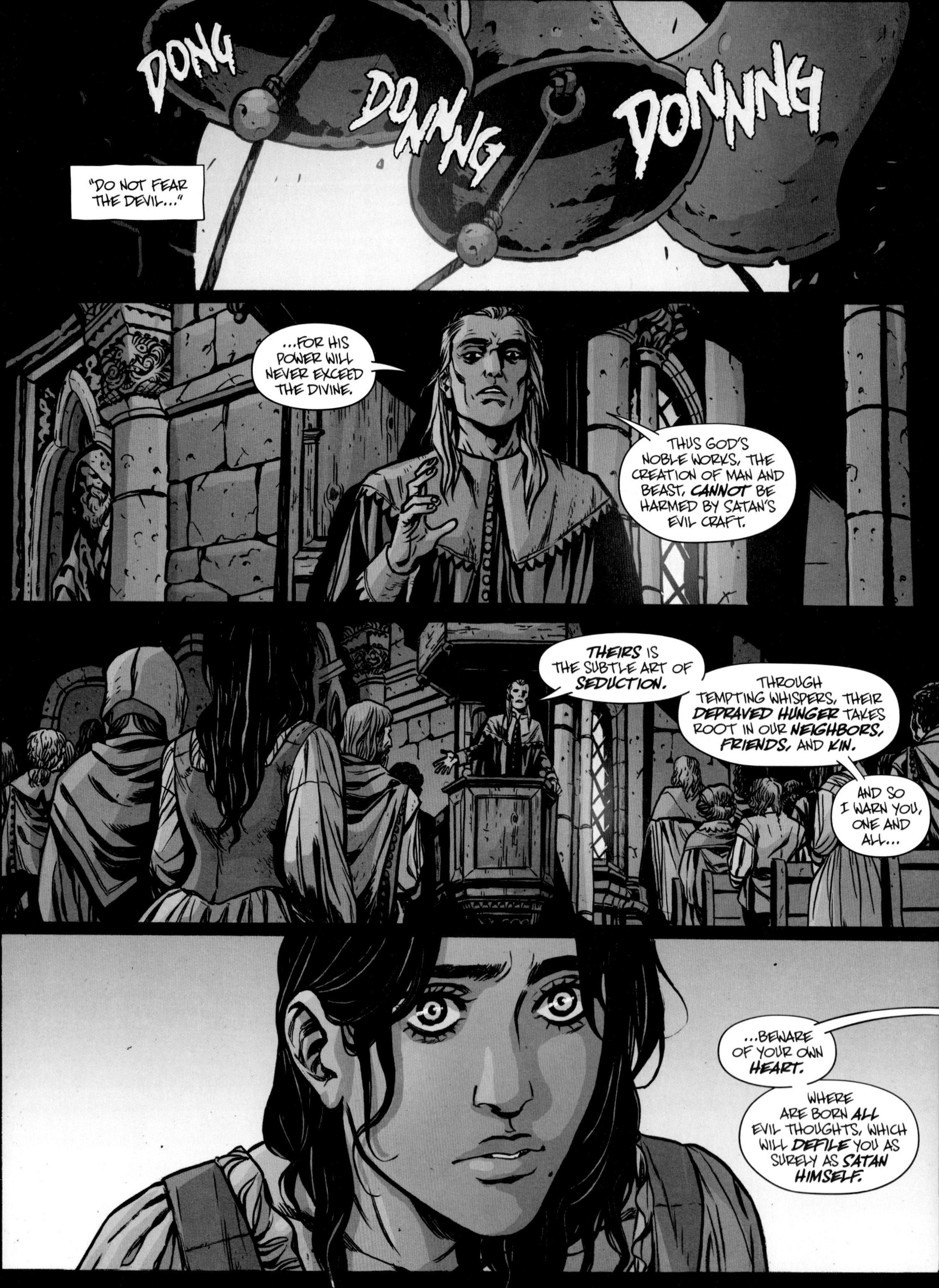
DONG
DONNNG
DONNNG
"DO NOT FEAR THE DEVIL..."
...FOR HIS POWER WILL NEVER EXCEED THE DIVINE.
THUS GOD'S NOBLE WORKS, THE CREATION OF MAN AND BEAST, CANNOT BE HARMED BY SATAN'S EVIL CRAFT.
THEIRS IS THE SUBTLE ART OF SEDUCTION.
THROUGH TEMPTING WHISPERS, THEIR DEPRAVED HUNGER TAKES ROOT IN OUR NEIGHBORS, FRIENDS, AND KIN.
AND SO I WARN YOU, ONE AND ALL...
...BEWARE OF YOUR OWN HEART.
WHERE ARE BORN ALL EVIL THOUGHTS, WHICH WILL DEFILE YOU AS SURELY AS SATAN HIMSELF.

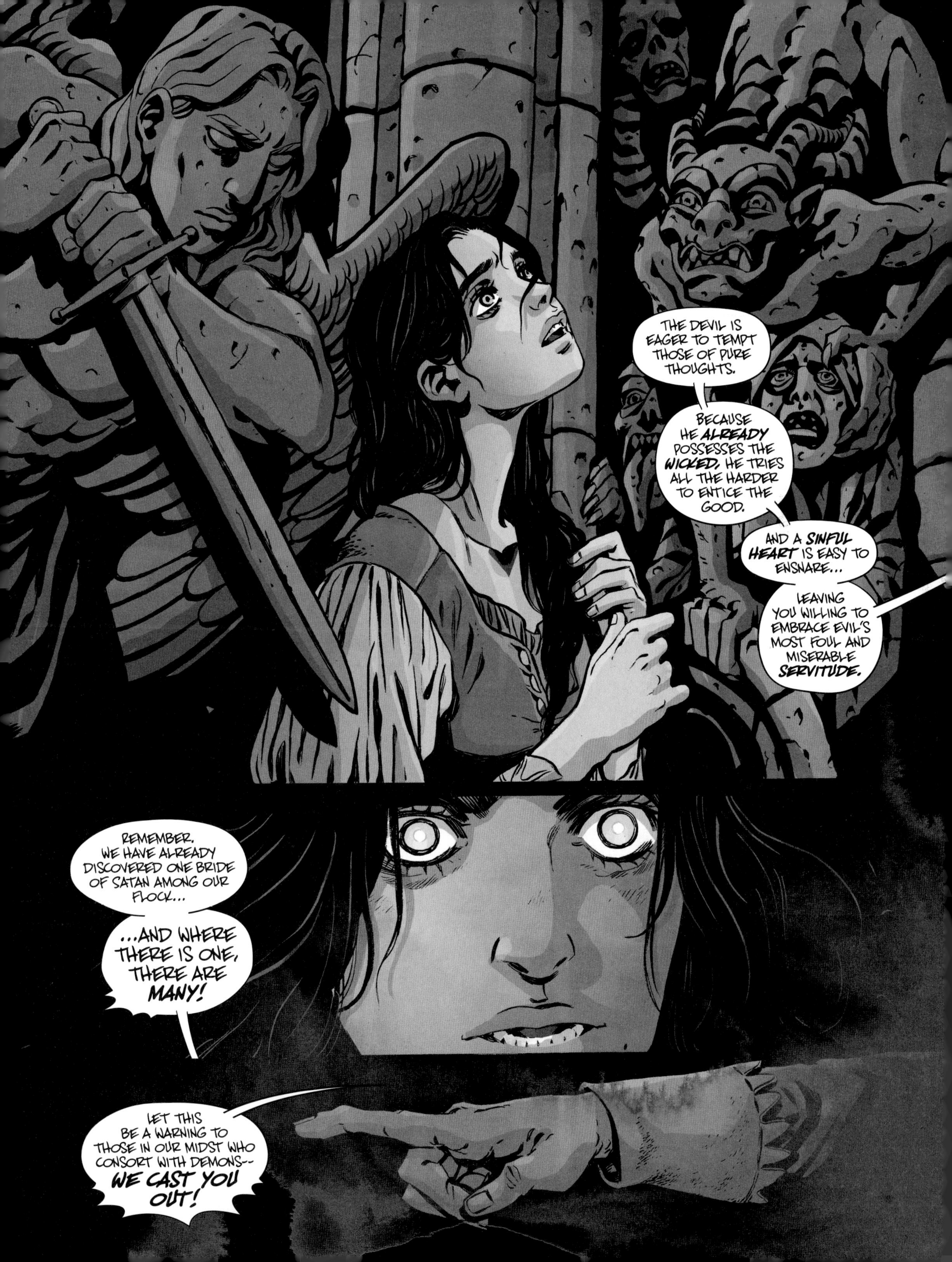
THE DEVIL IS EAGER TO TEMPT THOSE OF PURE THOUGHTS.
BECAUSE HE **ALREADY** POSSESSES THE **WICKED,** HE TRIES ALL THE HARDER TO ENTICE THE GOOD.
AND A **SINFUL HEART** IS EASY TO ENSNARE...
LEAVING YOU WILLING TO EMBRACE EVIL'S MOST FOUL AND MISERABLE **SERVITUDE.**
REMEMBER. WE HAVE ALREADY DISCOVERED ONE BRIDE OF SATAN AMONG OUR FLOCK...
...AND WHERE THERE IS ONE, THERE ARE **MANY!**
LET THIS BE A WARNING TO THOSE IN OUR MIDST WHO CONSORT WITH DEMONS--
WE CAST YOU OUT!

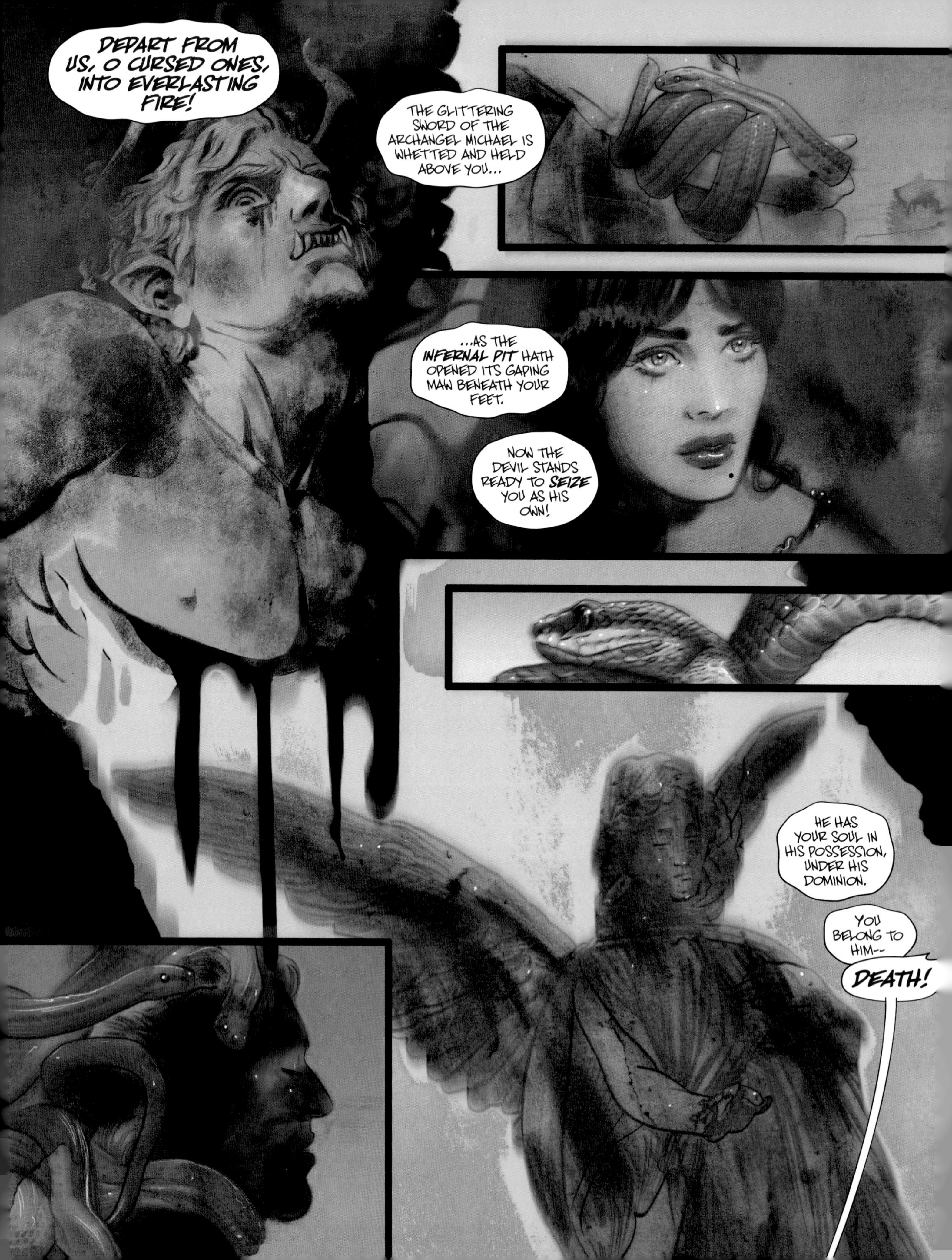
DEPART FROM US, O CURSED ONES, INTO EVERLASTING FIRE!
THE GLITTERING SWORD OF THE ARCHANGEL MICHAEL IS WHETTED AND HELD ABOVE YOU...
...AS THE INFERNAL PIT HATH OPENED ITS GAPING MAW BENEATH YOUR FEET.
NOW THE DEVIL STANDS READY TO SEIZE YOU AS HIS OWN!
HE HAS YOUR SOUL IN HIS POSSESSION, UNDER HIS DOMINION.
YOU BELONG TO HIM--
DEATH!

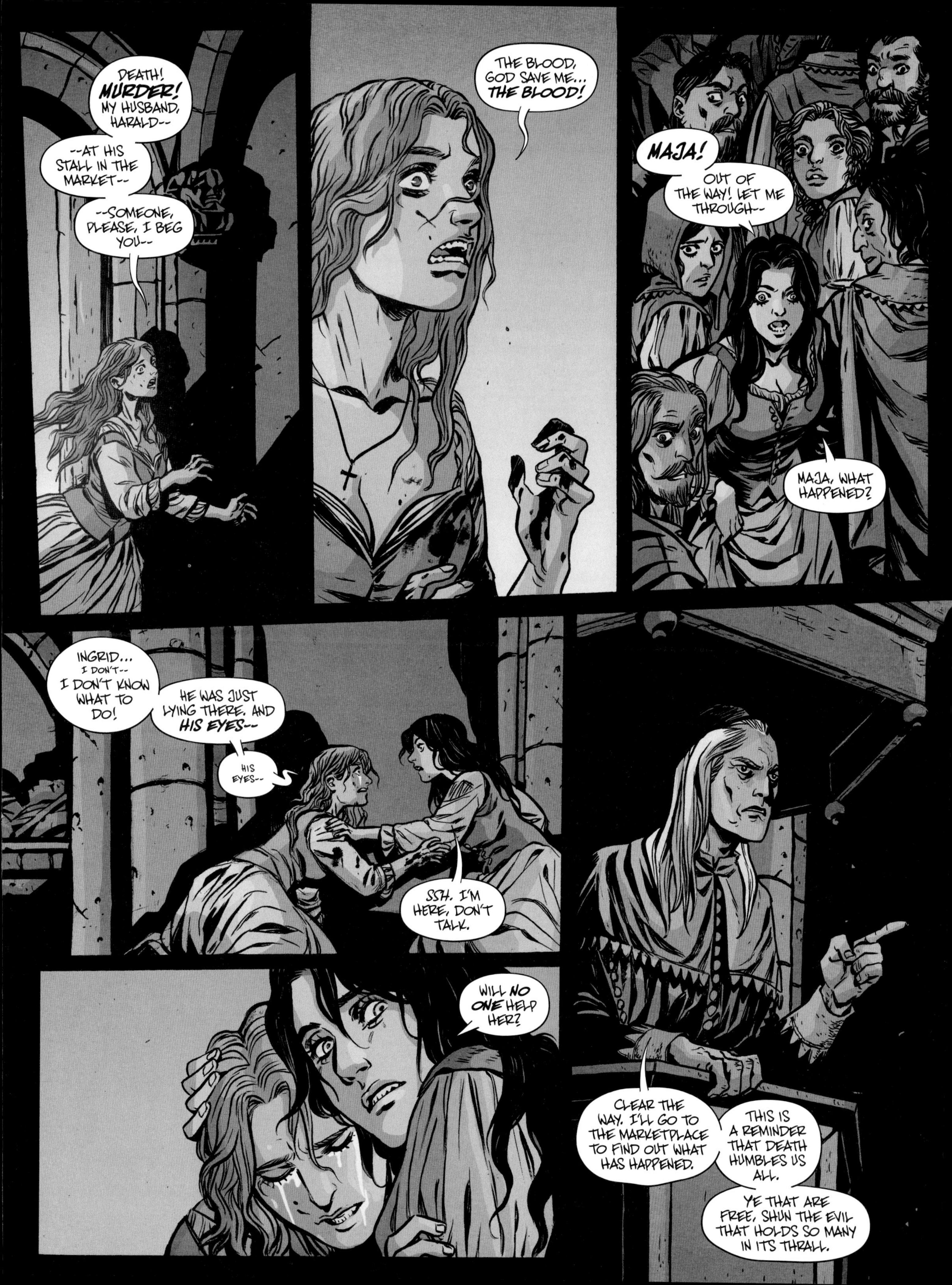
DEATH! MURDER! MY HUSBAND, HARALD--
--AT HIS STALL IN THE MARKET--
--SOMEONE, PLEASE, I BEG YOU--
THE BLOOD, GOD SAVE ME... THE BLOOD!
MAJA!
OUT OF THE WAY! LET ME THROUGH--
MAJA, WHAT HAPPENED?
INGRID... I DON'T-- I DON'T KNOW WHAT TO DO!
HE WAS JUST LYING THERE. AND HIS EYES--
HIS EYES--
SSH. I'M HERE, DON'T TALK.
WILL NO ONE HELP HER?
CLEAR THE WAY. I'LL GO TO THE MARKETPLACE TO FIND OUT WHAT HAS HAPPENED.
THIS IS A REMINDER THAT DEATH HUMBLES US ALL.
YE THAT ARE FREE, SHUN THE EVIL THAT HOLDS SO MANY IN ITS THRALL.

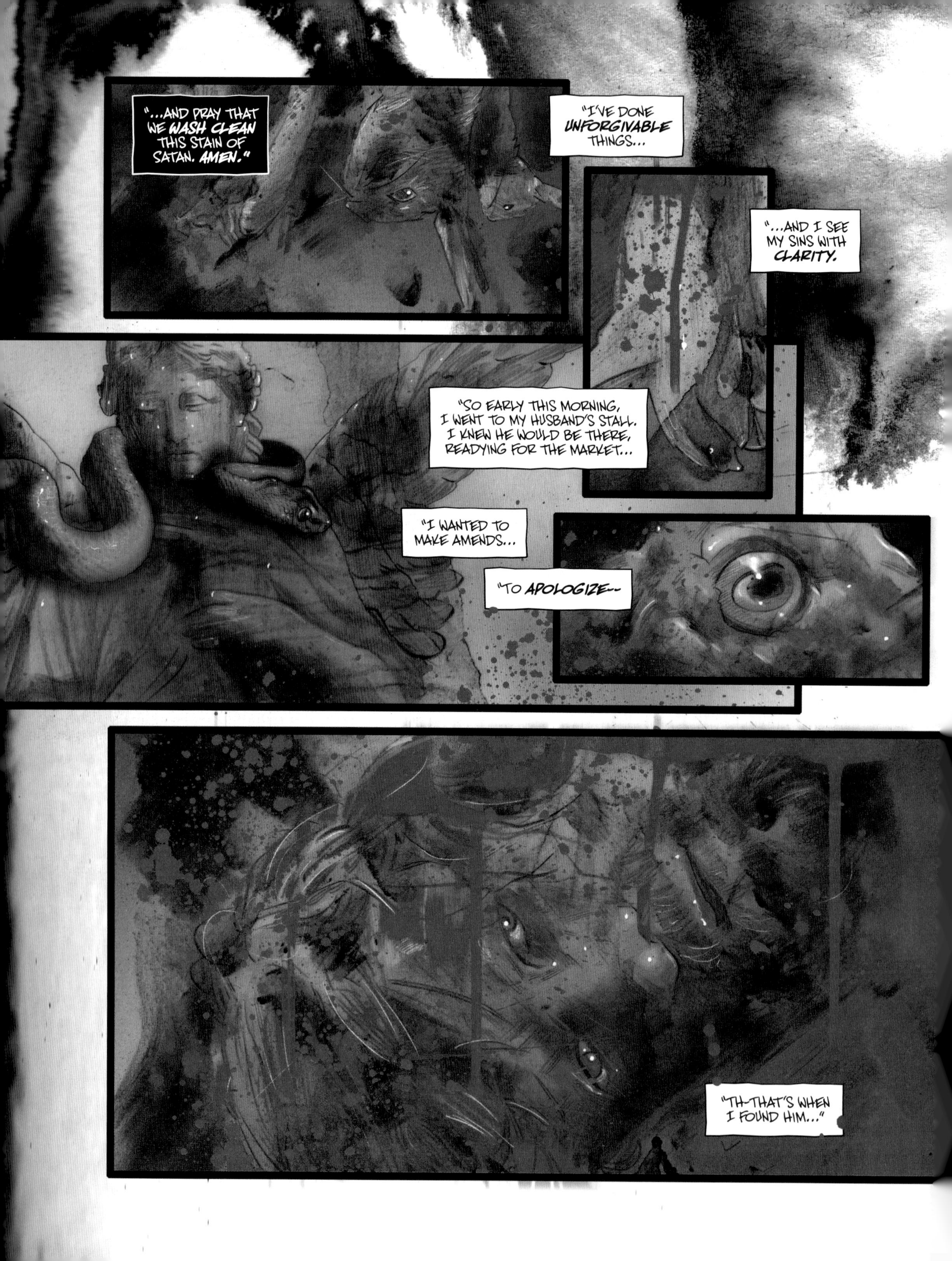
"...AND PRAY THAT WE WASH CLEAN THIS STAIN OF SATAN. AMEN."
"I'VE DONE UNFORGIVABLE THINGS...
"...AND I SEE MY SINS WITH CLARITY.
"SO EARLY THIS MORNING, I WENT TO MY HUSBAND'S STALL. I KNEW HE WOULD BE THERE, READYING FOR THE MARKET...
"I WANTED TO MAKE AMENDS...
"TO APOLOGIZE--
"TH-THAT'S WHEN I FOUND HIM..."

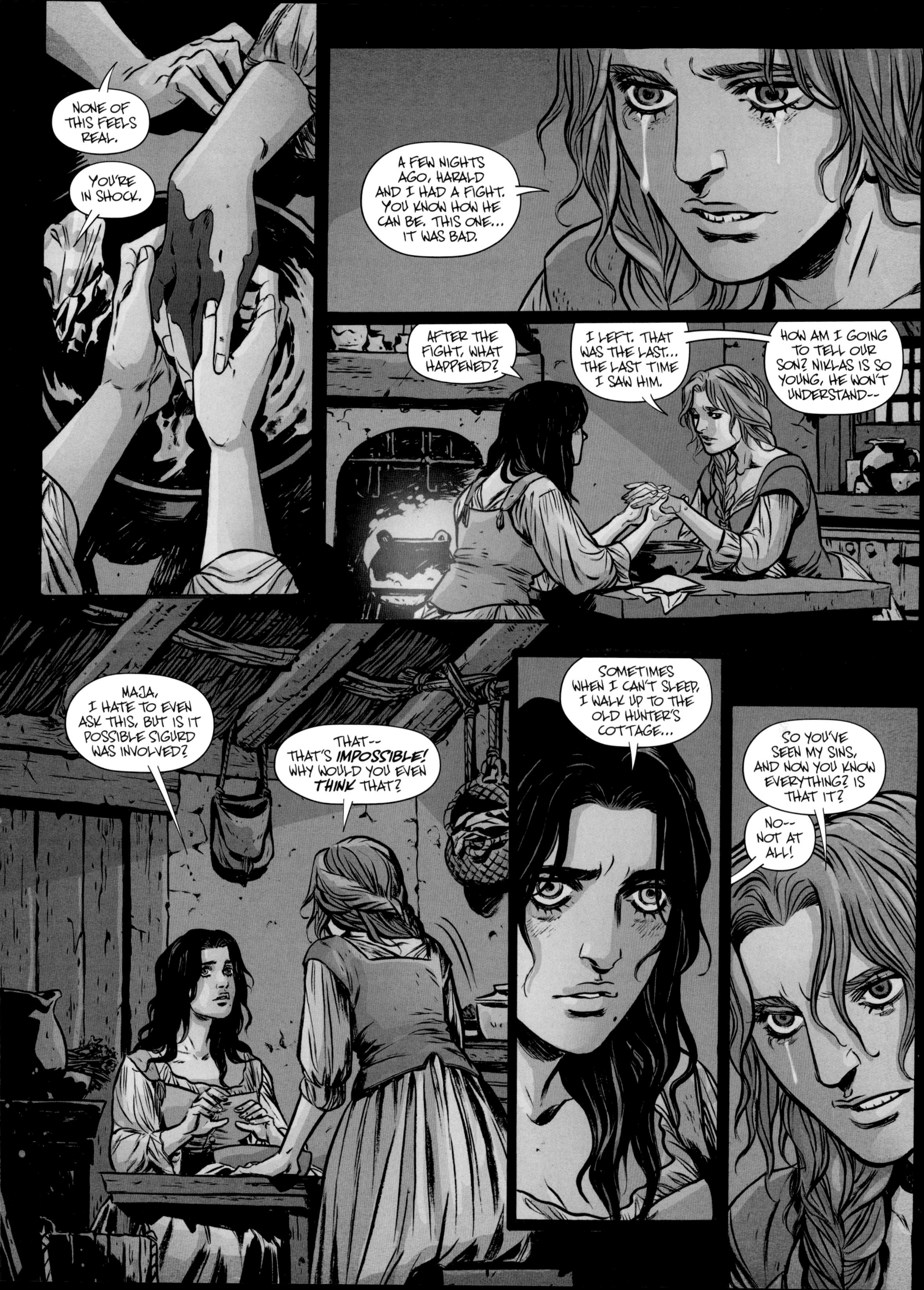
NONE OF THIS FEELS REAL.
YOU'RE IN SHOCK.
A FEW NIGHTS AGO, HARALD AND I HAD A FIGHT. YOU KNOW HOW HE CAN BE. THIS ONE... IT WAS BAD.
AFTER THE FIGHT, WHAT HAPPENED?
I LEFT. THAT WAS THE LAST... THE LAST TIME I SAW HIM.
HOW AM I GOING TO TELL OUR SON? NIKLAS IS SO YOUNG, HE WON'T UNDERSTAND--
MAJA, I HATE TO EVEN ASK THIS, BUT IS IT POSSIBLE SIGURD WAS INVOLVED?
THAT-- THAT'S **IMPOSSIBLE!** WHY WOULD YOU EVEN **THINK** THAT?
SOMETIMES WHEN I CAN'T SLEEP, I WALK UP TO THE OLD HUNTER'S COTTAGE...
SO YOU'VE SEEN MY SINS, AND NOW YOU KNOW EVERYTHING? IS THAT IT?
NO-- NOT AT ALL!

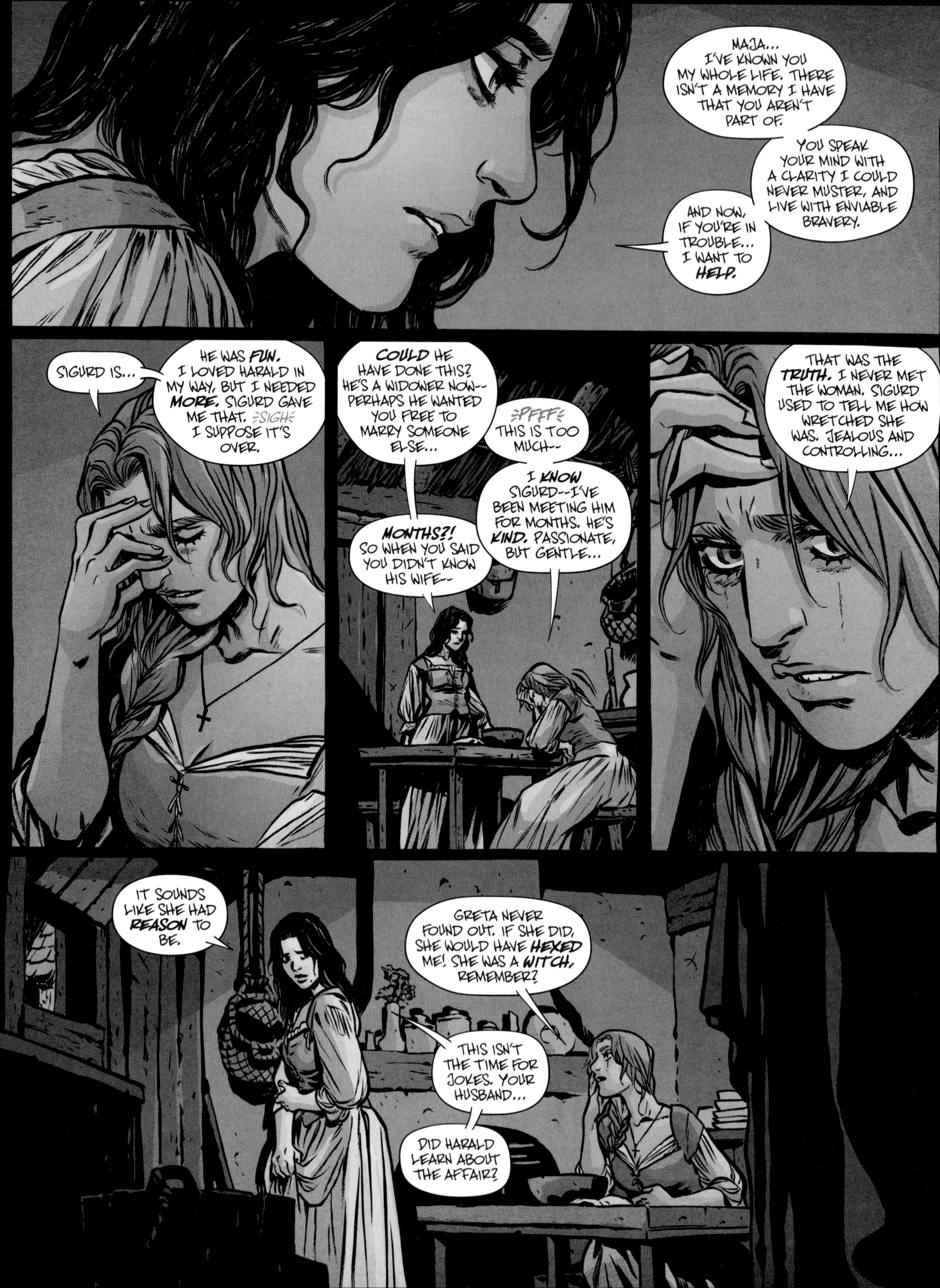
MAJA... I'VE KNOWN YOU MY WHOLE LIFE. THERE ISN'T A MEMORY I HAVE THAT YOU AREN'T PART OF.
YOU SPEAK YOUR MIND WITH A CLARITY I COULD NEVER MUSTER, AND LIVE WITH ENVIABLE BRAVERY.
AND NOW, IF YOU'RE IN TROUBLE... I WANT TO HELP.
SIGURD IS...
HE WAS FUN. I LOVED HARALD IN MY WAY, BUT I NEEDED MORE. SIGURD GAVE ME THAT. SIGH I SUPPOSE IT'S OVER.
COULD HE HAVE DONE THIS? HE'S A WIDOWER NOW--PERHAPS HE WANTED YOU FREE TO MARRY SOMEONE ELSE...
PFFF THIS IS TOO MUCH--
I KNOW SIGURD--I'VE BEEN MEETING HIM FOR MONTHS. HE'S KIND. PASSIONATE, BUT GENTLE...
MONTHS?! SO WHEN YOU SAID YOU DIDN'T KNOW HIS WIFE--
THAT WAS THE TRUTH. I NEVER MET THE WOMAN. SIGURD USED TO TELL ME HOW WRETCHED SHE WAS. JEALOUS AND CONTROLLING...
IT SOUNDS LIKE SHE HAD REASON TO BE.
GRETA NEVER FOUND OUT. IF SHE DID, SHE WOULD HAVE HEXED ME! SHE WAS A WITCH, REMEMBER?
THIS ISN'T THE TIME FOR JOKES. YOUR HUSBAND...
DID HARALD LEARN ABOUT THE AFFAIR?

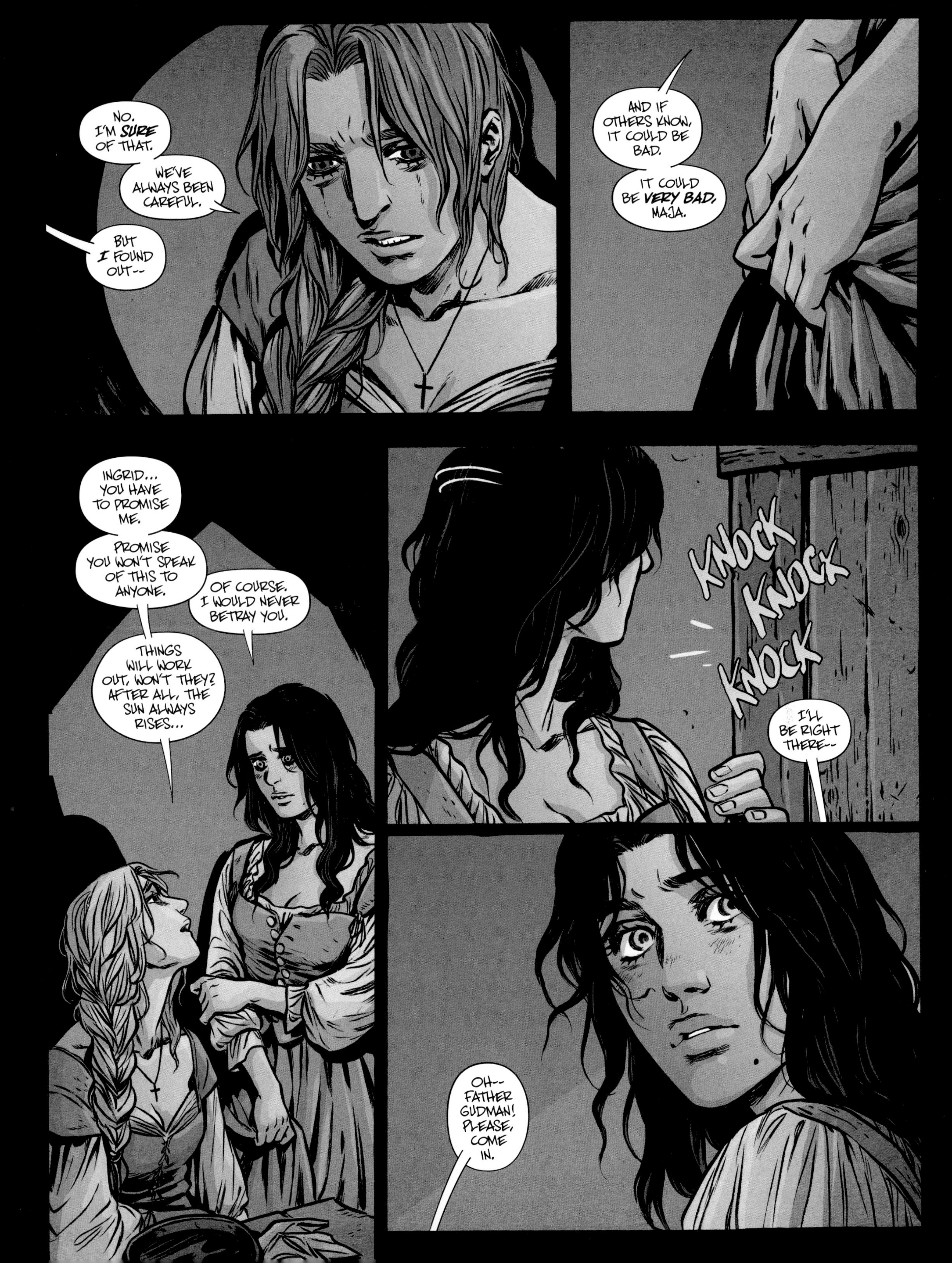

NO. I'M SURE OF THAT.
WE'VE ALWAYS BEEN CAREFUL.
BUT I FOUND OUT--
AND IF OTHERS KNOW, IT COULD BE BAD.
IT COULD BE VERY BAD, MAJA.
INGRID... YOU HAVE TO PROMISE ME.
PROMISE YOU WON'T SPEAK OF THIS TO ANYONE.
OF COURSE. I WOULD NEVER BETRAY YOU.
THINGS WILL WORK OUT, WON'T THEY? AFTER ALL, THE SUN ALWAYS RISES...
KNOCK KNOCK KNOCK
I'LL BE RIGHT THERE--
OH-- FATHER GUDMAN! PLEASE, COME IN.

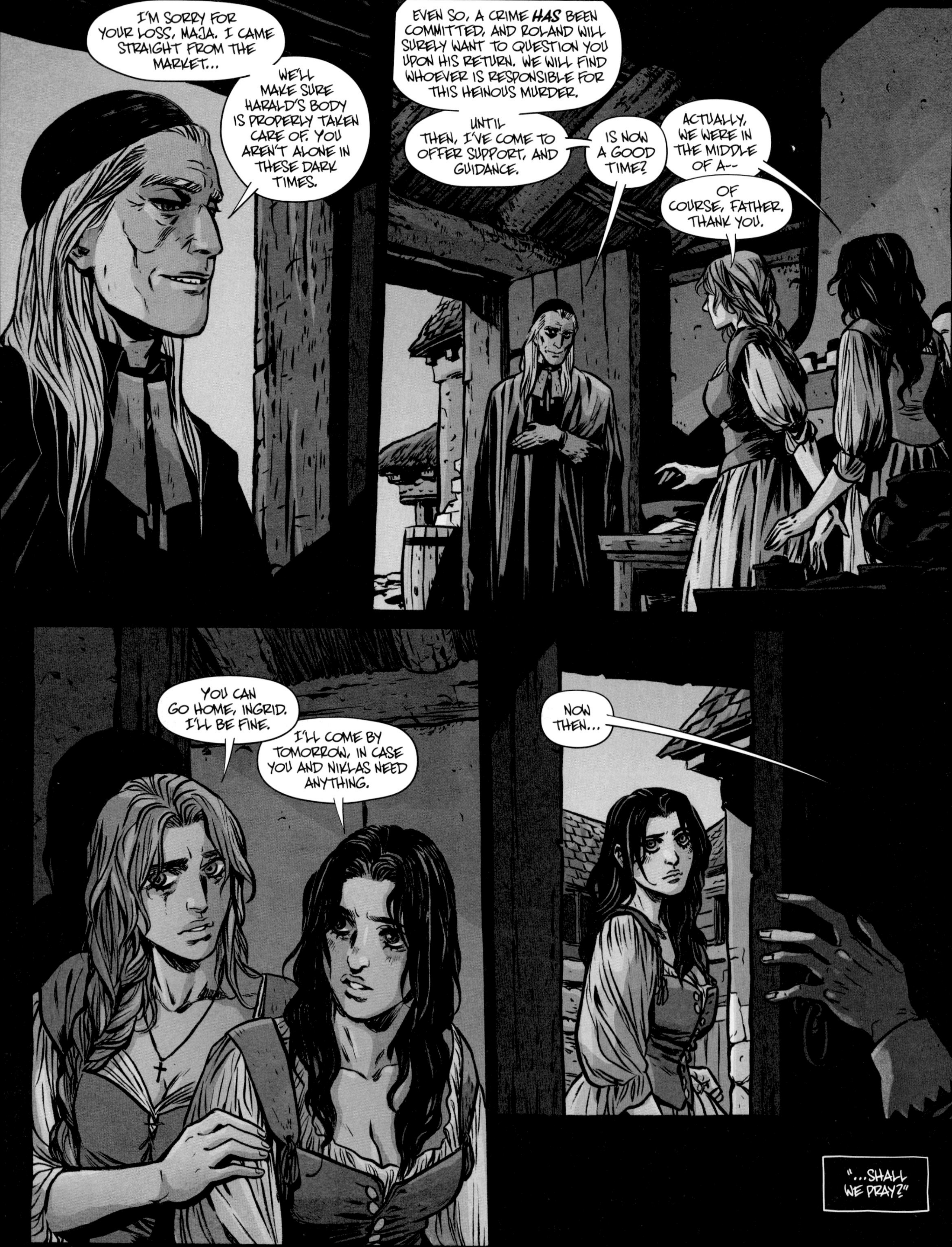
I'M SORRY FOR YOUR LOSS, MAJA. I CAME STRAIGHT FROM THE MARKET...
WE'LL MAKE SURE HARALD'S BODY IS PROPERLY TAKEN CARE OF. YOU AREN'T ALONE IN THESE DARK TIMES.
EVEN SO, A CRIME **HAS** BEEN COMMITTED, AND ROLAND WILL SURELY WANT TO QUESTION YOU UPON HIS RETURN. WE WILL FIND WHOEVER IS RESPONSIBLE FOR THIS HEINOUS MURDER.
UNTIL THEN, I'VE COME TO OFFER SUPPORT, AND GUIDANCE.
IS NOW A GOOD TIME?
ACTUALLY, WE WERE IN THE MIDDLE OF A--
OF COURSE, FATHER. THANK YOU.
YOU CAN GO HOME, INGRID. I'LL BE FINE.
I'LL COME BY TOMORROW, IN CASE YOU AND NIKLAS NEED ANYTHING.
NOW THEN...
"...SHALL WE PRAY?"

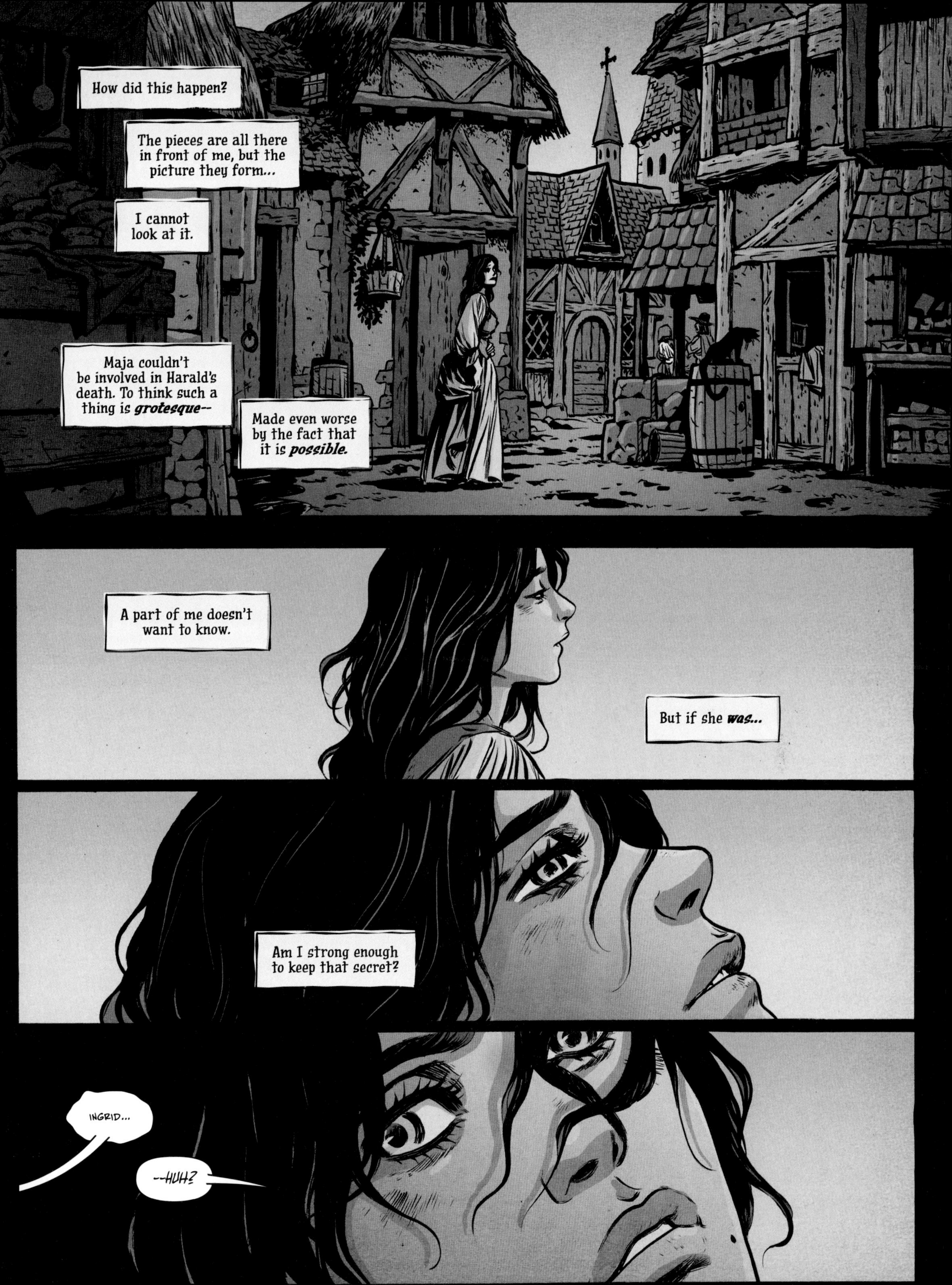
How did this happen?
The pieces are all there in front of me, but the picture they form...
I cannot look at it.
Maja couldn't be involved in Harald's death. To think such a thing is *grotesque*--
Made even worse by the fact that it is *possible*.
A part of me doesn't want to know.
But if she *was*...
Am I strong enough to keep that secret?
INGRID...
--HUH?

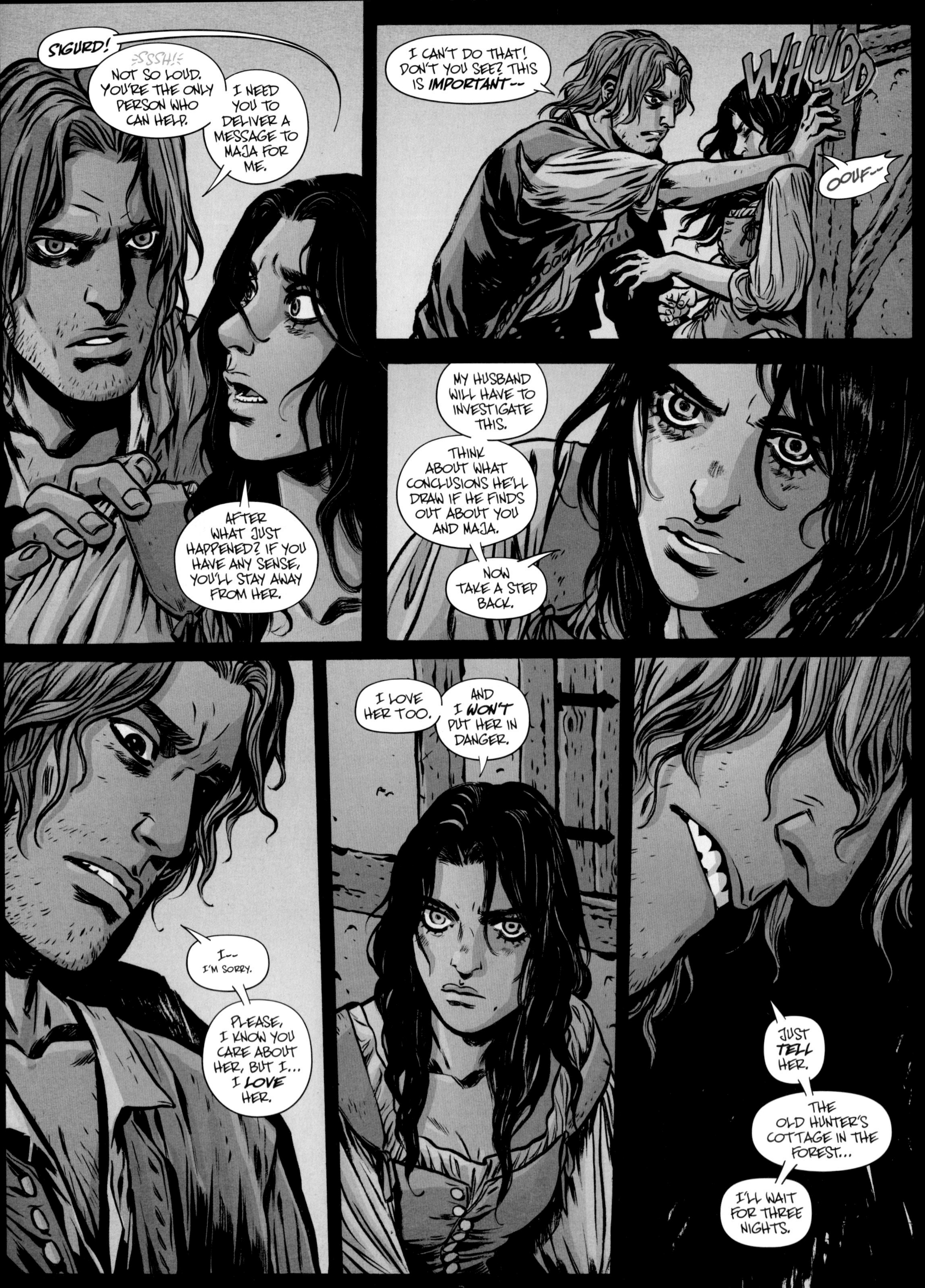

SIGURD!
SSSH!
NOT SO LOUD. YOU'RE THE ONLY PERSON WHO CAN HELP.
I NEED YOU TO DELIVER A MESSAGE TO MAJA FOR ME.
AFTER WHAT JUST HAPPENED? IF YOU HAVE ANY SENSE, YOU'LL STAY AWAY FROM HER.
I CAN'T DO THAT! DON'T YOU SEE? THIS IS IMPORTANT--
WHUDD
OOUF--
MY HUSBAND WILL HAVE TO INVESTIGATE THIS.
THINK ABOUT WHAT CONCLUSIONS HE'LL DRAW IF HE FINDS OUT ABOUT YOU AND MAJA.
NOW TAKE A STEP BACK.
I-- I'M SORRY.
PLEASE, I KNOW YOU CARE ABOUT HER, BUT I... I LOVE HER.
I LOVE HER TOO.
AND I WON'T PUT HER IN DANGER.
JUST TELL HER.
THE OLD HUNTER'S COTTAGE IN THE FOREST...
I'LL WAIT FOR THREE NIGHTS.

CHAPTER IV.
WHOSE HAND WAS AT THE LATCH

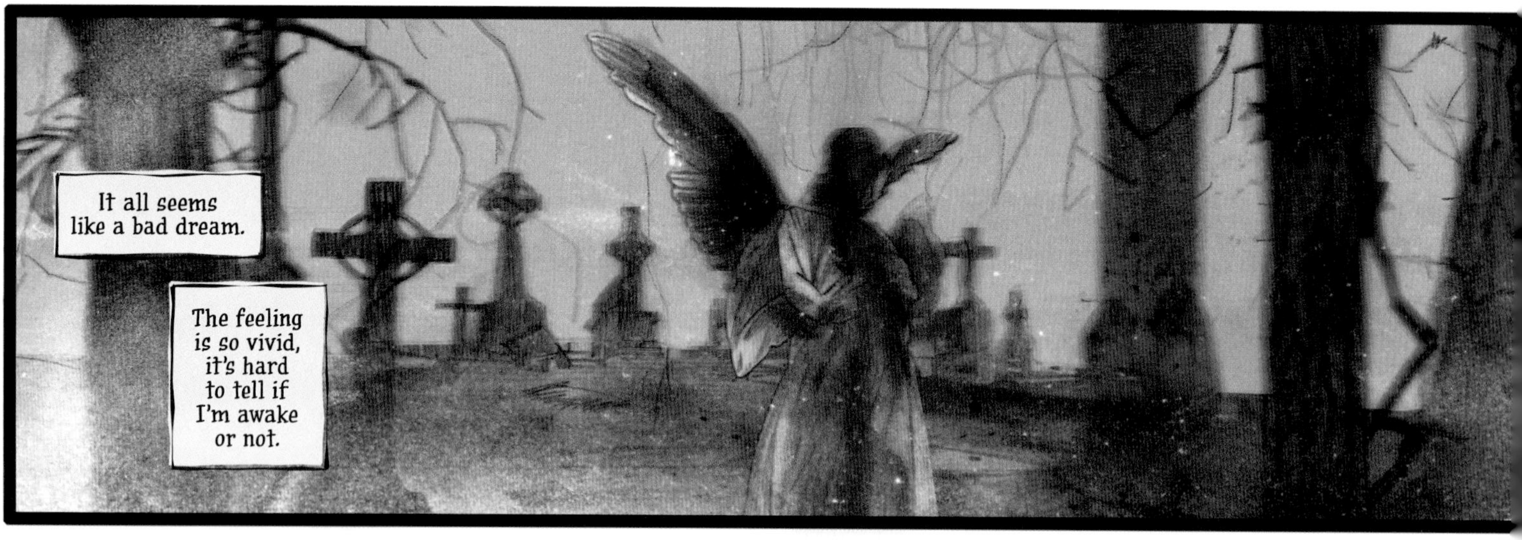
It all seems like a bad dream.
The feeling is so vivid, it's hard to tell if I'm awake or not.

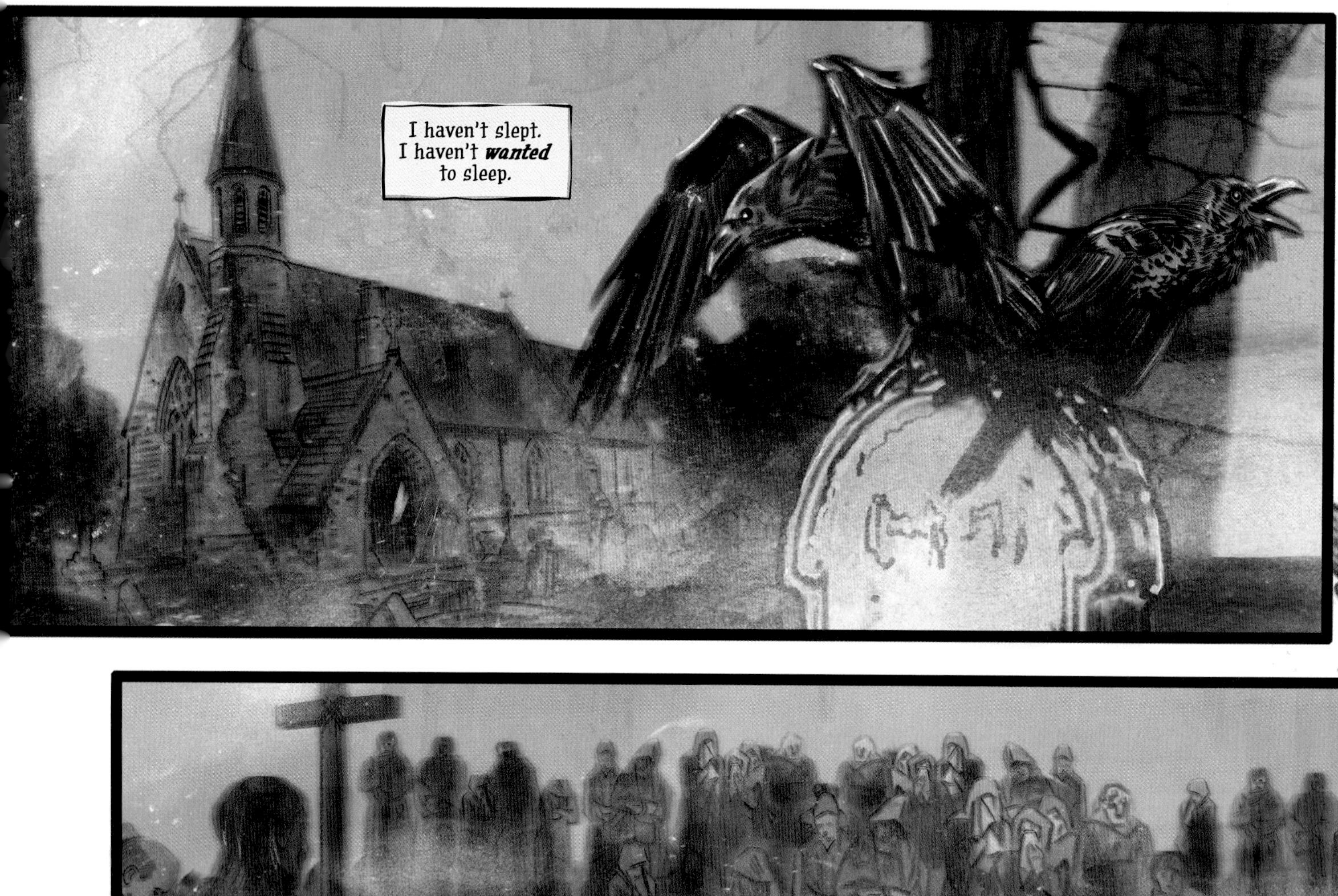
I haven't slept. I haven't ***wanted*** to sleep.

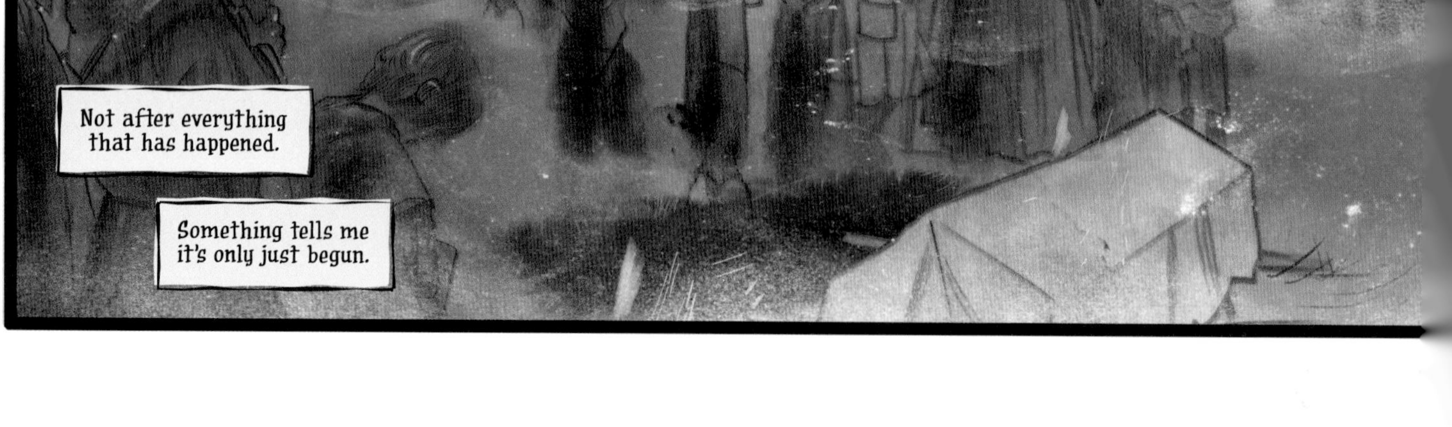
Not after everything that has happened.
Something tells me it's only just begun.

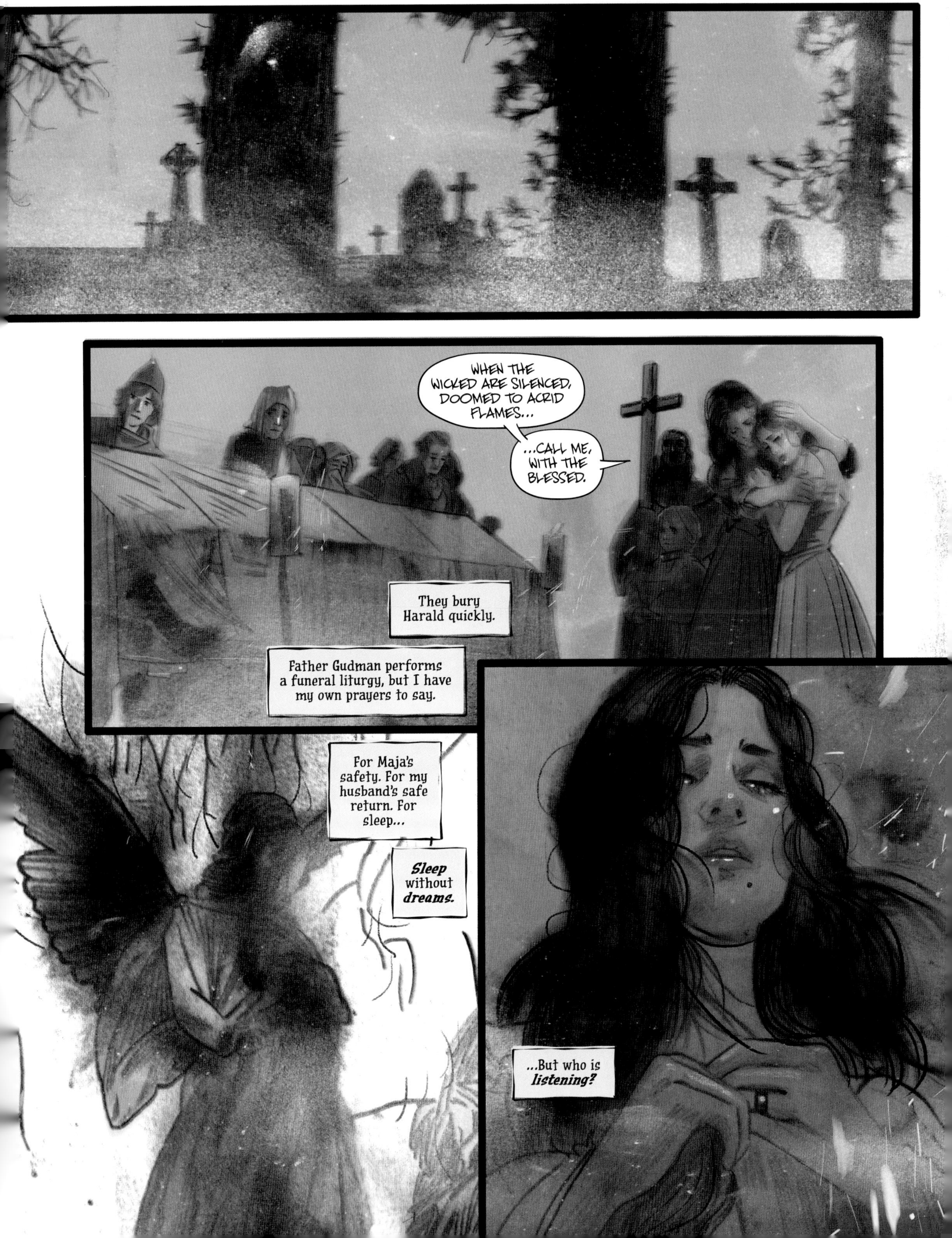
WHEN THE WICKED ARE SILENCED, DOOMED TO ACRID FLAMES...
...CALL ME, WITH THE BLESSED.
They bury Harald quickly.
Father Gudman performs a funeral liturgy, but I have my own prayers to say.
For Maja's safety. For my husband's safe return. For sleep...
Sleep without *dreams.*
...But who is *listening?*

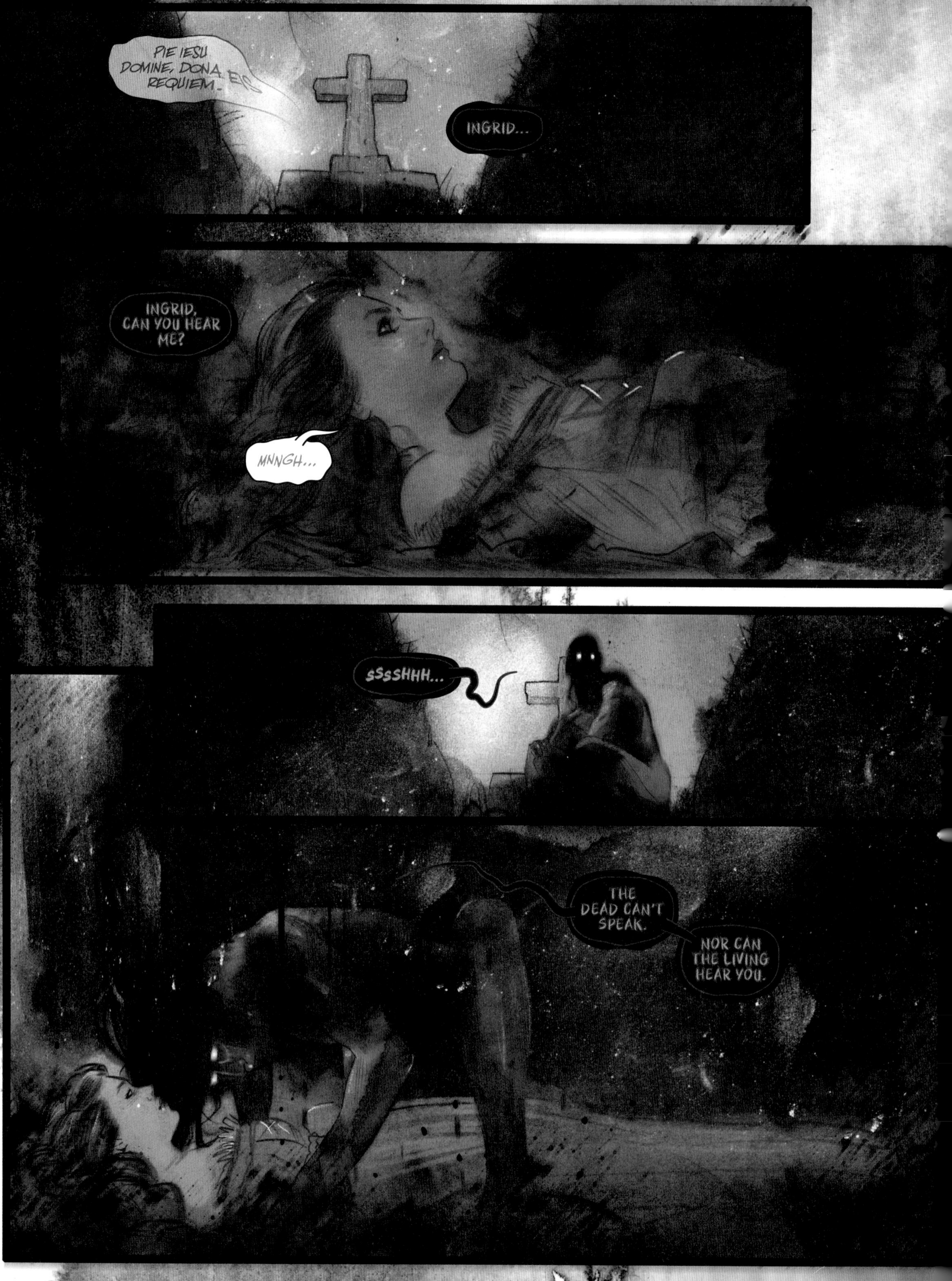
PIE IESU DOMINE, DONA EIS REQUIEM.
INGRID...
INGRID, CAN YOU HEAR ME?
MNNGH...
SSSSHHH...
THE DEAD CAN'T SPEAK.
NOR CAN THE LIVING HEAR YOU.

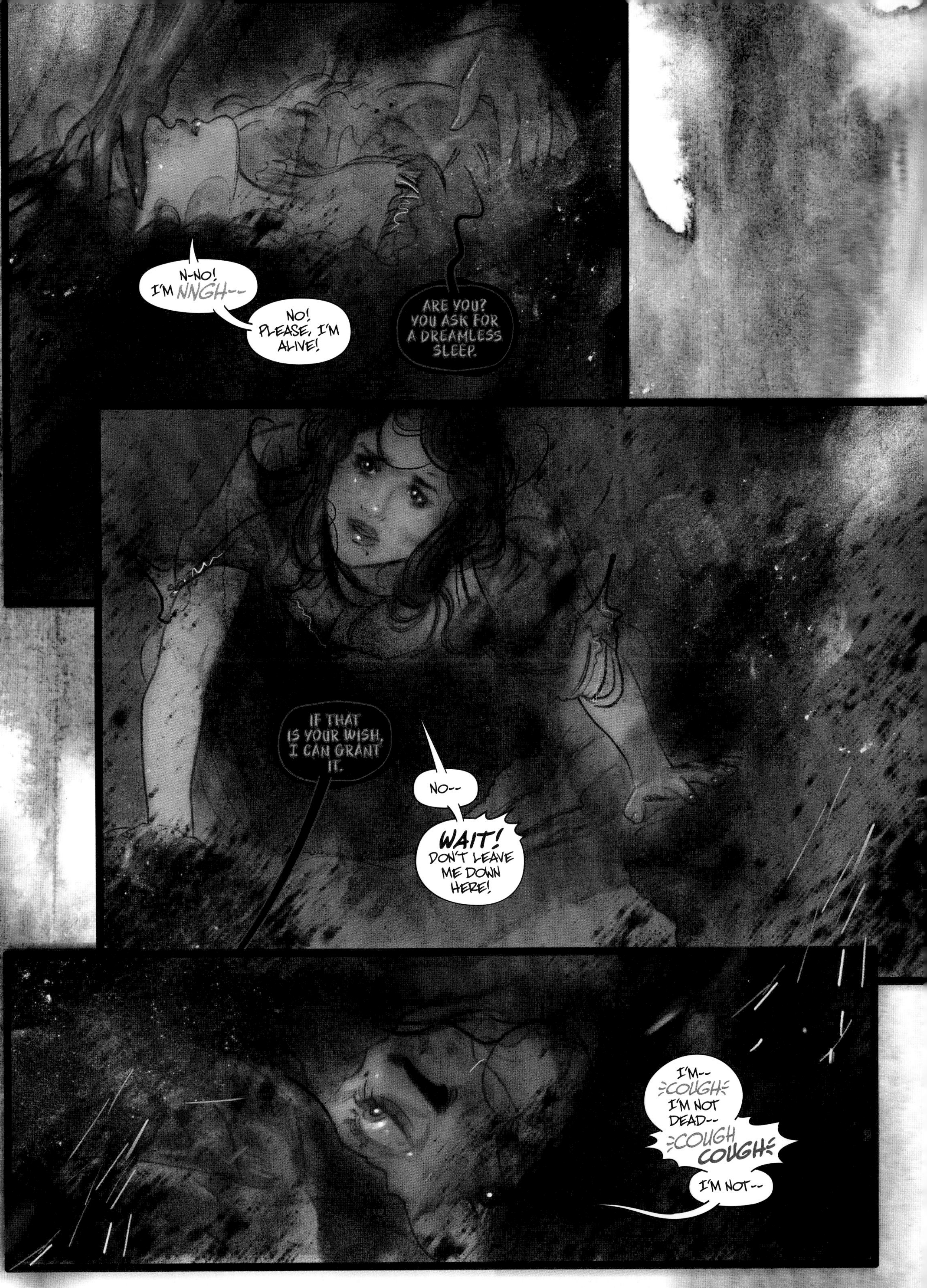
N-NO! I'M NNGH--
NO! PLEASE, I'M ALIVE!
ARE YOU? YOU ASK FOR A DREAMLESS SLEEP.
IF THAT IS YOUR WISH, I CAN GRANT IT.
NO--
WAIT! DON'T LEAVE ME DOWN HERE!
I'M-- COUGH I'M NOT DEAD-- COUGH COUGH
I'M NOT--

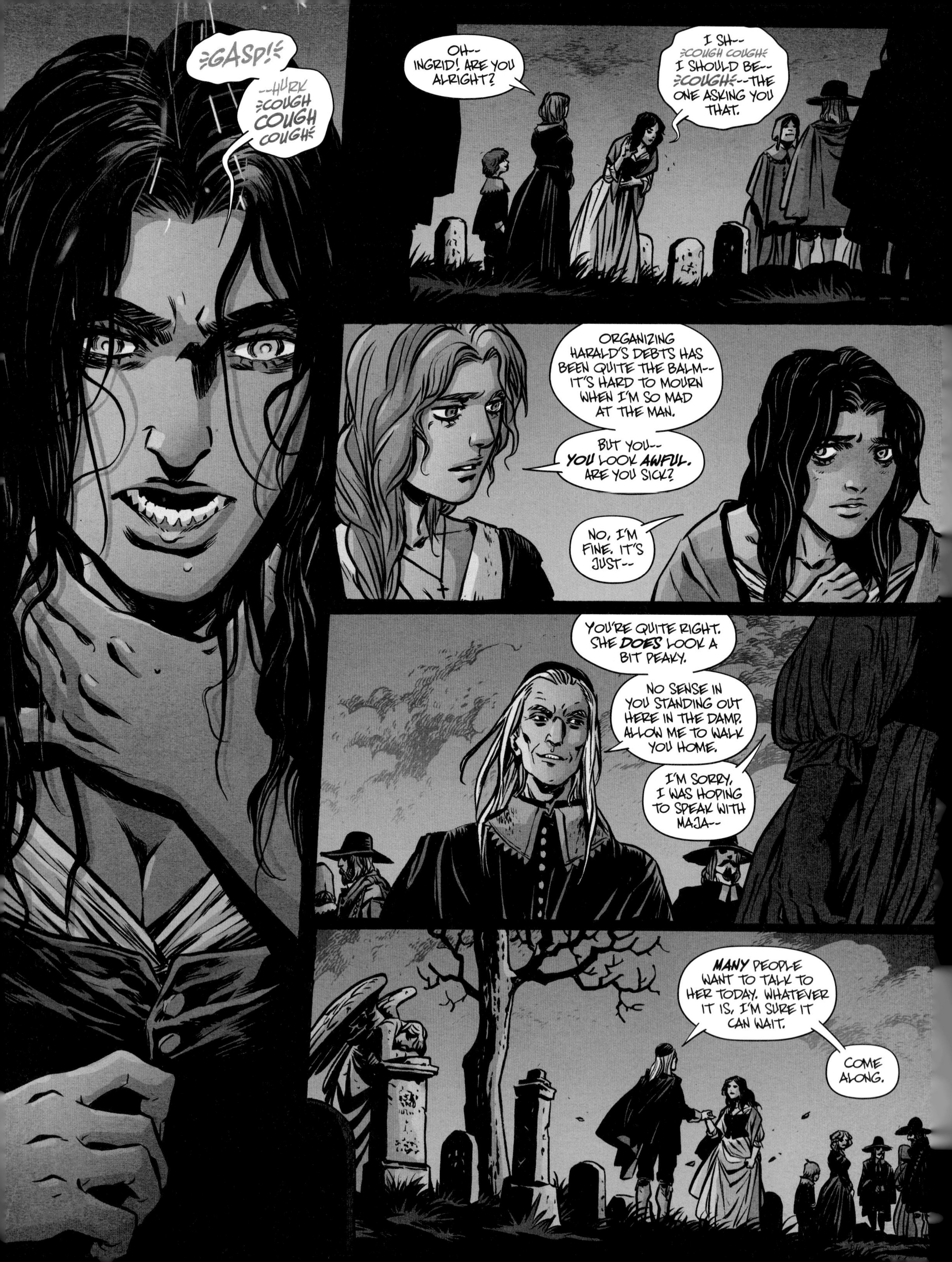
GASP!
--HURK COUGH COUGH COUGH
OH-- INGRID! ARE YOU ALRIGHT?
I SH-- COUGH COUGH I SHOULD BE-- COUGH --THE ONE ASKING YOU THAT.
ORGANIZING HARALD'S DEBTS HAS BEEN QUITE THE BALM-- IT'S HARD TO MOURN WHEN I'M SO MAD AT THE MAN.
BUT YOU-- YOU LOOK AWFUL. ARE YOU SICK?
NO, I'M FINE. IT'S JUST--
YOU'RE QUITE RIGHT. SHE DOES LOOK A BIT PEAKY.
NO SENSE IN YOU STANDING OUT HERE IN THE DAMP. ALLOW ME TO WALK YOU HOME.
I'M SORRY, I WAS HOPING TO SPEAK WITH MAJA--
MANY PEOPLE WANT TO TALK TO HER TODAY. WHATEVER IT IS, I'M SURE IT CAN WAIT.
COME ALONG.

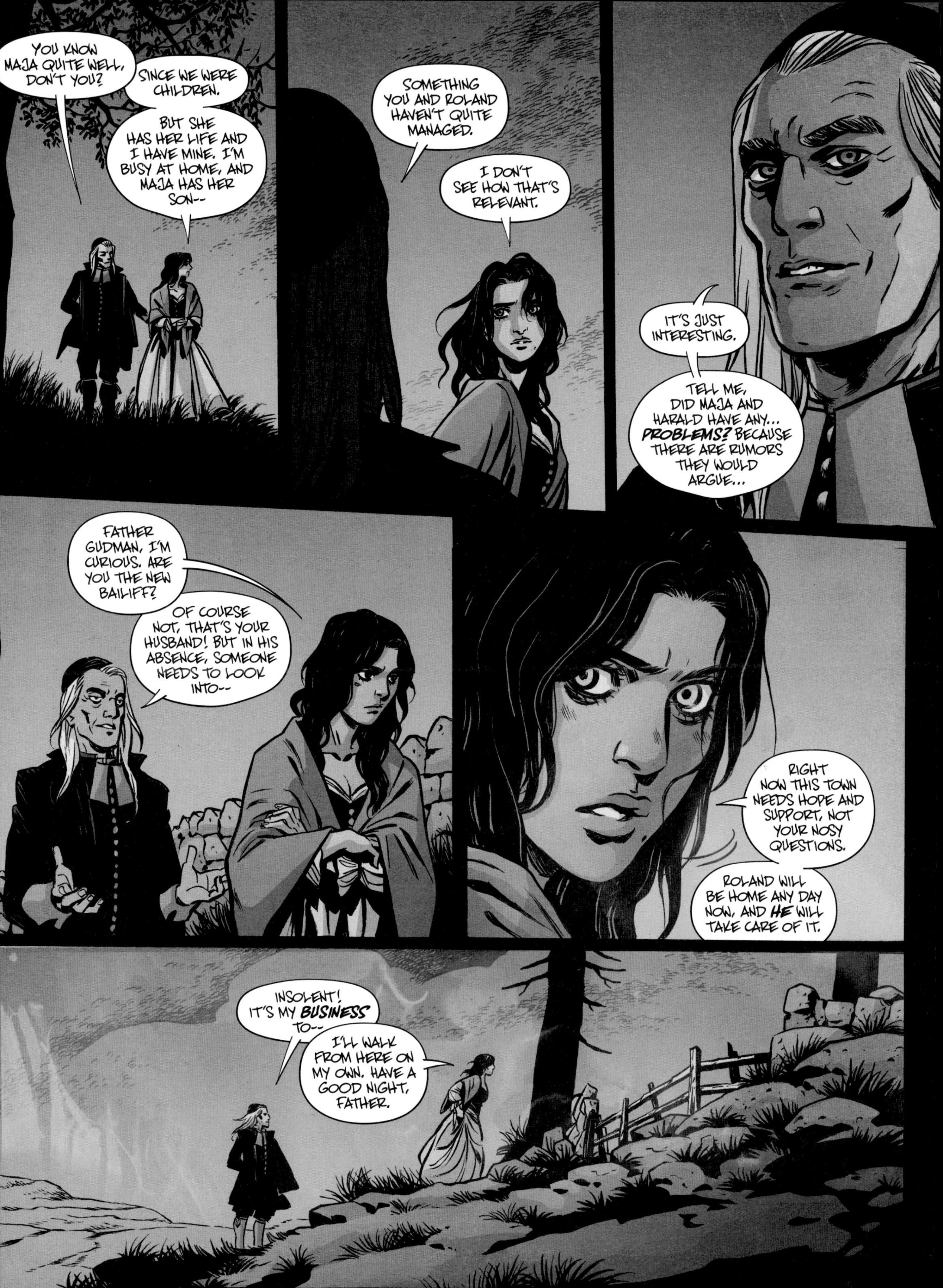
YOU KNOW MAJA QUITE WELL, DON'T YOU?
SINCE WE WERE CHILDREN.
BUT SHE HAS HER LIFE AND I HAVE MINE. I'M BUSY AT HOME, AND MAJA HAS HER SON--
SOMETHING YOU AND ROLAND HAVEN'T QUITE MANAGED.
I DON'T SEE HOW THAT'S RELEVANT.
IT'S JUST INTERESTING.
TELL ME, DID MAJA AND HARALD HAVE ANY... PROBLEMS? BECAUSE THERE ARE RUMORS THEY WOULD ARGUE...
FATHER GUDMAN, I'M CURIOUS. ARE YOU THE NEW BAILIFF?
OF COURSE NOT, THAT'S YOUR HUSBAND! BUT IN HIS ABSENCE, SOMEONE NEEDS TO LOOK INTO--
RIGHT NOW THIS TOWN NEEDS HOPE AND SUPPORT, NOT YOUR NOSY QUESTIONS.
ROLAND WILL BE HOME ANY DAY NOW, AND HE WILL TAKE CARE OF IT.
INSOLENT! IT'S MY BUSINESS TO--
I'LL WALK FROM HERE ON MY OWN. HAVE A GOOD NIGHT, FATHER.

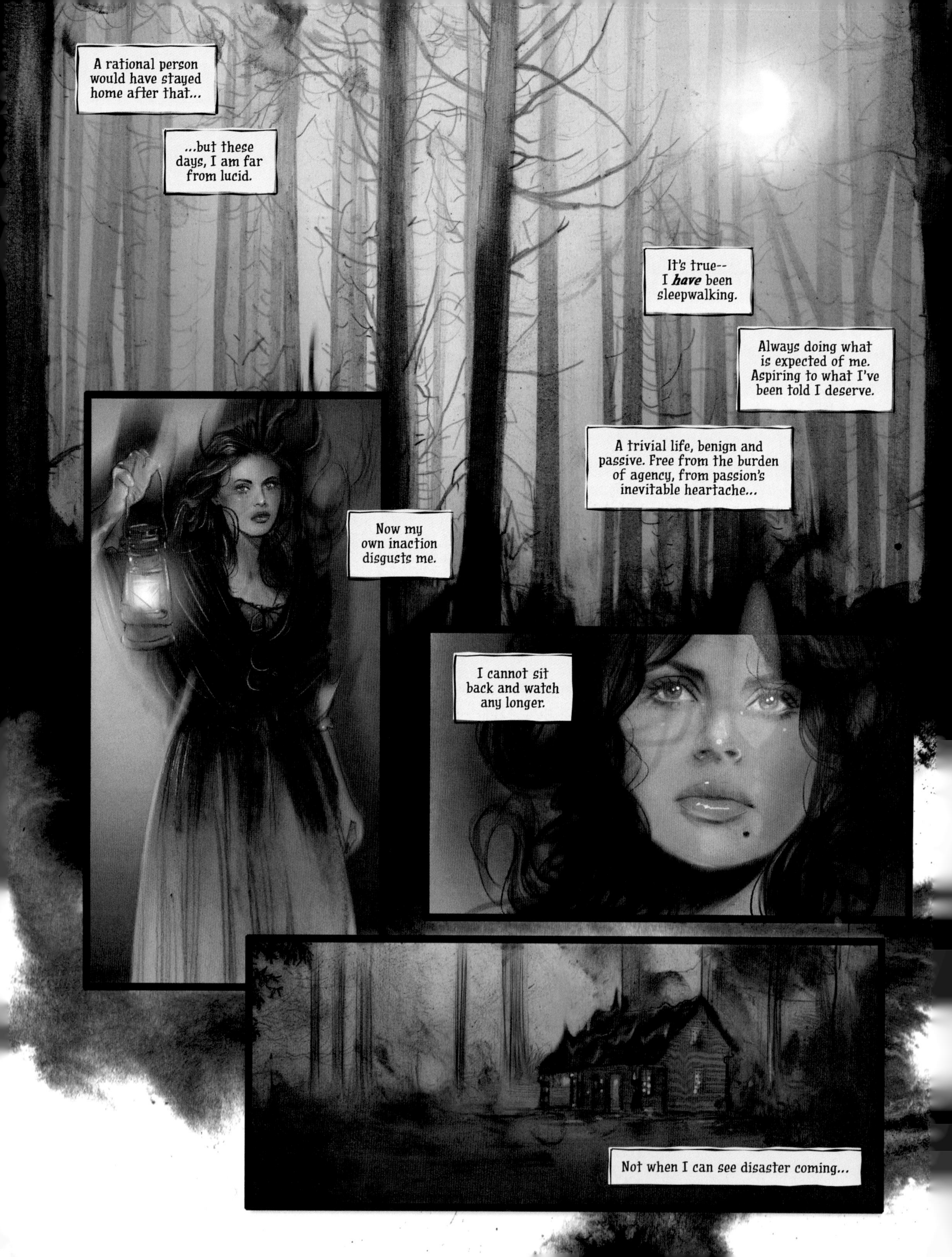
A rational person would have stayed home after that...
...but these days, I am far from lucid.
It's true-- I ***have*** been sleepwalking.
Always doing what is expected of me. Aspiring to what I've been told I deserve.
A trivial life, benign and passive. Free from the burden of agency, from passion's inevitable heartache...
Now my own inaction disgusts me.
I cannot sit back and watch any longer.
Not when I can see disaster coming...

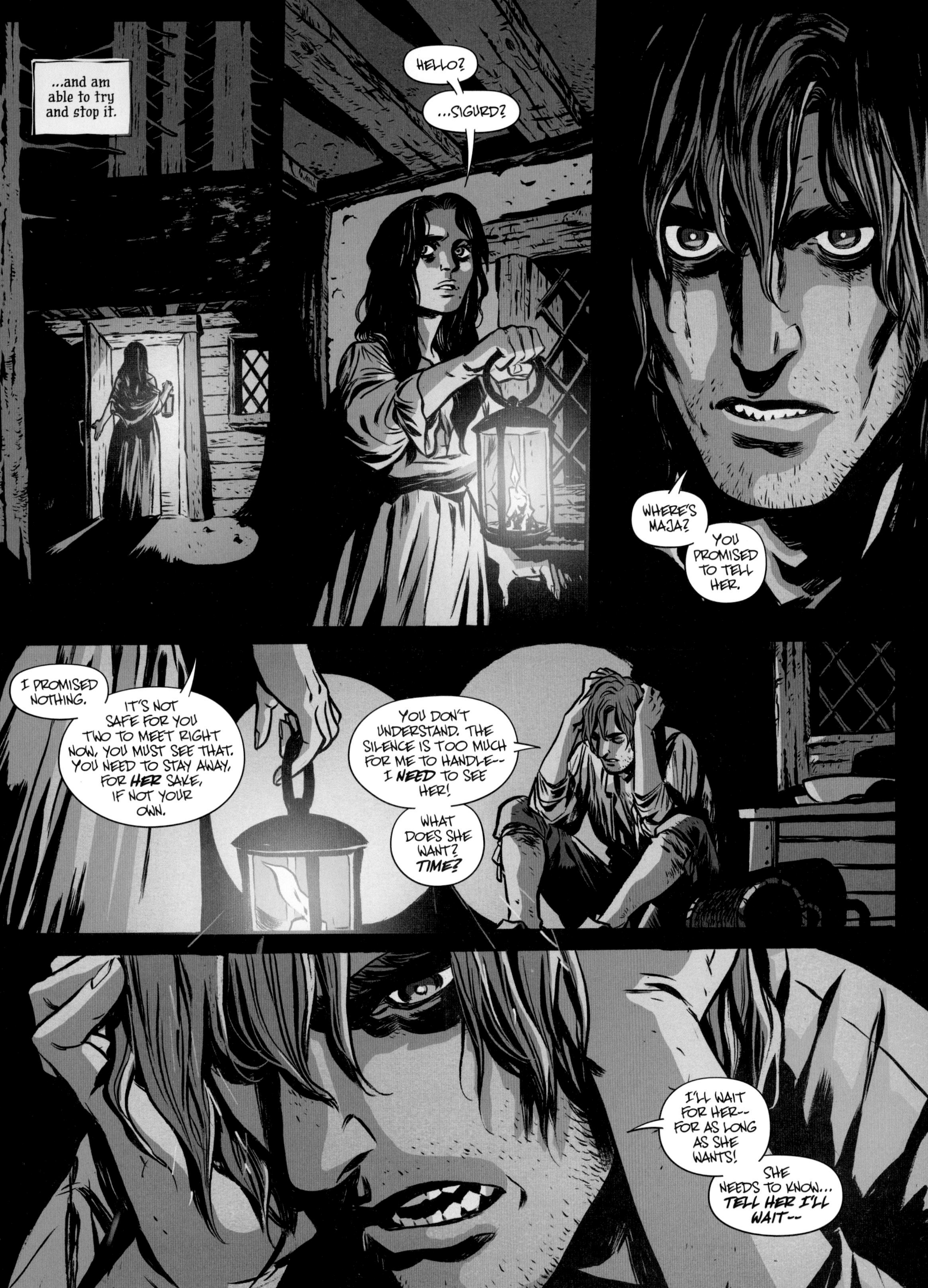
...and am able to try and stop it.
HELLO?
...SIGURD?
WHERE'S MAJA?
YOU PROMISED TO TELL HER.
I PROMISED NOTHING.
IT'S NOT SAFE FOR YOU TWO TO MEET RIGHT NOW, YOU MUST SEE THAT. YOU NEED TO STAY AWAY, FOR HER SAKE, IF NOT YOUR OWN.
YOU DON'T UNDERSTAND. THE SILENCE IS TOO MUCH FOR ME TO HANDLE-- I NEED TO SEE HER!
WHAT DOES SHE WANT? TIME?
I'LL WAIT FOR HER-- FOR AS LONG AS SHE WANTS!
SHE NEEDS TO KNOW... TELL HER I'LL WAIT--

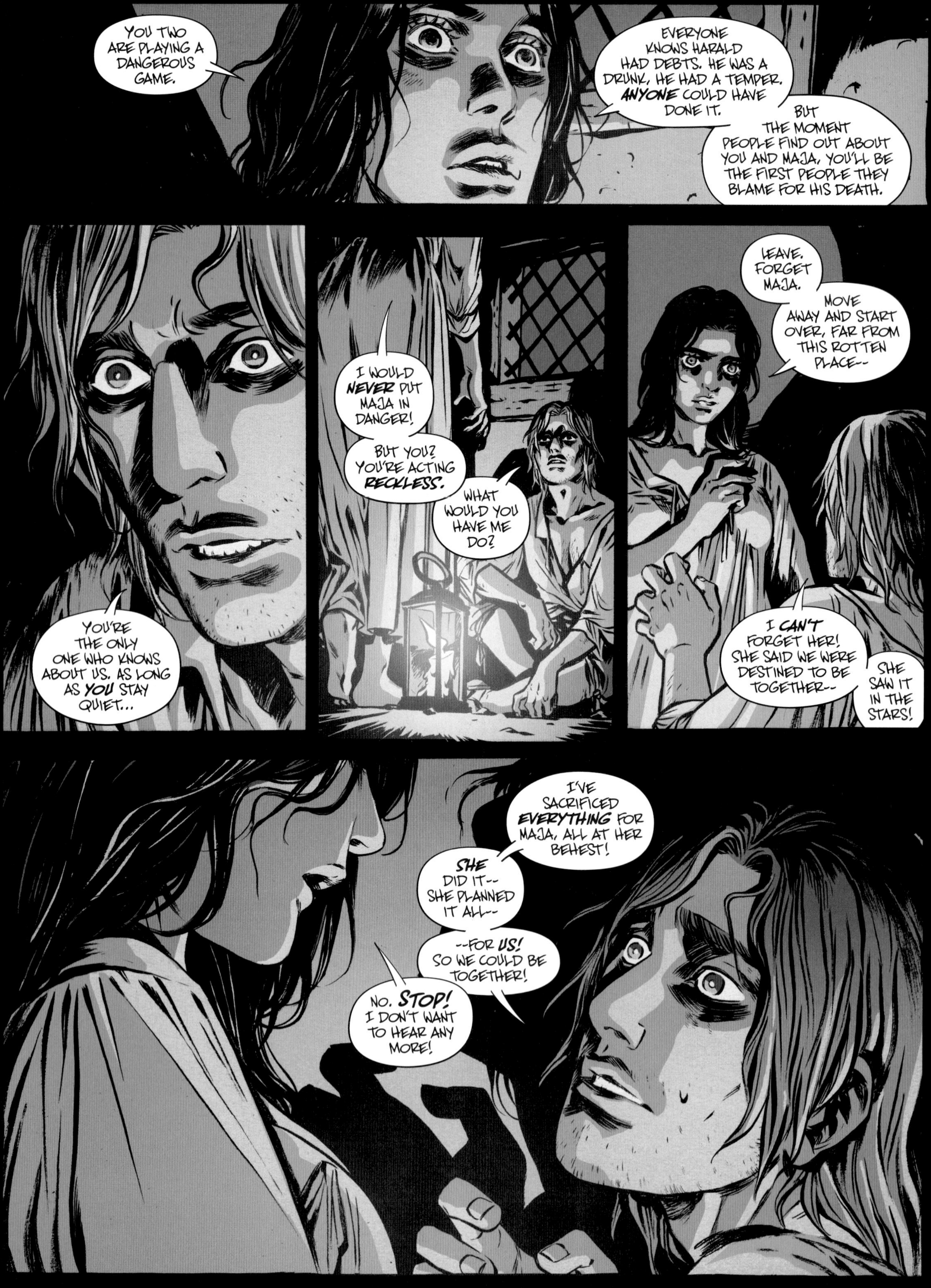
YOU TWO ARE PLAYING A DANGEROUS GAME.
EVERYONE KNOWS HARALD HAD DEBTS. HE WAS A DRUNK, HE HAD A TEMPER. ANYONE COULD HAVE DONE IT.
BUT THE MOMENT PEOPLE FIND OUT ABOUT YOU AND MAJA, YOU'LL BE THE FIRST PEOPLE THEY BLAME FOR HIS DEATH.
YOU'RE THE ONLY ONE WHO KNOWS ABOUT US. AS LONG AS YOU STAY QUIET...
I WOULD NEVER PUT MAJA IN DANGER!
BUT YOU? YOU'RE ACTING RECKLESS.
WHAT WOULD YOU HAVE ME DO?
LEAVE. FORGET MAJA.
MOVE AWAY AND START OVER, FAR FROM THIS ROTTEN PLACE--
I CAN'T FORGET HER! SHE SAID WE WERE DESTINED TO BE TOGETHER--
SHE SAW IT IN THE STARS!
I'VE SACRIFICED EVERYTHING FOR MAJA, ALL AT HER BEHEST!
SHE DID IT-- SHE PLANNED IT ALL--
--FOR US! SO WE COULD BE TOGETHER!
NO. STOP! I DON'T WANT TO HEAR ANY MORE!

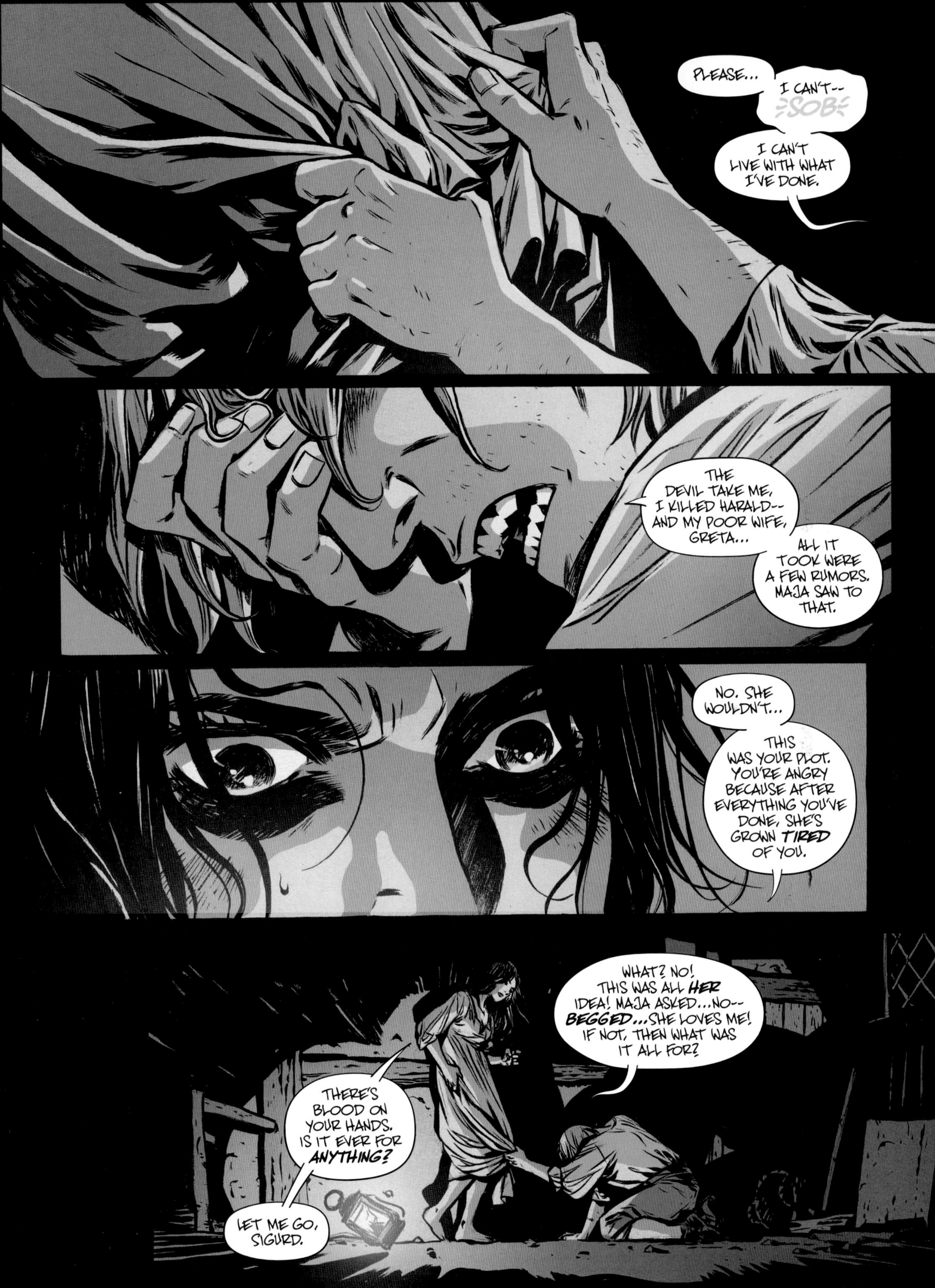
PLEASE...
I CAN'T--
SOB
I CAN'T LIVE WITH WHAT I'VE DONE.
THE DEVIL TAKE ME, I KILLED HARALD-- AND MY POOR WIFE, GRETA...
ALL IT TOOK WERE A FEW RUMORS. MAJA SAW TO THAT.
NO. SHE WOULDN'T...
THIS WAS YOUR PLOT. YOU'RE ANGRY BECAUSE AFTER EVERYTHING YOU'VE DONE, SHE'S GROWN **TIRED** OF YOU.
WHAT? NO! THIS WAS ALL **HER** IDEA! MAJA ASKED...NO-- **BEGGED...** SHE LOVES ME! IF NOT, THEN WHAT WAS IT ALL FOR?
THERE'S BLOOD ON YOUR HANDS. IS IT EVER FOR **ANYTHING?**
LET ME GO, SIGURD.

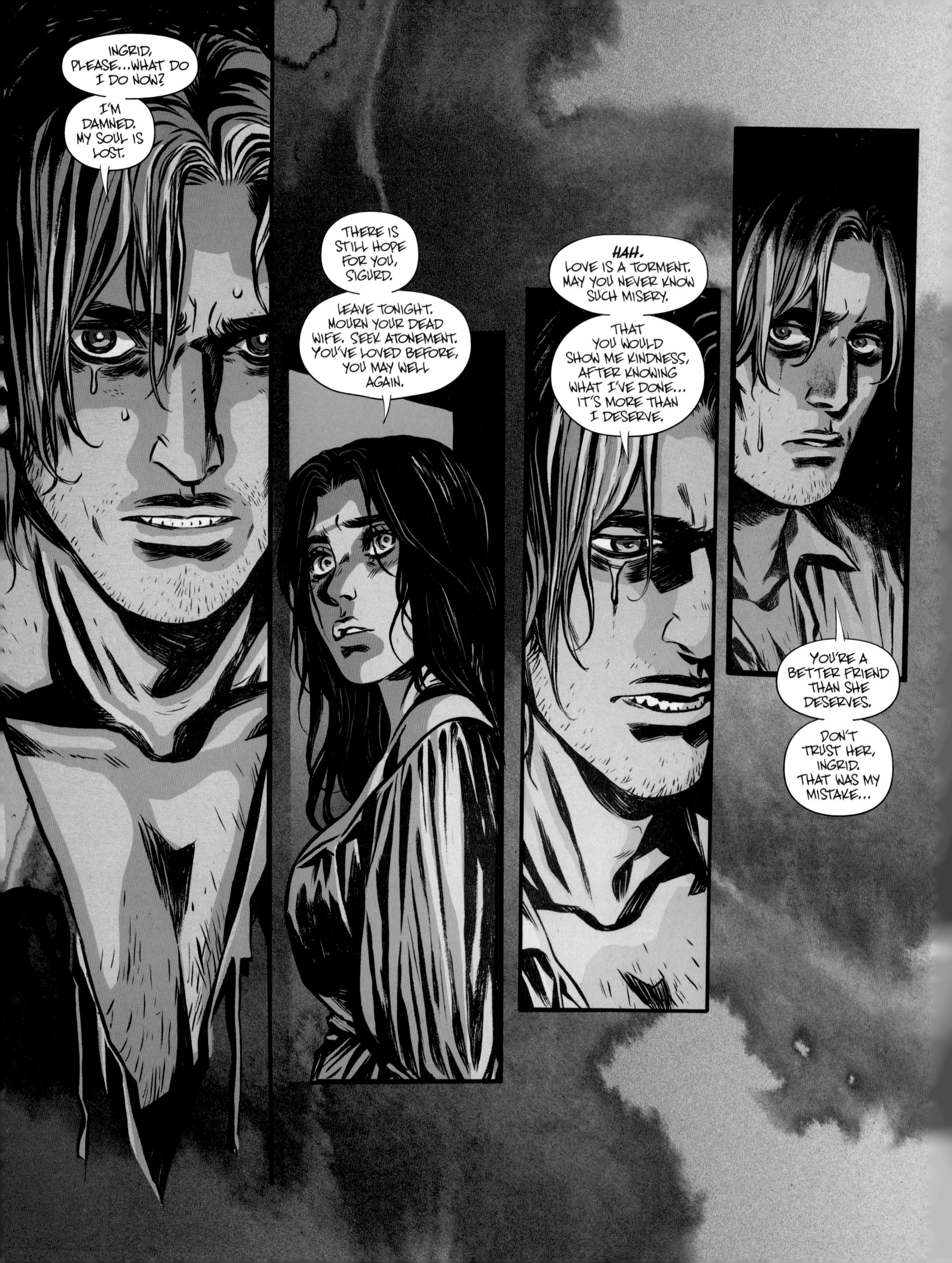
INGRID, PLEASE...WHAT DO I DO NOW?
I'M DAMNED. MY SOUL IS LOST.
THERE IS STILL HOPE FOR YOU, SIGURD.
LEAVE TONIGHT. MOURN YOUR DEAD WIFE. SEEK ATONEMENT. YOU'VE LOVED BEFORE, YOU MAY WELL AGAIN.
HAH. LOVE IS A TORMENT. MAY YOU NEVER KNOW SUCH MISERY.
THAT YOU WOULD SHOW ME KINDNESS, AFTER KNOWING WHAT I'VE DONE... IT'S MORE THAN I DESERVE.
YOU'RE A BETTER FRIEND THAN SHE DESERVES.
DON'T TRUST HER, INGRID. THAT WAS MY MISTAKE...

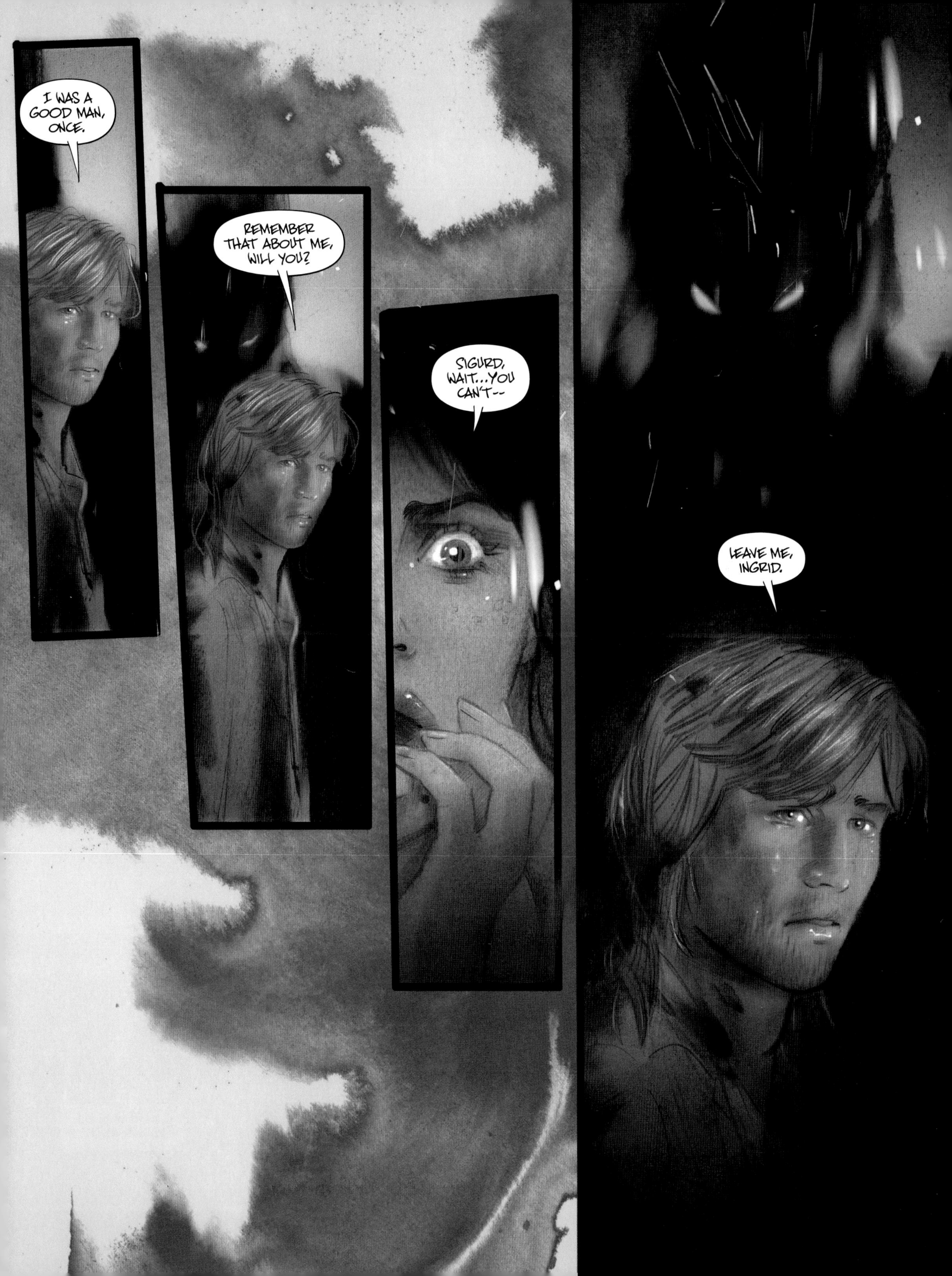
I WAS A GOOD MAN, ONCE.
REMEMBER THAT ABOUT ME, WILL YOU?
SIGURD, WAIT...YOU CAN'T--
LEAVE ME, INGRID.

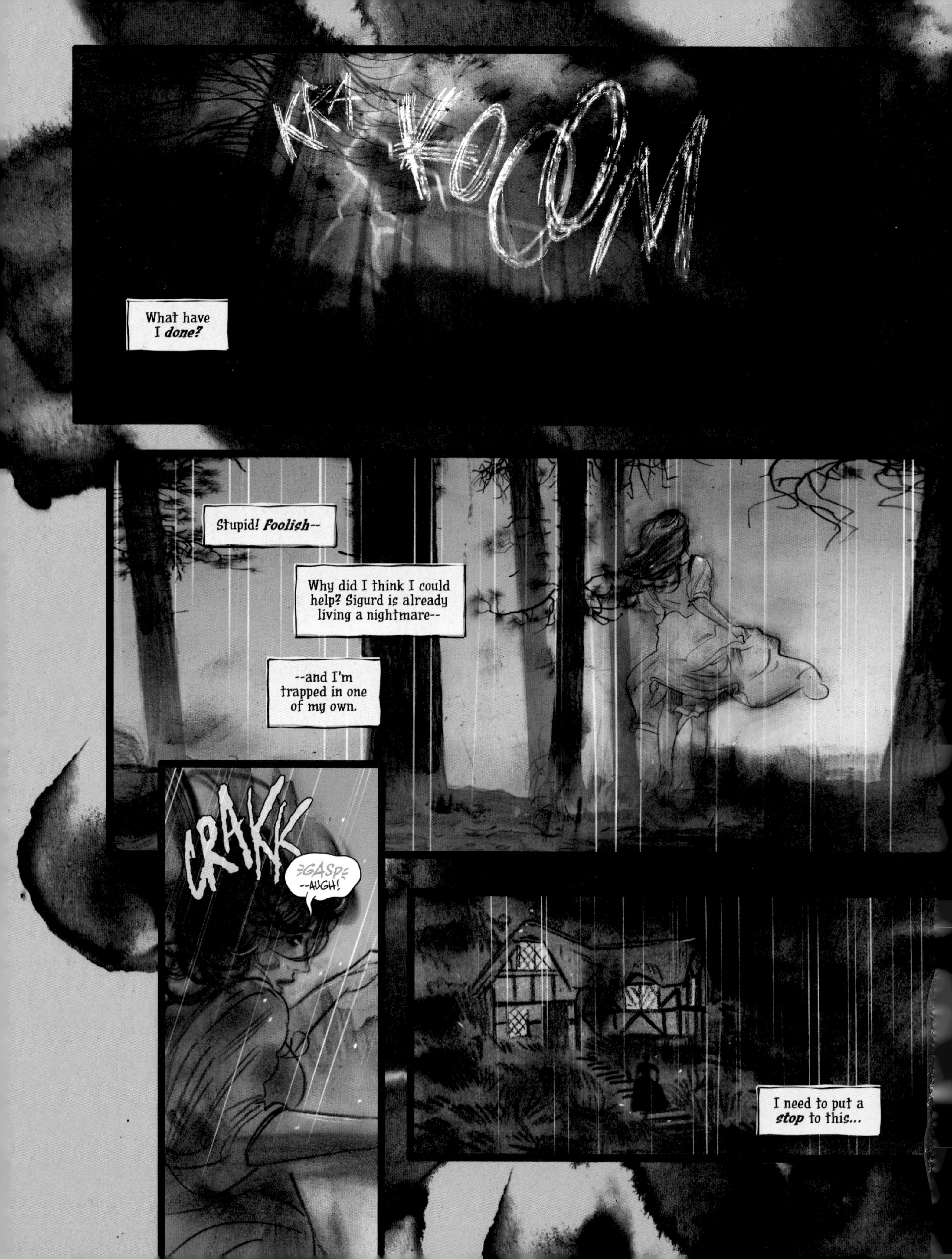
KRA-KOOOM
What have I done?
Stupid! Foolish--
Why did I think I could help? Sigurd is already living a nightmare--
--and I'm trapped in one of my own.
CRAKK
GASP --AUGH!
I need to put a stop to this...

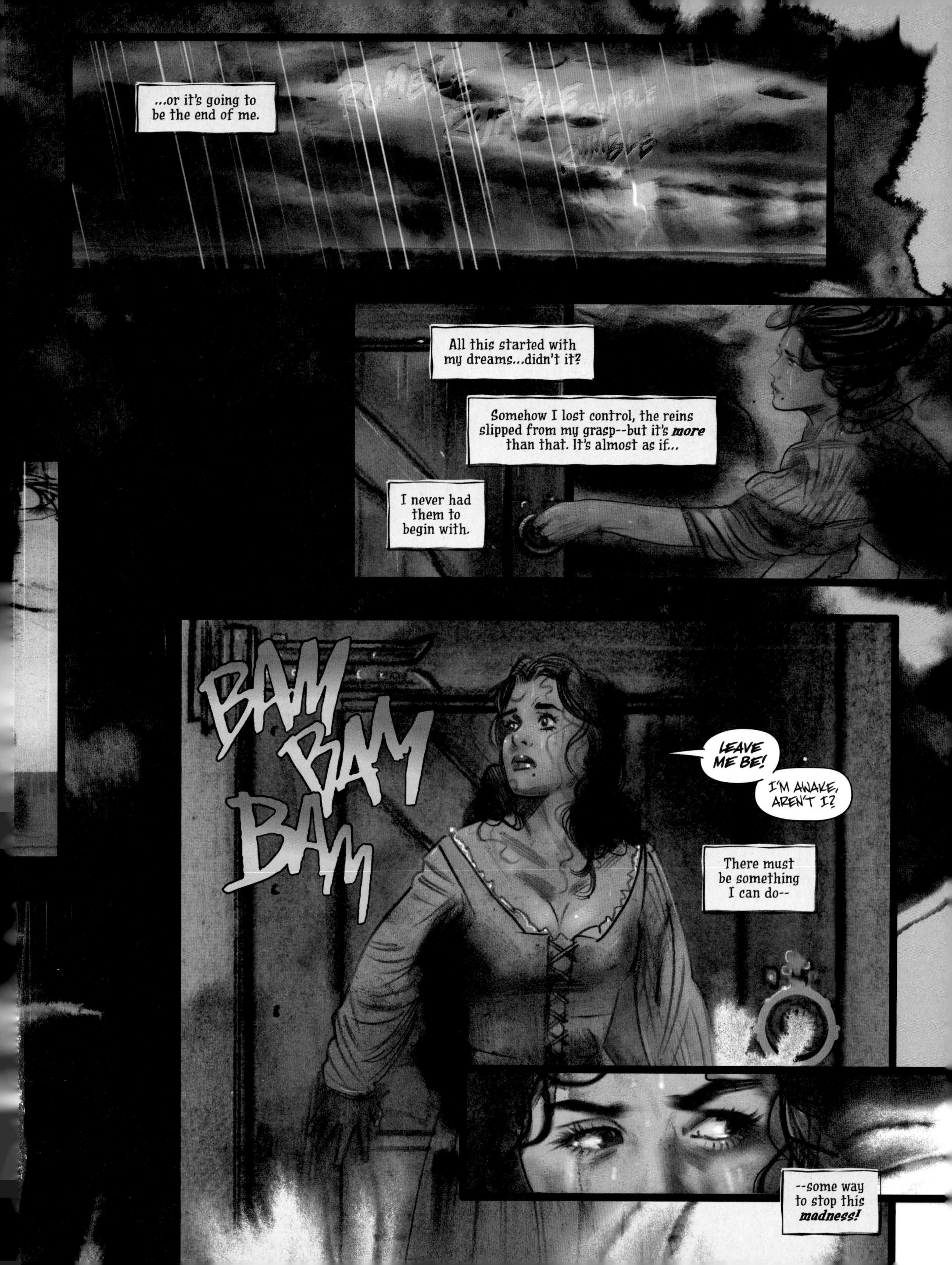
...or it's going to be the end of me.
All this started with my dreams...didn't it?
Somehow I lost control, the reins slipped from my grasp--but it's **more** than that. It's almost as if...
I never had them to begin with.
BAM BAM BAM
LEAVE ME BE!
I'M AWAKE, AREN'T I?
There must be something I can do--
--some way to stop this **madness!**

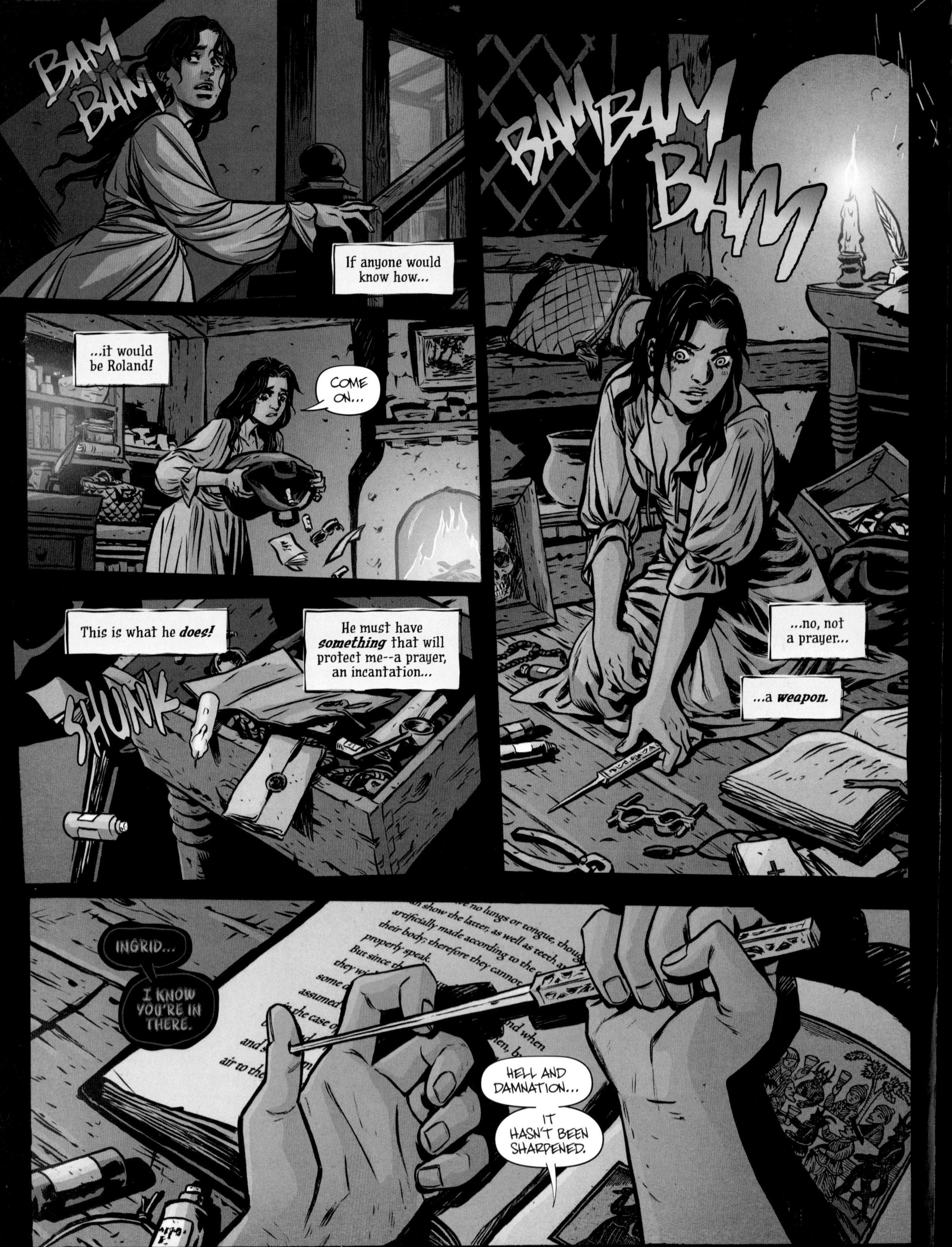
BAM BAM
If anyone would know how...
...it would be Roland!
COME ON...
This is what he *does!*
He must have *something* that will protect me--a prayer, an incantation...
SHUNK
BAM BAM BAM
...no, not a prayer...
...a *weapon.*
INGRID...
I KNOW YOU'RE IN THERE.
HELL AND DAMNATION...
IT HASN'T BEEN SHARPENED.

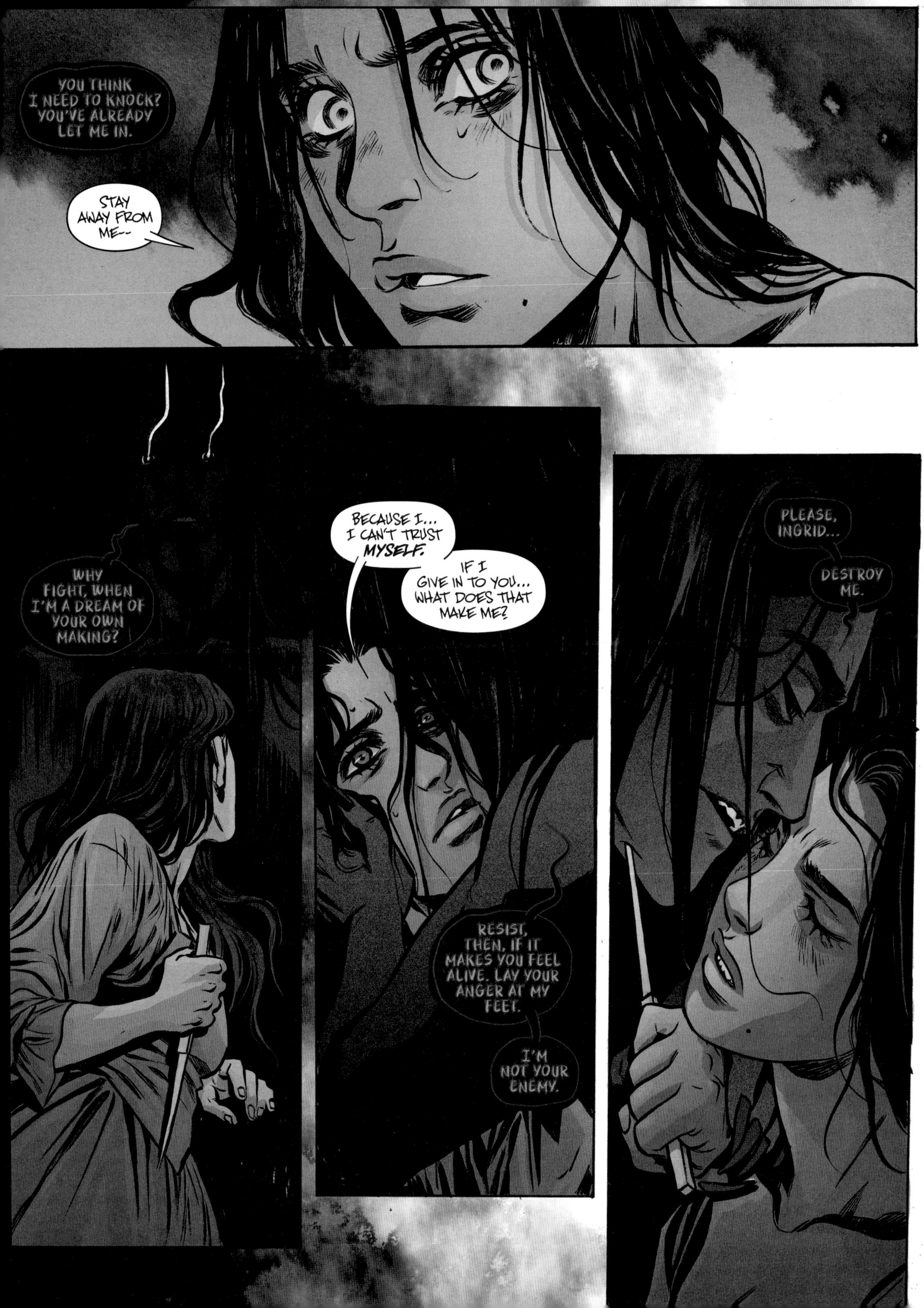
YOU THINK I NEED TO KNOCK? YOU'VE ALREADY LET ME IN.
STAY AWAY FROM ME--
WHY FIGHT, WHEN I'M A DREAM OF YOUR OWN MAKING?
BECAUSE I... I CAN'T TRUST MYSELF.
IF I GIVE IN TO YOU... WHAT DOES THAT MAKE ME?
RESIST, THEN, IF IT MAKES YOU FEEL ALIVE. LAY YOUR ANGER AT MY FEET.
I'M NOT YOUR ENEMY.
PLEASE, INGRID...
DESTROY ME.

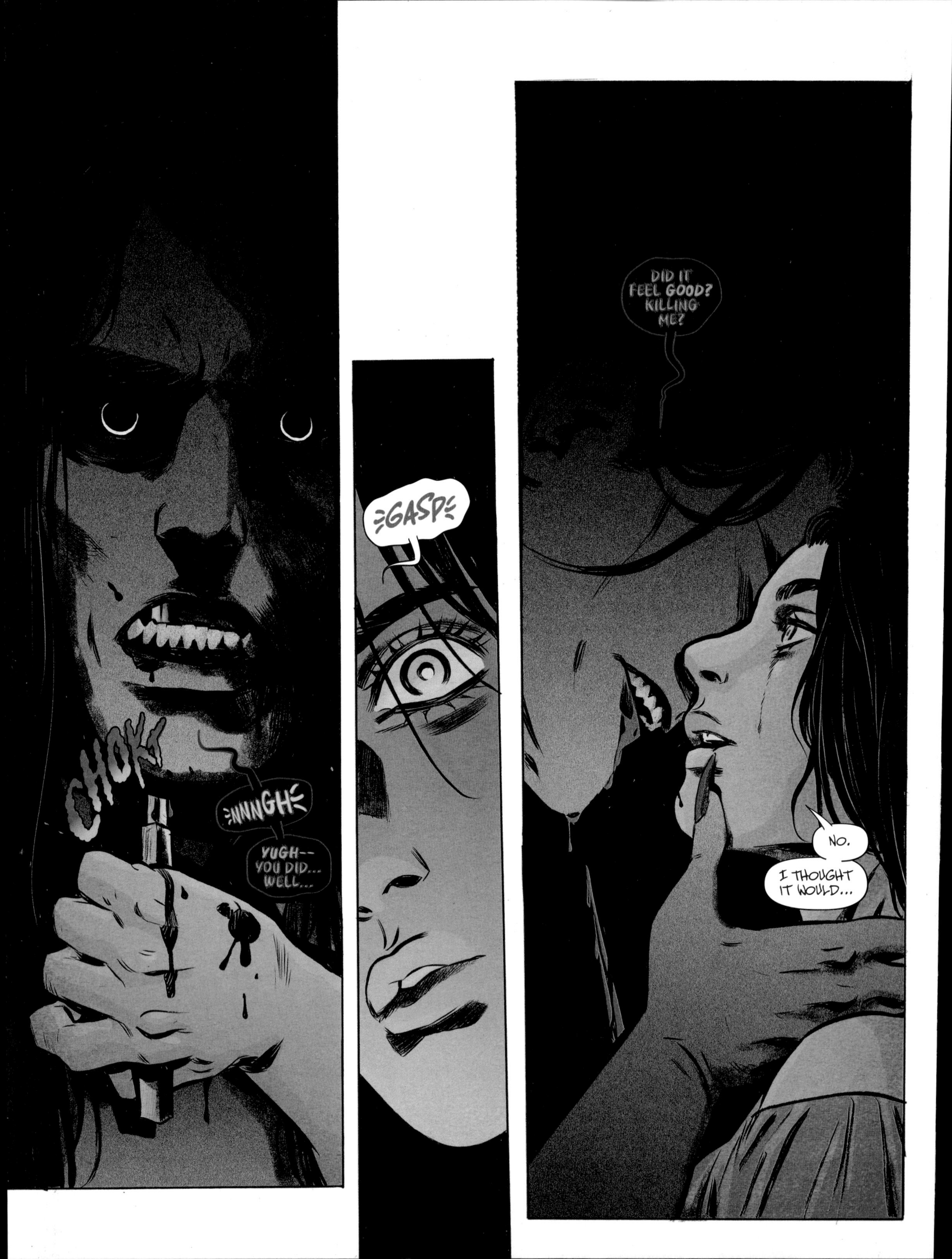
CHOK
NNNGH
YUGH-- YOU DID... WELL...
GASP
DID IT FEEL GOOD? KILLING ME?
NO.
I THOUGHT IT WOULD...

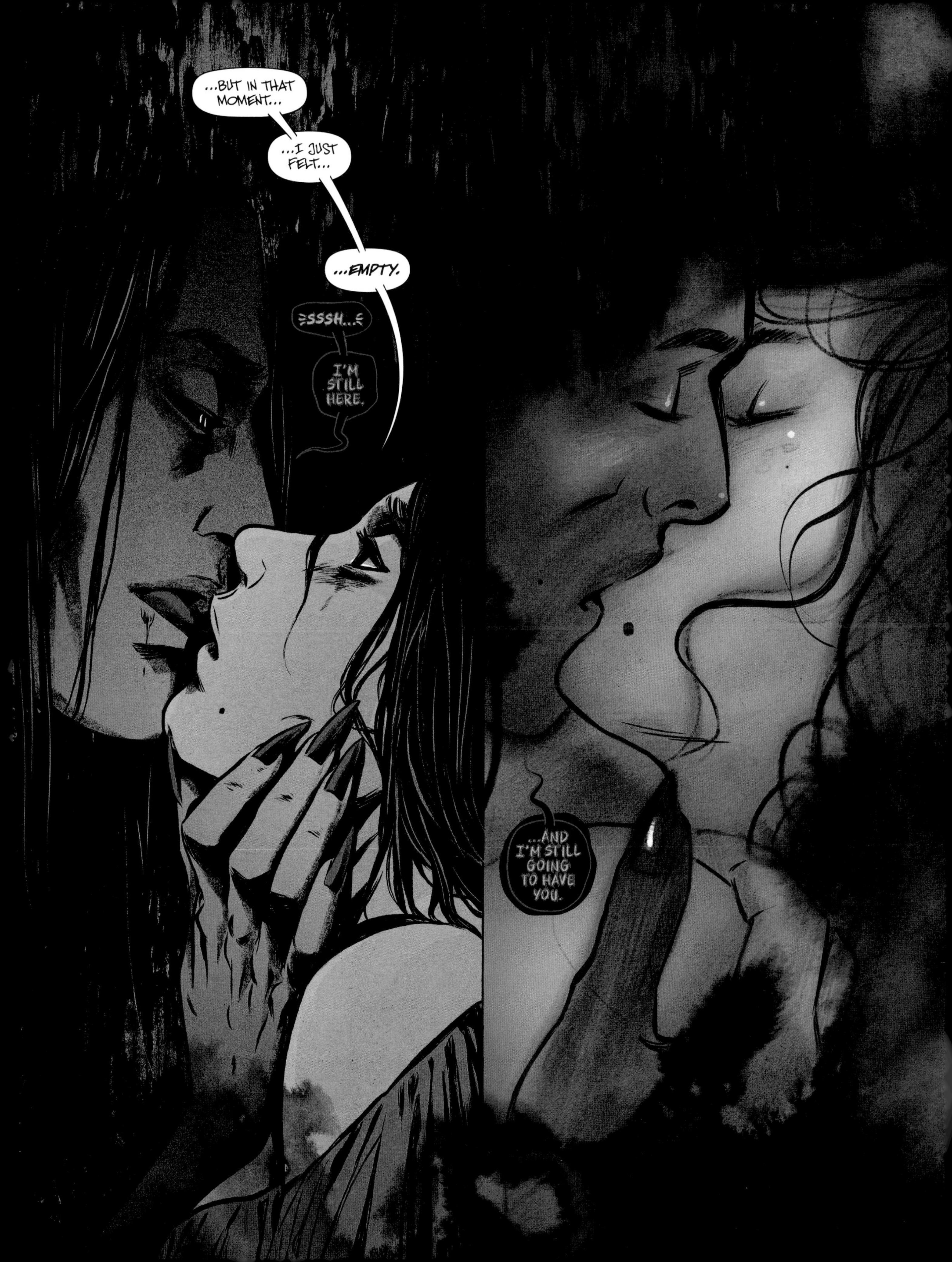
...BUT IN THAT MOMENT...
...I JUST FELT...
...EMPTY.
SSSH...
I'M STILL HERE.
...AND I'M STILL GOING TO HAVE YOU.

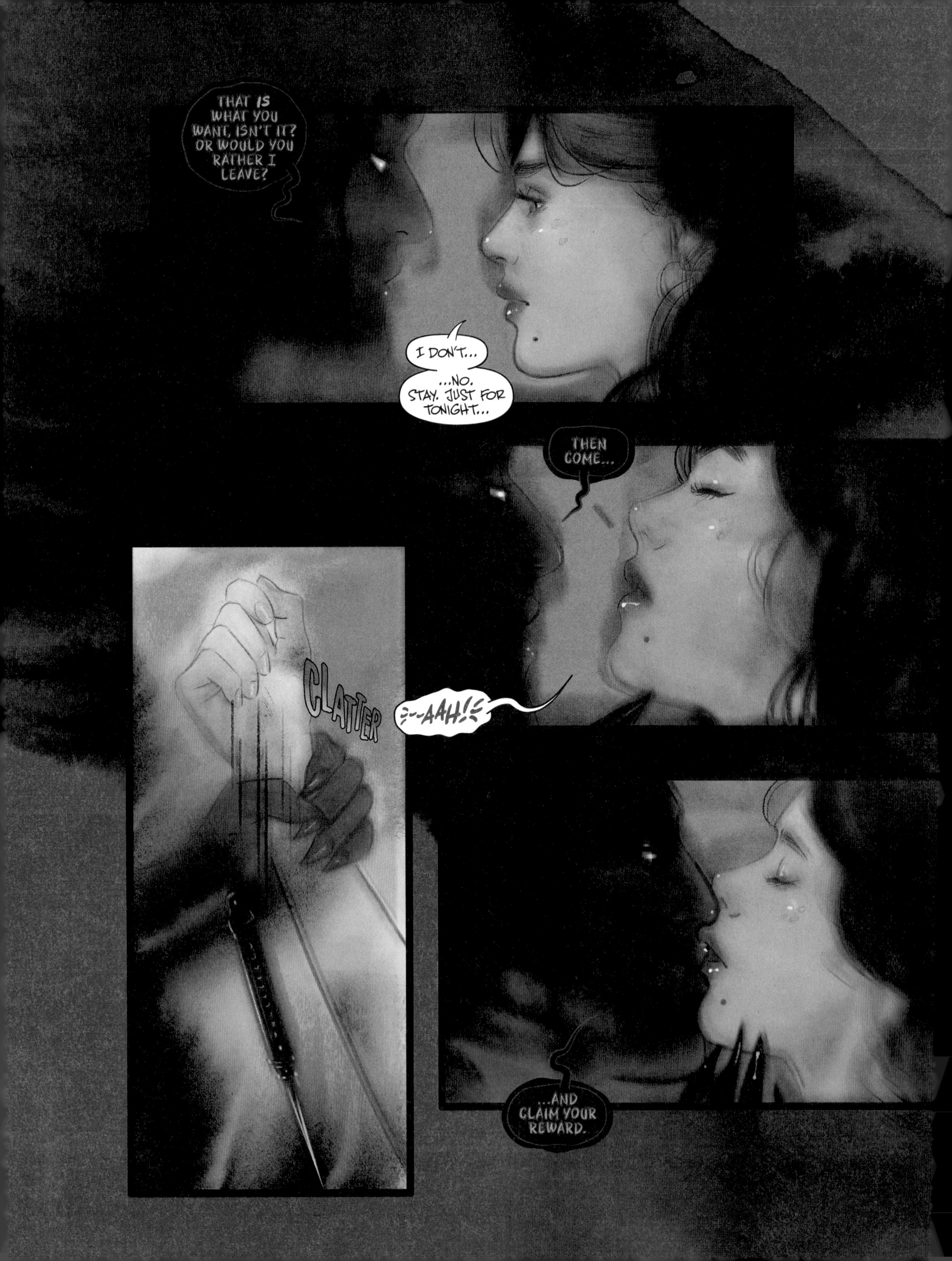
THAT IS WHAT YOU WANT, ISN'T IT? OR WOULD YOU RATHER I LEAVE?
I DON'T...
...NO. STAY. JUST FOR TONIGHT...
THEN COME...
CLATTER
--AAH!
...AND CLAIM YOUR REWARD.

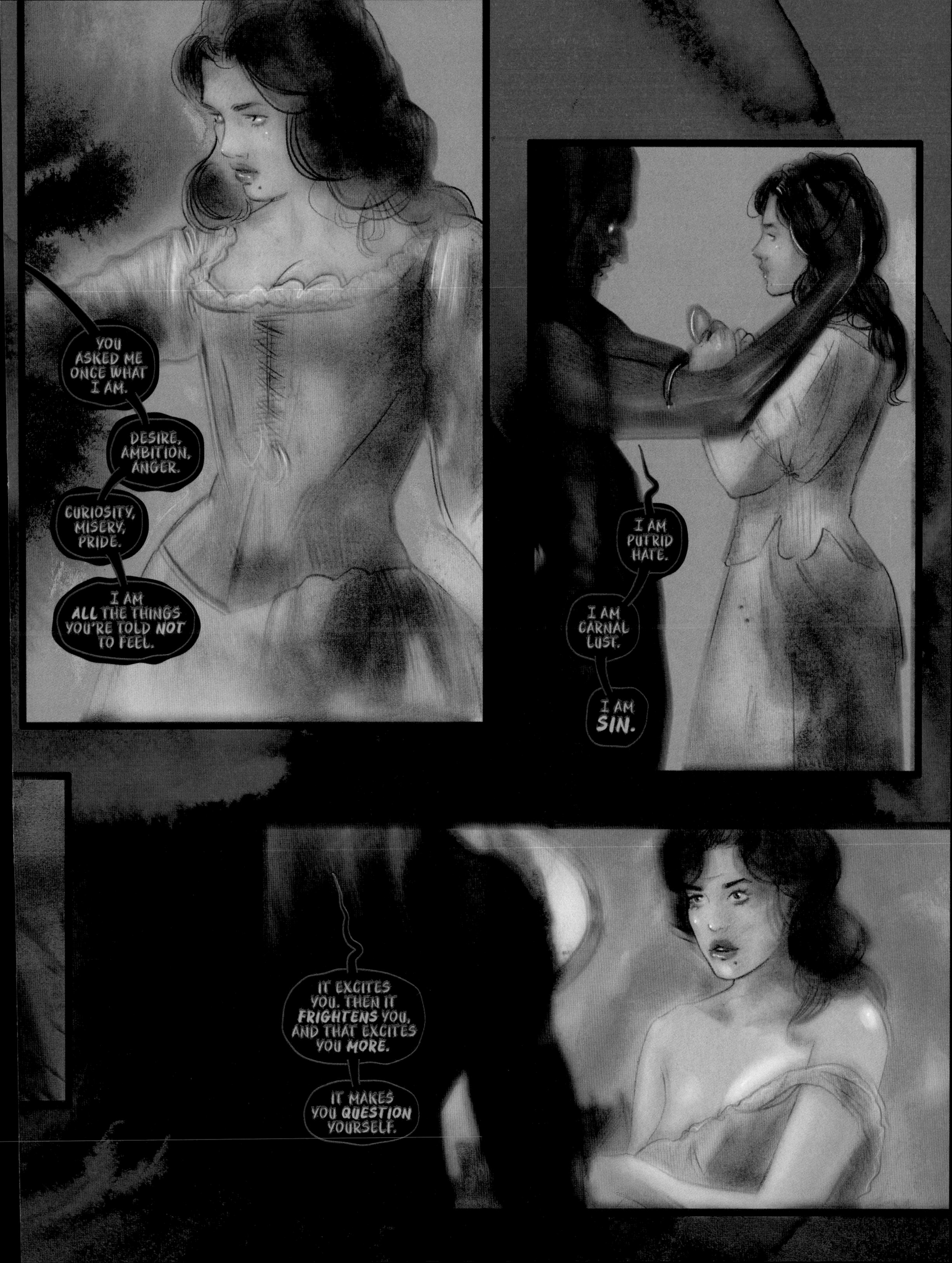
YOU ASKED ME ONCE WHAT I AM.
DESIRE, AMBITION, ANGER.
CURIOSITY, MISERY, PRIDE.
I AM **ALL** THE THINGS YOU'RE TOLD **NOT** TO FEEL.
I AM PUTRID HATE.
I AM CARNAL LUST.
I AM **SIN.**
IT EXCITES YOU. THEN IT **FRIGHTENS** YOU, AND THAT EXCITES YOU **MORE.**
IT MAKES YOU **QUESTION** YOURSELF.

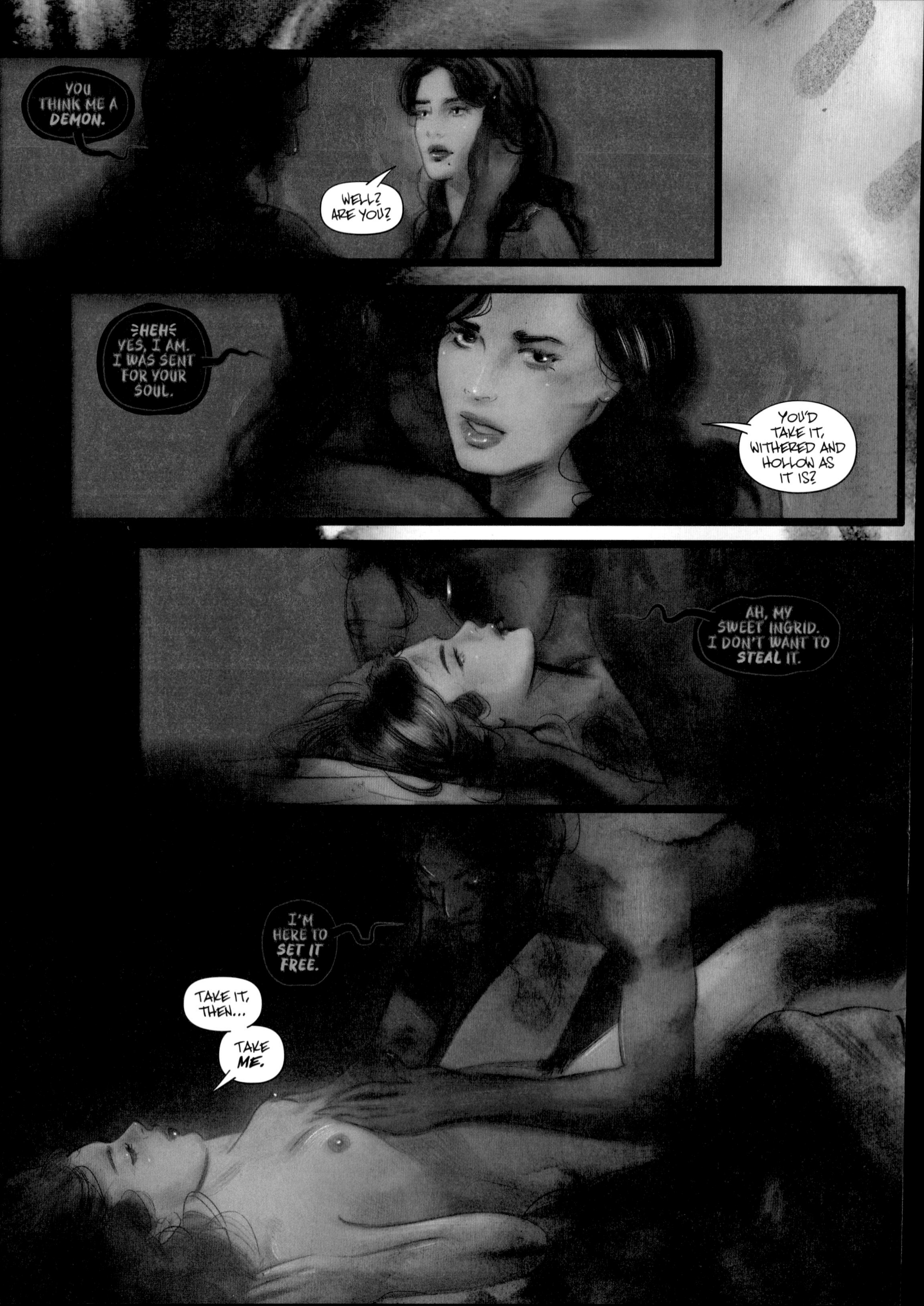
YOU THINK ME A DEMON.
WELL? ARE YOU?
≡HEH≡ YES, I AM. I WAS SENT FOR YOUR SOUL.
YOU'D TAKE IT, WITHERED AND HOLLOW AS IT IS?
AH, MY SWEET INGRID. I DON'T WANT TO STEAL IT.
I'M HERE TO SET IT FREE.
TAKE IT, THEN...
TAKE ME.

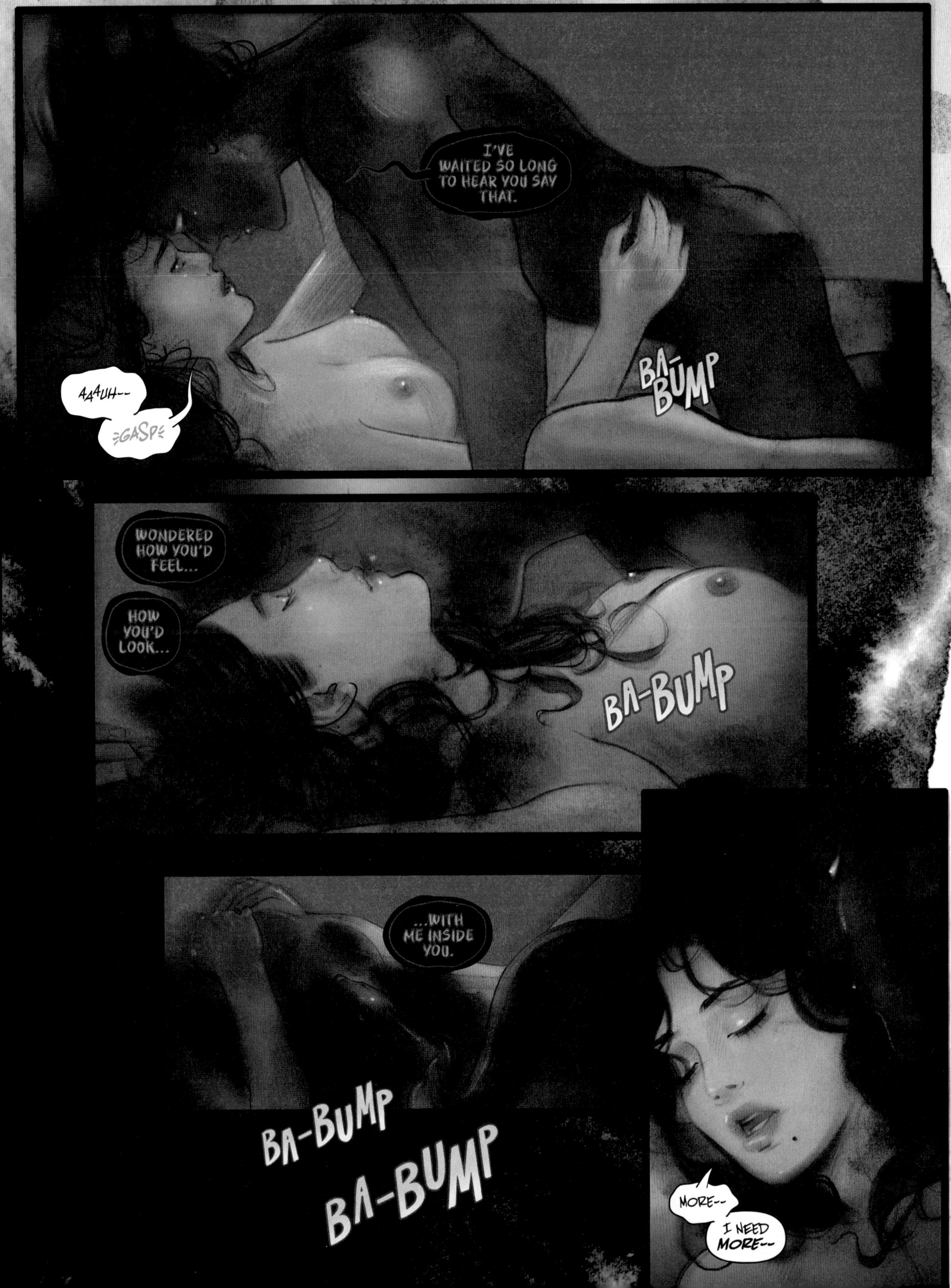
I'VE WAITED SO LONG TO HEAR YOU SAY THAT.
AAAUH--
GASP
BA-BUMP
WONDERED HOW YOU'D FEEL...
HOW YOU'D LOOK...
BA-BUMP
...WITH ME INSIDE YOU.
BA-BUMP
BA-BUMP
MORE--
I NEED MORE--

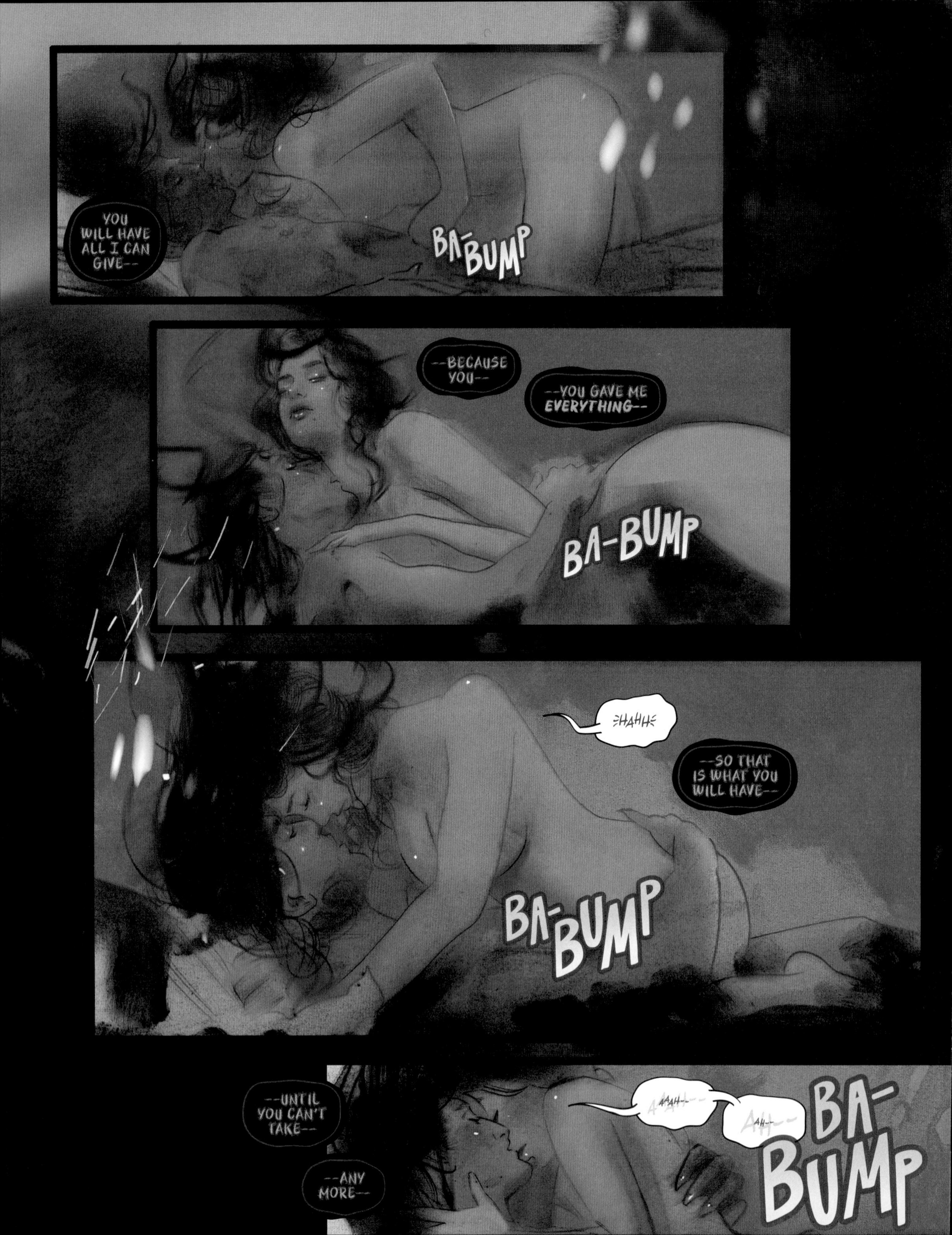
YOU WILL HAVE ALL I CAN GIVE--
BA-BUMP
--BECAUSE YOU--
--YOU GAVE ME EVERYTHING--
BA-BUMP
HAHH
--SO THAT IS WHAT YOU WILL HAVE--
BA-BUMP
--UNTIL YOU CAN'T TAKE--
--ANY MORE--
AAAH--
AH--
BA-BUMP

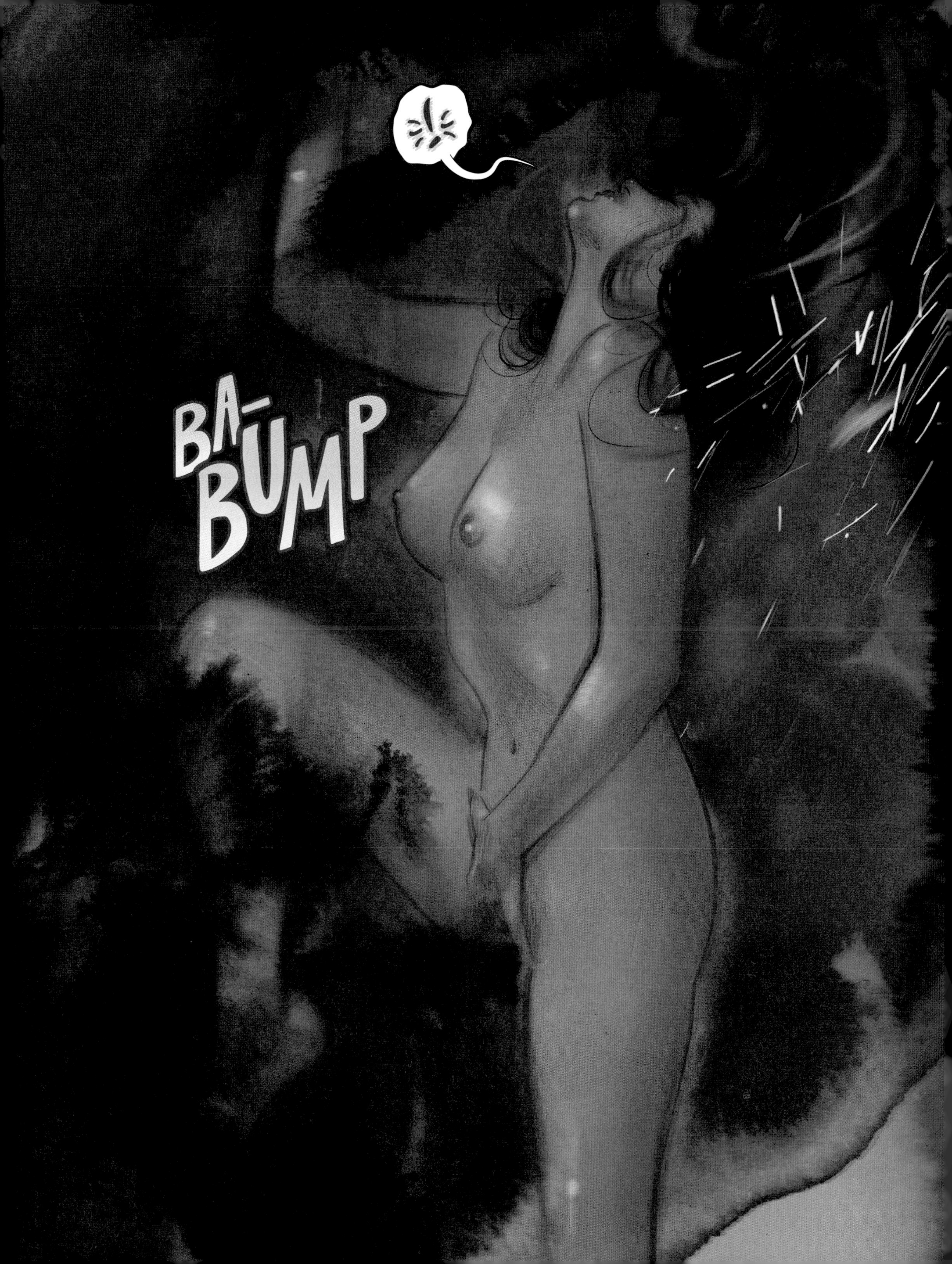
!
BA-BUMP

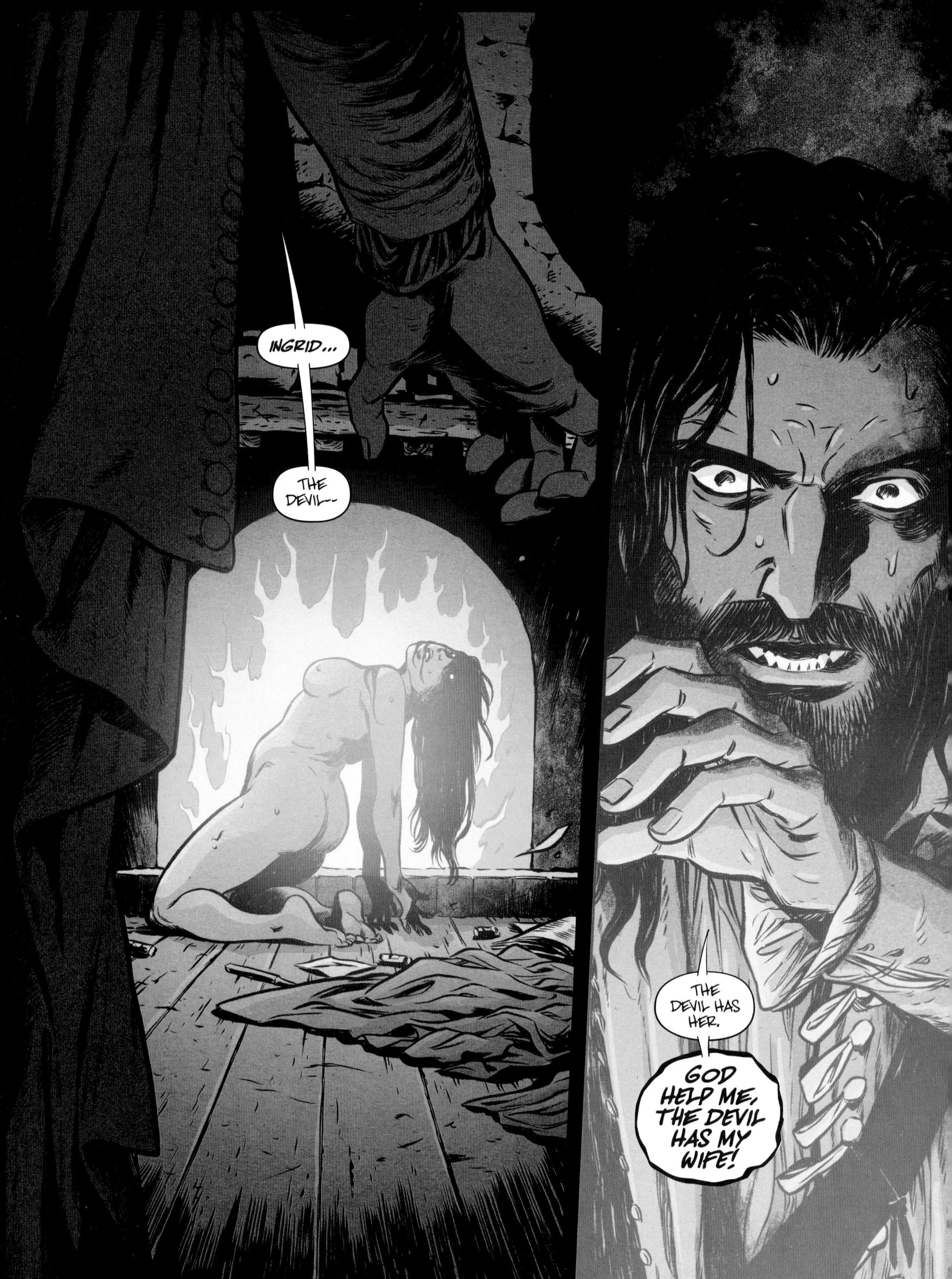
INGRID...
THE DEVIL--
THE DEVIL HAS HER.
GOD HELP ME, THE DEVIL HAS MY WIFE!

CHAPTER V.
LET ME BE THY CHOIR

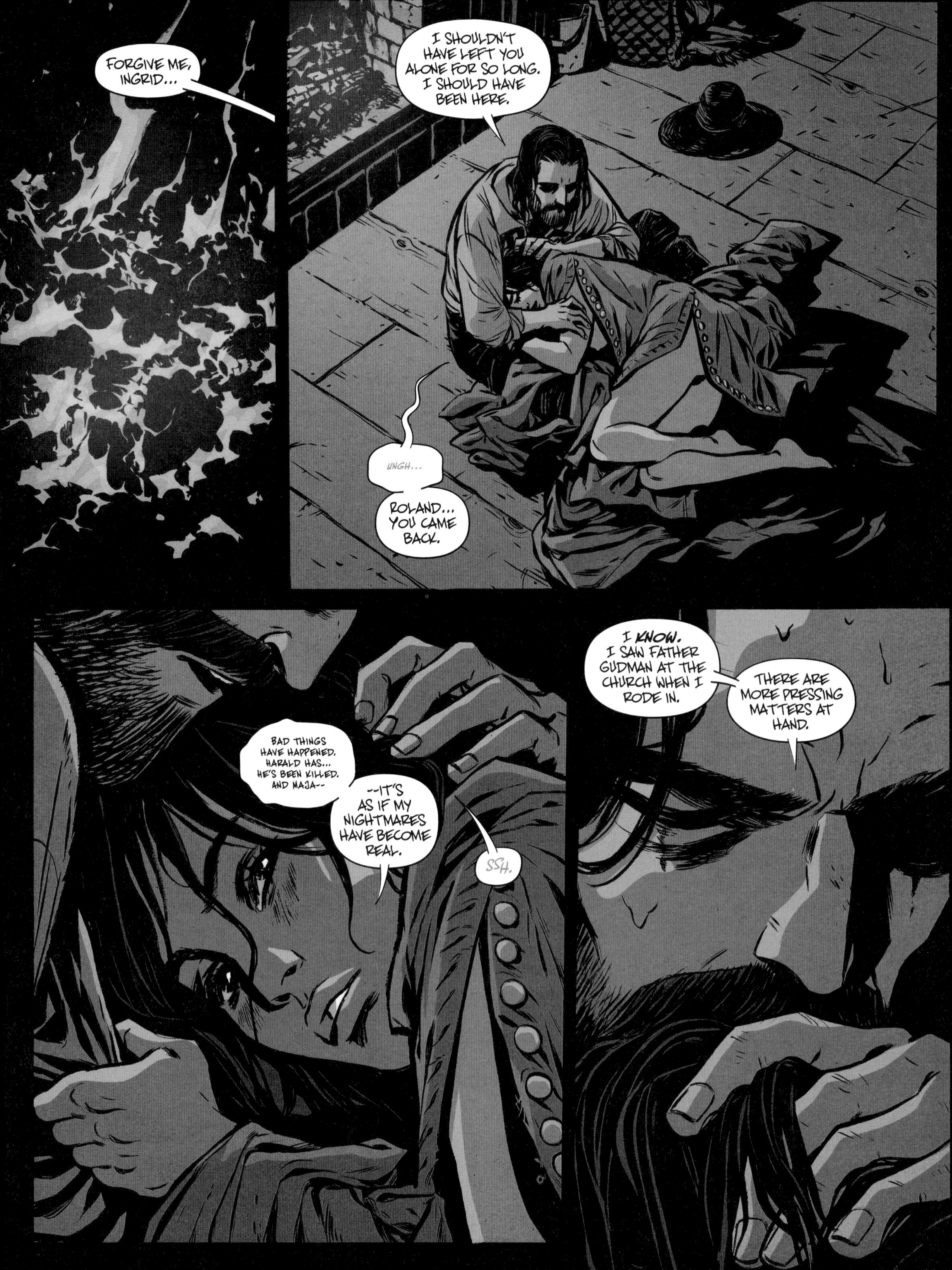
FORGIVE ME, INGRID...
I SHOULDN'T HAVE LEFT YOU ALONE FOR SO LONG. I SHOULD HAVE BEEN HERE.
UNGH...
ROLAND... YOU CAME BACK.
BAD THINGS HAVE HAPPENED. HARALD HAS... HE'S BEEN KILLED. AND MAJA--
--IT'S AS IF MY NIGHTMARES HAVE BECOME REAL.
SSH.
I KNOW. I SAW FATHER GUDMAN AT THE CHURCH WHEN I RODE IN.
THERE ARE MORE PRESSING MATTERS AT HAND.

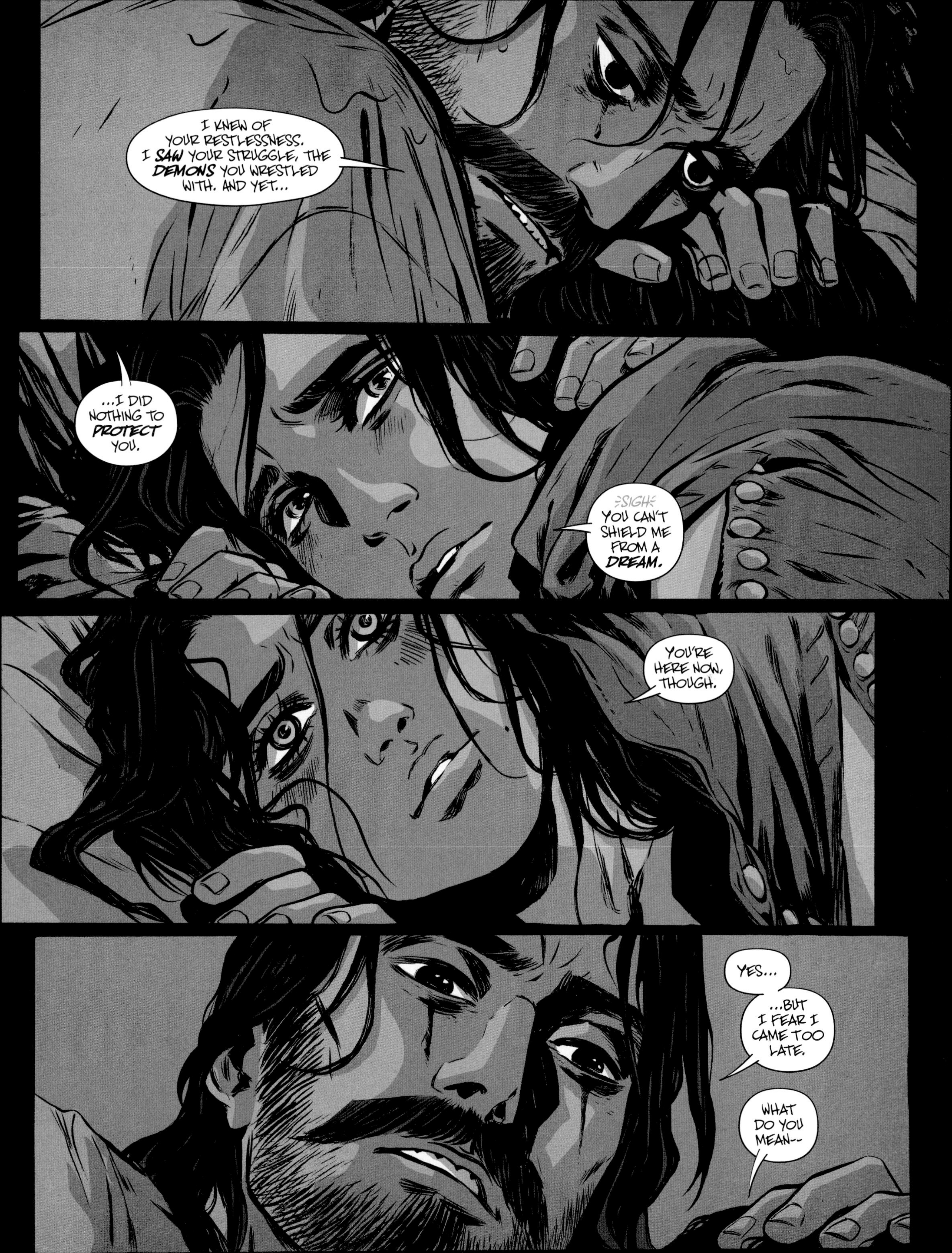
I KNEW OF YOUR RESTLESSNESS. I SAW YOUR STRUGGLE, THE DEMONS YOU WRESTLED WITH. AND YET...
...I DID NOTHING TO PROTECT YOU.
SIGH
YOU CAN'T SHIELD ME FROM A DREAM.
YOU'RE HERE NOW, THOUGH.
YES...
...BUT I FEAR I CAME TOO LATE.
WHAT DO YOU MEAN--

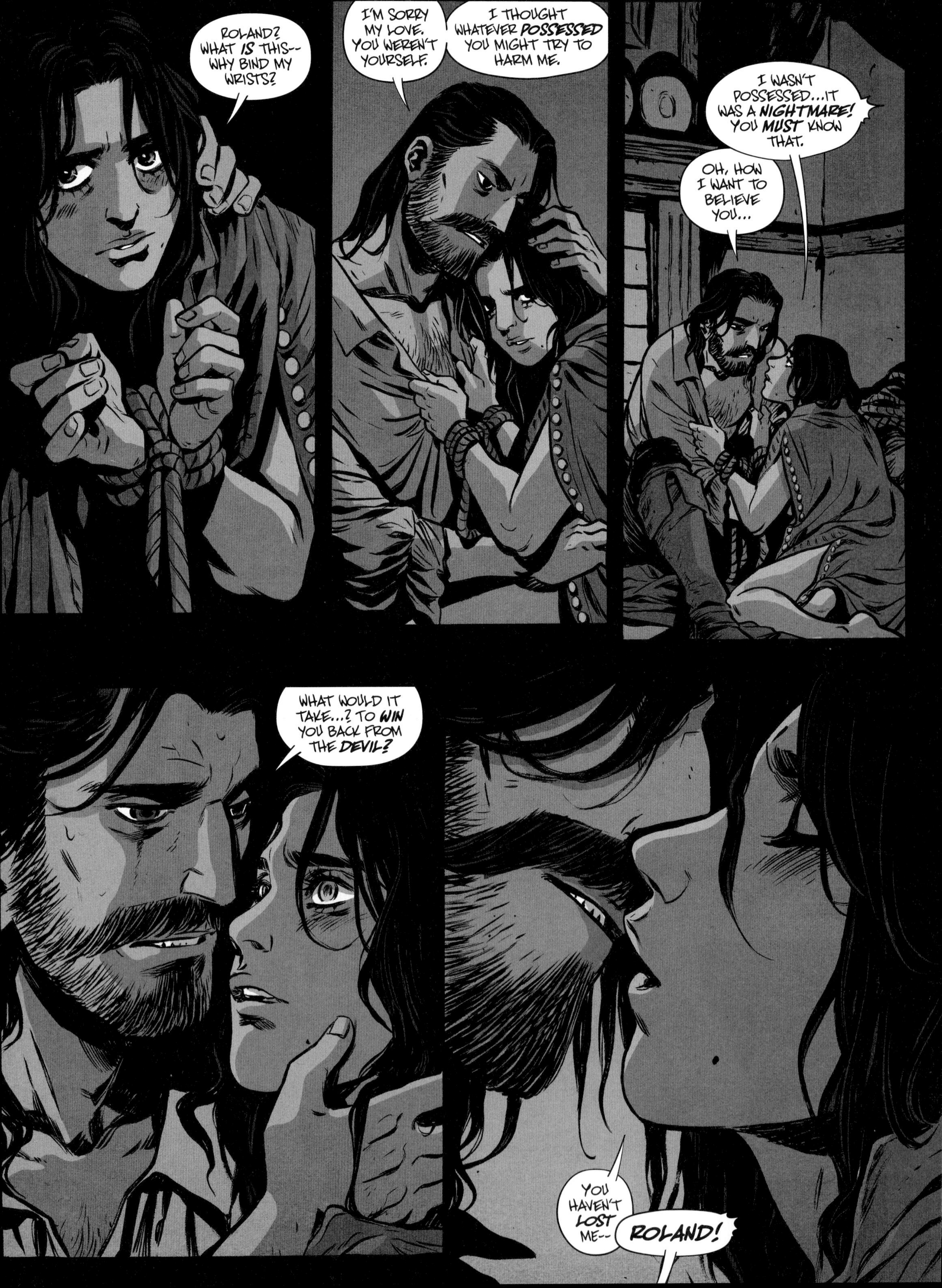
ROLAND? WHAT IS THIS-- WHY BIND MY WRISTS?
I'M SORRY MY LOVE. YOU WEREN'T YOURSELF.
I THOUGHT WHATEVER POSSESSED YOU MIGHT TRY TO HARM ME.
I WASN'T POSSESSED...IT WAS A NIGHTMARE! YOU MUST KNOW THAT.
OH, HOW I WANT TO BELIEVE YOU...
WHAT WOULD IT TAKE...? TO WIN YOU BACK FROM THE DEVIL?
YOU HAVEN'T LOST ME--
ROLAND!

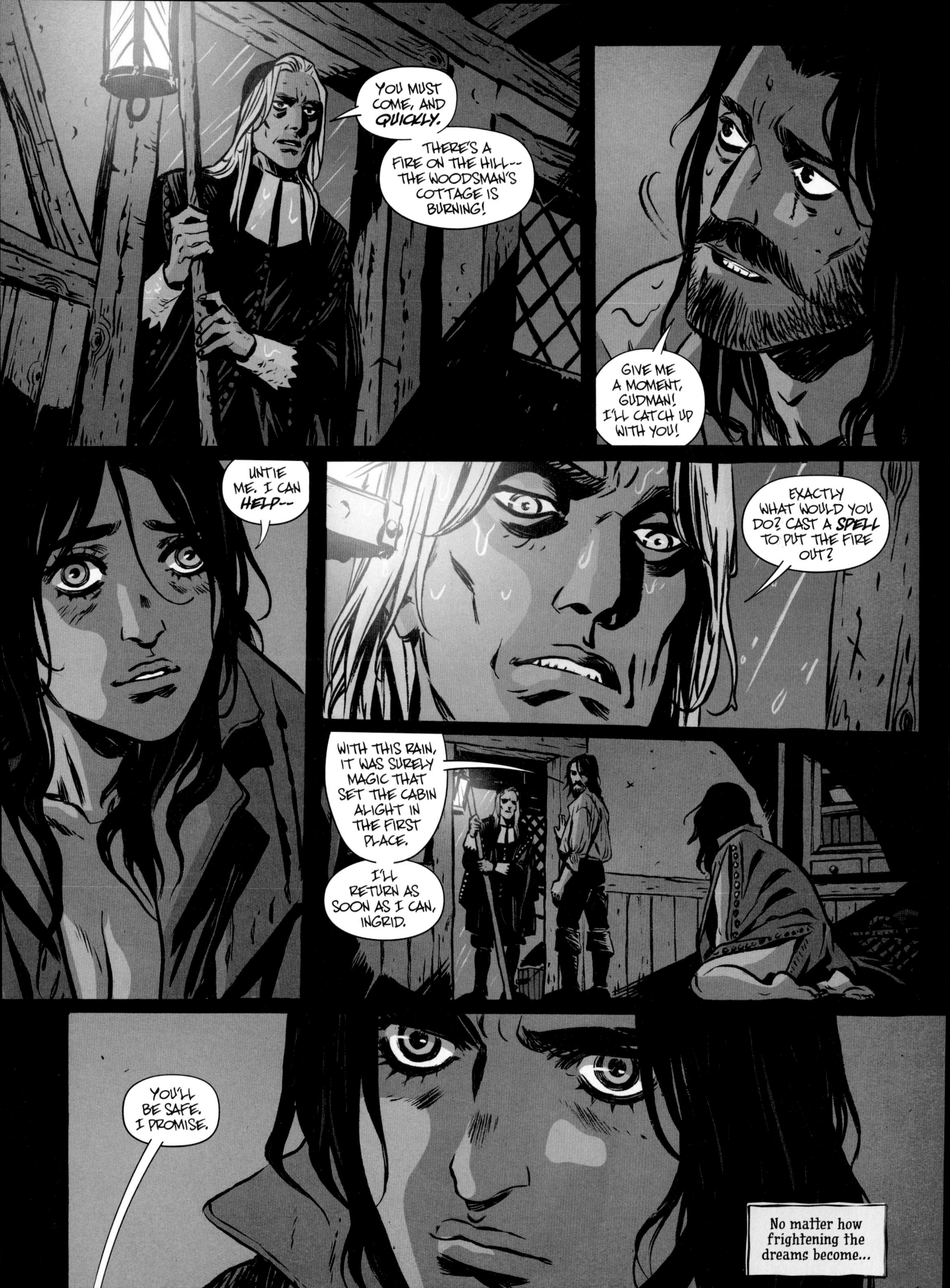
YOU MUST COME, AND **QUICKLY.**
THERE'S A FIRE ON THE HILL-- THE WOODSMAN'S COTTAGE IS BURNING!
GIVE ME A MOMENT, GUDMAN! I'LL CATCH UP WITH YOU!
UNTIE ME. I CAN **HELP--**
EXACTLY WHAT WOULD YOU DO? CAST A **SPELL** TO PUT THE FIRE OUT?
WITH THIS RAIN, IT WAS SURELY MAGIC THAT SET THE CABIN ALIGHT IN THE FIRST PLACE.
I'LL RETURN AS SOON AS I CAN, INGRID.
YOU'LL BE SAFE. I PROMISE.
No matter how frightening the dreams become...

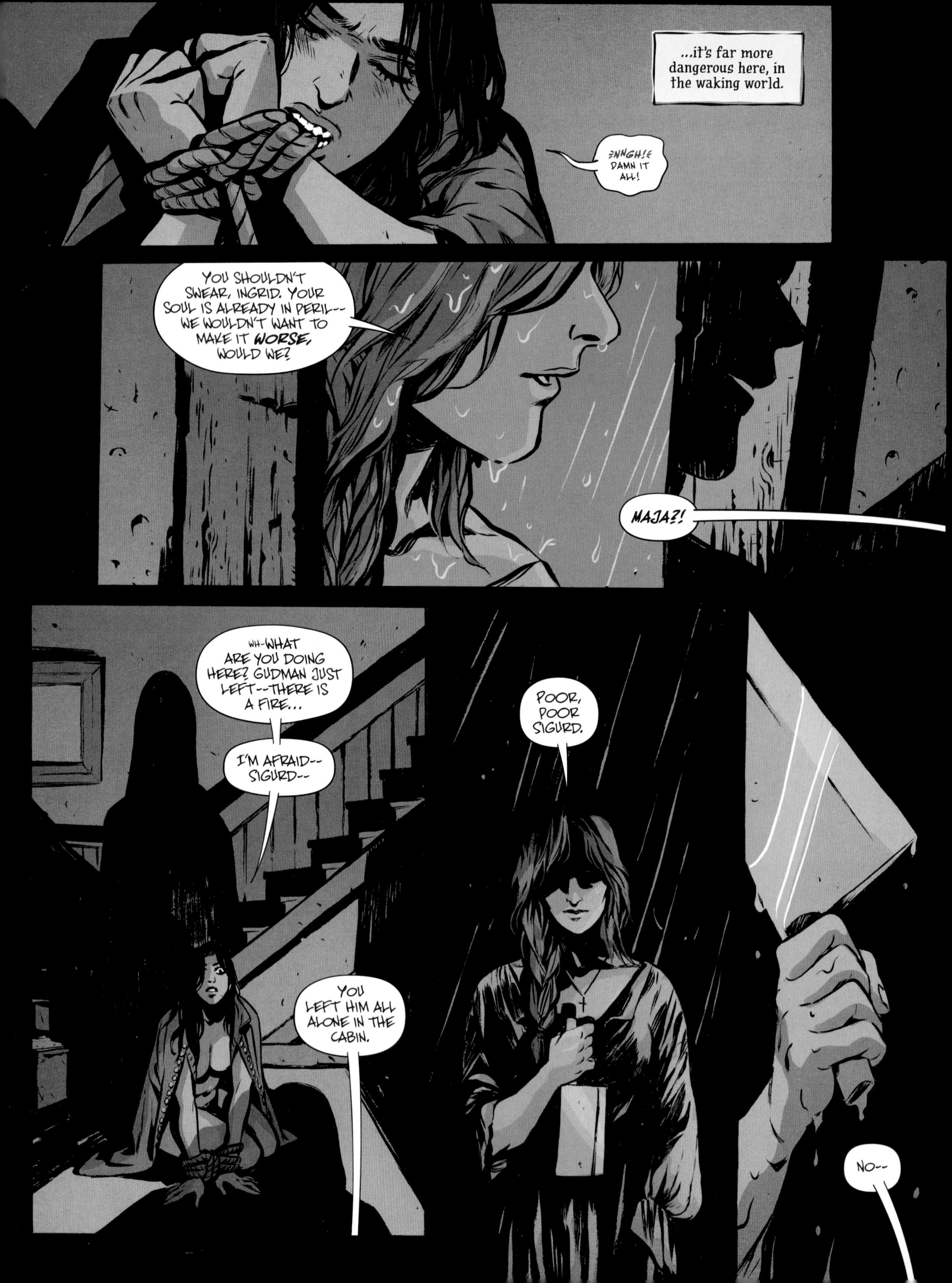
...it's far more dangerous here, in the waking world.
ƐNNGH!Ǝ DAMN IT ALL!
YOU SHOULDN'T SWEAR, INGRID. YOUR SOUL IS ALREADY IN PERIL-- WE WOULDN'T WANT TO MAKE IT WORSE, WOULD WE?
MAJA?!
WH-WHAT ARE YOU DOING HERE? GUDMAN JUST LEFT--THERE IS A FIRE...
I'M AFRAID-- SIGURD--
POOR, POOR SIGURD.
YOU LEFT HIM ALL ALONE IN THE CABIN.
NO--

--STOP--

CHOKT

=HNGH=

DON'T MAKE THIS MORE DIFFICULT THAN IT NEEDS TO BE.

HAVE YOU GONE MAD?! I SWORE TO KEEP YOUR SECRETS-- I HAVEN'T TOLD ANYONE!

THAT'S EXACTLY WHAT SIGURD SAID, YET HE STILL TOLD YOU.

YOU'RE A LOOSE THREAD, INGRID. YOU NEED TO BE CUT!

WHUKt

AUGH!

I KNOW ABOUT HARALD. AND SIGURD'S WIFE, GRETA...

YOU'VE BECOME SOMEONE I DON'T RECOGNIZE. OR PERHAPS YOU WERE ALWAYS A MONSTER?

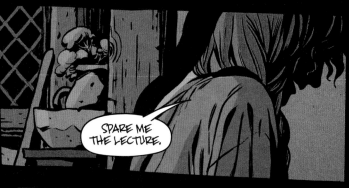

SPARE ME THE LECTURE.

THERE ARE NO INNOCENTS--

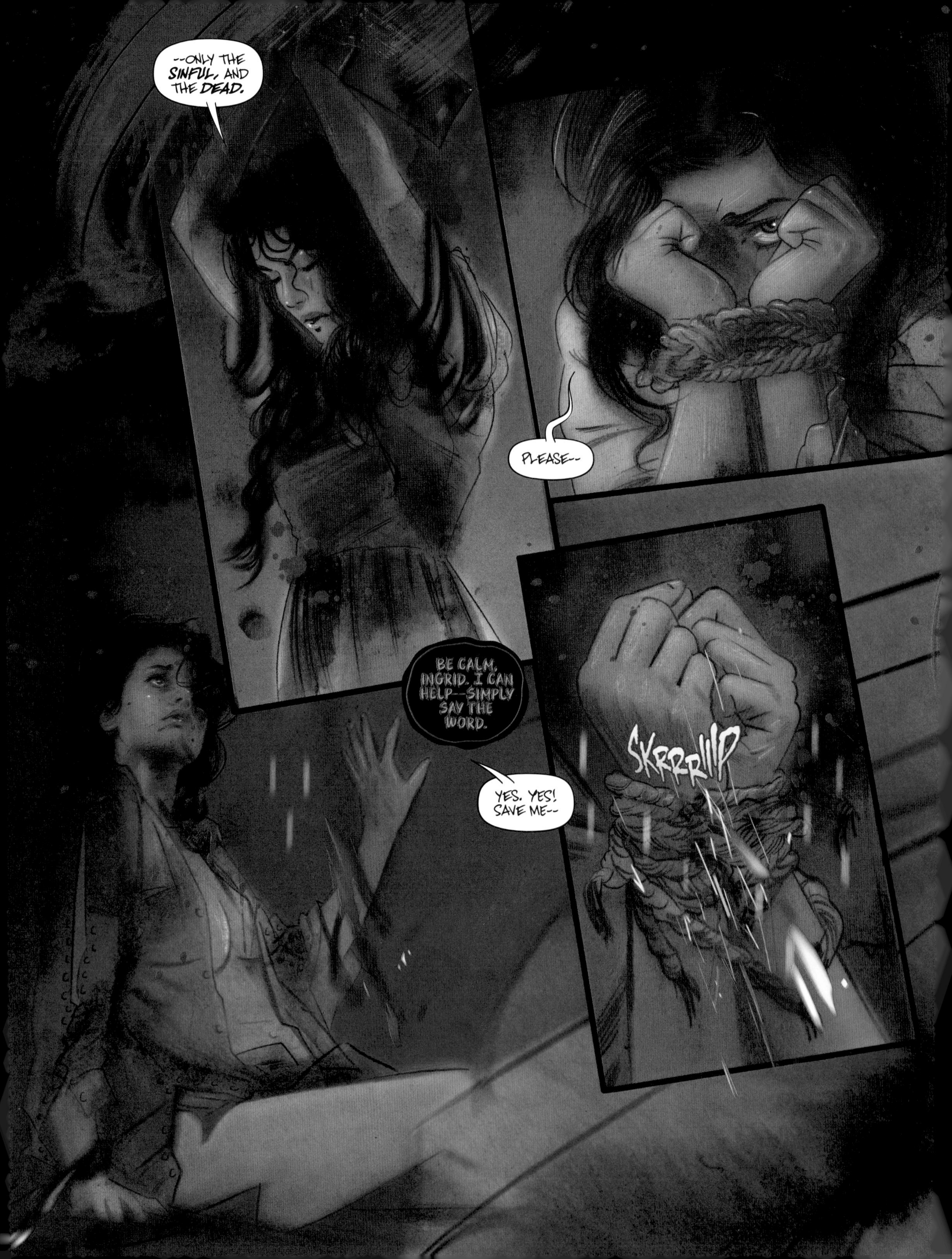
--ONLY THE *SINFUL*, AND THE *DEAD.*
PLEASE--
BE CALM, INGRID. I CAN HELP--SIMPLY SAY THE WORD.
YES. YES! SAVE ME--
SKRRRIIIP

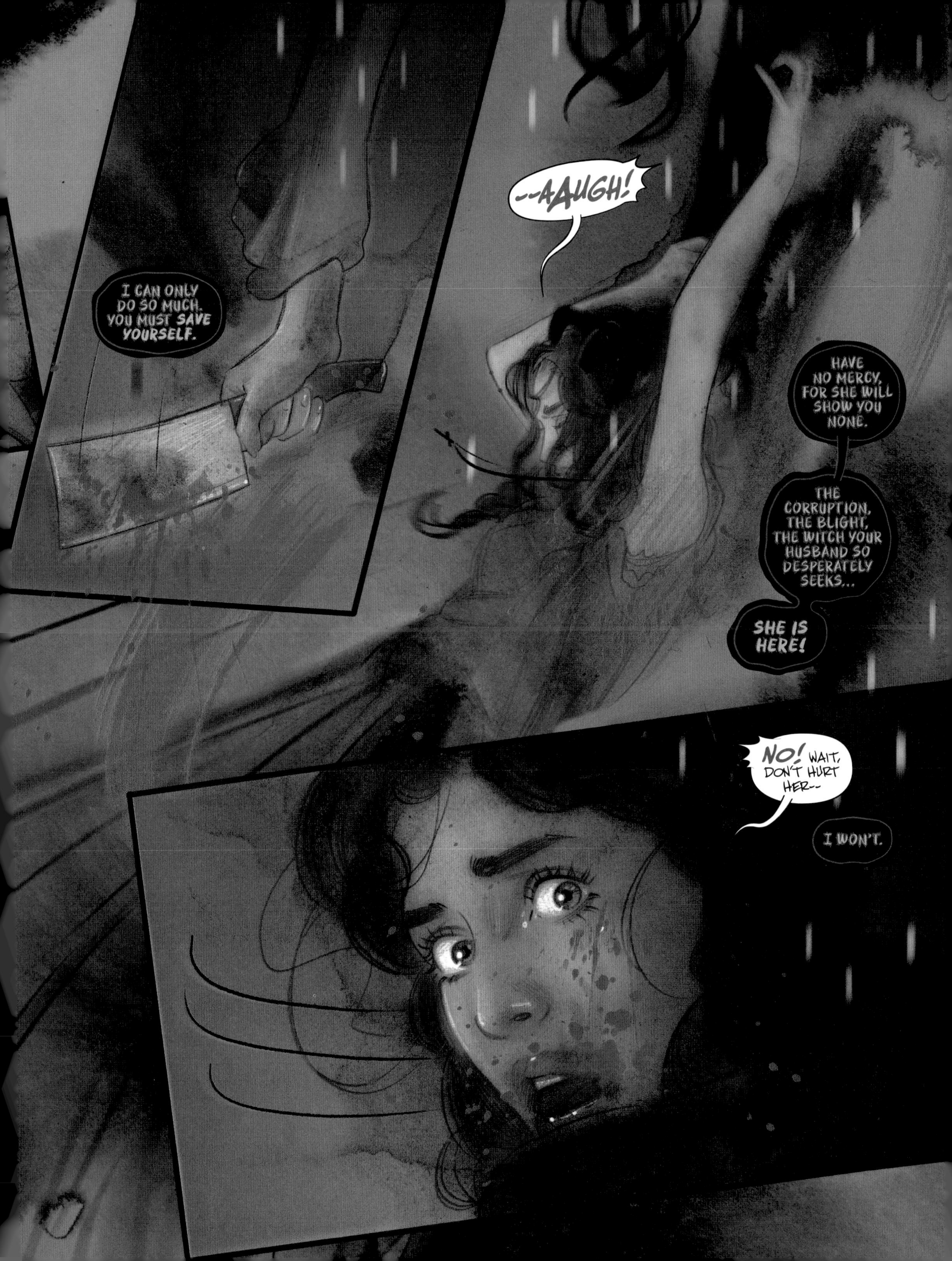

I CAN ONLY DO SO MUCH. YOU MUST SAVE YOURSELF.
--AAUGH!
HAVE NO MERCY, FOR SHE WILL SHOW YOU NONE.
THE CORRUPTION, THE BLIGHT, THE WITCH YOUR HUSBAND SO DESPERATELY SEEKS...
SHE IS HERE!
NO! WAIT, DON'T HURT HER--
I WON'T.

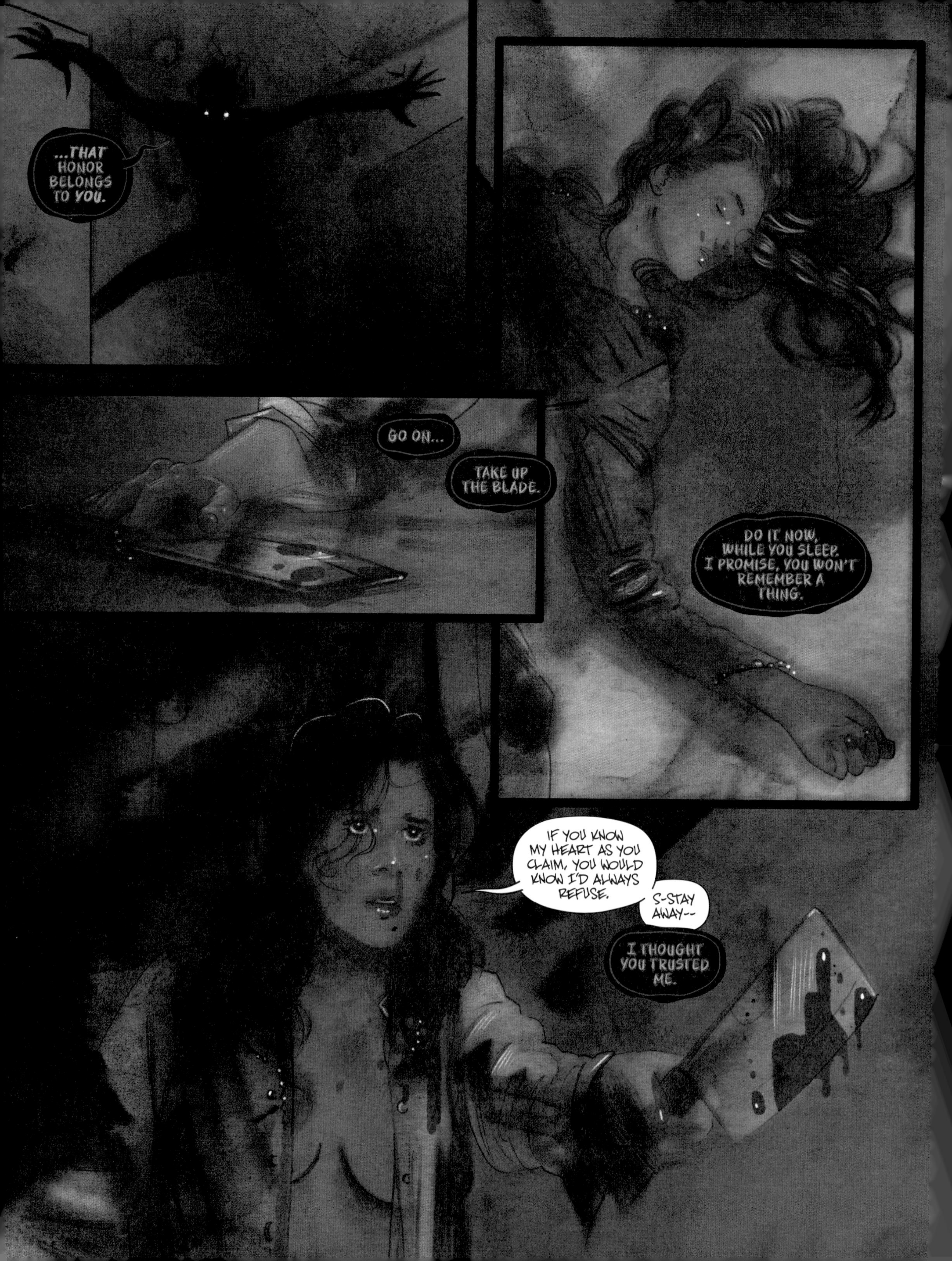
...THAT HONOR BELONGS TO YOU.
GO ON...
TAKE UP THE BLADE.
DO IT NOW, WHILE YOU SLEEP. I PROMISE, YOU WON'T REMEMBER A THING.
IF YOU KNOW MY HEART AS YOU CLAIM, YOU WOULD KNOW I'D ALWAYS REFUSE.
S-STAY AWAY--
I THOUGHT YOU TRUSTED ME.

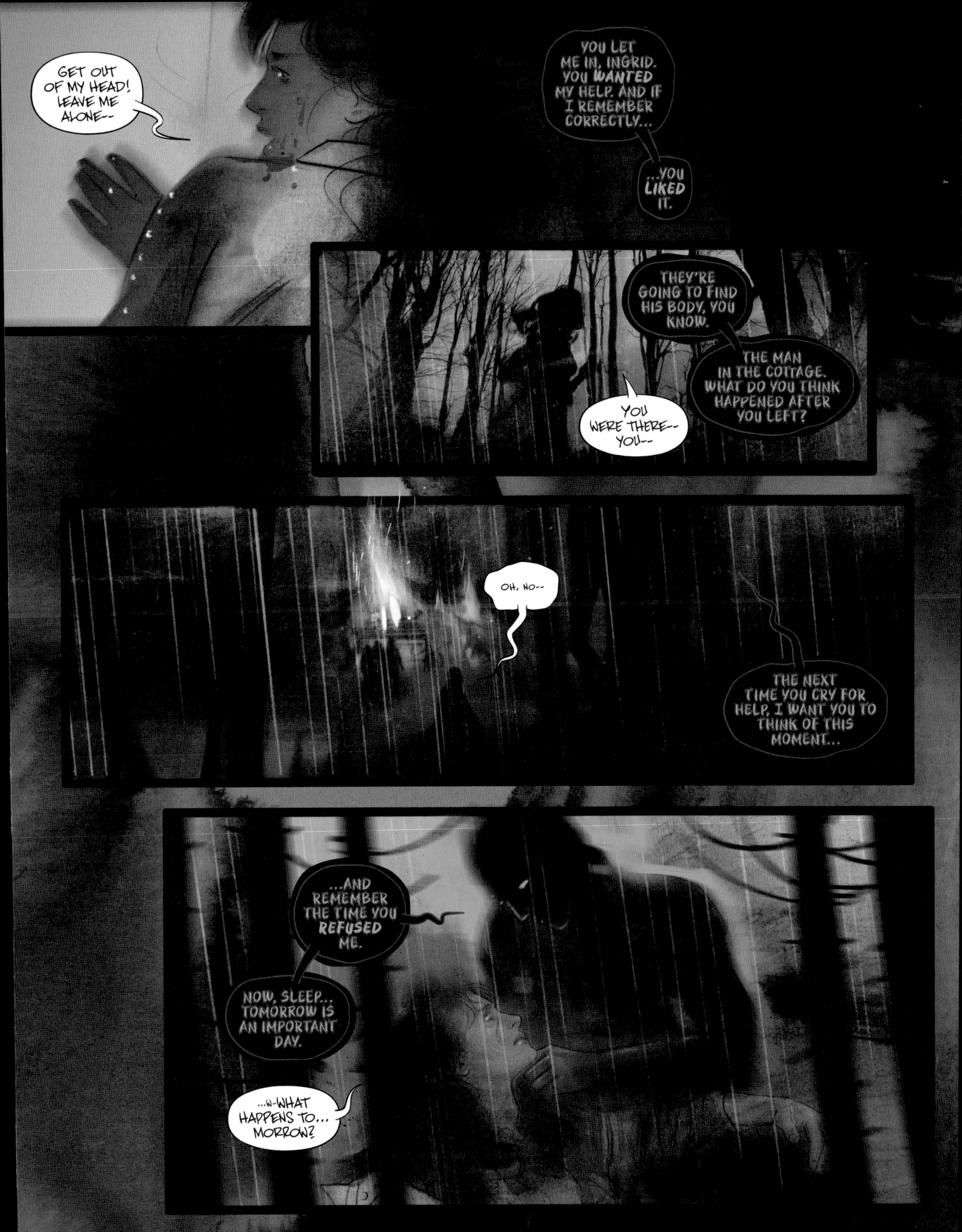
GET OUT OF MY HEAD! LEAVE ME ALONE--
YOU LET ME IN, INGRID. YOU WANTED MY HELP. AND IF I REMEMBER CORRECTLY...
...YOU LIKED IT.
THEY'RE GOING TO FIND HIS BODY, YOU KNOW.
THE MAN IN THE COTTAGE. WHAT DO YOU THINK HAPPENED AFTER YOU LEFT?
YOU WERE THERE-- YOU--
OH, NO--
THE NEXT TIME YOU CRY FOR HELP, I WANT YOU TO THINK OF THIS MOMENT...
...AND REMEMBER THE TIME YOU REFUSED ME.
NOW, SLEEP... TOMORROW IS AN IMPORTANT DAY.
...W-WHAT HAPPENS TO... MORROW?

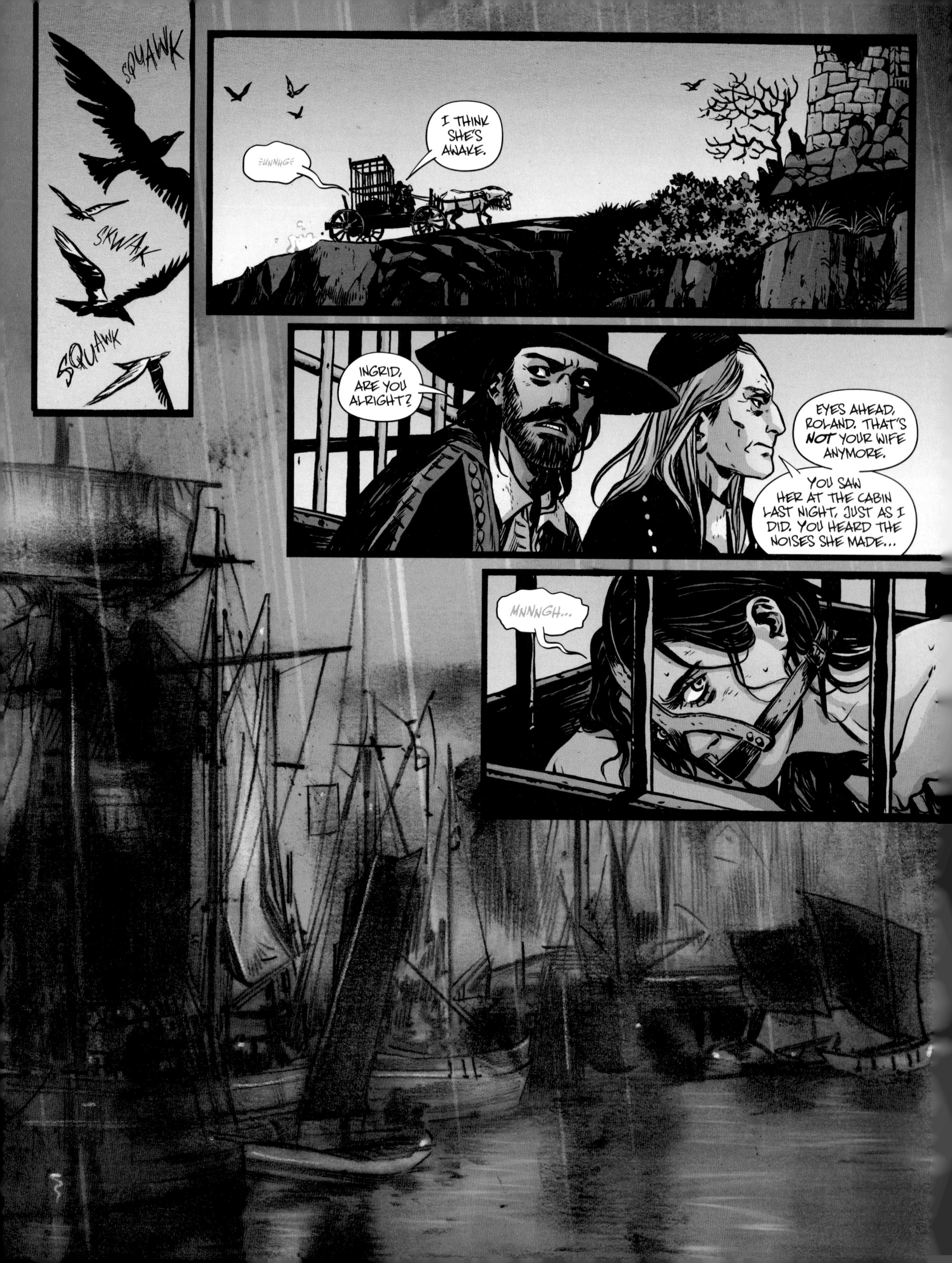
SQUAWK
SKWAK
SQUAWK
UNNHG
I THINK SHE'S AWAKE.
INGRID, ARE YOU ALRIGHT?
EYES AHEAD, ROLAND. THAT'S NOT YOUR WIFE ANYMORE.
YOU SAW HER AT THE CABIN LAST NIGHT, JUST AS I DID. YOU HEARD THE NOISES SHE MADE...
MNNNGH...

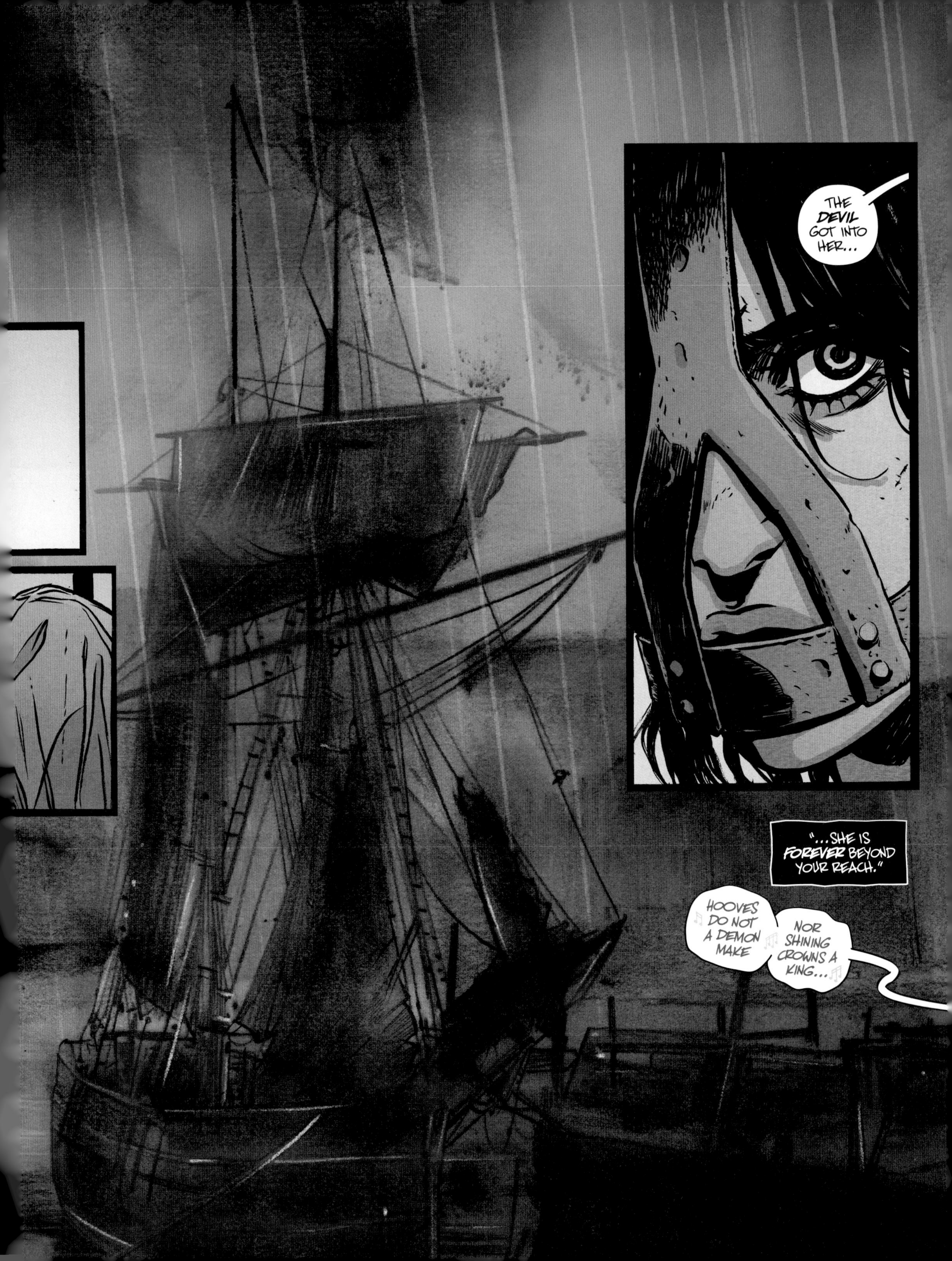
THE DEVIL GOT INTO HER...
"...SHE IS FOREVER BEYOND YOUR REACH."
HOOVES DO NOT A DEMON MAKE
NOR SHINING CROWNS A KING...

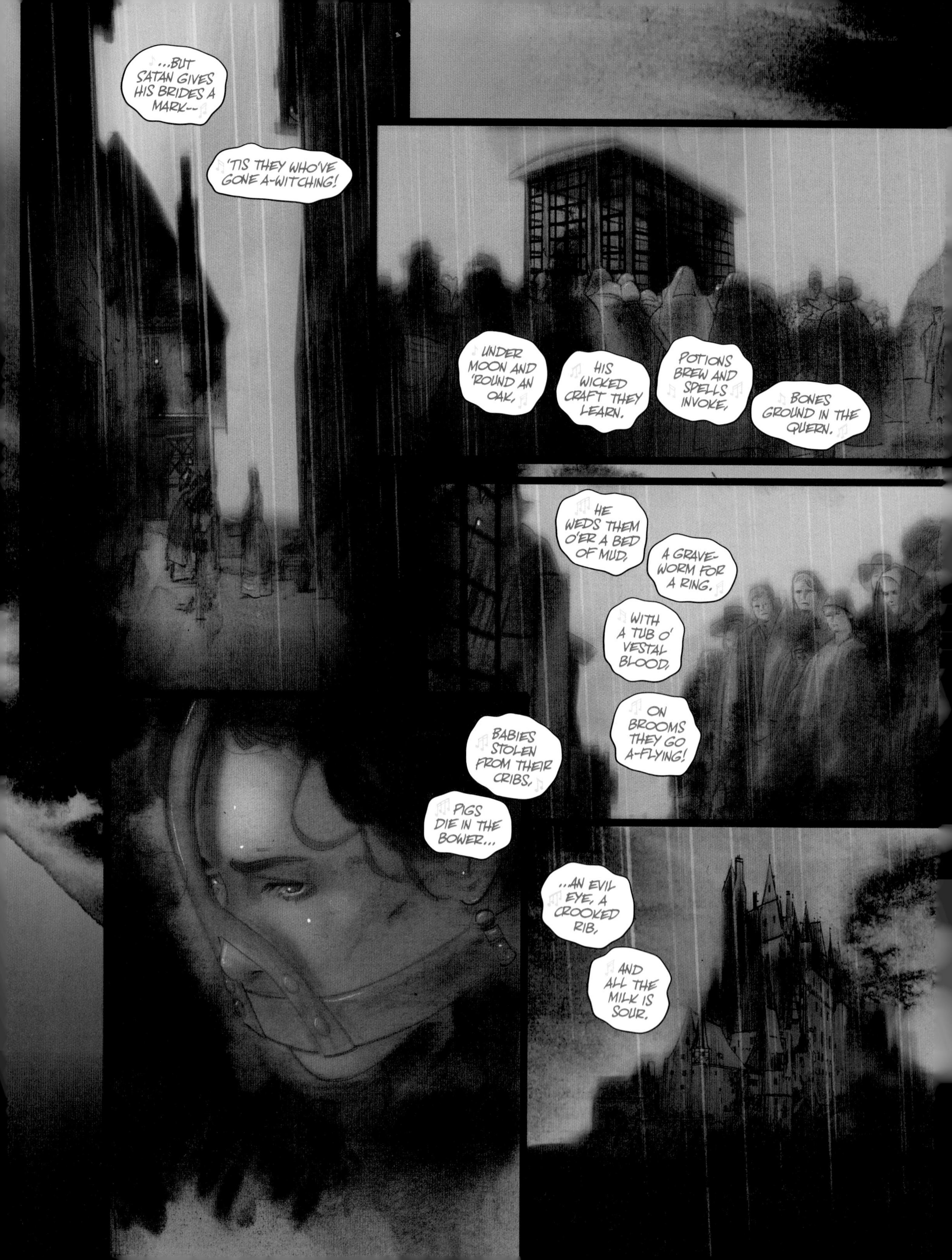
...BUT SATAN GIVES HIS BRIDES A MARK--
'TIS THEY WHO'VE GONE A-WITCHING!
UNDER MOON AND 'ROUND AN OAK,
HIS WICKED CRAFT THEY LEARN.
POTIONS BREW AND SPELLS INVOKE,
BONES GROUND IN THE QUERN.
HE WEDS THEM O'ER A BED OF MUD,
A GRAVE-WORM FOR A RING.
WITH A TUB O' VESTAL BLOOD,
ON BROOMS THEY GO A-FLYING!
BABIES STOLEN FROM THEIR CRIBS,
PIGS DIE IN THE BOWER...
...AN EVIL EYE, A CROOKED RIB,
AND ALL THE MILK IS SOUR.

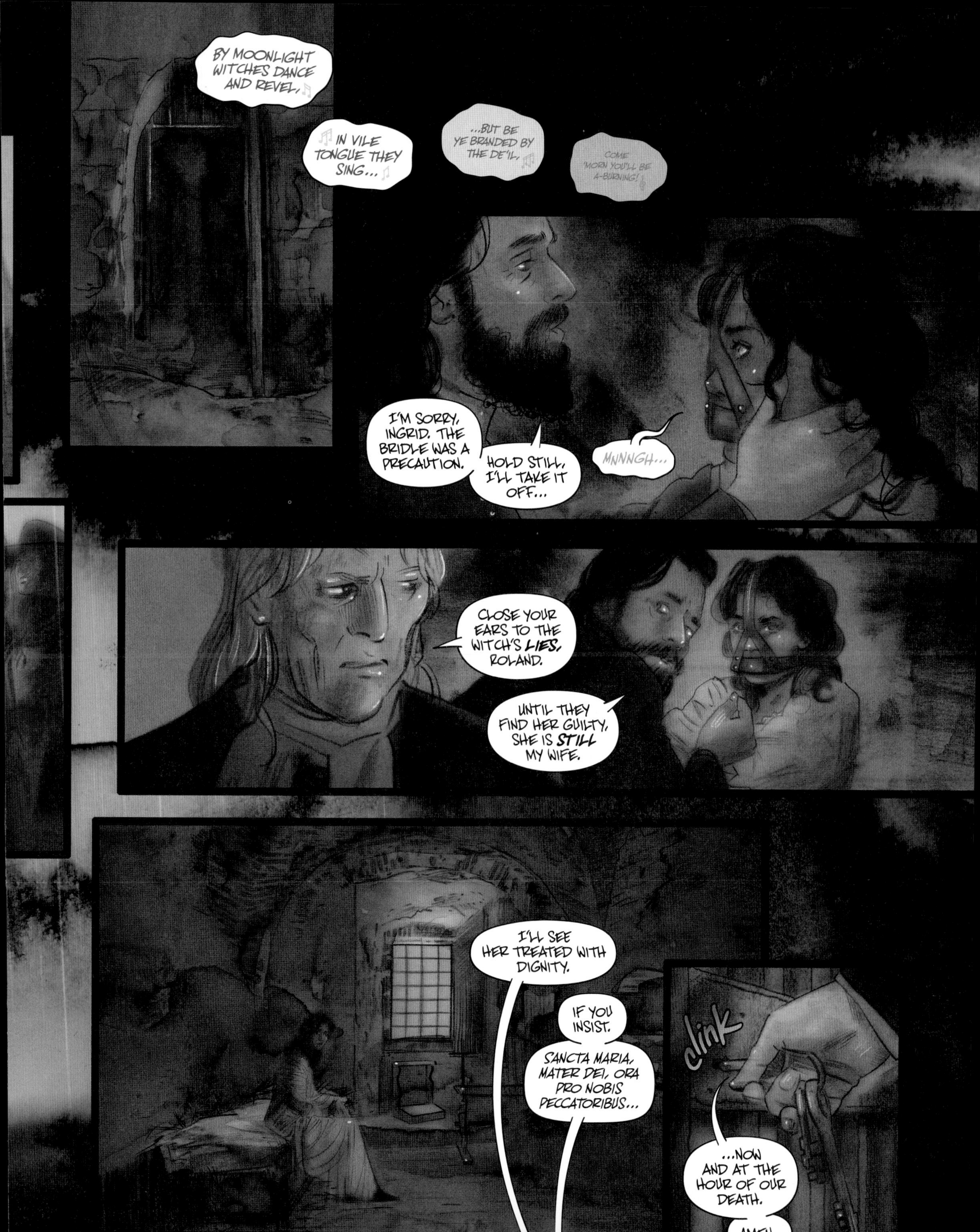
BY MOONLIGHT WITCHES DANCE AND REVEL,
IN VILE TONGUE THEY SING...
...BUT BE YE BRANDED BY THE DE'IL,
COME 'MORN YOU'LL BE A-BURNING!
I'M SORRY, INGRID. THE BRIDLE WAS A PRECAUTION.
HOLD STILL, I'LL TAKE IT OFF...
MNNNGH...
CLOSE YOUR EARS TO THE WITCH'S **LIES,** ROLAND.
UNTIL THEY FIND HER GUILTY, SHE IS **STILL** MY WIFE.
I'LL SEE HER TREATED WITH DIGNITY.
IF YOU INSIST.
SANCTA MARIA, MATER DEI, ORA PRO NOBIS PECCATORIBUS...
clink
...NOW AND AT THE HOUR OF OUR DEATH.

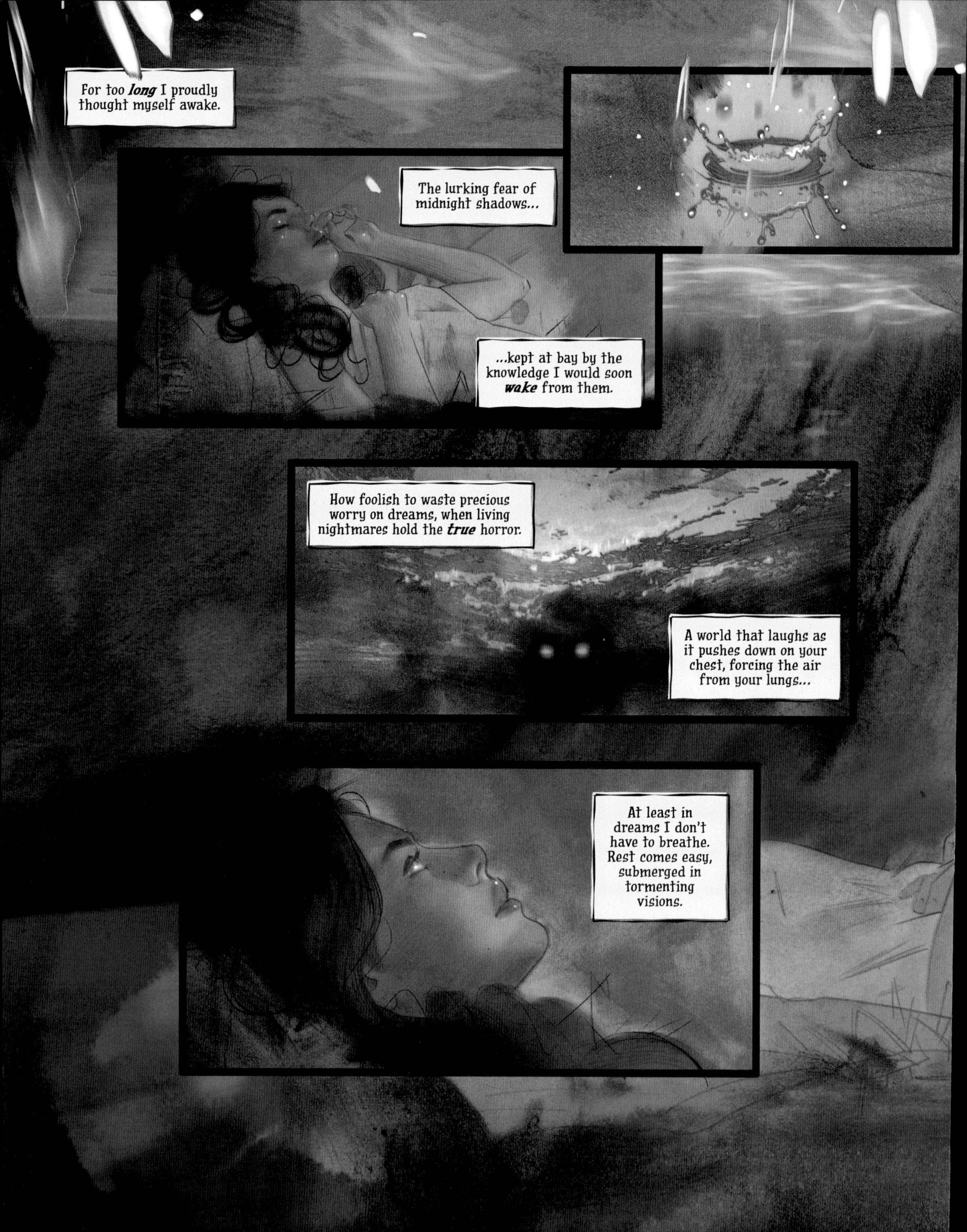
For too *long* I proudly thought myself awake.
The lurking fear of midnight shadows...
...kept at bay by the knowledge I would soon *wake* from them.
How foolish to waste precious worry on dreams, when living nightmares hold the *true* horror.
A world that laughs as it pushes down on your chest, forcing the air from your lungs...
At least in dreams I don't have to breathe. Rest comes easy, submerged in tormenting visions.

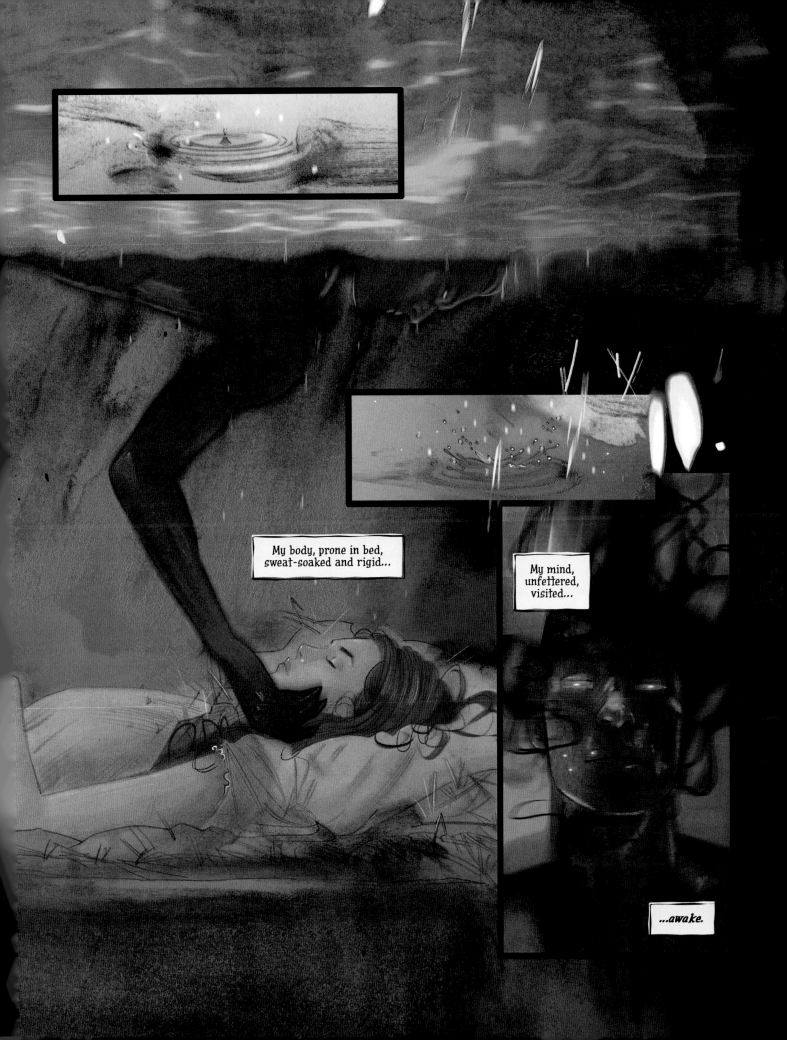

My body, prone in bed, sweat-soaked and rigid...

My mind, unfettered, visited...

...awake.

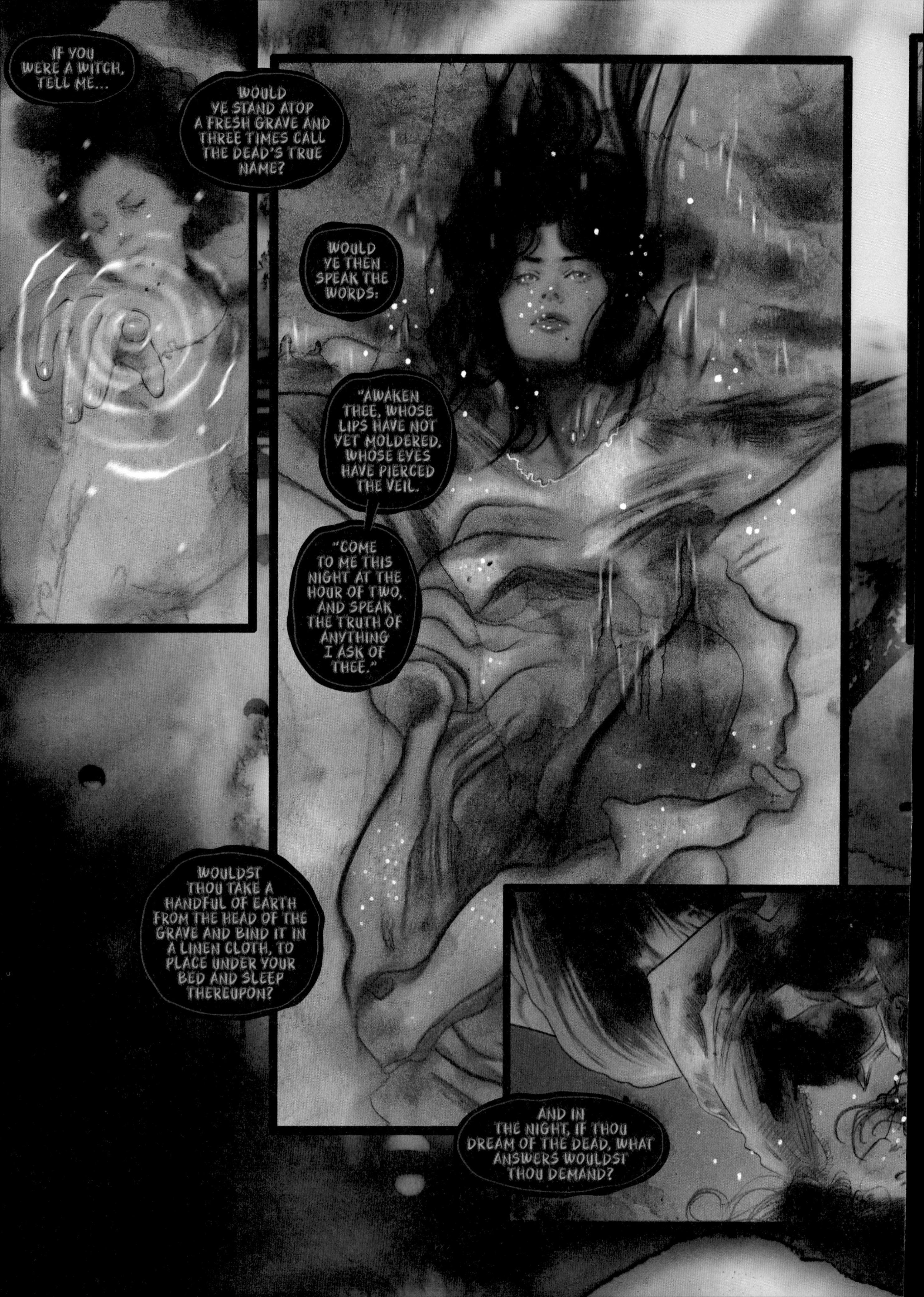
IF YOU WERE A WITCH, TELL ME...
WOULD YE STAND ATOP A FRESH GRAVE AND THREE TIMES CALL THE DEAD'S TRUE NAME?
WOULD YE THEN SPEAK THE WORDS:
"AWAKEN THEE, WHOSE LIPS HAVE NOT YET MOLDERED, WHOSE EYES HAVE PIERCED THE VEIL.
"COME TO ME THIS NIGHT AT THE HOUR OF TWO, AND SPEAK THE TRUTH OF ANYTHING I ASK OF THEE."
WOULDST THOU TAKE A HANDFUL OF EARTH FROM THE HEAD OF THE GRAVE AND BIND IT IN A LINEN CLOTH, TO PLACE UNDER YOUR BED AND SLEEP THEREUPON?
AND IN THE NIGHT, IF THOU DREAM OF THE DEAD, WHAT ANSWERS WOULDST THOU DEMAND?

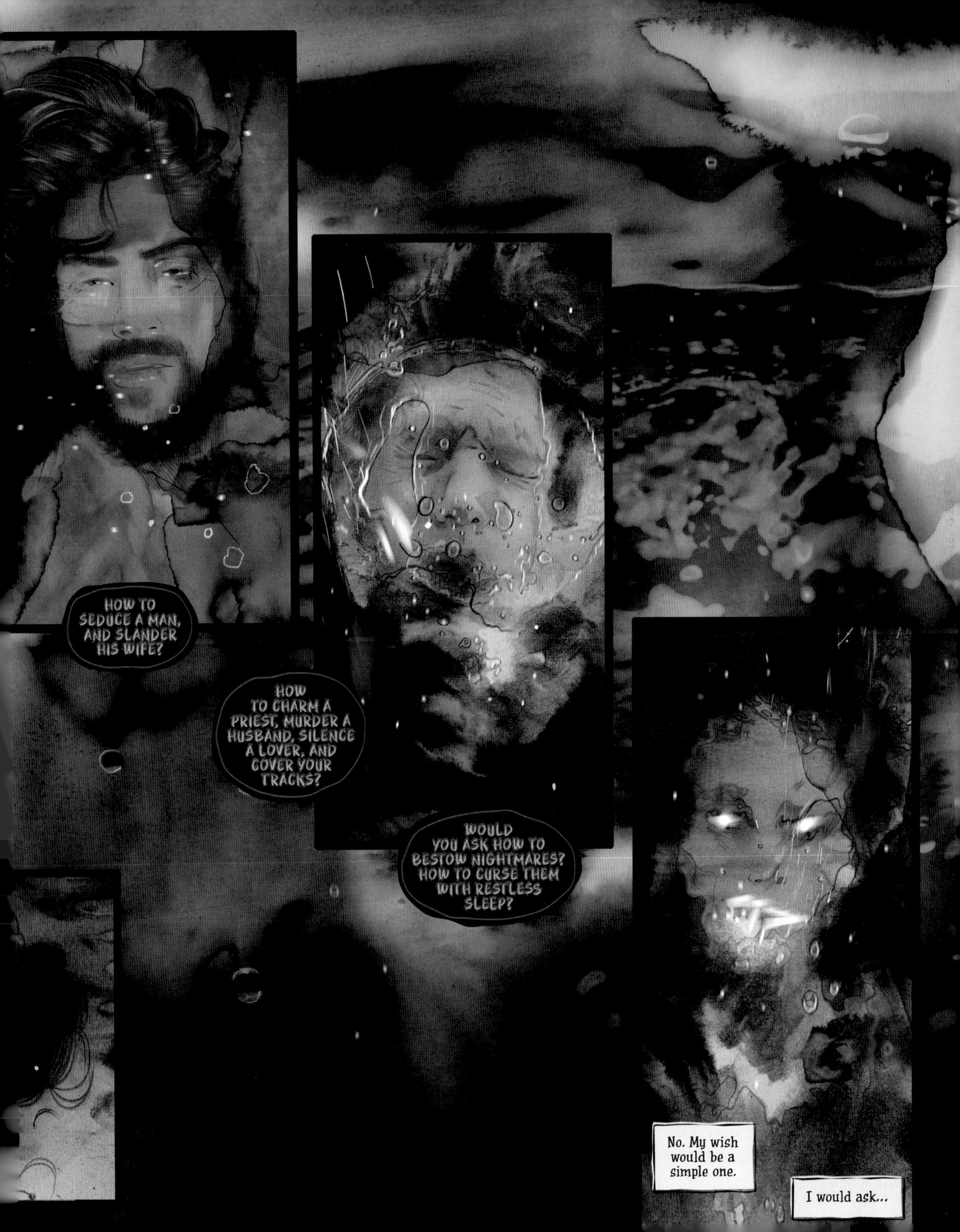
HOW TO SEDUCE A MAN, AND SLANDER HIS WIFE?
HOW TO CHARM A PRIEST, MURDER A HUSBAND, SILENCE A LOVER, AND COVER YOUR TRACKS?
WOULD YOU ASK HOW TO BESTOW NIGHTMARES? HOW TO CURSE THEM WITH RESTLESS SLEEP?
No. My wish would be a simple one.
I would ask...

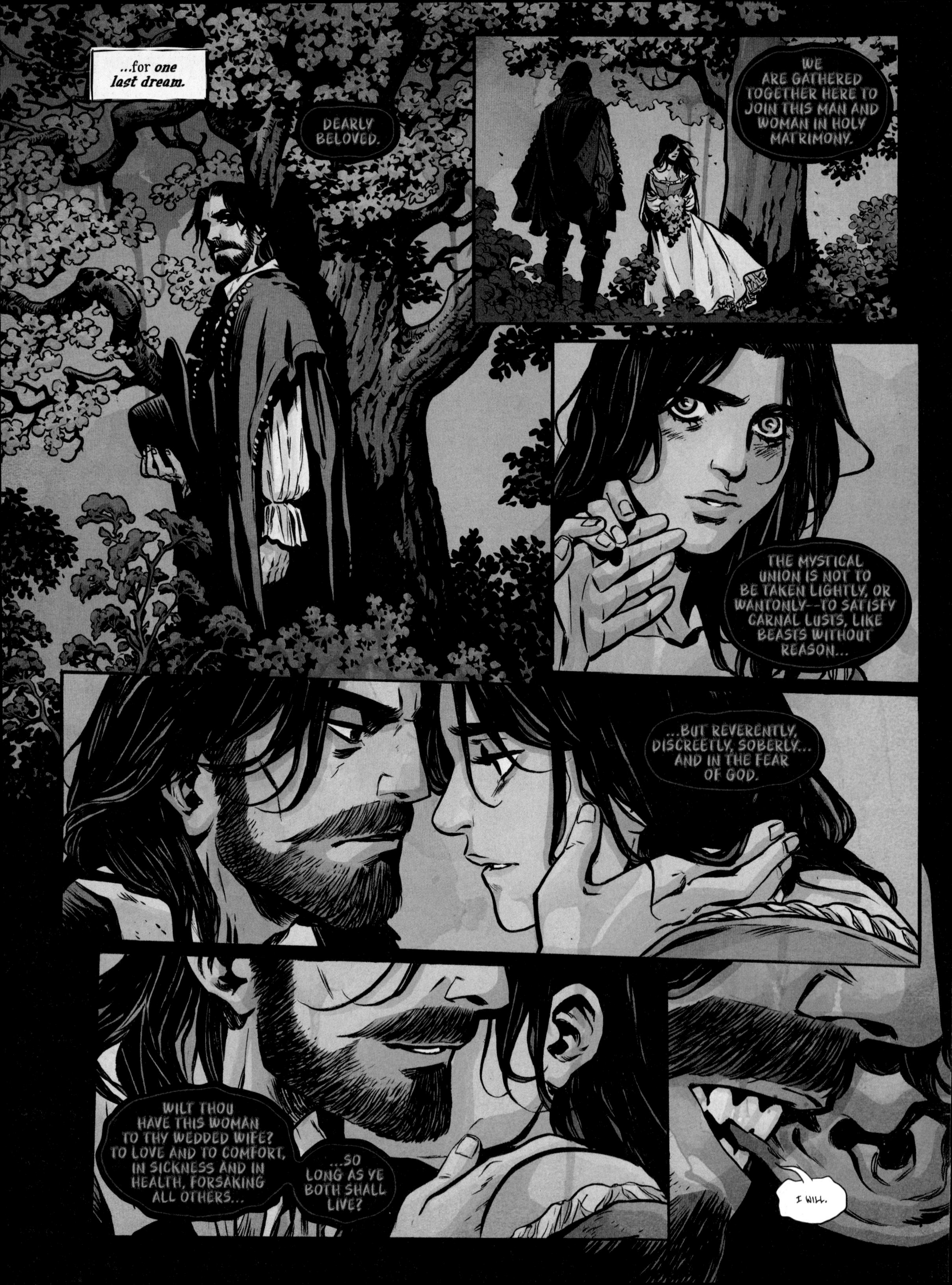
...for one last dream.
DEARLY BELOVED.
WE ARE GATHERED TOGETHER HERE TO JOIN THIS MAN AND WOMAN IN HOLY MATRIMONY.
THE MYSTICAL UNION IS NOT TO BE TAKEN LIGHTLY, OR WANTONLY--TO SATISFY CARNAL LUSTS, LIKE BEASTS WITHOUT REASON...
...BUT REVERENTLY, DISCREETLY, SOBERLY... AND IN THE FEAR OF GOD.
WILT THOU HAVE THIS WOMAN TO THY WEDDED WIFE? TO LOVE AND TO COMFORT, IN SICKNESS AND IN HEALTH, FORSAKING ALL OTHERS...
...SO LONG AS YE BOTH SHALL LIVE?
I WILL.

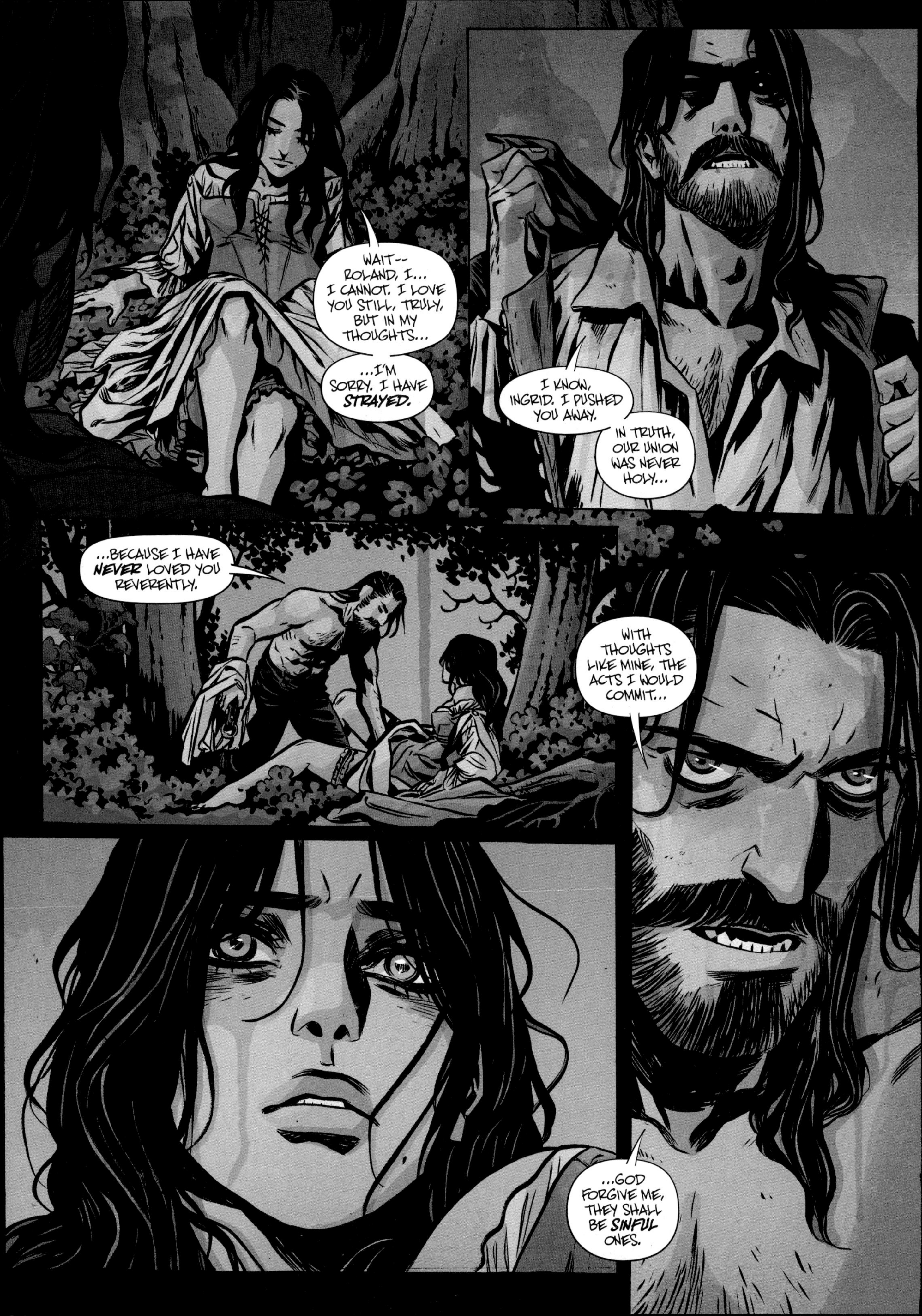
WAIT-- ROLAND, I... I CANNOT. I LOVE YOU STILL, TRULY, BUT IN MY THOUGHTS...
...I'M SORRY. I HAVE **STRAYED.**
I KNOW, INGRID. I PUSHED YOU AWAY.
IN TRUTH, OUR UNION WAS NEVER HOLY...
...BECAUSE I HAVE **NEVER** LOVED YOU REVERENTLY.
WITH THOUGHTS LIKE MINE, THE ACTS I WOULD COMMIT...
...GOD FORGIVE ME, THEY SHALL BE **SINFUL** ONES.

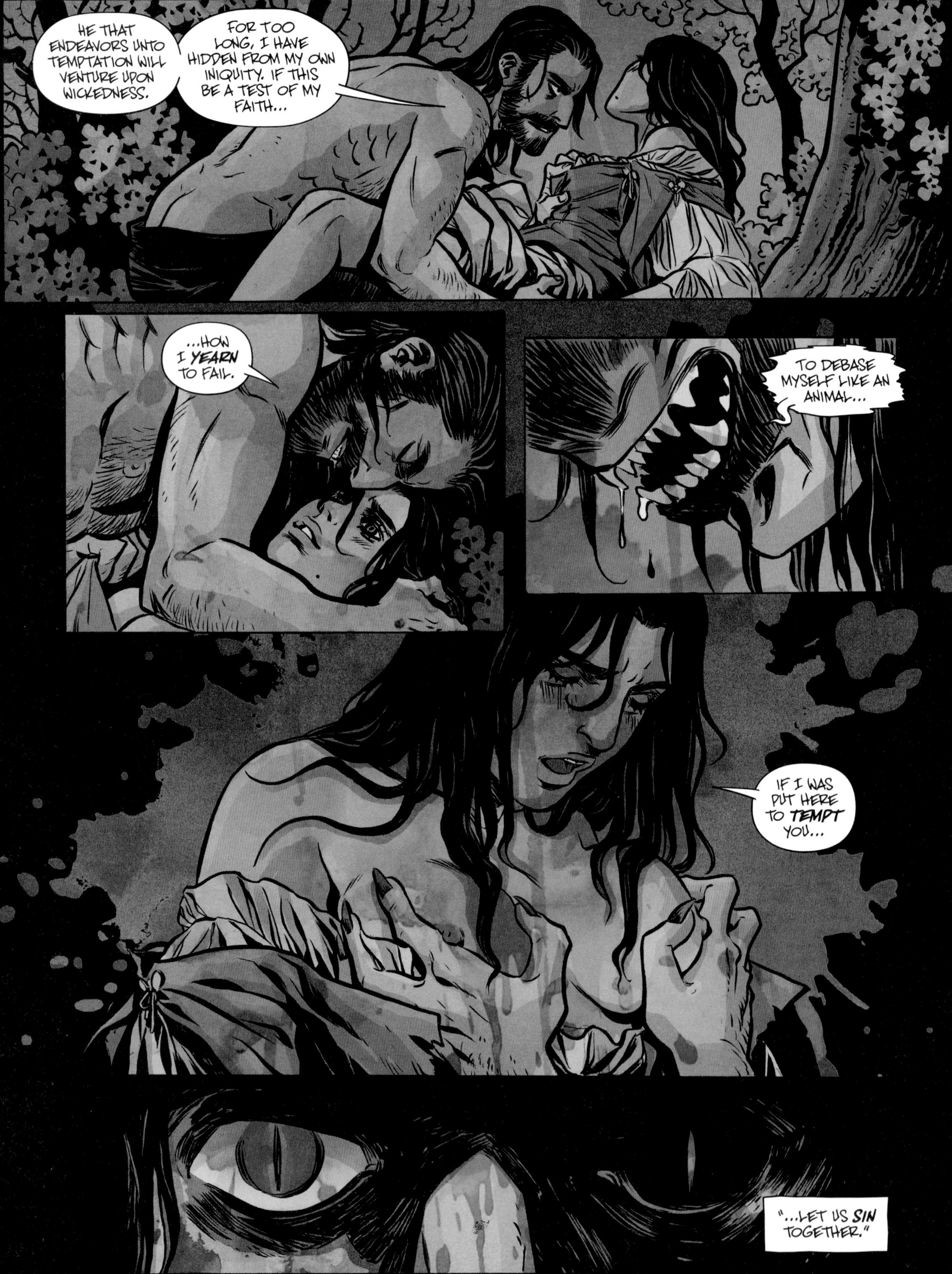
HE THAT ENDEAVORS UNTO TEMPTATION WILL VENTURE UPON WICKEDNESS.
FOR TOO LONG, I HAVE HIDDEN FROM MY OWN INIQUITY. IF THIS BE A TEST OF MY FAITH...
...HOW I YEARN TO FAIL.
TO DEBASE MYSELF LIKE AN ANIMAL...
IF I WAS PUT HERE TO TEMPT YOU...
"...LET US SIN TOGETHER."

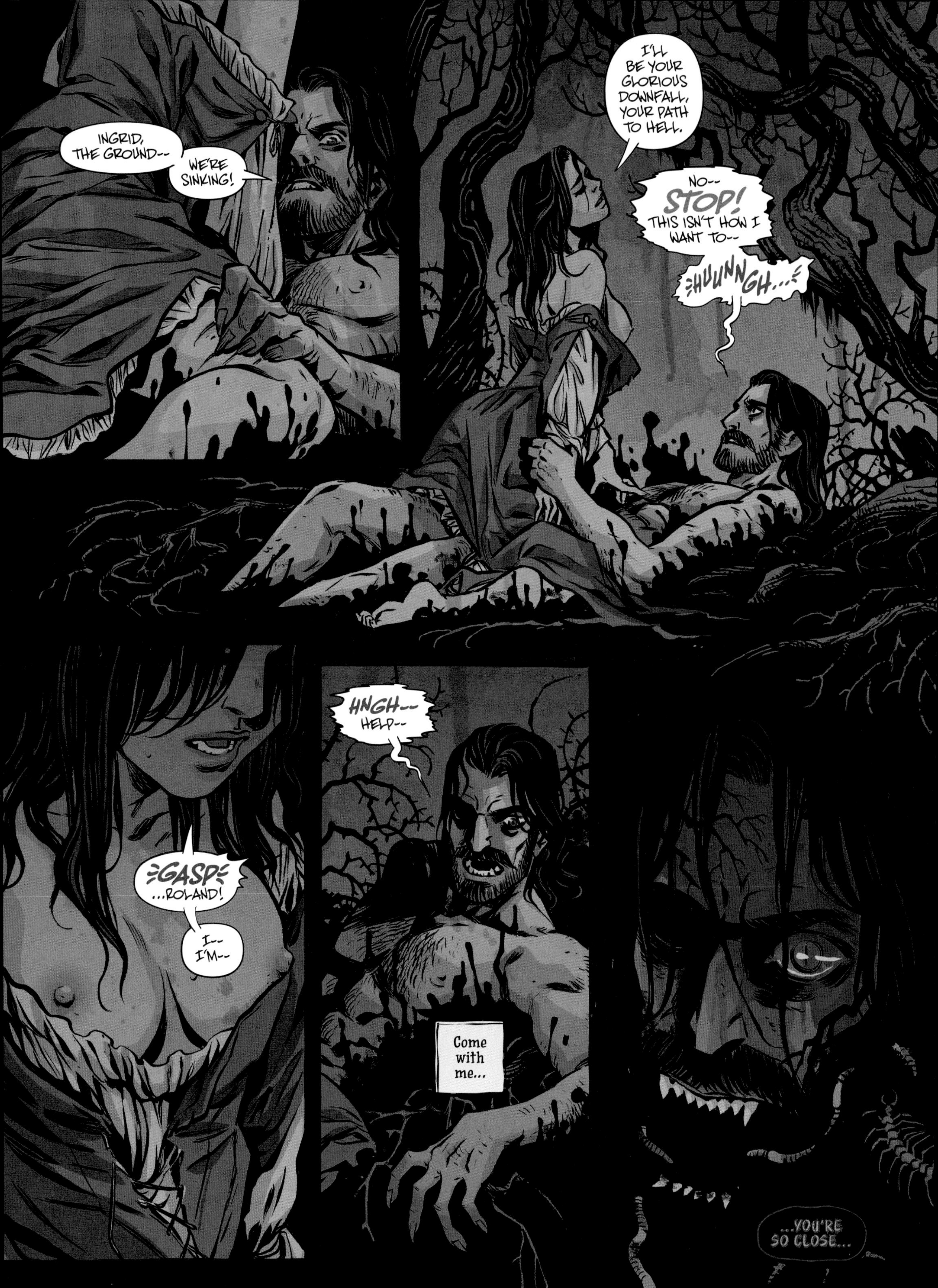
INGRID, THE GROUND--
WE'RE SINKING!
I'LL BE YOUR GLORIOUS DOWNFALL, YOUR PATH TO HELL.
NO-- STOP! THIS ISN'T HOW I WANT TO--
HUUNNGH...
GASP ...ROLAND!
I-- I'M--
HNGH-- HELP--
Come with me...
...YOU'RE SO CLOSE...

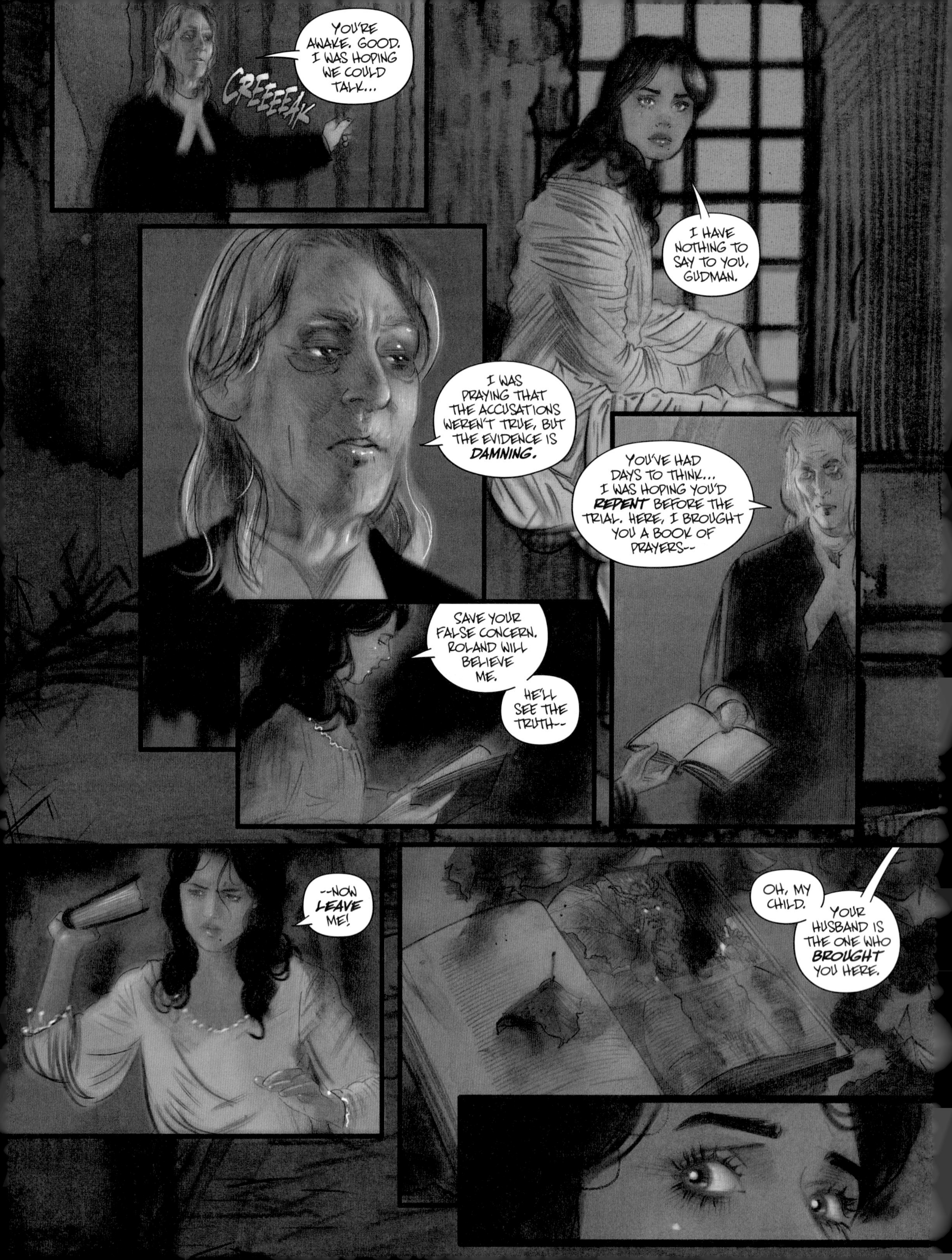

YOU'RE AWAKE. GOOD. I WAS HOPING WE COULD TALK...
CREEEEEAK
I HAVE NOTHING TO SAY TO YOU, GUDMAN.
I WAS PRAYING THAT THE ACCUSATIONS WEREN'T TRUE, BUT THE EVIDENCE IS DAMNING.
YOU'VE HAD DAYS TO THINK... I WAS HOPING YOU'D REPENT BEFORE THE TRIAL. HERE, I BROUGHT YOU A BOOK OF PRAYERS--
SAVE YOUR FALSE CONCERN. ROLAND WILL BELIEVE ME.
HE'LL SEE THE TRUTH--
--NOW LEAVE ME!
OH, MY CHILD.
YOUR HUSBAND IS THE ONE WHO BROUGHT YOU HERE.

CHAPTER VI.
A PRICK OF THE TONGUE

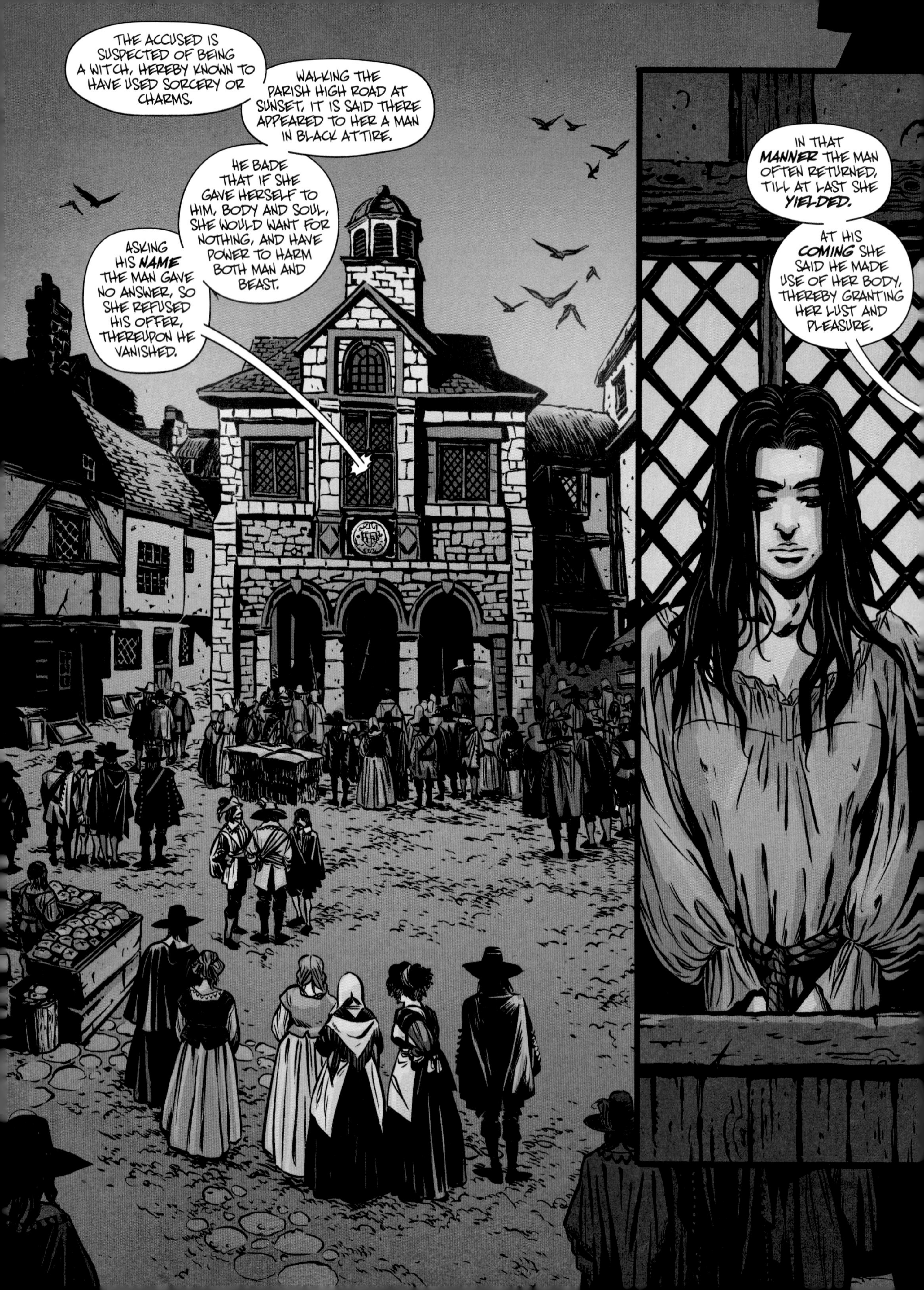
THE ACCUSED IS SUSPECTED OF BEING A WITCH, HEREBY KNOWN TO HAVE USED SORCERY OR CHARMS.
WALKING THE PARISH HIGH ROAD AT SUNSET, IT IS SAID THERE APPEARED TO HER A MAN IN BLACK ATTIRE.
HE BADE THAT IF SHE GAVE HERSELF TO HIM, BODY AND SOUL, SHE WOULD WANT FOR NOTHING, AND HAVE POWER TO HARM BOTH MAN AND BEAST.
ASKING HIS NAME THE MAN GAVE NO ANSWER, SO SHE REFUSED HIS OFFER, THEREUPON HE VANISHED.
IN THAT MANNER THE MAN OFTEN RETURNED, TILL AT LAST SHE YIELDED.
AT HIS COMING SHE SAID HE MADE USE OF HER BODY, THEREBY GRANTING HER LUST AND PLEASURE.

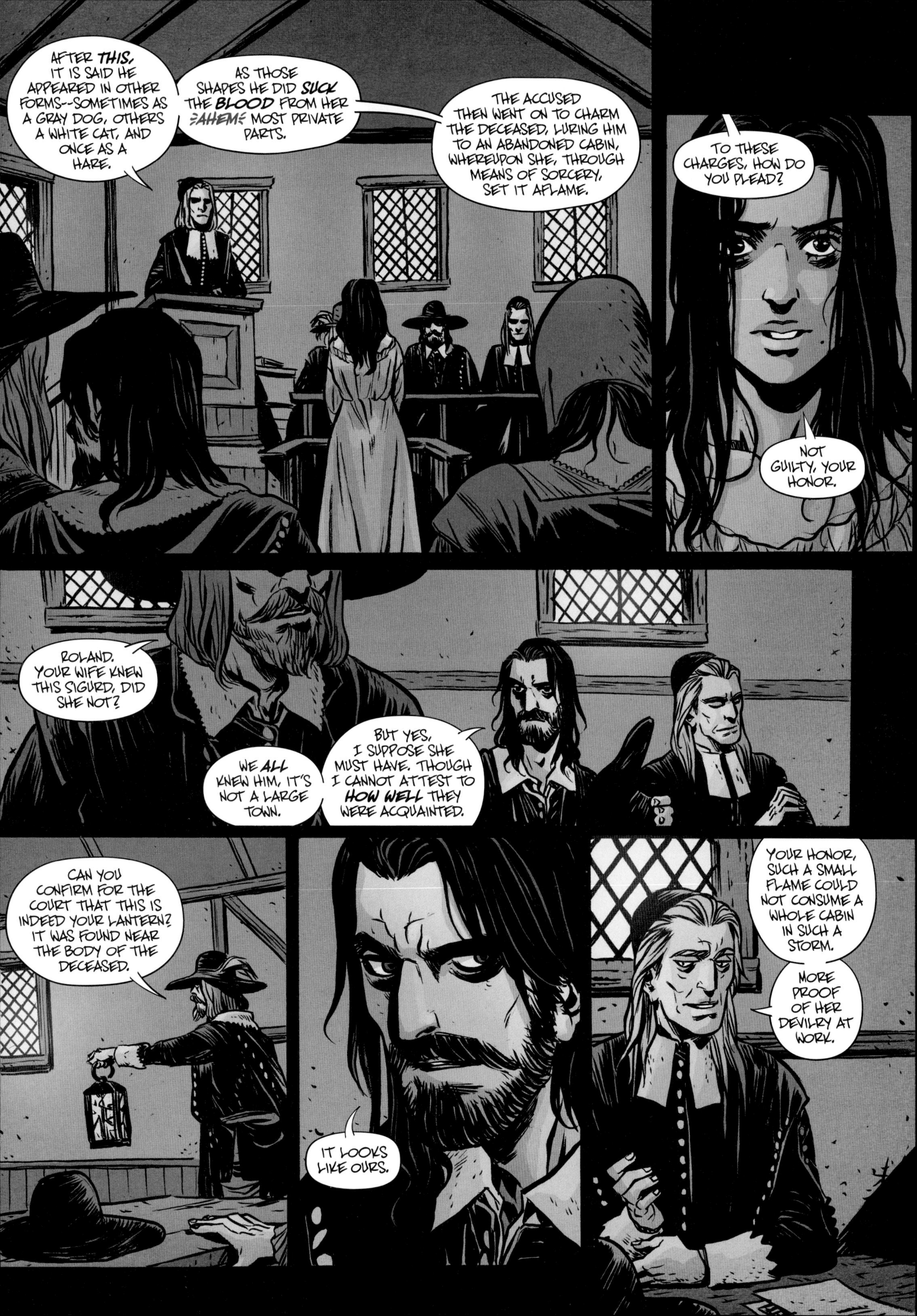
AFTER THIS, IT IS SAID HE APPEARED IN OTHER FORMS--SOMETIMES AS A GRAY DOG, OTHERS A WHITE CAT, AND ONCE AS A HARE.
AS THOSE SHAPES HE DID SUCK THE BLOOD FROM HER AHEM MOST PRIVATE PARTS.
THE ACCUSED THEN WENT ON TO CHARM THE DECEASED, LURING HIM TO AN ABANDONED CABIN, WHEREUPON SHE, THROUGH MEANS OF SORCERY, SET IT AFLAME.
TO THESE CHARGES, HOW DO YOU PLEAD?
NOT GUILTY, YOUR HONOR.
ROLAND. YOUR WIFE KNEW THIS SIGURD, DID SHE NOT?
WE ALL KNEW HIM, IT'S NOT A LARGE TOWN.
BUT YES, I SUPPOSE SHE MUST HAVE. THOUGH I CANNOT ATTEST TO HOW WELL THEY WERE ACQUAINTED.
CAN YOU CONFIRM FOR THE COURT THAT THIS IS INDEED YOUR LANTERN? IT WAS FOUND NEAR THE BODY OF THE DECEASED.
IT LOOKS LIKE OURS.
YOUR HONOR, SUCH A SMALL FLAME COULD NOT CONSUME A WHOLE CABIN IN SUCH A STORM.
MORE PROOF OF HER DEVILRY AT WORK.

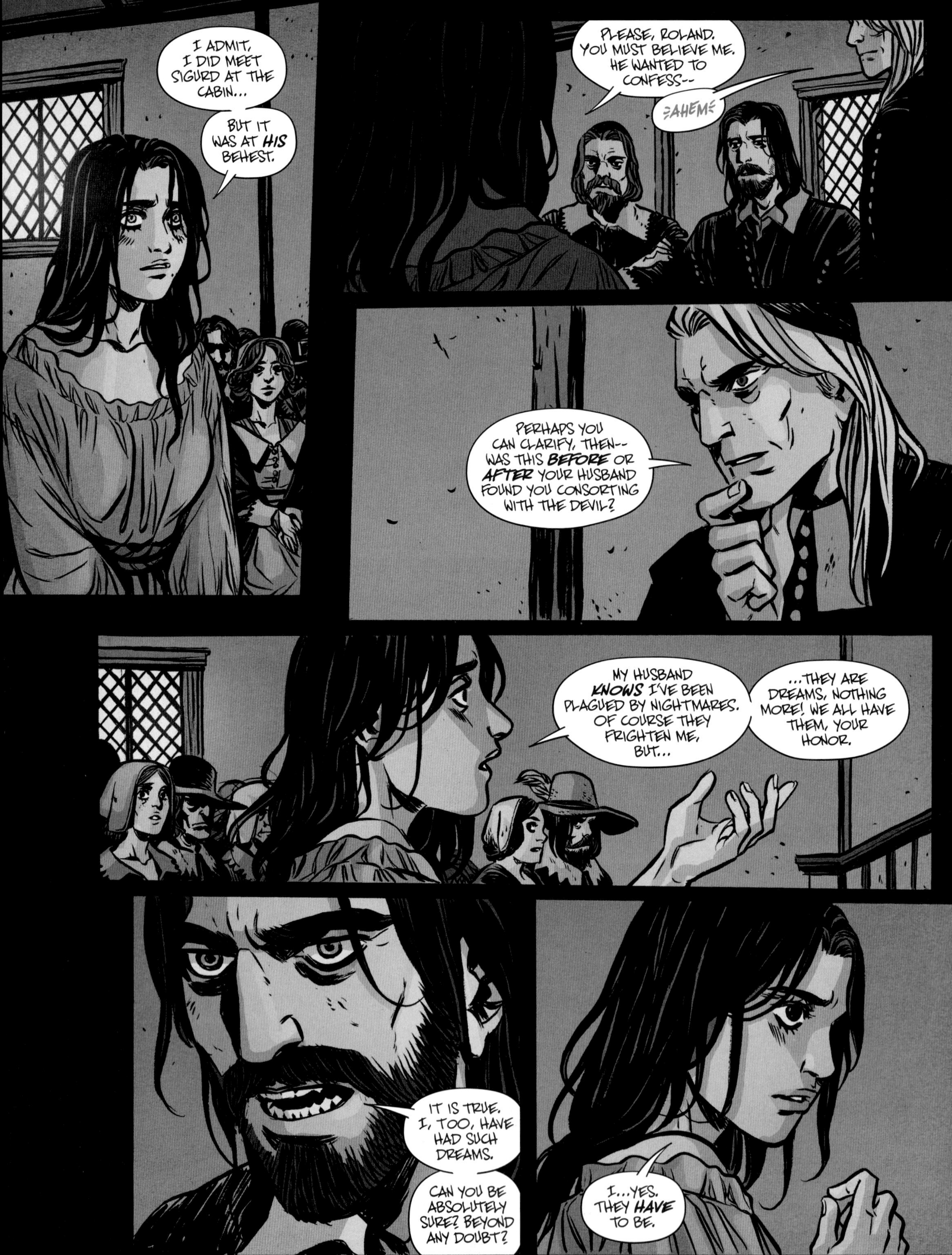
I ADMIT, I DID MEET SIGURD AT THE CABIN...
BUT IT WAS AT HIS BEHEST.
PLEASE, ROLAND. YOU MUST BELIEVE ME. HE WANTED TO CONFESS--
AHEM
PERHAPS YOU CAN CLARIFY, THEN-- WAS THIS BEFORE OR AFTER YOUR HUSBAND FOUND YOU CONSORTING WITH THE DEVIL?
MY HUSBAND KNOWS I'VE BEEN PLAGUED BY NIGHTMARES. OF COURSE THEY FRIGHTEN ME, BUT...
...THEY ARE DREAMS, NOTHING MORE! WE ALL HAVE THEM, YOUR HONOR.
IT IS TRUE. I, TOO, HAVE HAD SUCH DREAMS.
CAN YOU BE ABSOLUTELY SURE? BEYOND ANY DOUBT?
I...YES. THEY HAVE TO BE.

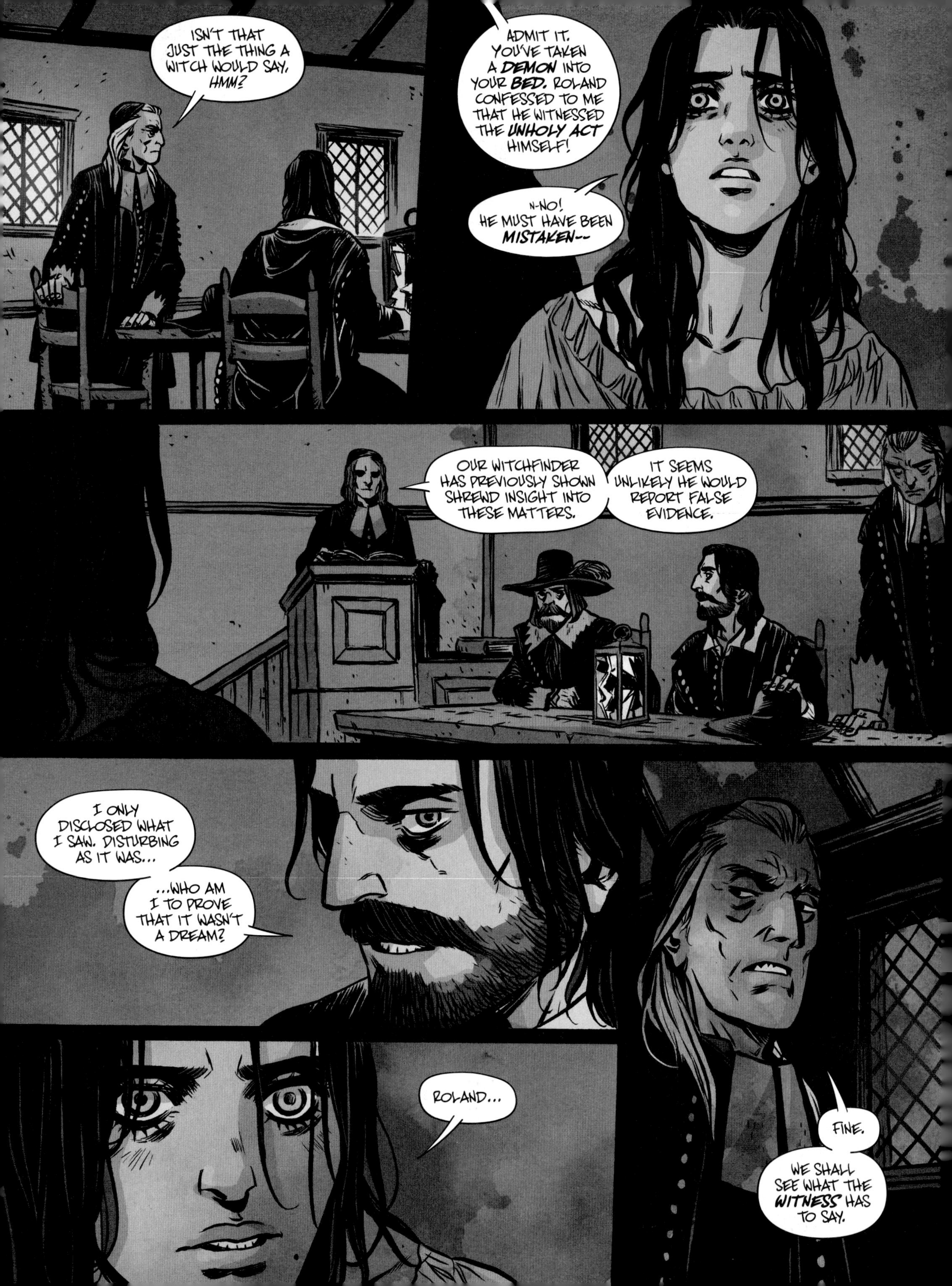

ISN'T THAT JUST THE THING A WITCH WOULD SAY, HMM?
ADMIT IT. YOU'VE TAKEN A **DEMON** INTO YOUR **BED.** ROLAND CONFESSED TO ME THAT HE WITNESSED THE **UNHOLY ACT** HIMSELF!
N-NO! HE MUST HAVE BEEN **MISTAKEN--**
OUR WITCHFINDER HAS PREVIOUSLY SHOWN SHREWD INSIGHT INTO THESE MATTERS.
IT SEEMS UNLIKELY HE WOULD REPORT FALSE EVIDENCE.
I ONLY DISCLOSED WHAT I SAW. DISTURBING AS IT WAS...
...WHO AM I TO PROVE THAT IT WASN'T A DREAM?
ROLAND...
FINE.
WE SHALL SEE WHAT THE **WITNESS** HAS TO SAY.

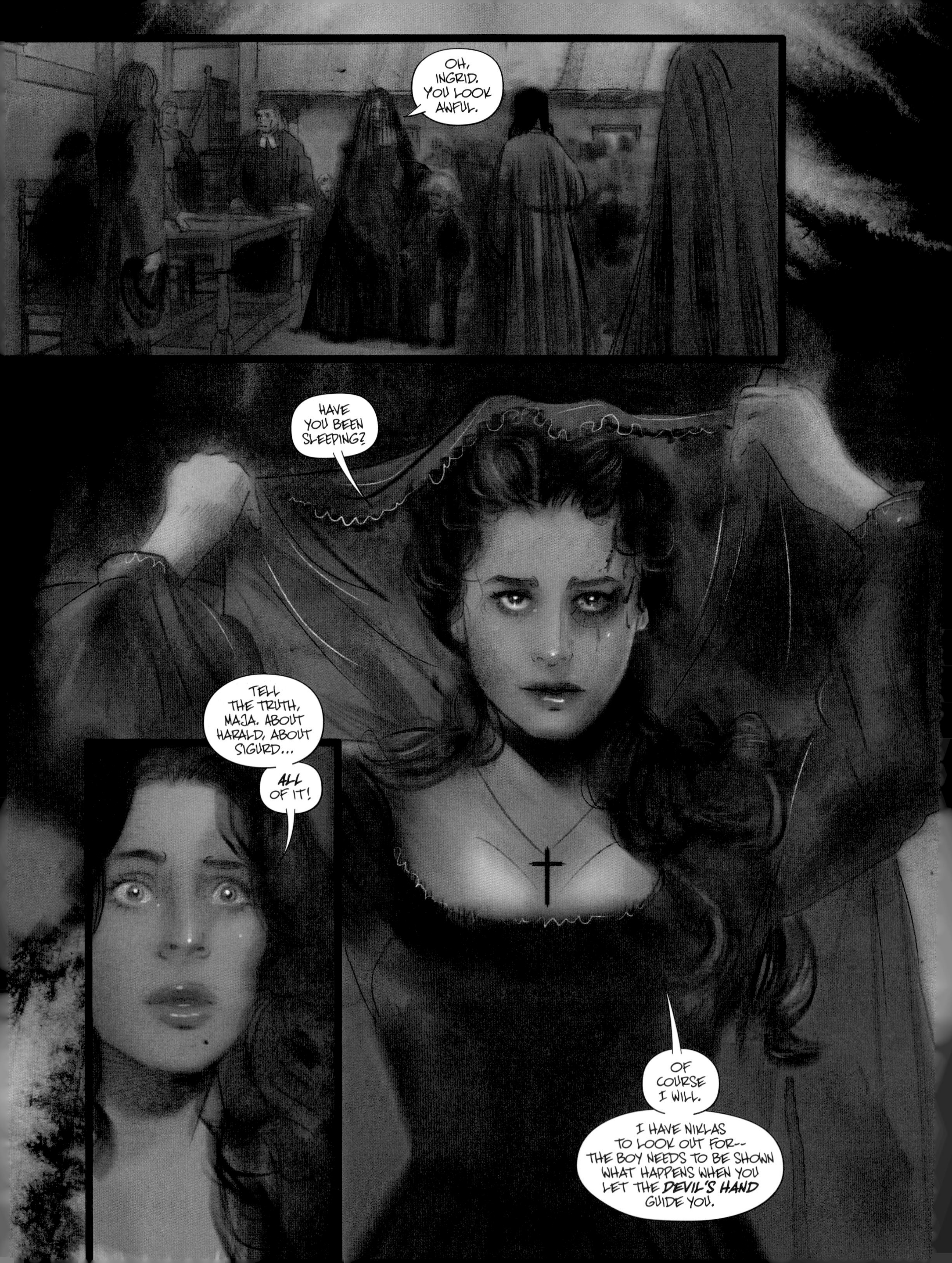
OH, INGRID. YOU LOOK AWFUL.
HAVE YOU BEEN SLEEPING?
TELL THE TRUTH, MAJA. ABOUT HARALD, ABOUT SIGURD...
ALL OF IT!
OF COURSE I WILL.
I HAVE NIKLAS TO LOOK OUT FOR-- THE BOY NEEDS TO BE SHOWN WHAT HAPPENS WHEN YOU LET THE DEVIL'S HAND GUIDE YOU.

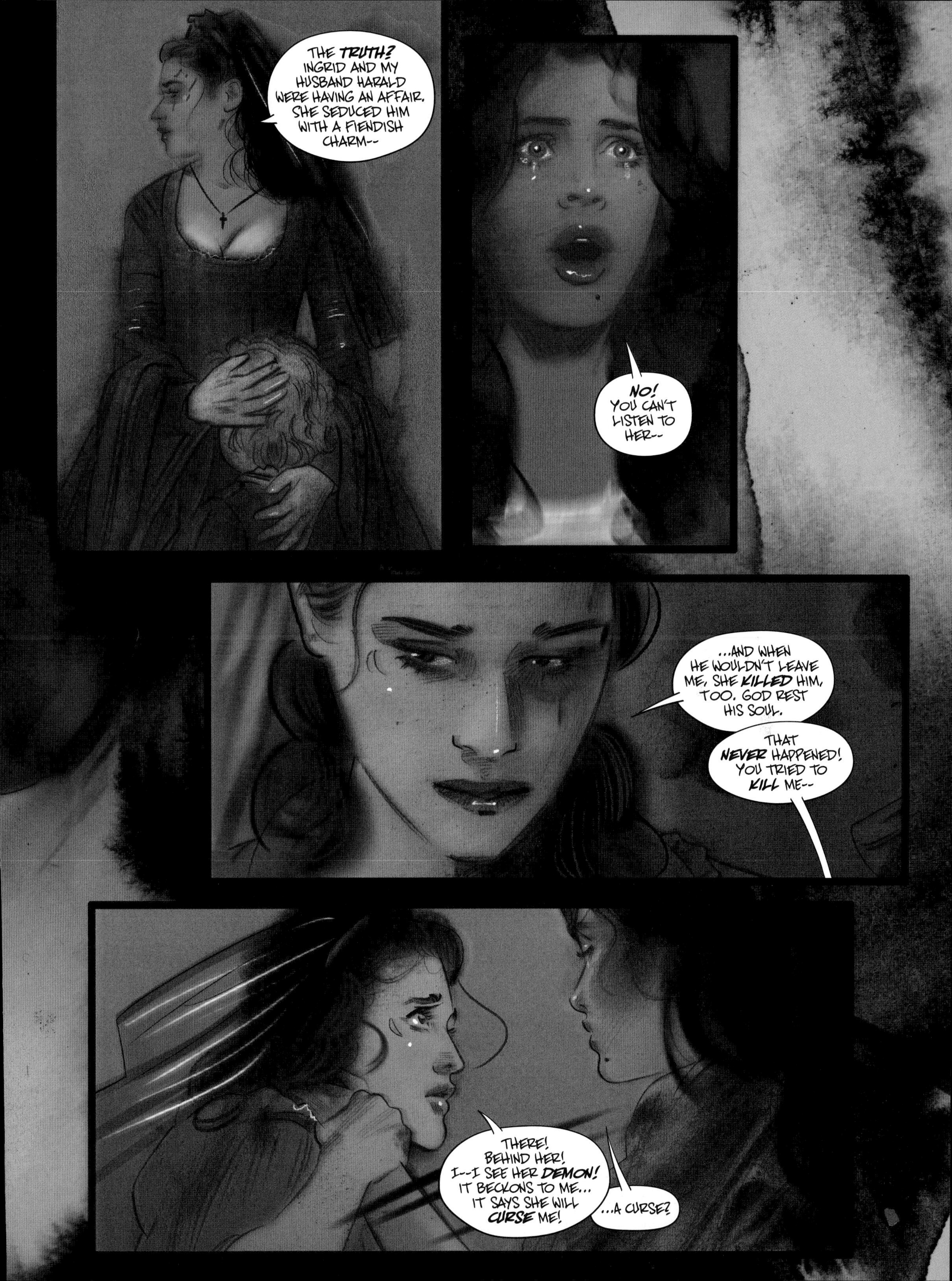
THE TRUTH? INGRID AND MY HUSBAND HARALD WERE HAVING AN AFFAIR. SHE SEDUCED HIM WITH A FIENDISH CHARM--
NO! YOU CAN'T LISTEN TO HER--
...AND WHEN HE WOULDN'T LEAVE ME, SHE KILLED HIM, TOO. GOD REST HIS SOUL.
THAT NEVER HAPPENED! YOU TRIED TO KILL ME--
THERE! BEHIND HER! I--I SEE HER DEMON! IT BECKONS TO ME... IT SAYS SHE WILL CURSE ME!
...A CURSE?

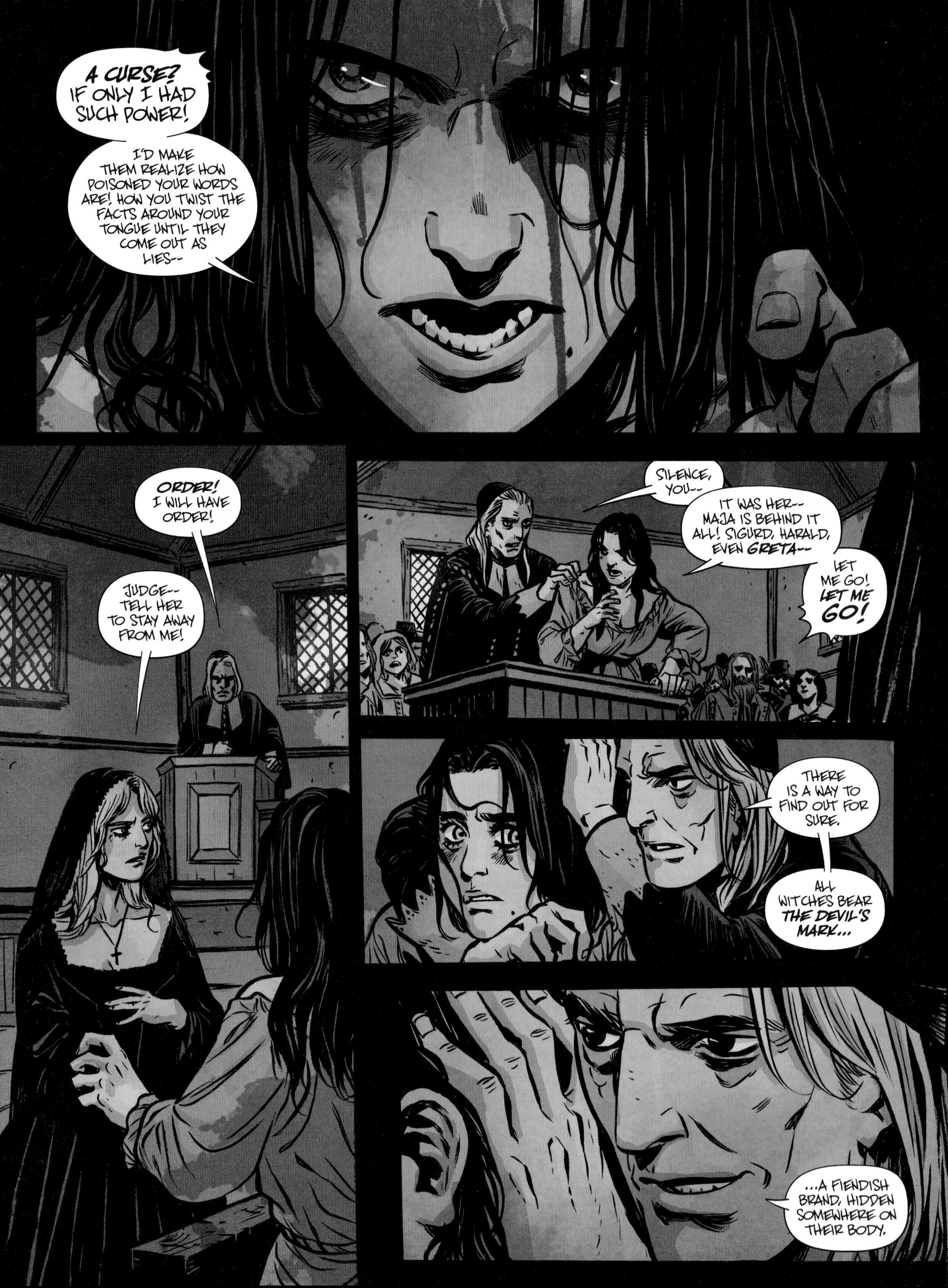
A CURSE? IF ONLY I HAD SUCH POWER!
I'D MAKE THEM REALIZE HOW POISONED YOUR WORDS ARE! HOW YOU TWIST THE FACTS AROUND YOUR TONGUE UNTIL THEY COME OUT AS LIES--
ORDER! I WILL HAVE ORDER!
JUDGE-- TELL HER TO STAY AWAY FROM ME!
SILENCE, YOU--
IT WAS HER-- MAJA IS BEHIND IT ALL! SIGURD, HARALD, EVEN GRETA--
LET ME GO! LET ME GO!
THERE IS A WAY TO FIND OUT FOR SURE.
ALL WITCHES BEAR THE DEVIL'S MARK...
...A FIENDISH BRAND, HIDDEN SOMEWHERE ON THEIR BODY.

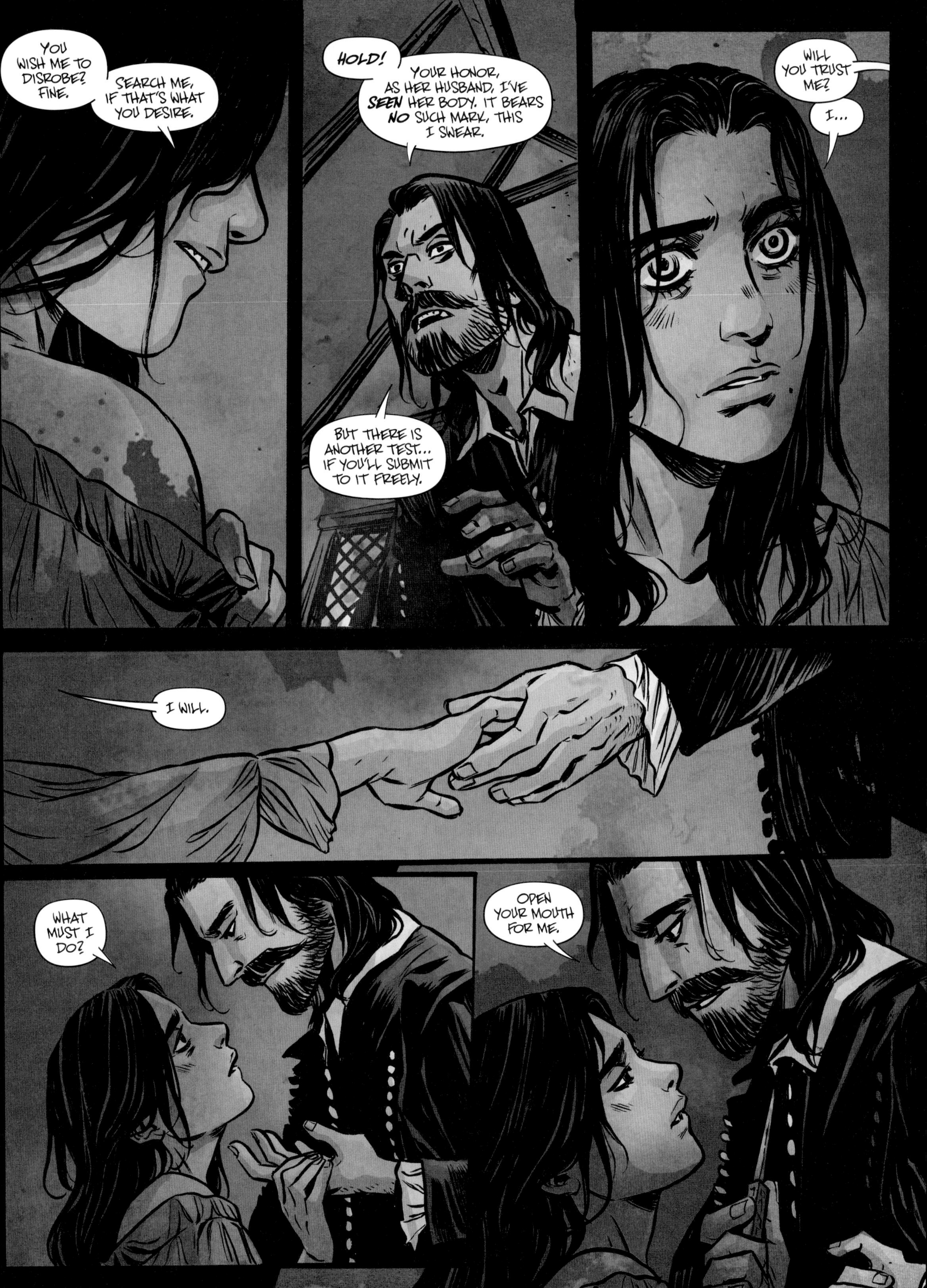
YOU WISH ME TO DISROBE? FINE.
SEARCH ME, IF THAT'S WHAT YOU DESIRE.
HOLD!
YOUR HONOR, AS HER HUSBAND, I'VE SEEN HER BODY. IT BEARS NO SUCH MARK, THIS I SWEAR.
BUT THERE IS ANOTHER TEST... IF YOU'LL SUBMIT TO IT FREELY.
WILL YOU TRUST ME?
I...
I WILL.
WHAT MUST I DO?
OPEN YOUR MOUTH FOR ME.

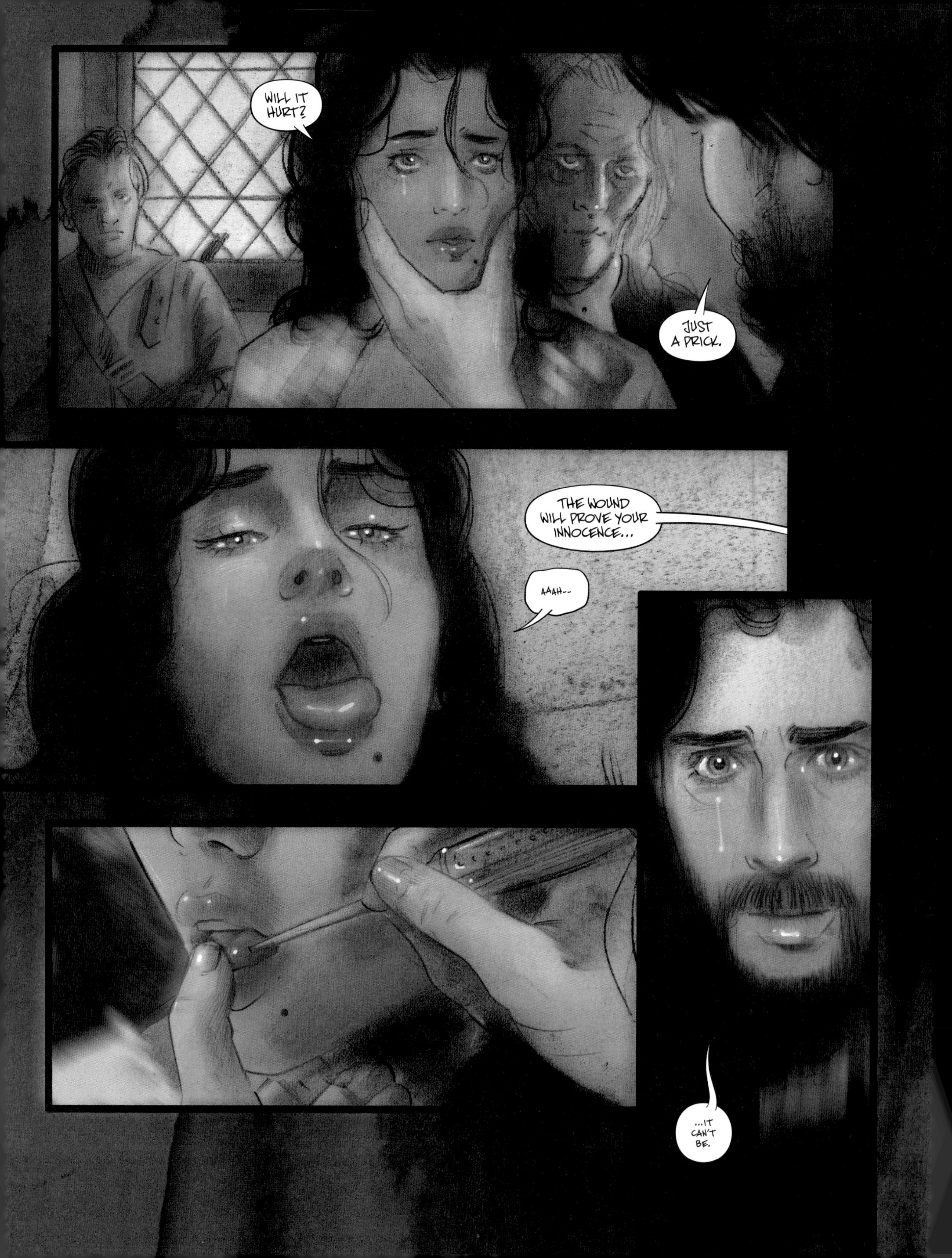
WILL IT HURT?
JUST A PRICK.
THE WOUND WILL PROVE YOUR INNOCENCE...
AAAH--
...IT CAN'T BE.

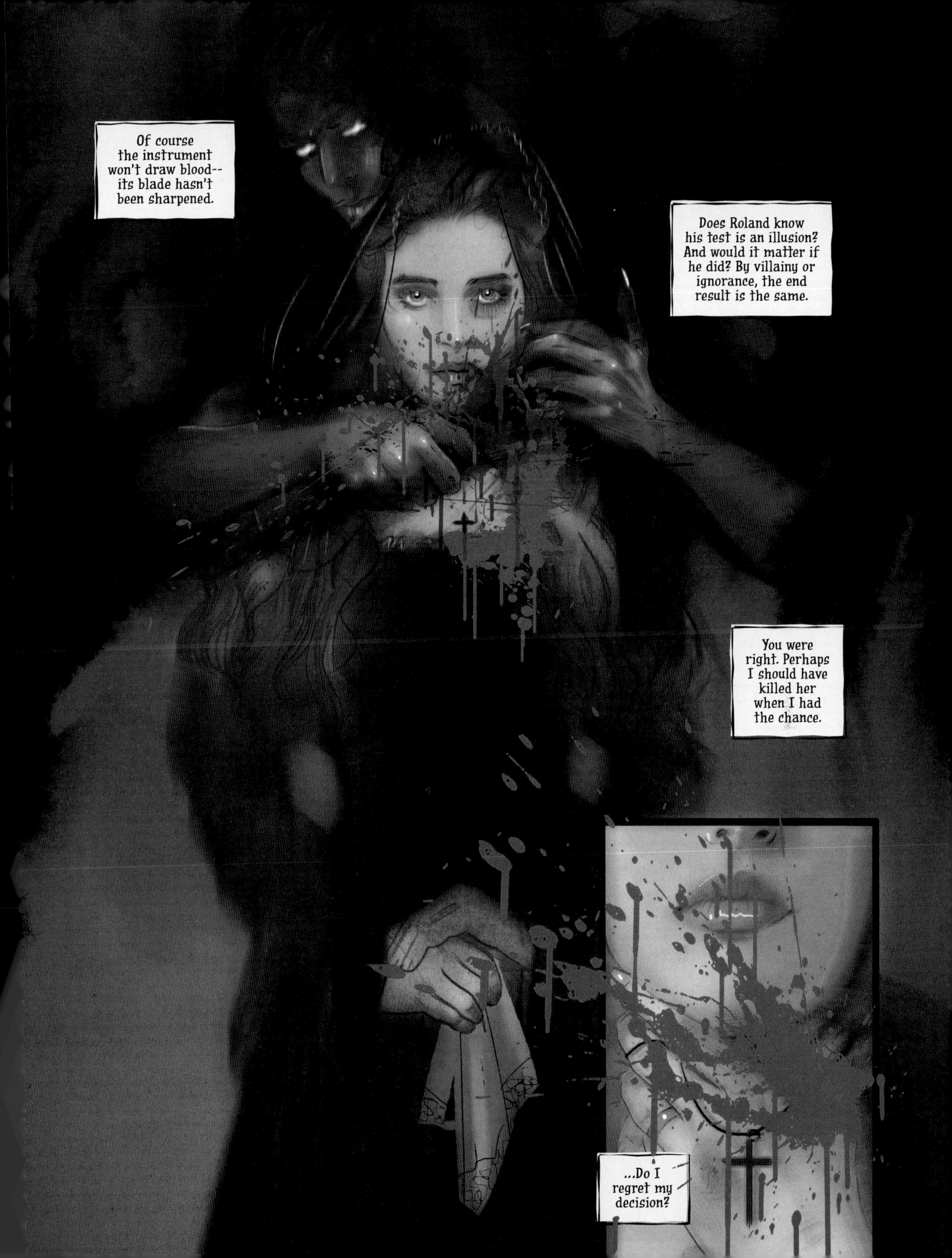
Of course the instrument won't draw blood-- its blade hasn't been sharpened.
Does Roland know his test is an illusion? And would it matter if he did? By villainy or ignorance, the end result is the same.
You were right. Perhaps I should have killed her when I had the chance.
...Do I regret my decision?

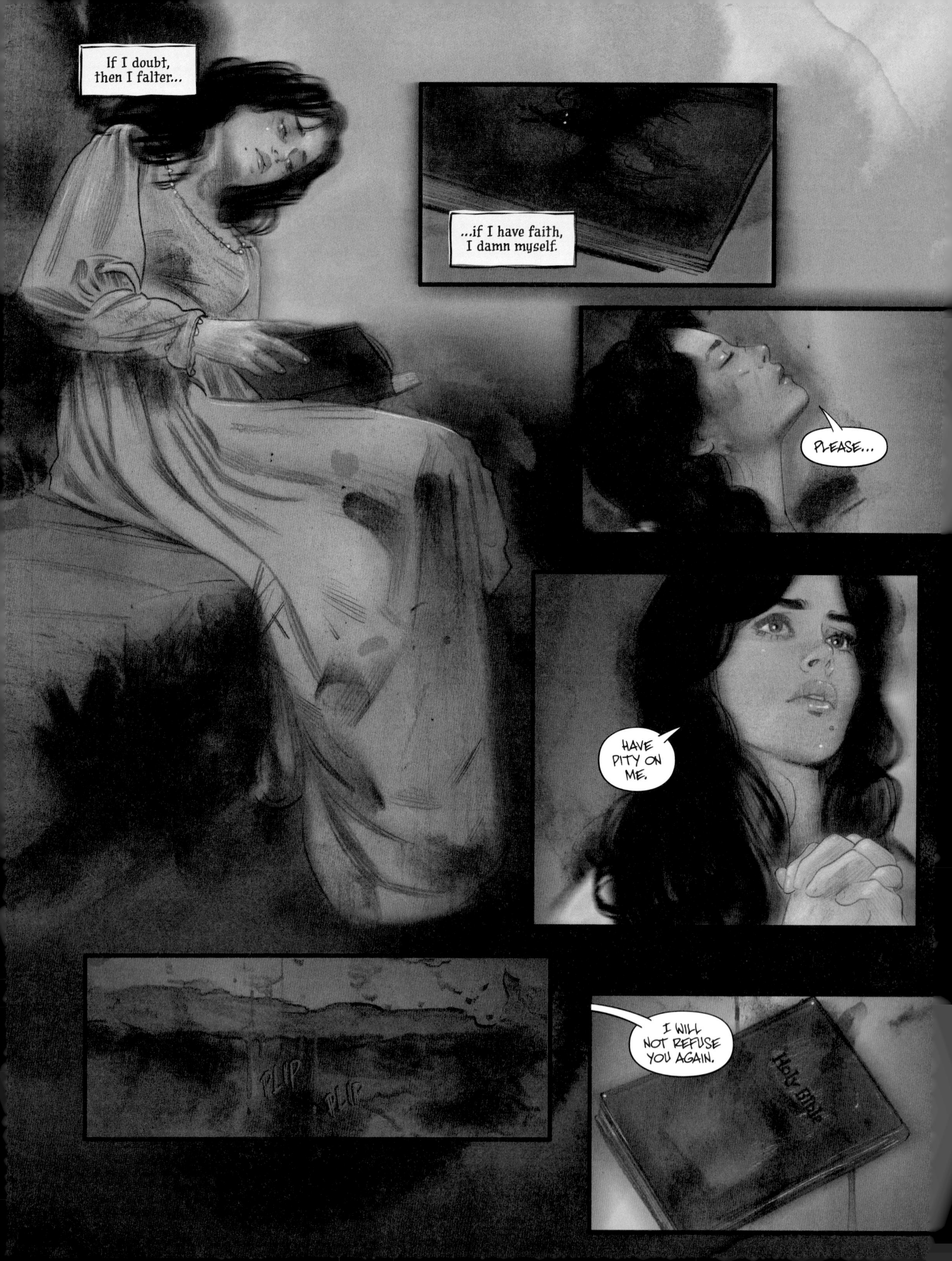
If I doubt, then I falter...
...if I have faith, I damn myself.
PLEASE...
HAVE PITY ON ME.
PLIP
PLIP
I WILL NOT REFUSE YOU AGAIN.
Holy Bible

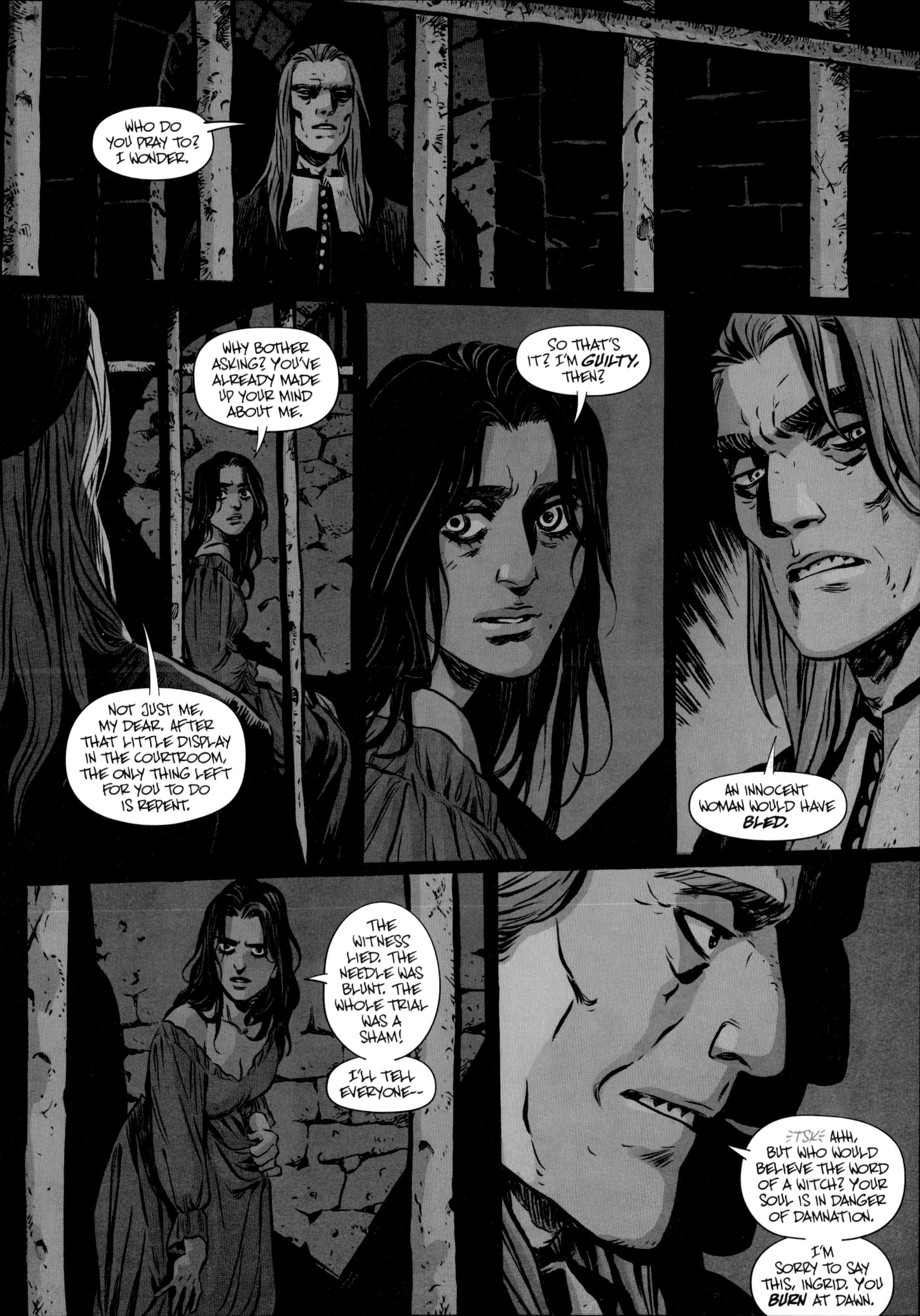
WHO DO YOU PRAY TO? I WONDER.
WHY BOTHER ASKING? YOU'VE ALREADY MADE UP YOUR MIND ABOUT ME.
NOT JUST ME, MY DEAR. AFTER THAT LITTLE DISPLAY IN THE COURTROOM, THE ONLY THING LEFT FOR YOU TO DO IS REPENT.
SO THAT'S IT? I'M GUILTY, THEN?
AN INNOCENT WOMAN WOULD HAVE BLED.
THE WITNESS LIED. THE NEEDLE WAS BLUNT. THE WHOLE TRIAL WAS A SHAM!
I'LL TELL EVERYONE--
TSK AHH, BUT WHO WOULD BELIEVE THE WORD OF A WITCH? YOUR SOUL IS IN DANGER OF DAMNATION.
I'M SORRY TO SAY THIS, INGRID. YOU BURN AT DAWN.

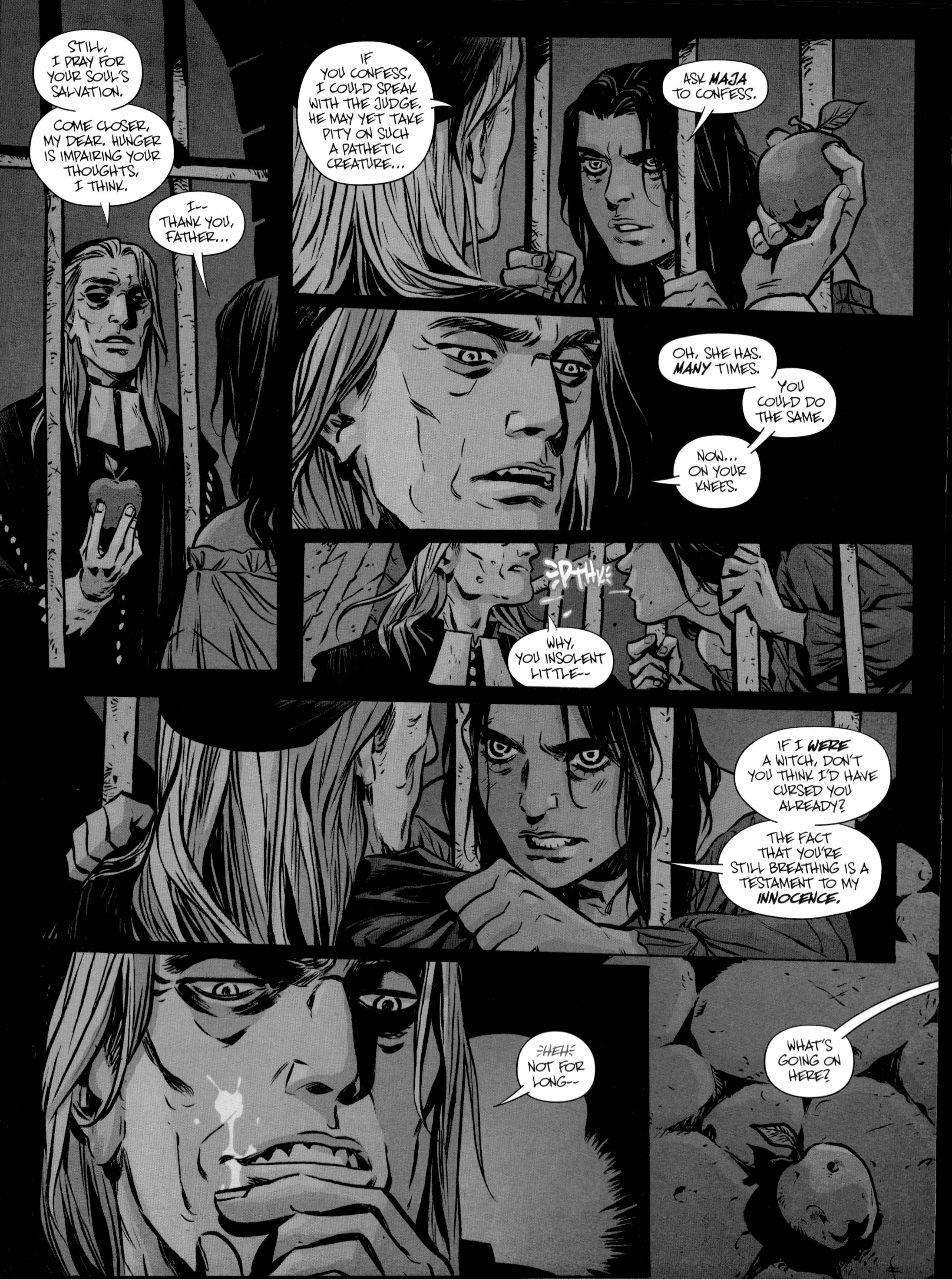

STILL, I PRAY FOR YOUR SOUL'S SALVATION.
COME CLOSER, MY DEAR. HUNGER IS IMPAIRING YOUR THOUGHTS, I THINK.
I-- THANK YOU, FATHER...
IF YOU CONFESS, I COULD SPEAK WITH THE JUDGE. HE MAY YET TAKE PITY ON SUCH A PATHETIC CREATURE...
ASK MAJA TO CONFESS.
OH, SHE HAS. MANY TIMES.
YOU COULD DO THE SAME.
NOW... ON YOUR KNEES.
PTHK
WHY, YOU INSOLENT LITTLE--
IF I WERE A WITCH, DON'T YOU THINK I'D HAVE CURSED YOU ALREADY?
THE FACT THAT YOU'RE STILL BREATHING IS A TESTAMENT TO MY INNOCENCE.
HEH NOT FOR LONG--
WHAT'S GOING ON HERE?

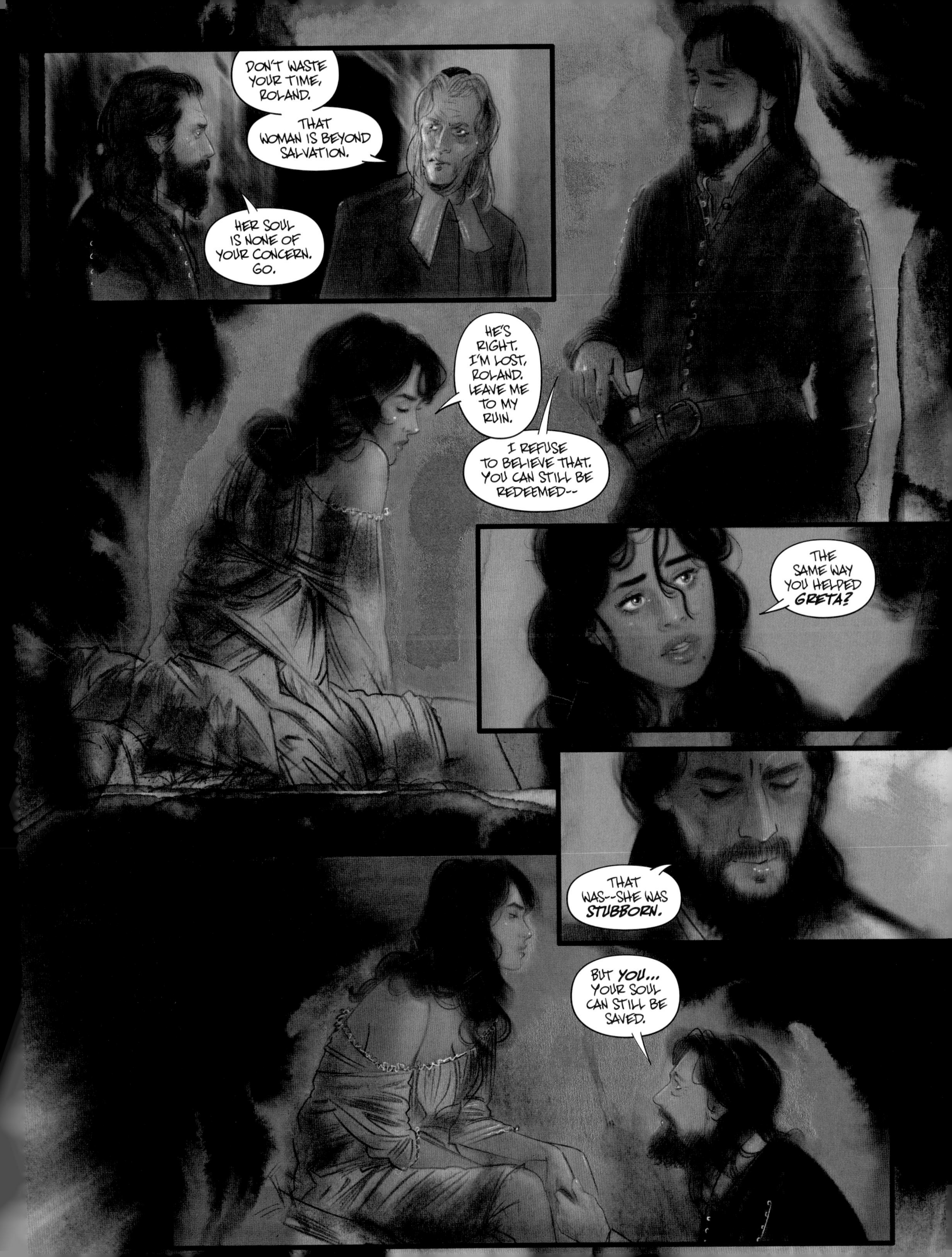
DON'T WASTE YOUR TIME, ROLAND.
THAT WOMAN IS BEYOND SALVATION.
HER SOUL IS NONE OF YOUR CONCERN. GO.
HE'S RIGHT. I'M LOST, ROLAND. LEAVE ME TO MY RUIN.
I REFUSE TO BELIEVE THAT. YOU CAN STILL BE REDEEMED--
THE SAME WAY YOU HELPED GRETA?
THAT WAS--SHE WAS STUBBORN.
BUT YOU... YOUR SOUL CAN STILL BE SAVED.

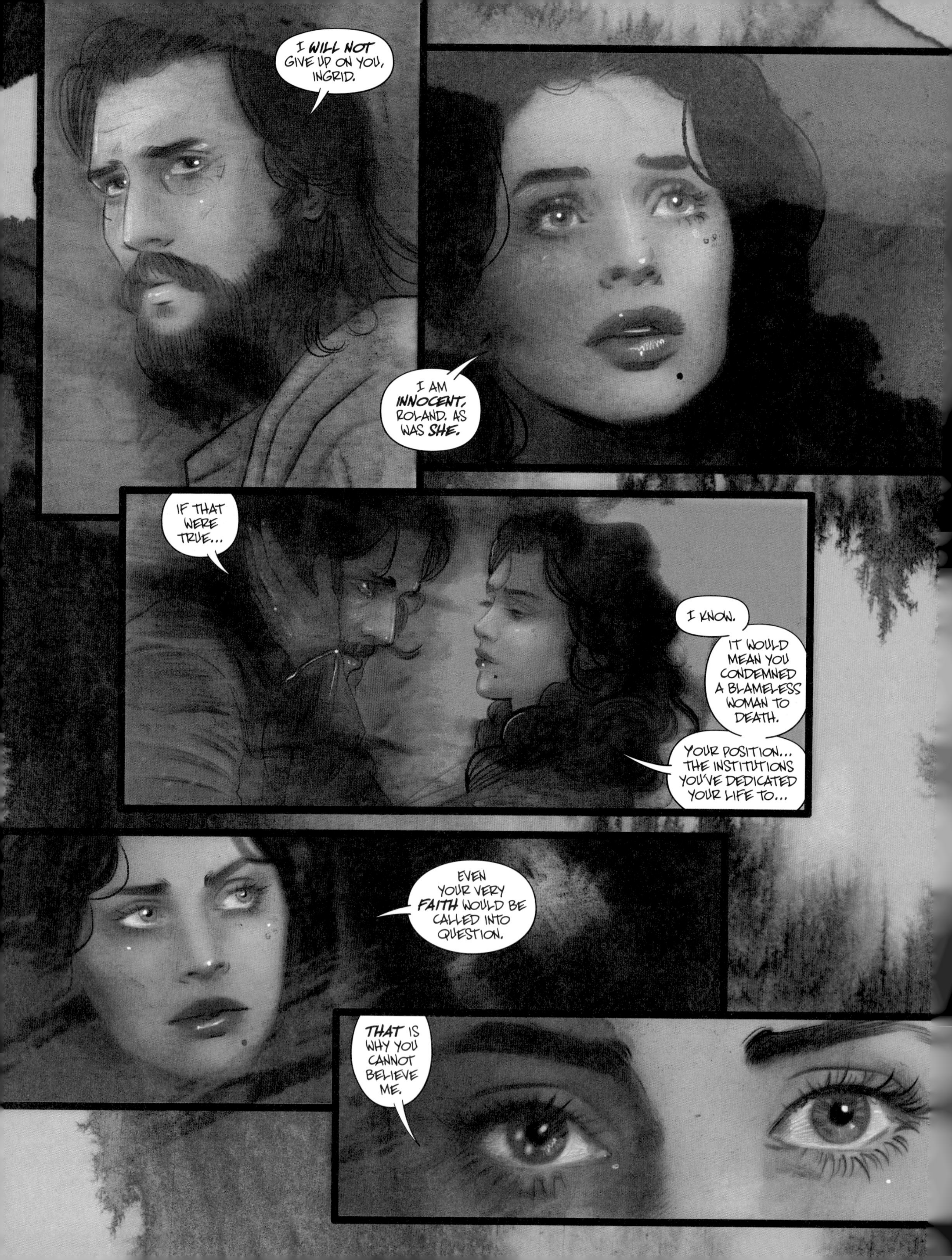
I WILL NOT GIVE UP ON YOU, INGRID.
I AM INNOCENT, ROLAND. AS WAS SHE.
IF THAT WERE TRUE...
I KNOW.
IT WOULD MEAN YOU CONDEMNED A BLAMELESS WOMAN TO DEATH.
YOUR POSITION... THE INSTITUTIONS YOU'VE DEDICATED YOUR LIFE TO...
EVEN YOUR VERY FAITH WOULD BE CALLED INTO QUESTION.
THAT IS WHY YOU CANNOT BELIEVE ME.

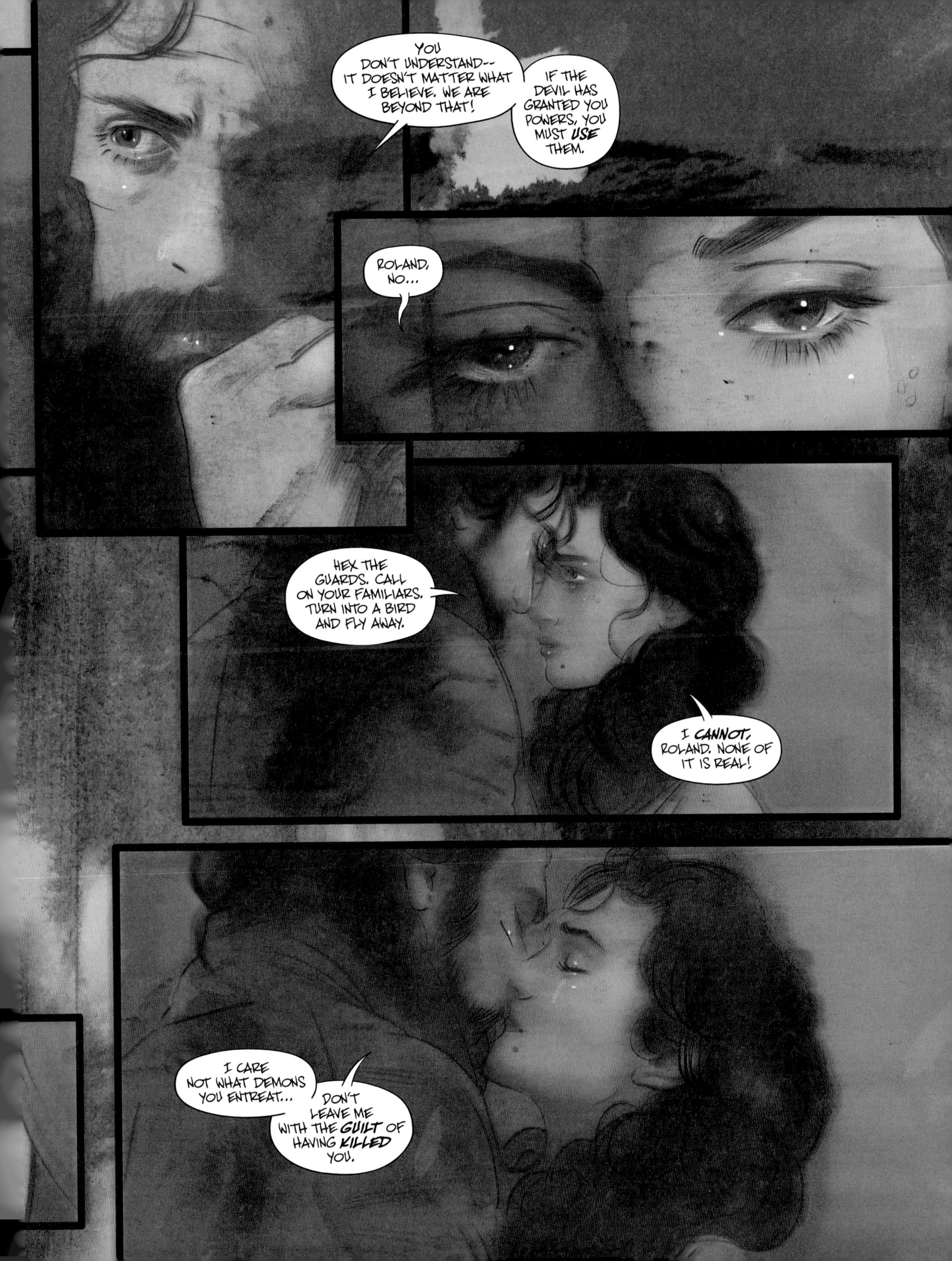
YOU DON'T UNDERSTAND-- IT DOESN'T MATTER WHAT I BELIEVE. WE ARE BEYOND THAT!
IF THE DEVIL HAS GRANTED YOU POWERS, YOU MUST USE THEM.
ROLAND, NO...
HEX THE GUARDS. CALL ON YOUR FAMILIARS. TURN INTO A BIRD AND FLY AWAY.
I CANNOT, ROLAND. NONE OF IT IS REAL!
I CARE NOT WHAT DEMONS YOU ENTREAT...
DON'T LEAVE ME WITH THE GUILT OF HAVING KILLED YOU.

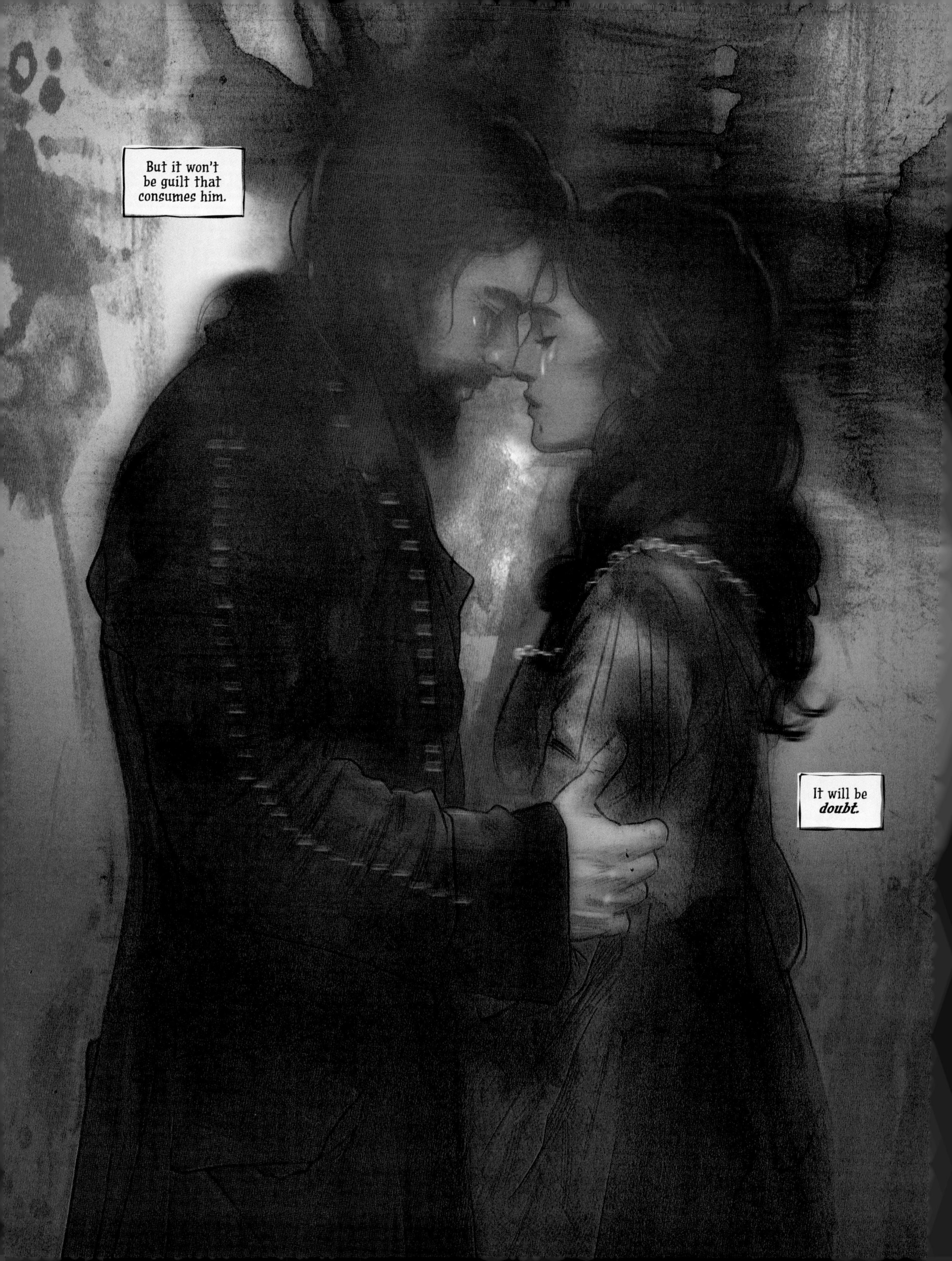
But it won't be guilt that consumes him.
It will be *doubt.*

CHAPTER VII.
AWAKE IN SWEET UNREST

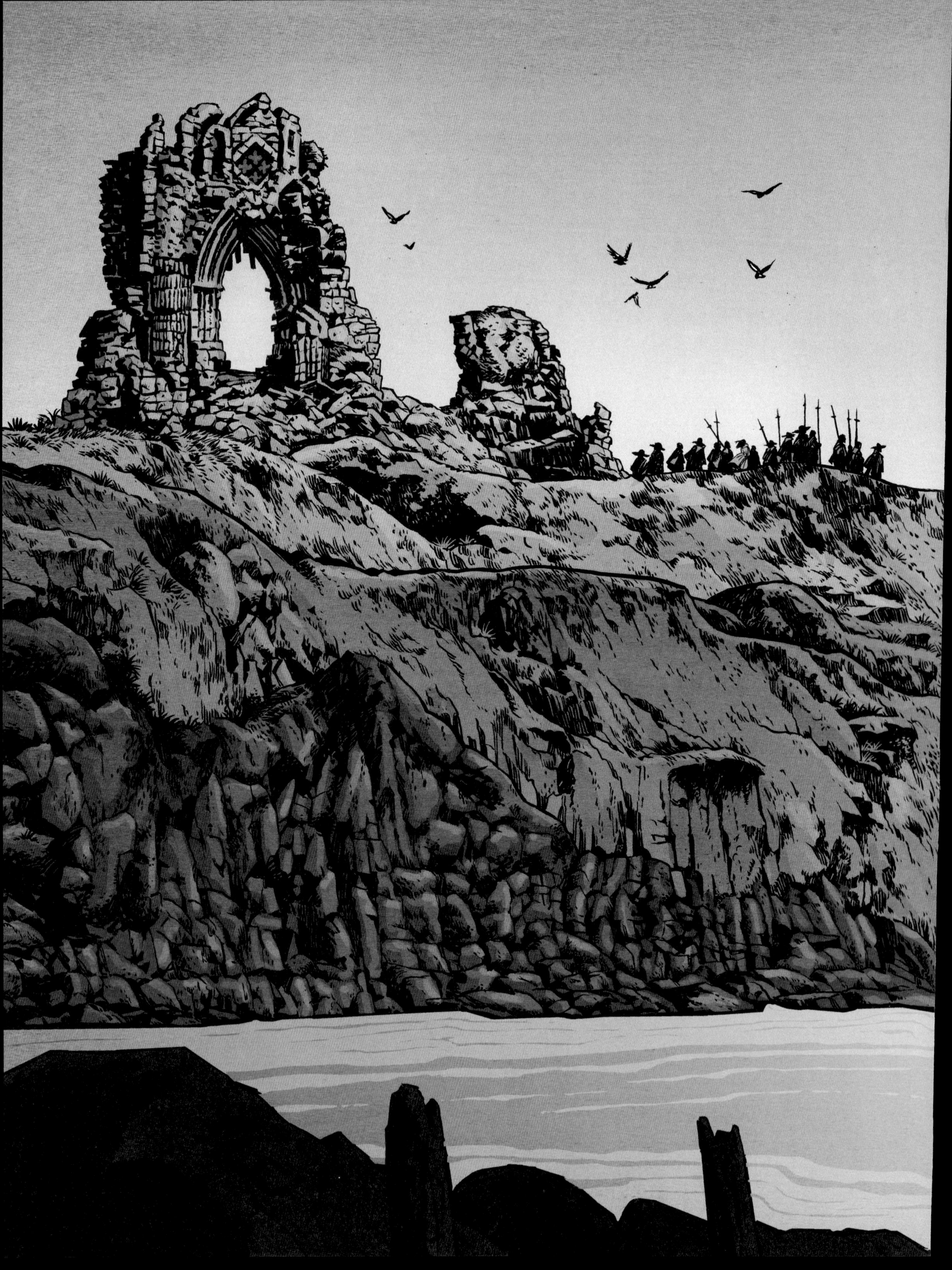

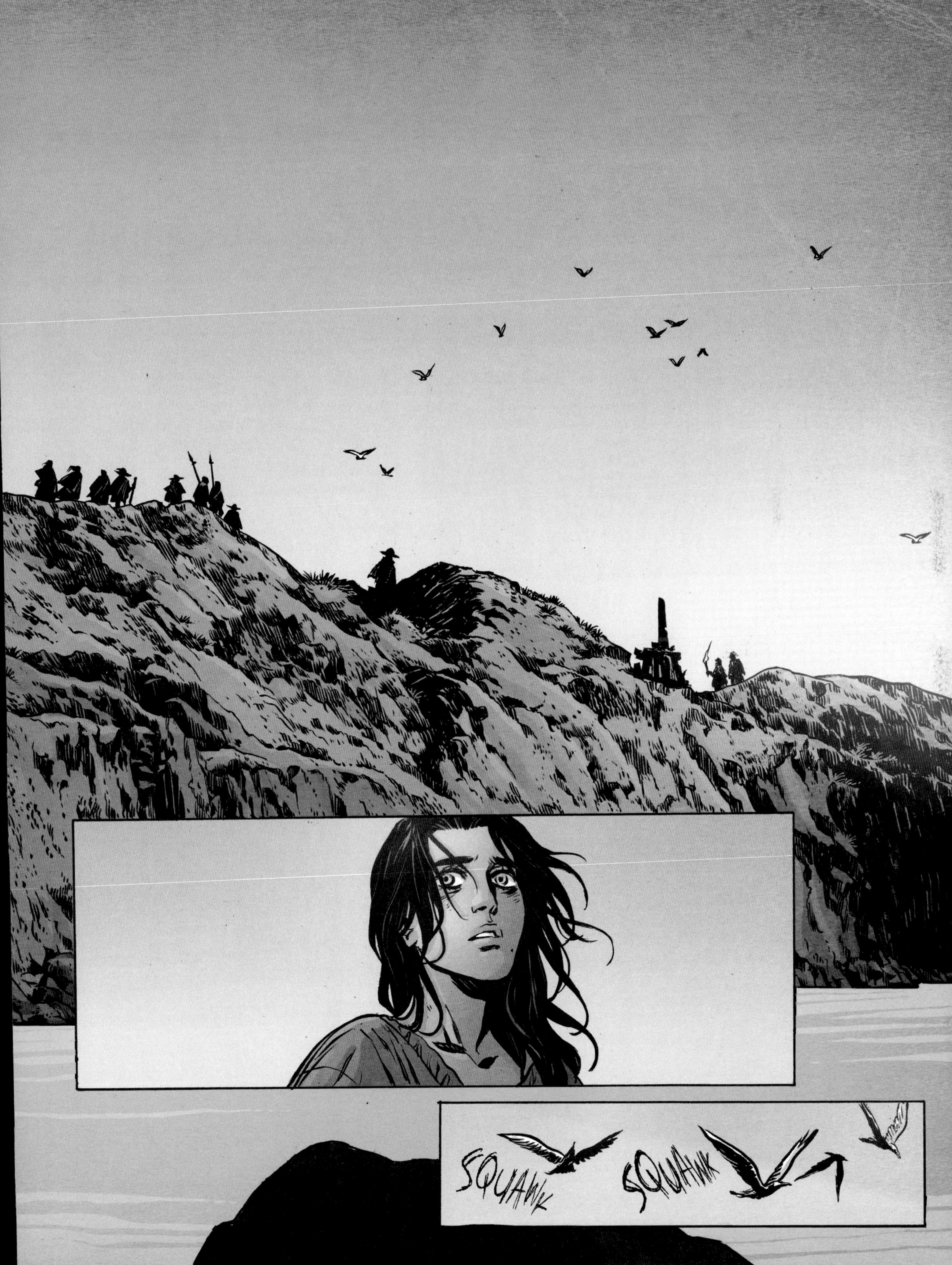
SQUAWK
SQUAWK

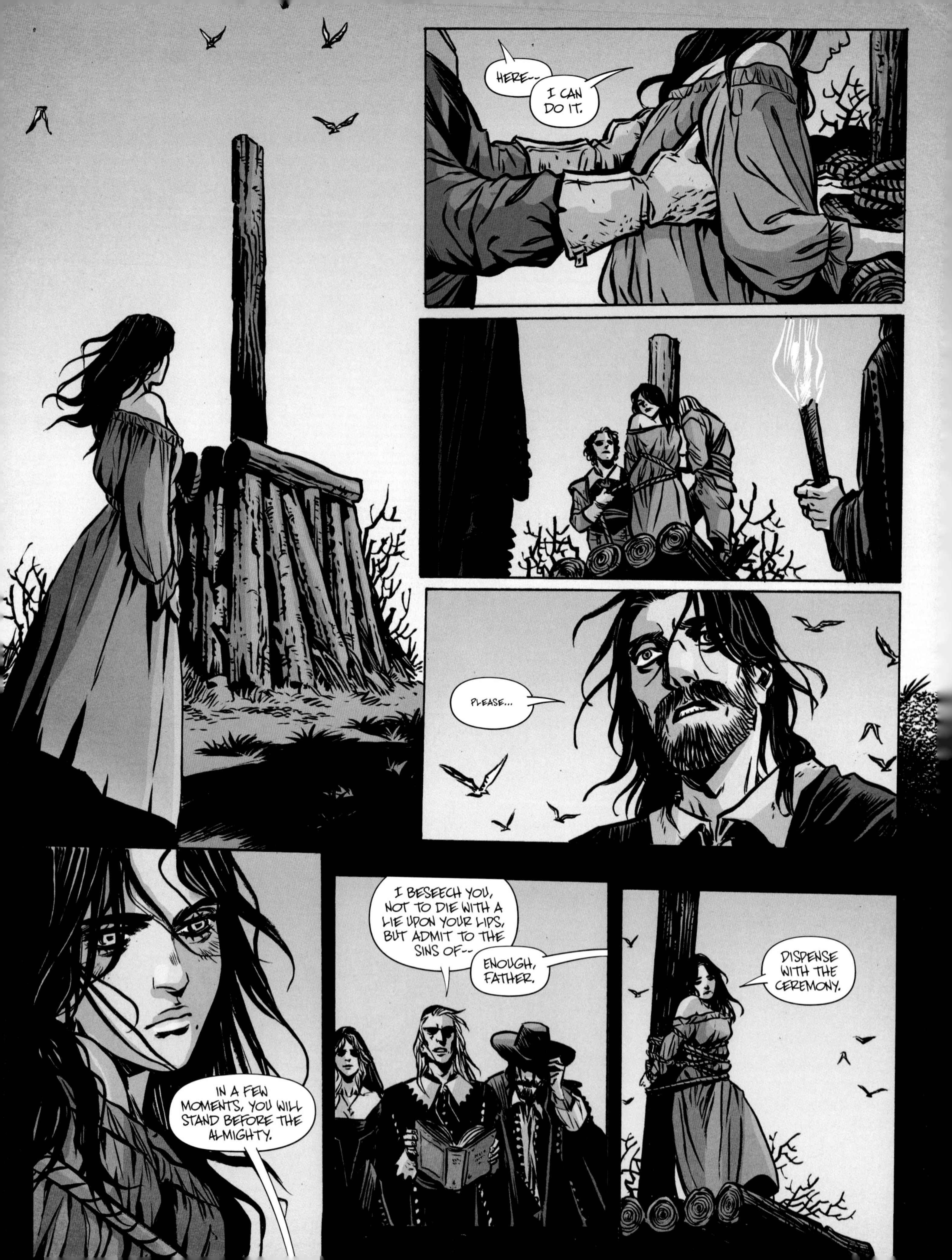
HERE--
I CAN DO IT.
PLEASE...
IN A FEW MOMENTS, YOU WILL STAND BEFORE THE ALMIGHTY.
I BESEECH YOU, NOT TO DIE WITH A LIE UPON YOUR LIPS, BUT ADMIT TO THE SINS OF--
ENOUGH, FATHER.
DISPENSE WITH THE CEREMONY.

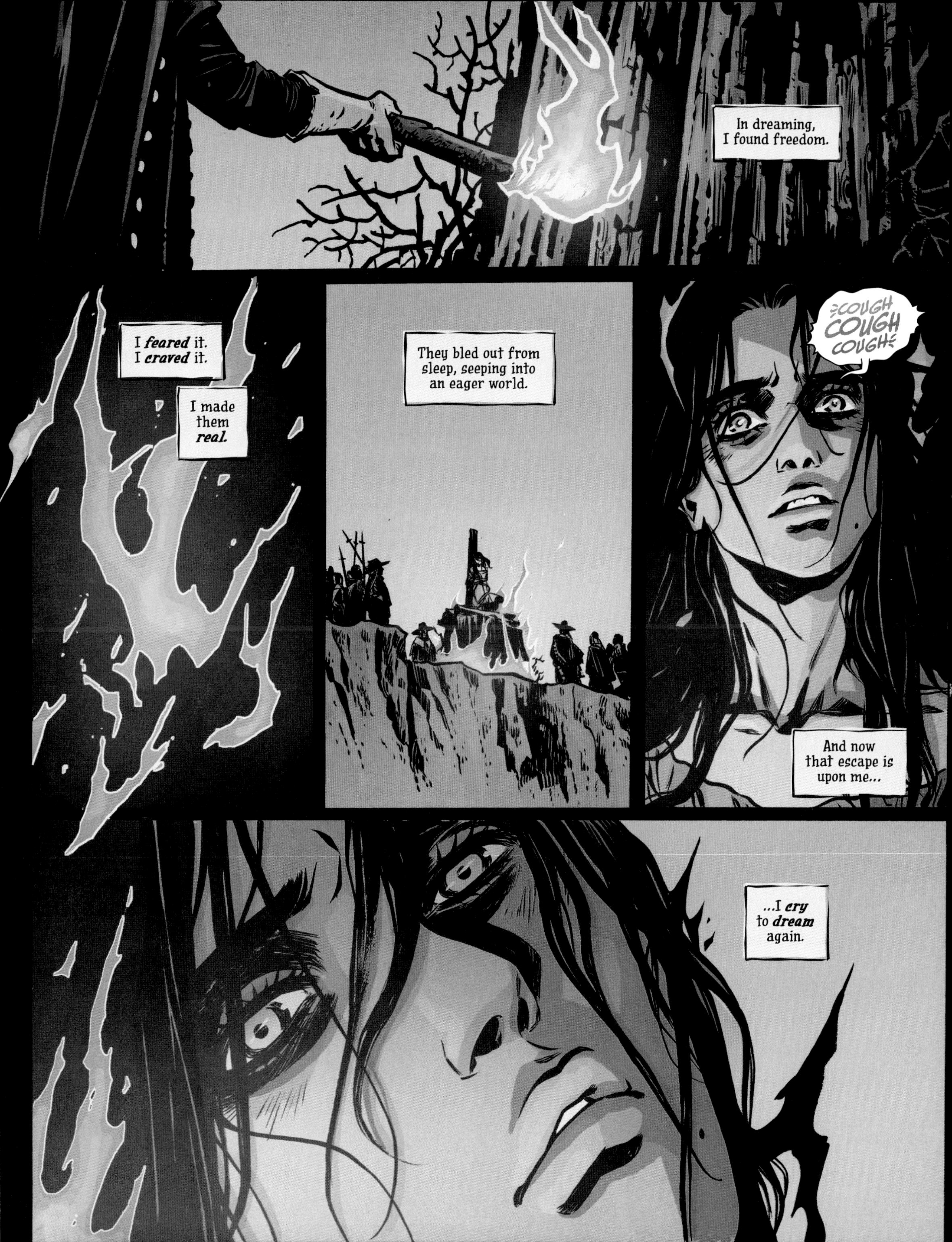

In dreaming, I found freedom.
I **feared** it. I **craved** it.
I made them **real.**
They bled out from sleep, seeping into an eager world.
COUGH COUGH COUGH
And now that escape is upon me...
...I **cry** to **dream** again.

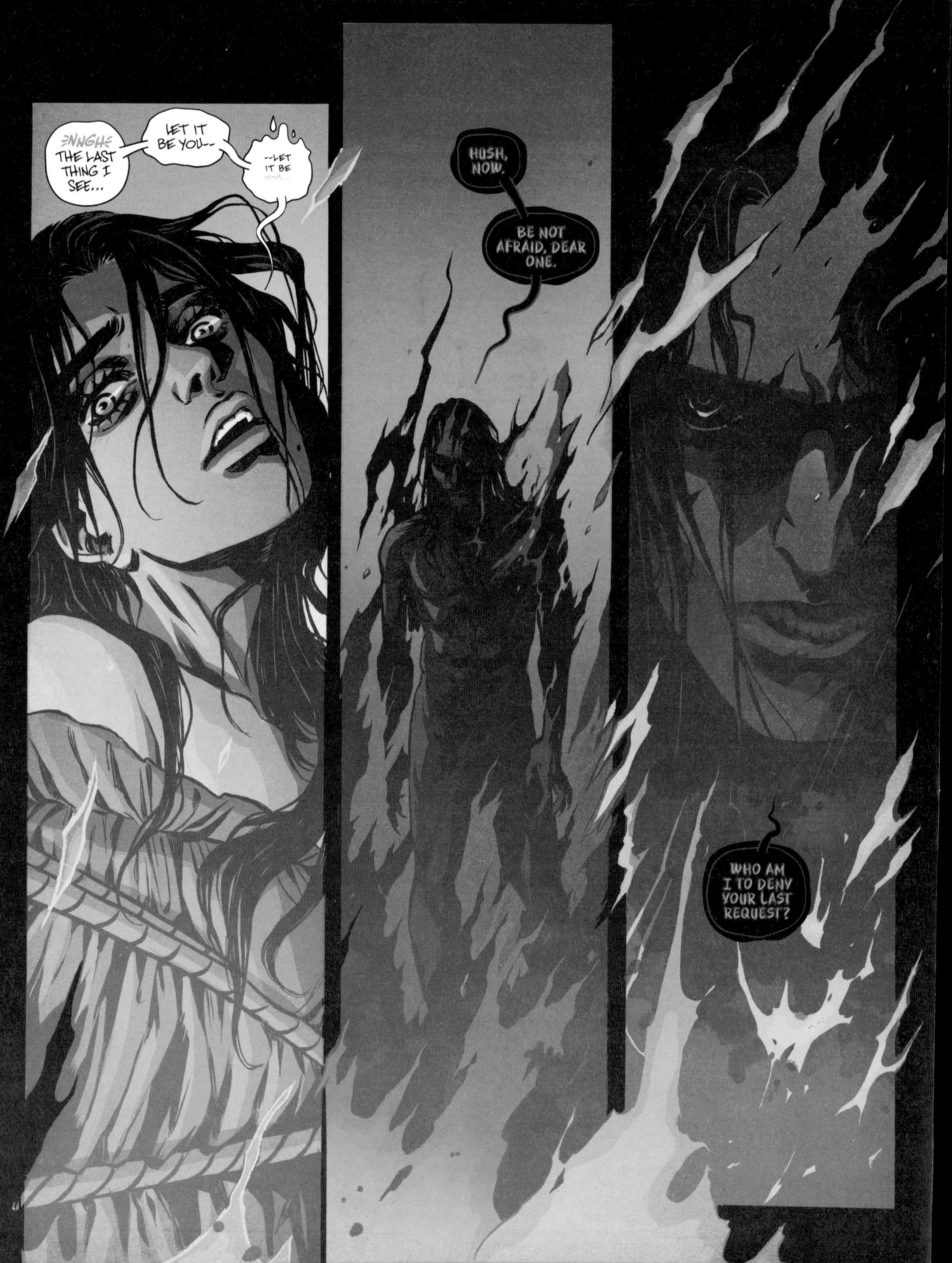
NNGH THE LAST THING I SEE...
LET IT BE YOU--
--LET IT BE YOU!--
HUSH, NOW.
BE NOT AFRAID, DEAR ONE.
WHO AM I TO DENY YOUR LAST REQUEST?

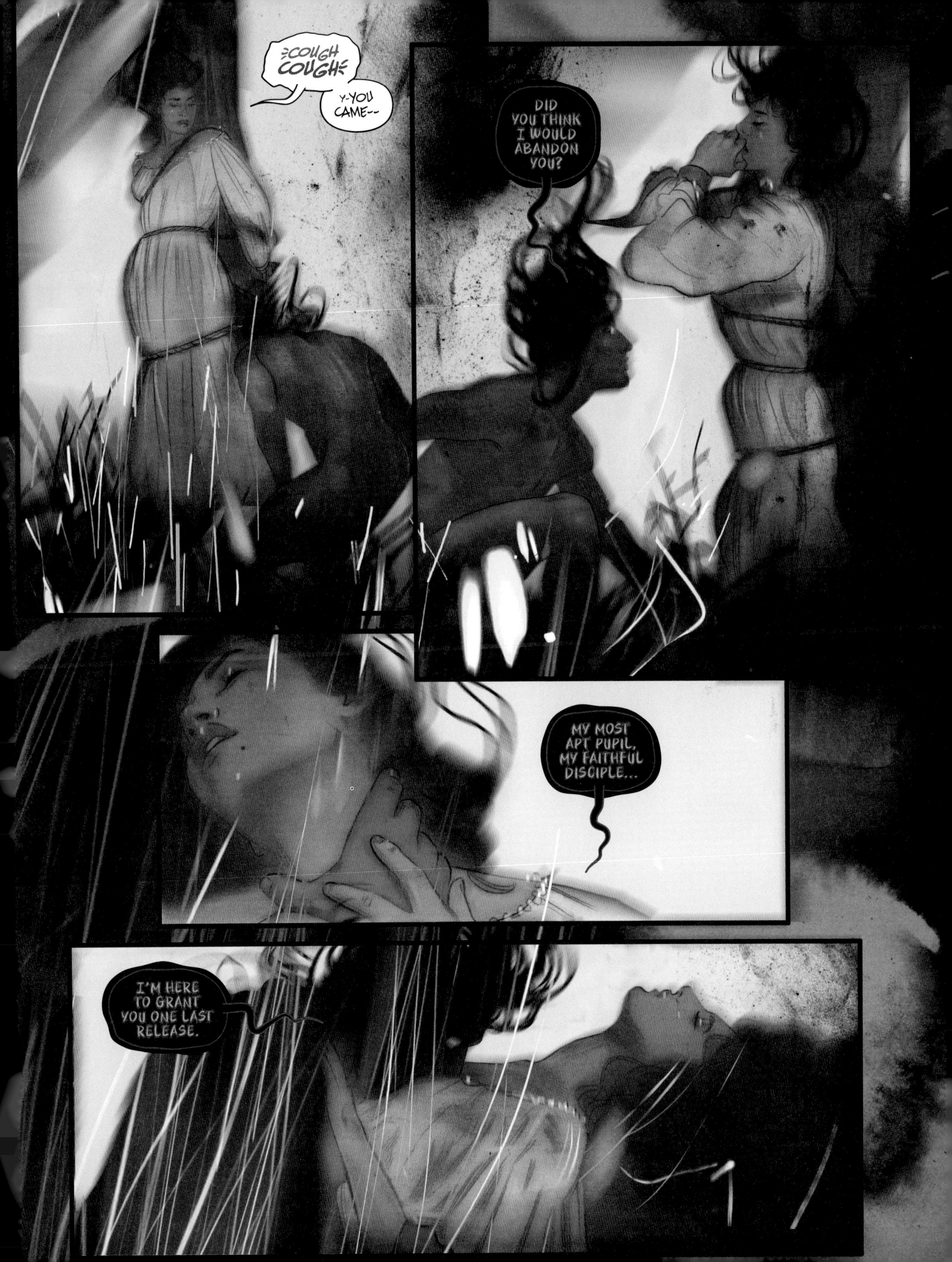
COUGH COUGH
Y-YOU CAME--
DID YOU THINK I WOULD ABANDON YOU?
MY MOST APT PUPIL, MY FAITHFUL DISCIPLE...
I'M HERE TO GRANT YOU ONE LAST RELEASE.

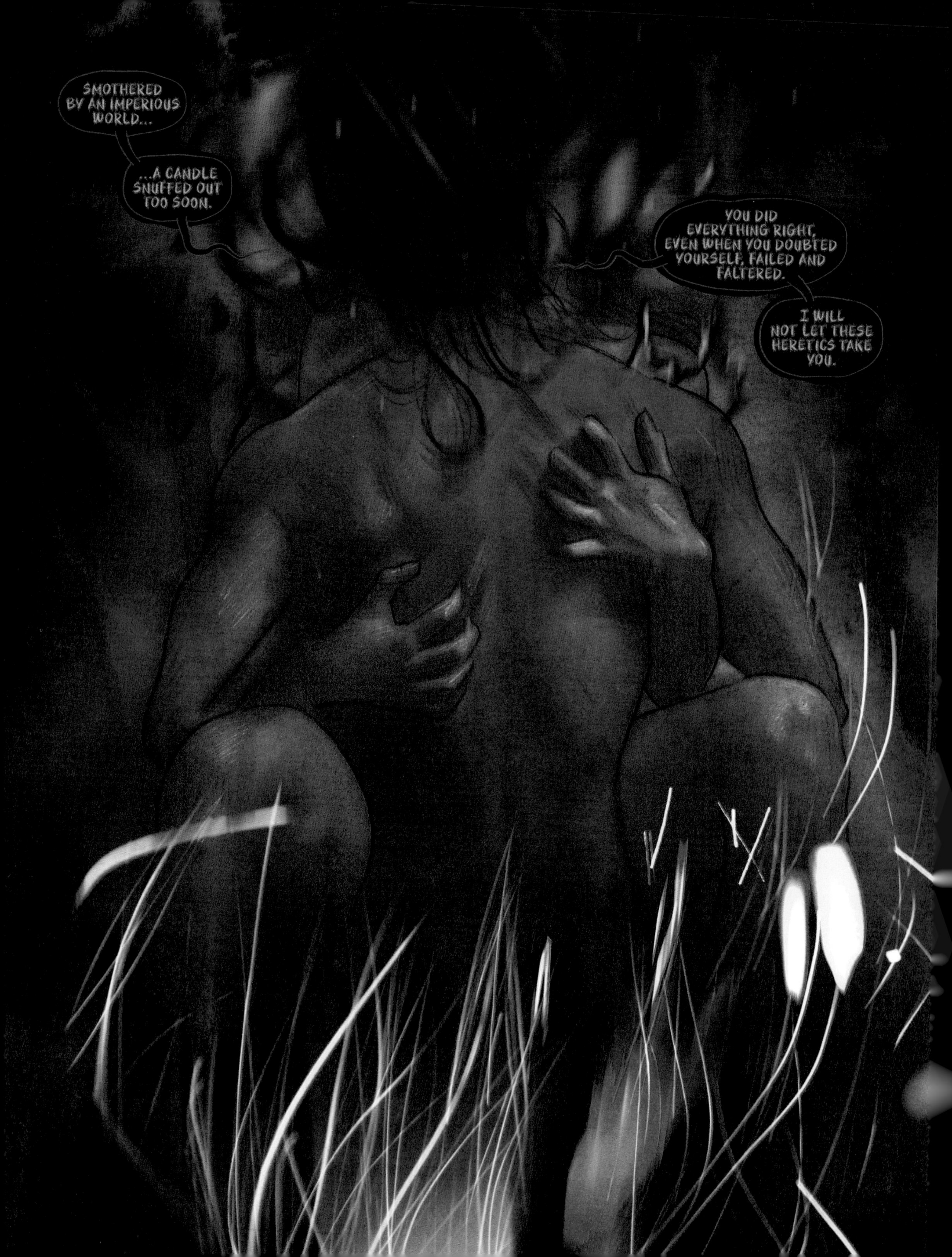
SMOTHERED BY AN IMPERIOUS WORLD...
...A CANDLE SNUFFED OUT TOO SOON.
YOU DID EVERYTHING RIGHT, EVEN WHEN YOU DOUBTED YOURSELF, FAILED AND FALTERED.
I WILL NOT LET THESE HERETICS TAKE YOU.

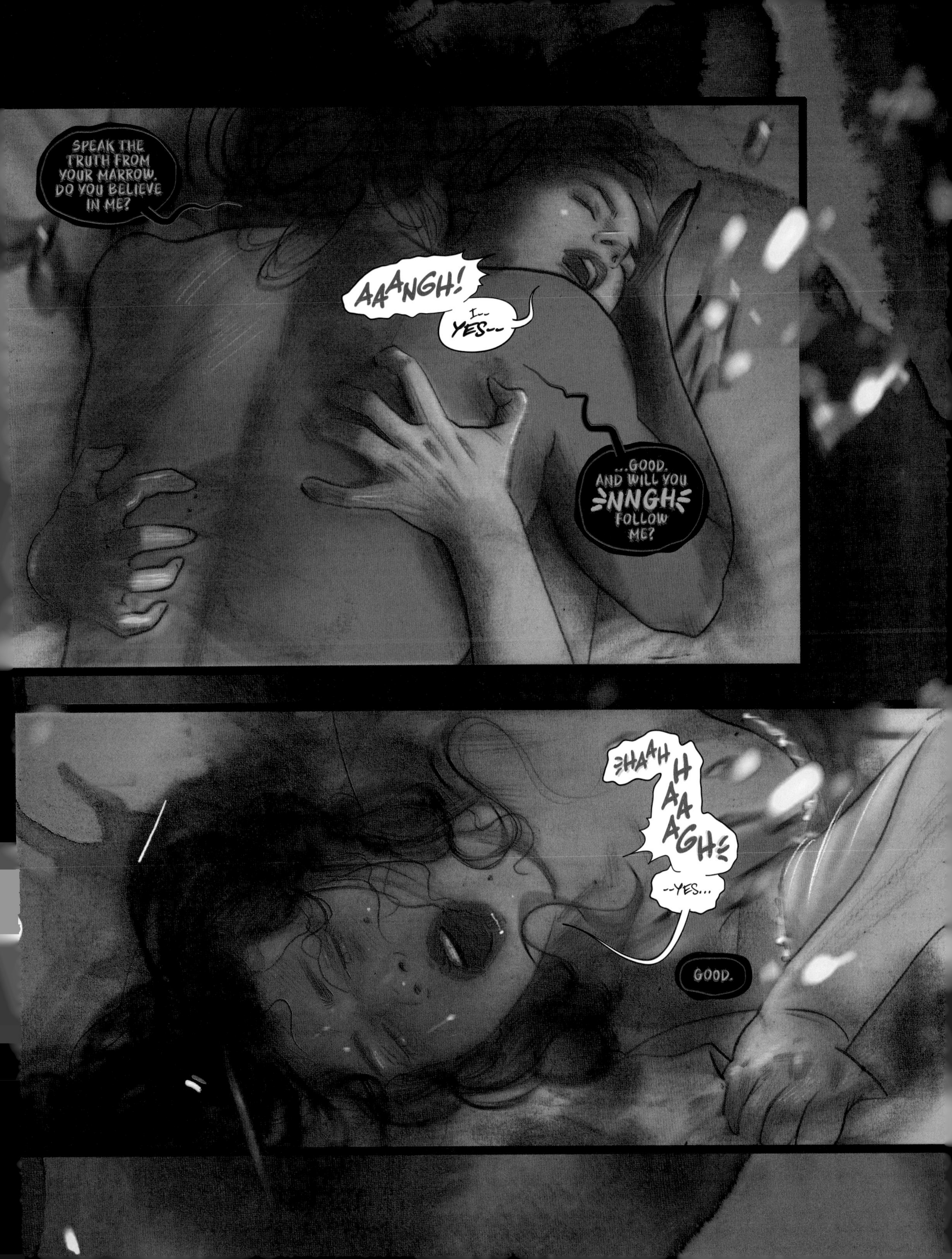
SPEAK THE TRUTH FROM YOUR MARROW. DO YOU BELIEVE IN ME?
AAANGH!
I-- YES--
...GOOD. AND WILL YOU NNGH FOLLOW ME?
HAAH HAAAGH
--YES...
GOOD.

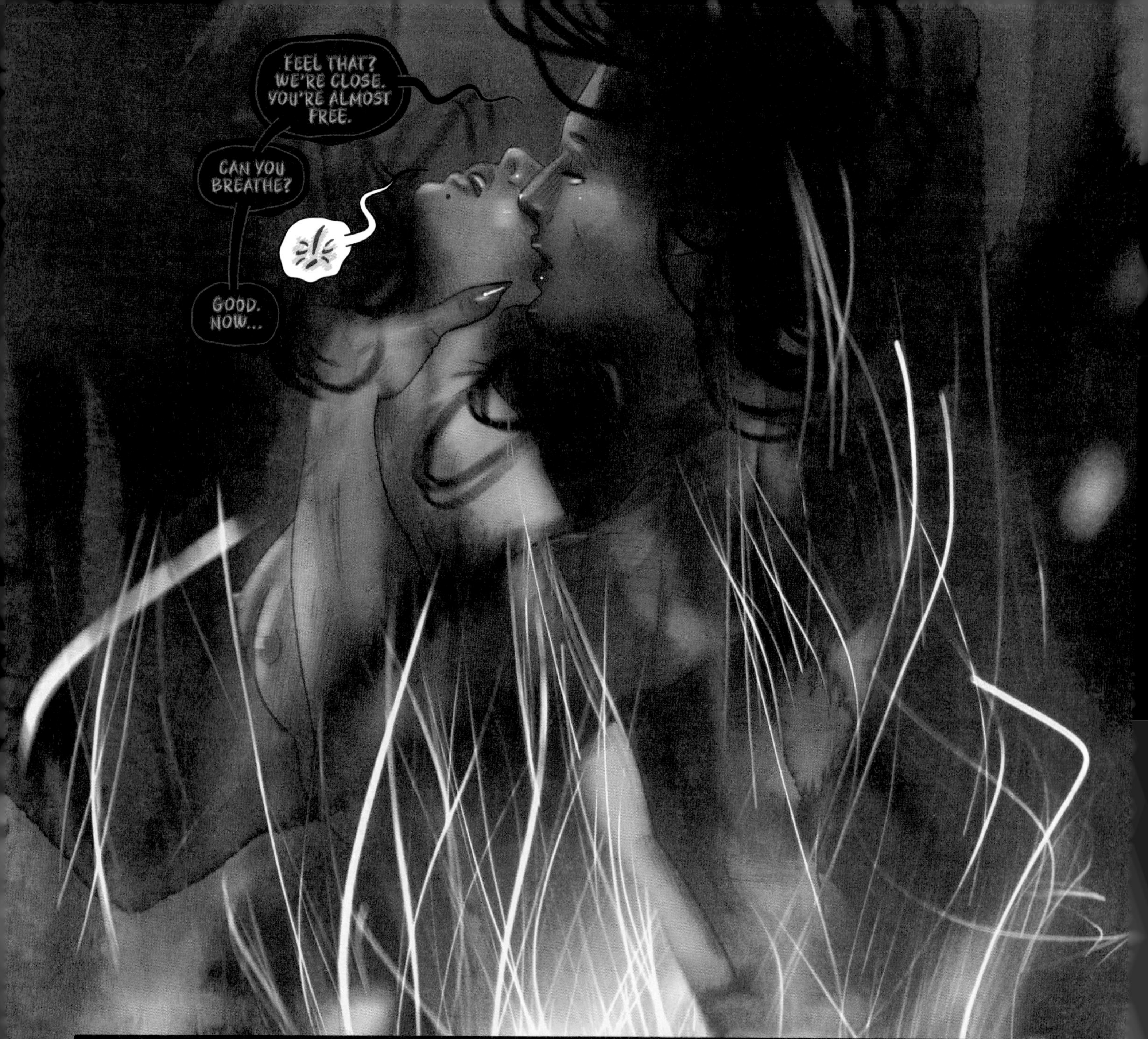
FEEL THAT? WE'RE CLOSE. YOU'RE ALMOST FREE.
CAN YOU BREATHE?
!
GOOD. NOW...

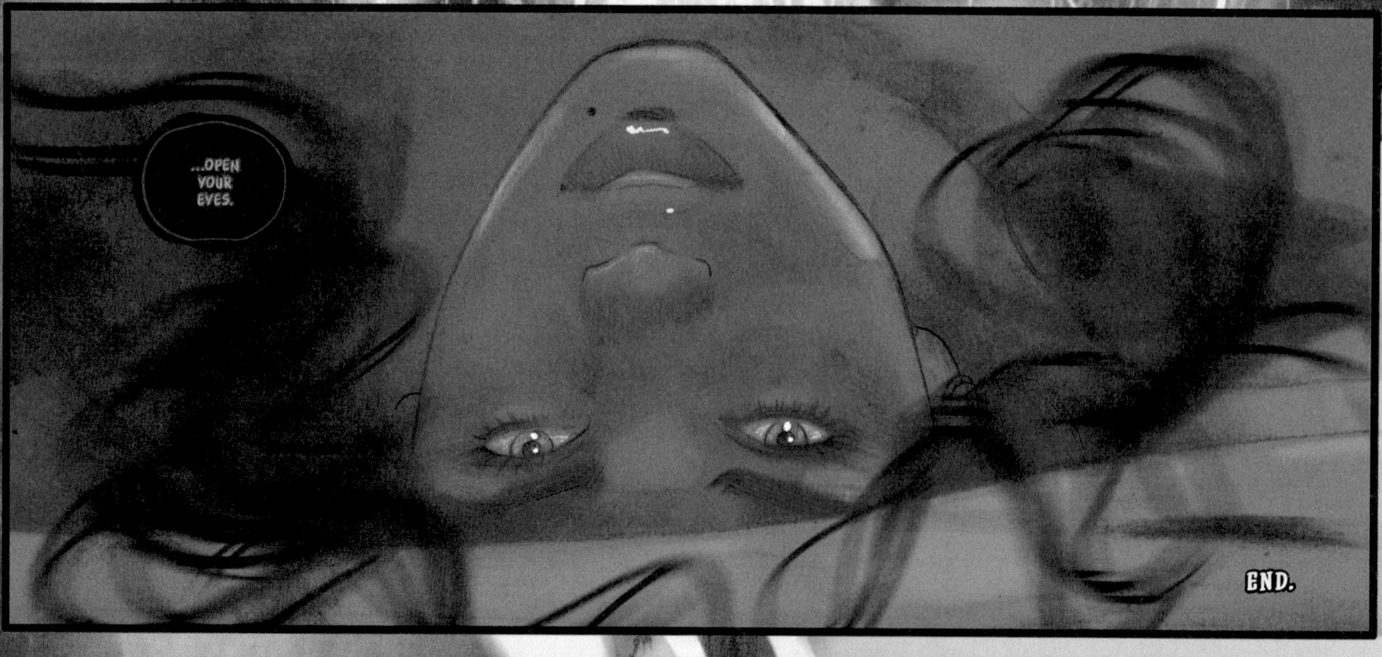
...OPEN YOUR EYES.
END.

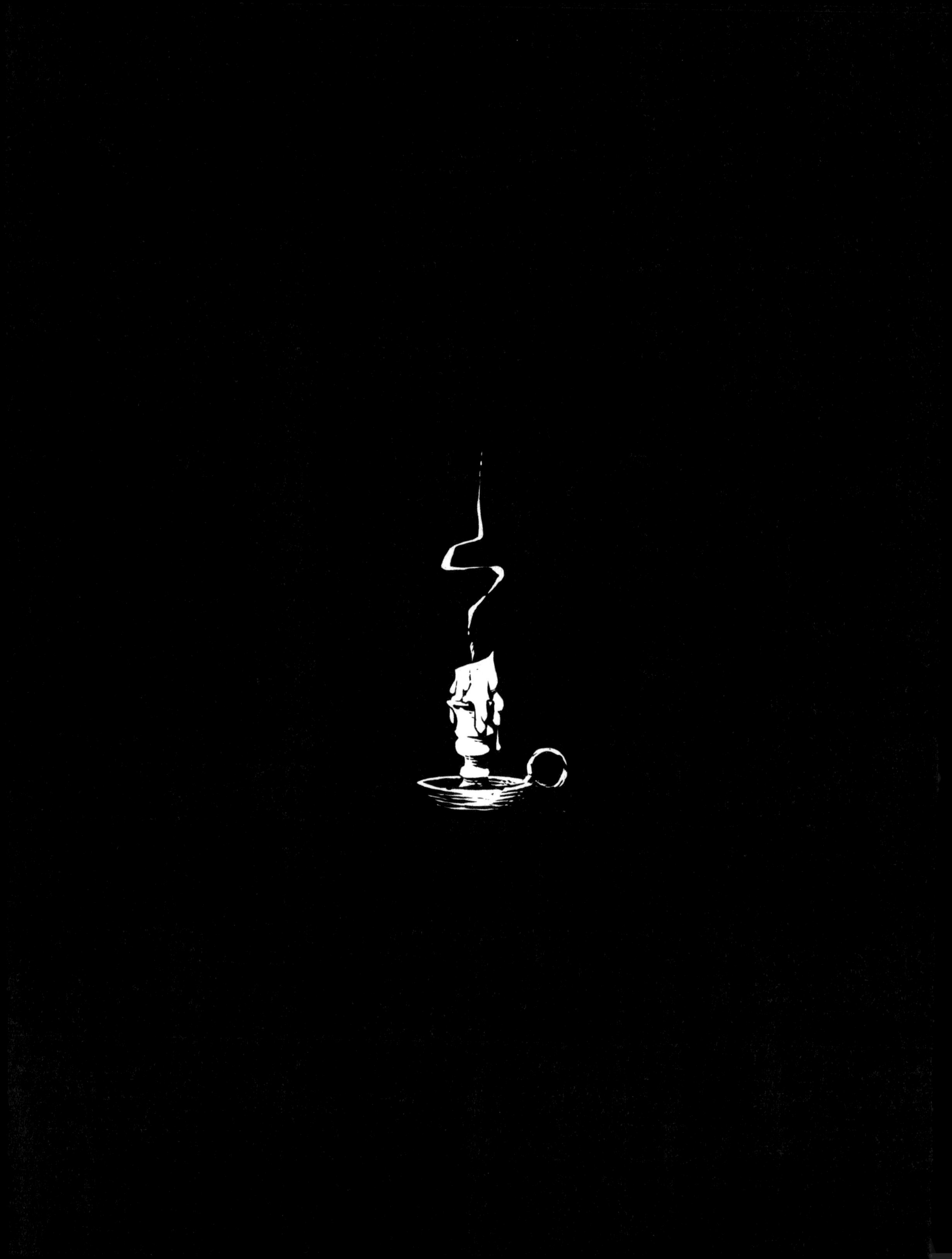

❧ EXTRAS ❧

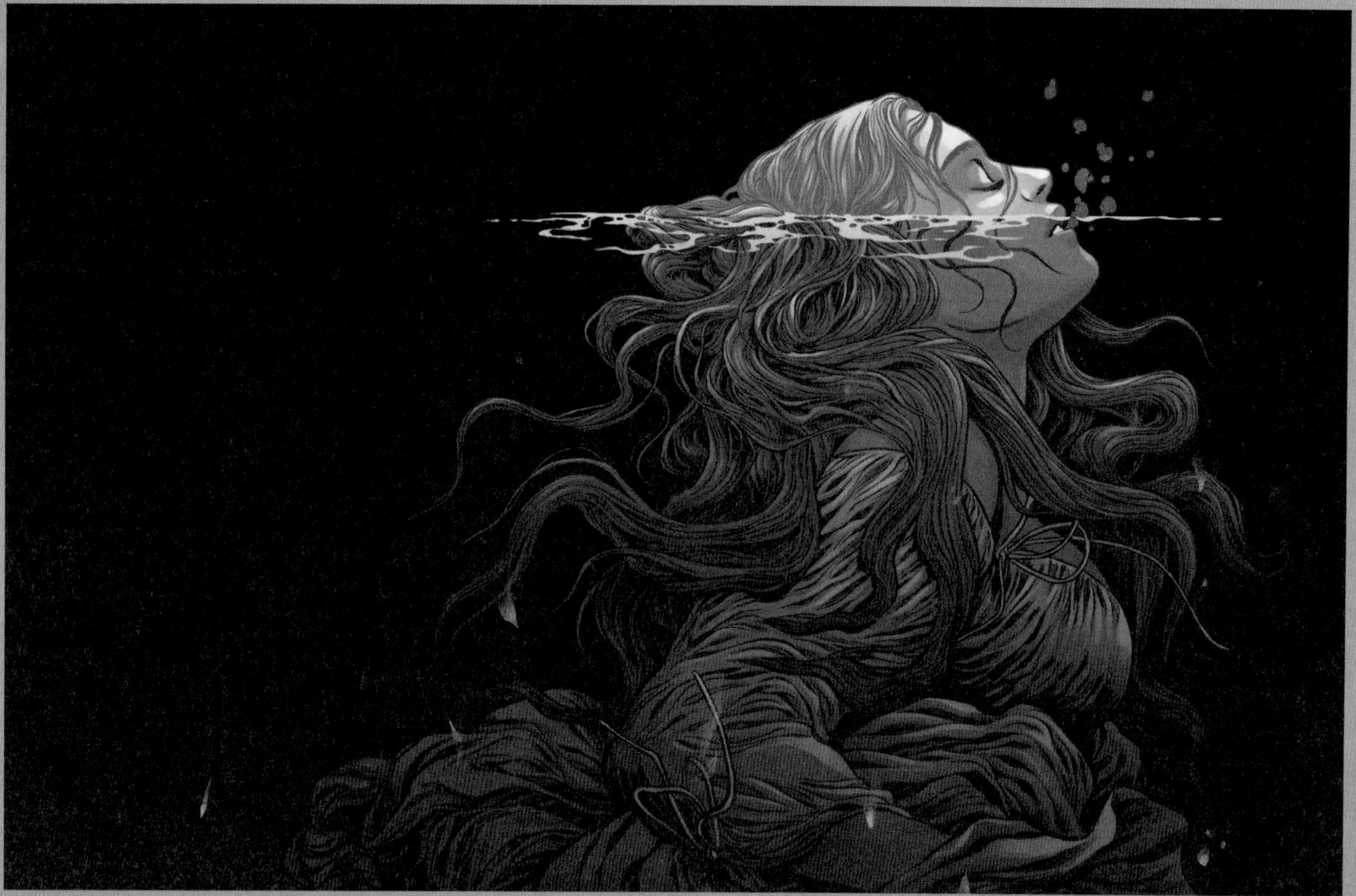

above: issue one cover by Becky Cloonan

below: issue one cover by Tula Lotay

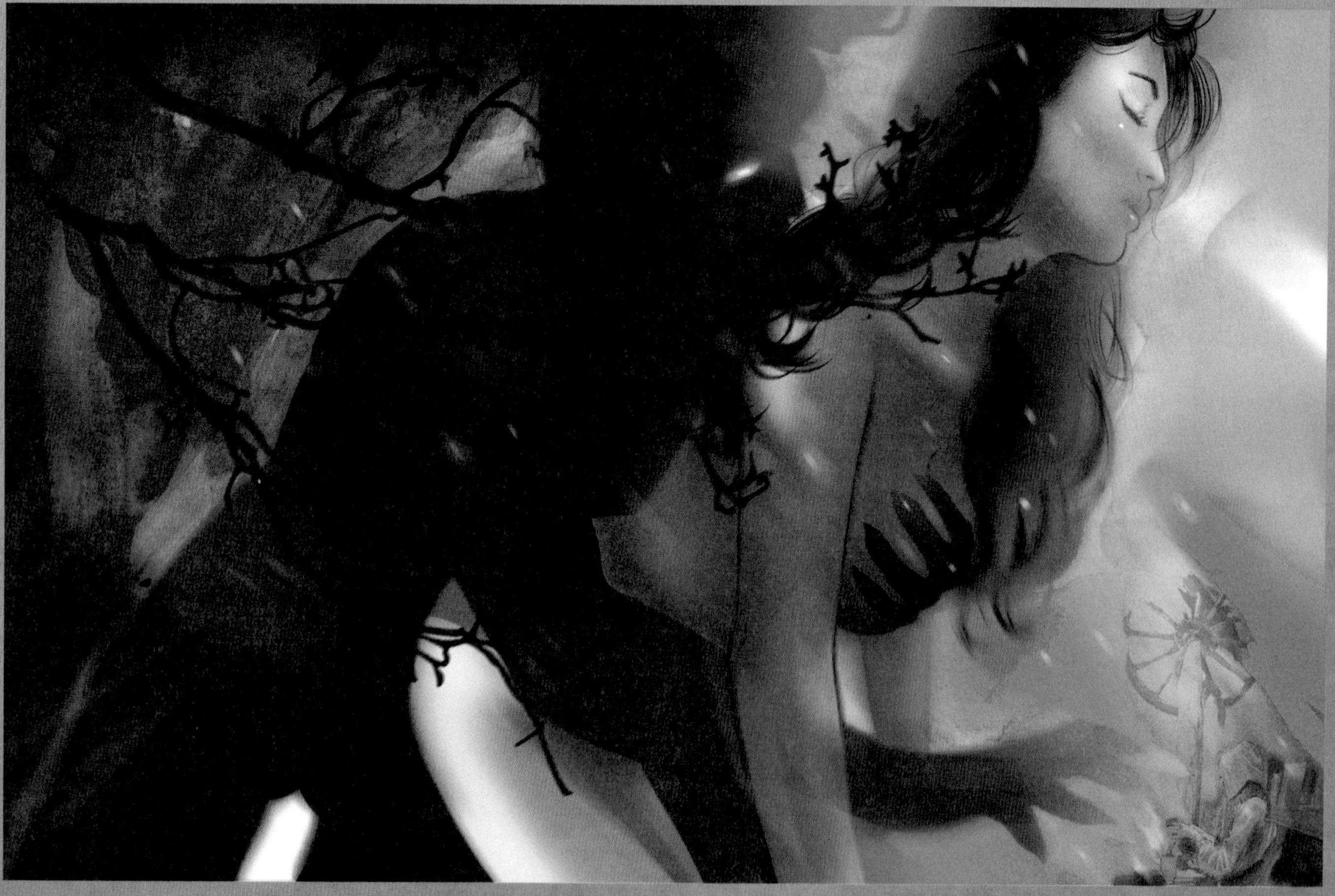

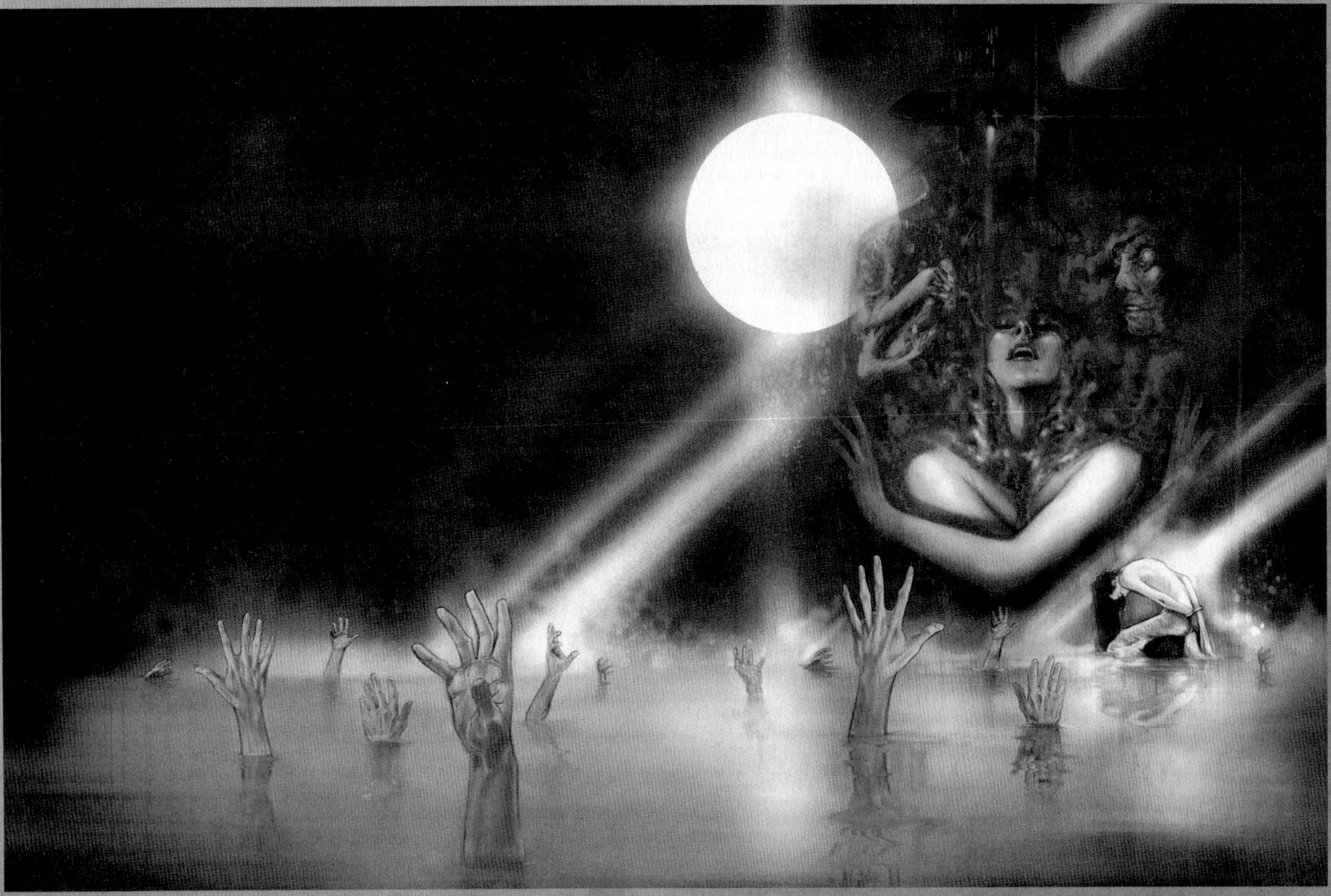

above: issue one variant by Joëlle Jones

below: issue one variant by Junko Mizuno

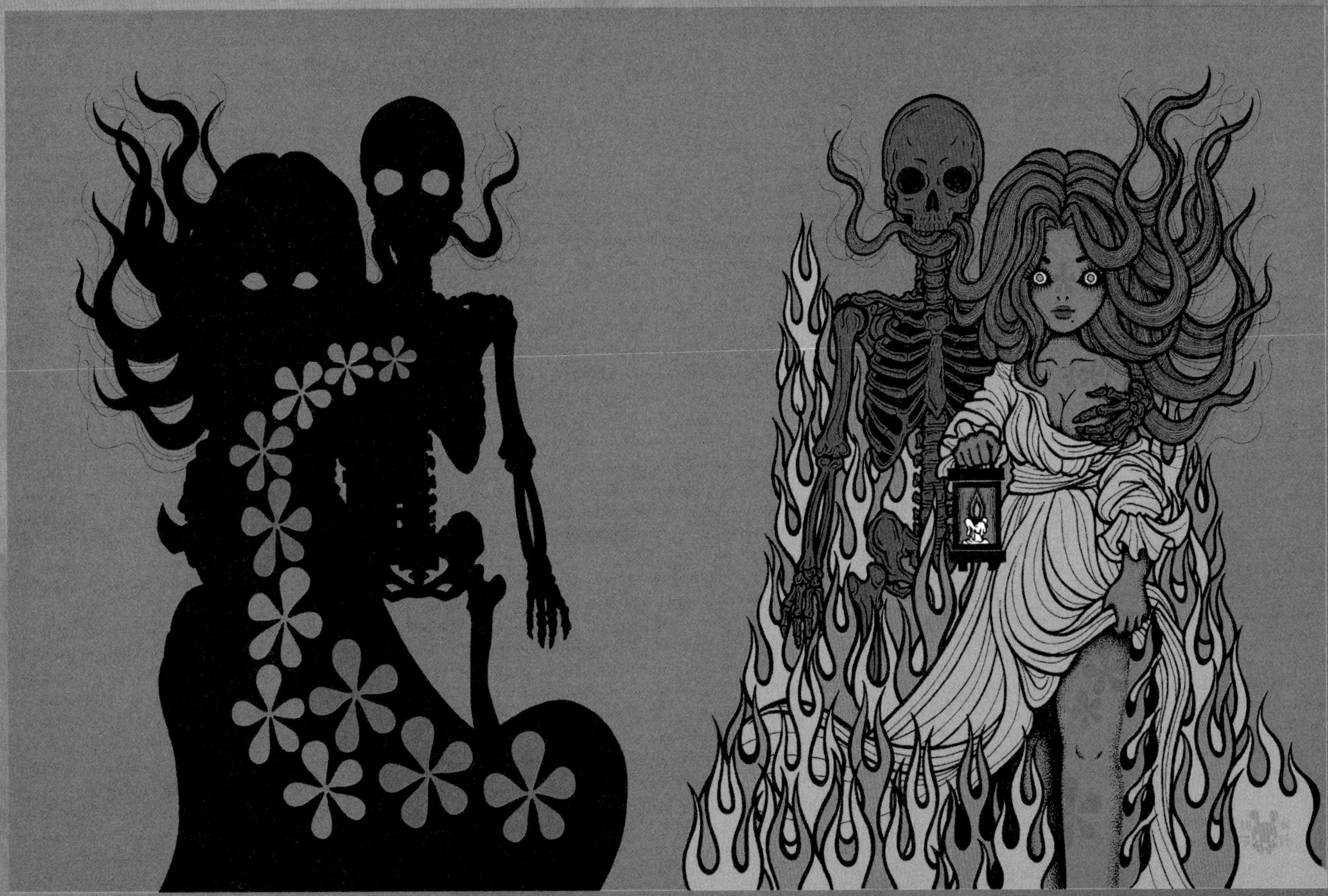

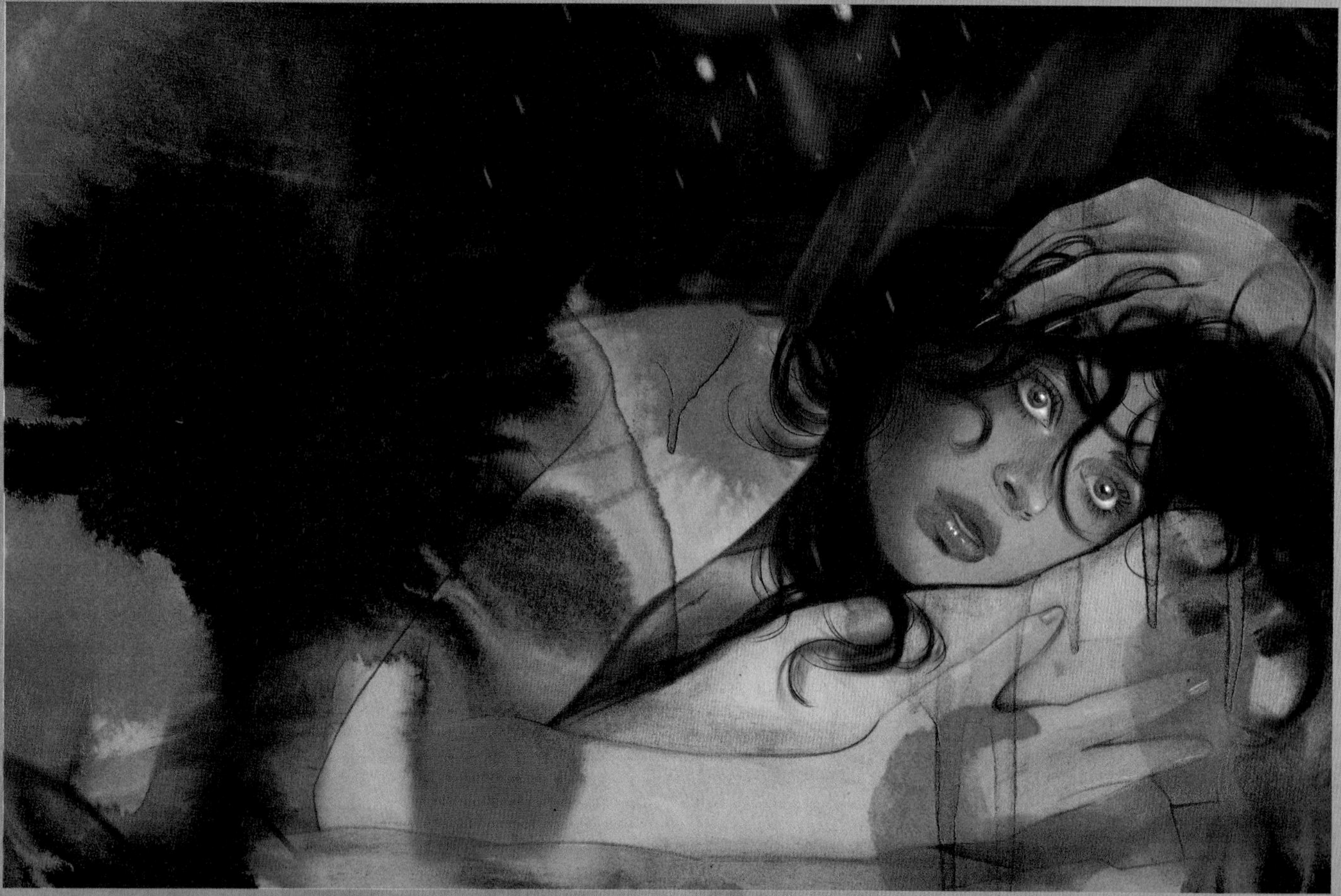

above: issue two cover by Tula Lotay

below: issue two cover by Becky Cloonan

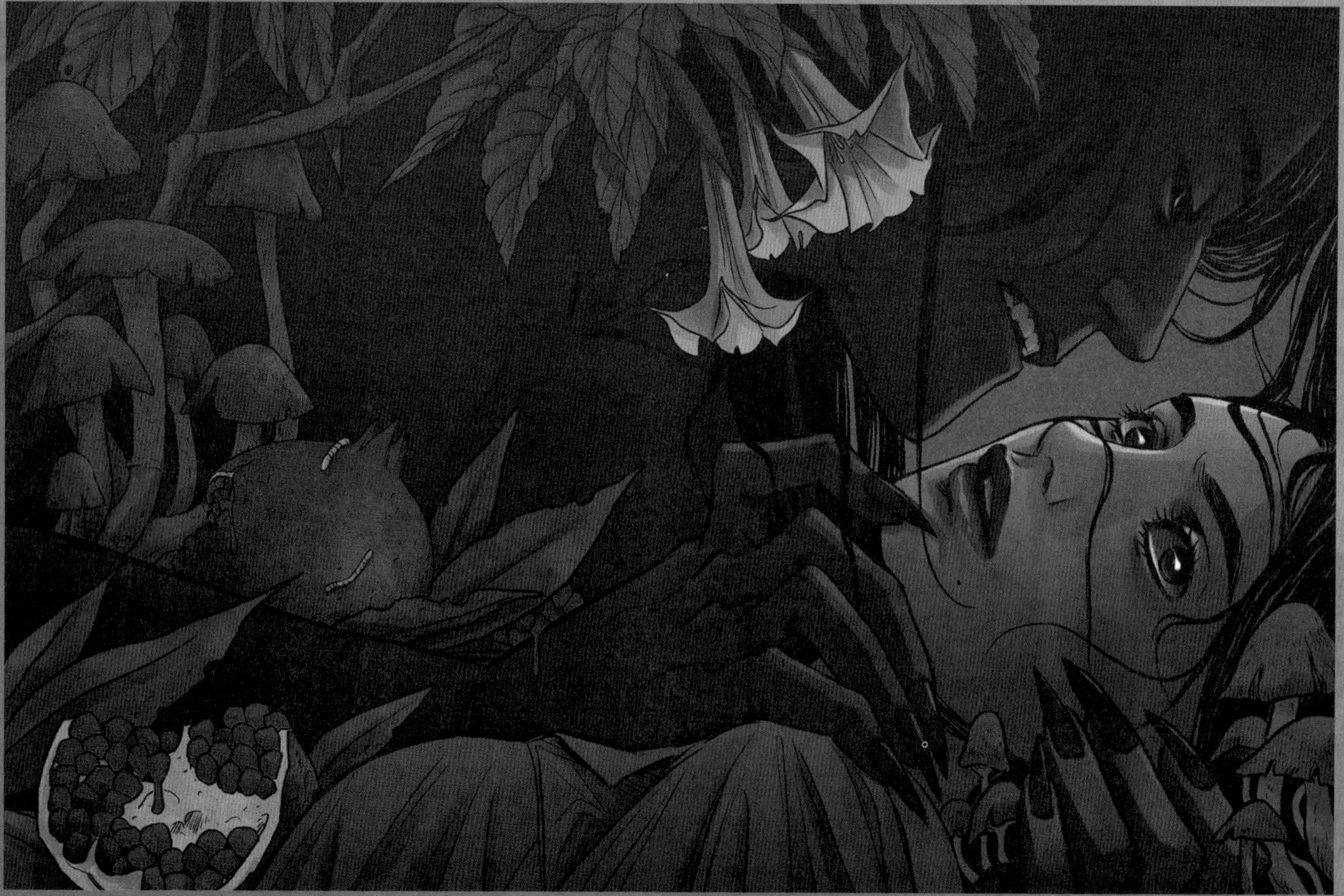

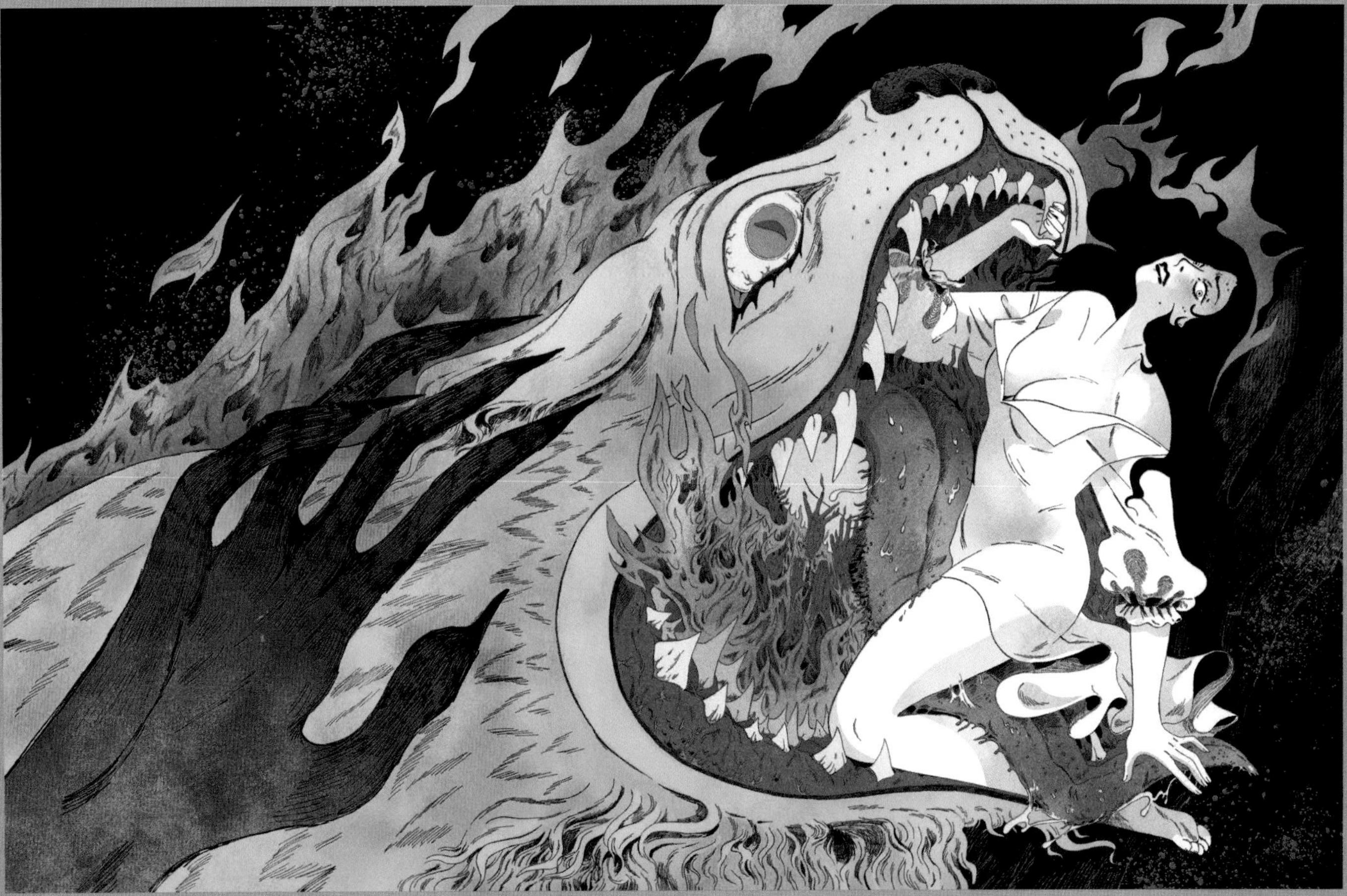

above: issue two variant by E.M. Carroll

below: issue two variant by Julian Totino Tedesco

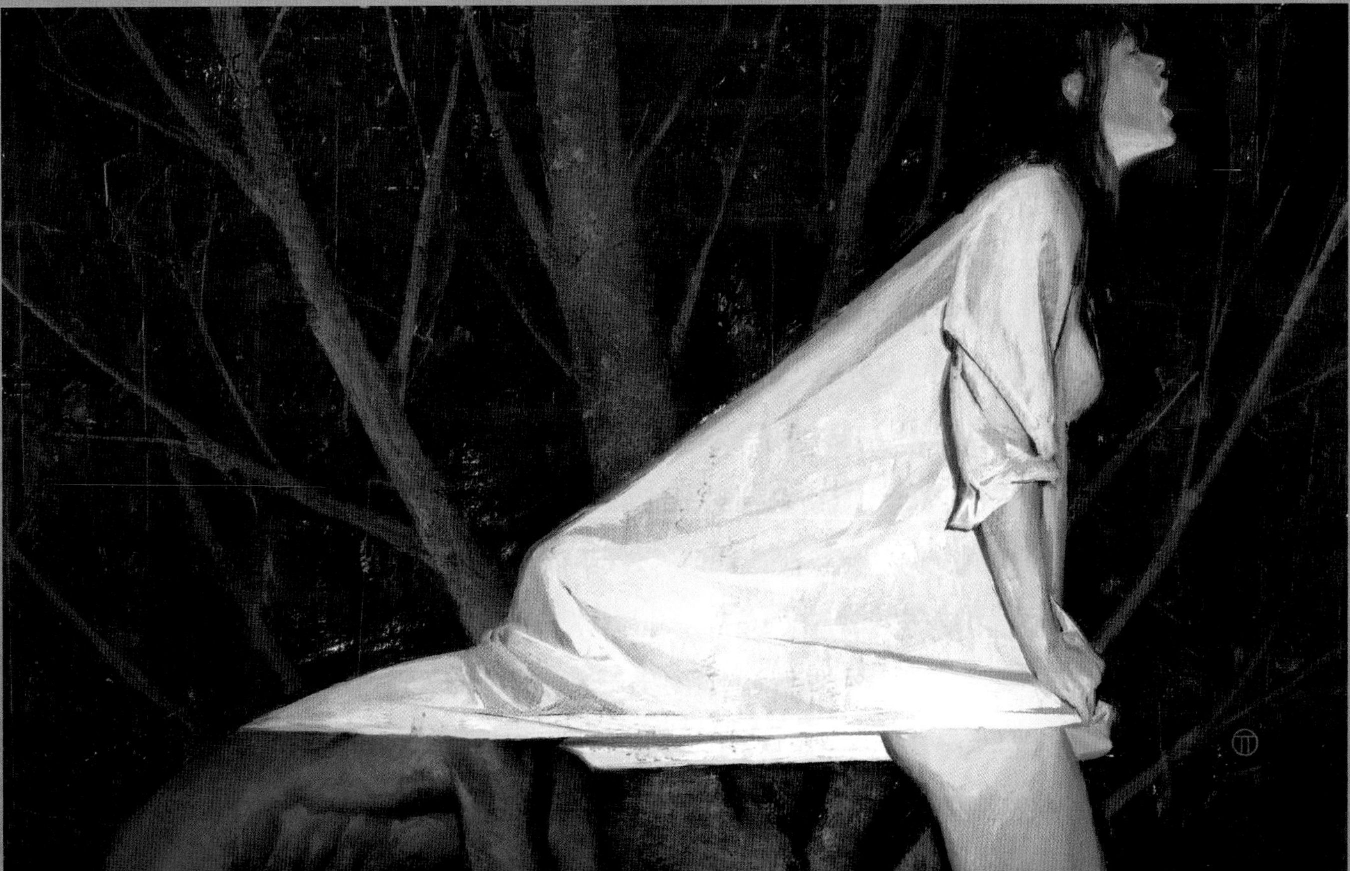

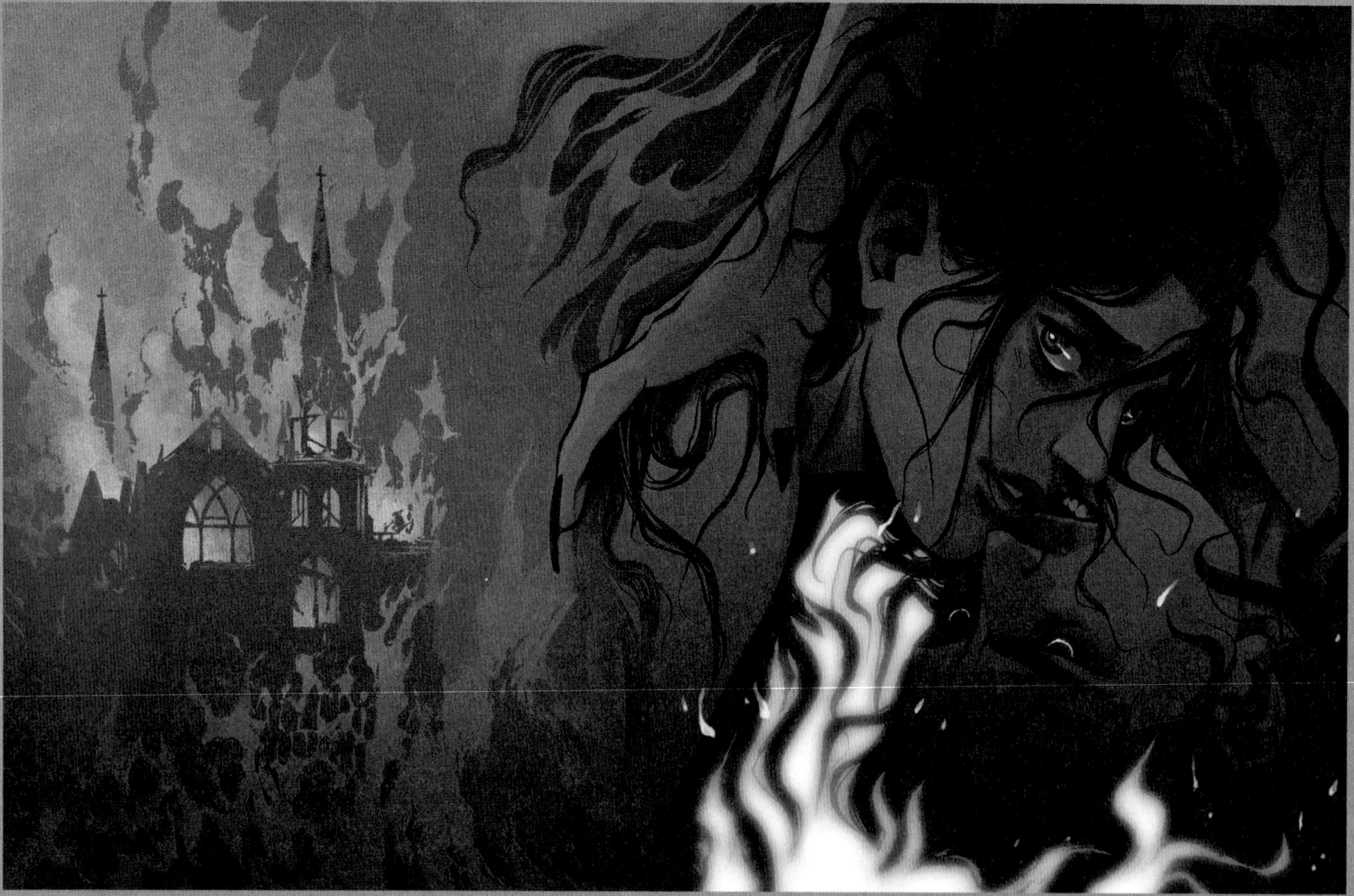

above: issue three cover by Becky Cloonan

below: issue three cover by Tula Lotay

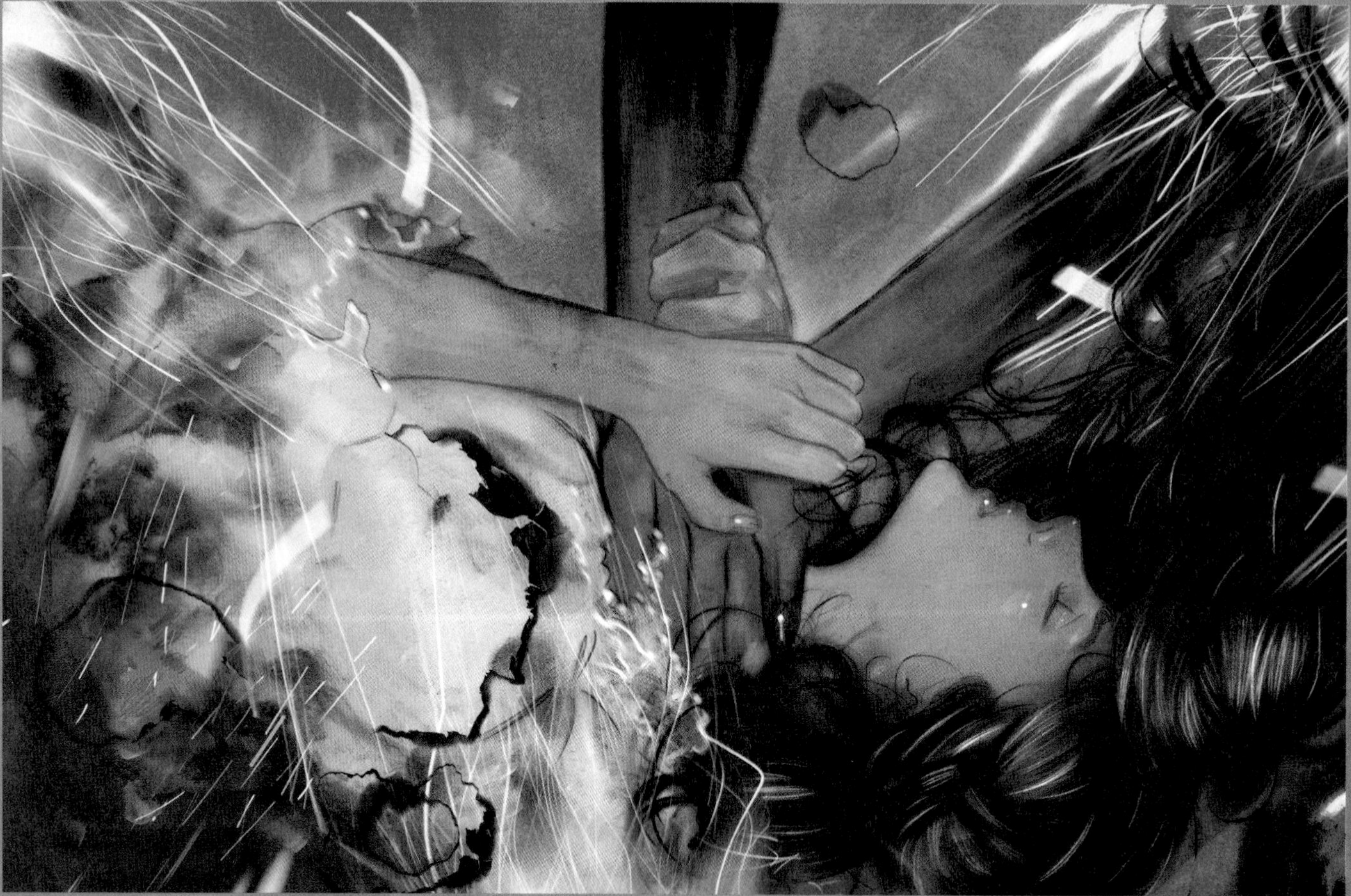

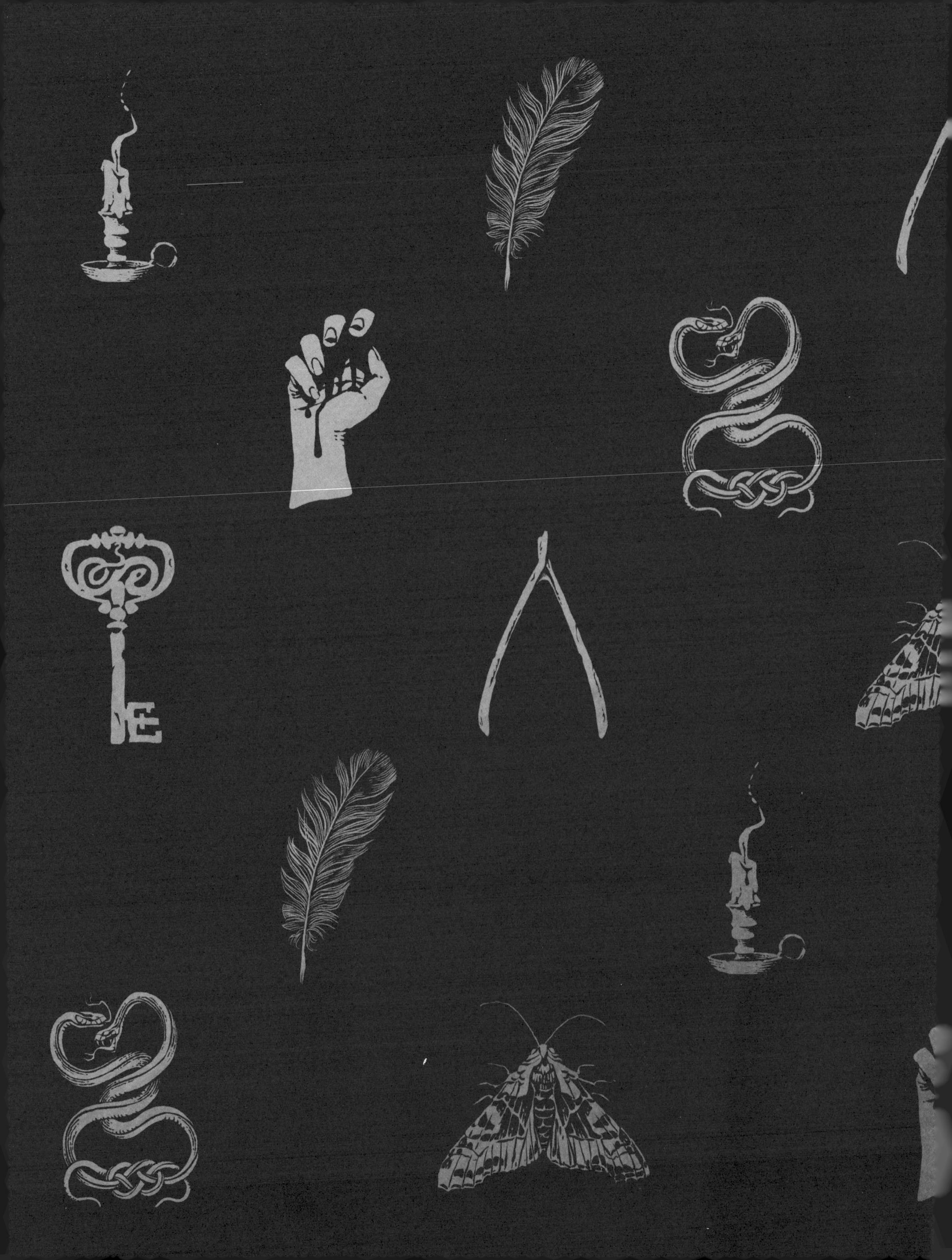